RACE
THE
DARKNESS

ABBIE ROADS

sourcebooks
casablanca

Published by Sourcebooks Casablanca, an imprint of Sourcebooks, Inc.
P.O. Box 4410, Naperville, Illinois 60567-4410
(630) 961-3900
Fax: (630) 961-2168
www.sourcebooks.com

Printed and bound in Canada.
MBP 10 9 8 7 6 5 4 3 2 1

To all the people who've been hurt or broken by life...

Never stop believing in your happy ending.

Individuals with Auditory Perception Syndrome claim to hear more than sound. They allegedly possess the ability to hear thoughts. These assertions have never been scientifically proven and should be treated as an auditory hallucination.

—Dr. M. J. Franklin, *Journal of Sound and Mind*

Chapter 1

XANDER STONE STOPPED OUTSIDE INTERROGATION Room B, shoved his ear up to the seam of the closed soundproof door, and listened. Supercharged hearing had only one benefit, and this was it. From inside the other room, he heard the slow, easy breathing of someone who thought he'd never be caught or prosecuted or imprisoned. Xander's favorite kind of criminal.

He pushed open the door and made sure to display his scars to the suspect. The disfigurement was a neon sign on a starless and moonless night, pointing and flashing *freak, freak, freak*. A caution to all who dared speak to him. Wasn't his fault if no one listened to the warning.

Yeah, life was a saggy-assed, fun bag of laughs since he'd been zapped with more than 50,000 volts of lightning. But the forehead-to-calf scarring didn't even rank on the Richter scale of shit when compared to the bizarre sensation of no longer being alone inside his head. And then there was the issue of his amplified hearing. He couldn't ignore the way his brain now tuned in to the frequency of thoughts.

The familiar pounding—like a basketball upside the head—slammed into Xander's right temple. He winced. Always did with the first thump, no matter how hard he tried not to react. Tuning in to the frequency of people's thoughts fucking hurt. He washed his features of expression.

Holy shit. What happened to the dude's face? Xander heard the words even though they hadn't been spoken aloud. The suspect—a kid, really—snickered, his gaze riveted to the puckered striation and the network of branch-like scars that stretched up Xander's neck, spread over his cheek, and finally ceased on his forehead.

"Good Cop–Bad Cop didn't work, so now they're sending in Ugly Cop?" The kid slouched back in his chair as if he were in his dorm watching the latest episode of some show glamorizing stupid people, instead of in an interrogation room at a Bureau of Criminal Investigation field office. He looked like every other cocky college kid—hair too long, clothes too preppy, ego too large. He didn't look like the leader of a sex gang.

"Ugly Cop? The last guy said the same thing. The asshole before him too, and the one before him. See how boring that gets? If you really want to insult someone, you've got to get creative. Try again. Lay a real good one on me. One I've never heard before." Xander couldn't remember the kid's name—wasn't important anyway. He took a seat at the table and settled his notepad squarely in front of him with his pen diagonal across the clean sheets of paper.

Scar face. Fugly motherfucker.

The kid opened his mouth, but Xander cut him off. "'Scar face' and 'fugly motherfucker.' Seriously? That's the best you got?" Most suspects expected him to be offended or outraged. They didn't expect his total acceptance.

The kid tilted his head like a dog trying to understand a new command. *That's weird.*

Yeah, it was weird. "My name is Xander Stone, and

just so you know for your insult planning, I'm not a cop. Never been a cop. Never wanted to be a cop. Don't even like cops. They're all pricks. And these guys"—Xander jabbed his thumb over his shoulder at the mirrored glass of the interrogation room—"are some of the biggest pricks of all."

No one could accuse him of lying. It was no secret he didn't do well with authority. The only reason the BCI put up with him was because they *needed* him and his unique style of interrogation.

A smile padded with self-satisfied smugness hitched up the kid's mouth. *We're back to Good Cop.*

"What is he doing in there?" The superintendent's words came to Xander from beyond the mirrored glass. With his supercharged hearing, the soundproofing separating the rooms was little more than a cotton swab on a spurting artery.

He turned in his seat to face the mirror. Everyone knew about his rule of absolute quiet if they were going to observe. "Silence. I need complete silence. Or I'm out of here and you can let the kid walk." He glared at the mirror, daring someone to speak.

This dude is certifiable cray-cray.

Xander faced the kid. "I think you might be on to something with that cray-cray bit."

The kid jerked upright like someone had goosed his gonads. *How'd he know what I was thinking?* His attention bull's-eyed on Xander. The kid was just starting to realize Xander had changed the game from checkers to chess.

"I know what you're thinking because I'm the guy the BCI calls in when they've got a difficult case."

Referring to gang rape as merely a *difficult case* was like painting a pile of shit just to make it look better. It was still shit. It still stank.

The kid laughed a blatantly fake laugh, the kind that was code for "fuck you." *He's trying to mess with me. Ain't gonna work.*

"I'm not trying to mess with you." *Well, maybe just a little.* Disbelief in his ability was a universal rule. Hell, he barely believed in it himself. "I just want to get this done so I can get out of here. Like I said, I hate cops. And I've got a headache." The vision in his right eye pulsed with each thump inside his brain. He wanted to press his palm against the pounding, but didn't. Show no pain. Show no weakness. Show no emotion.

No more dicking around with the kid. Xander needed to get answers to the questions he'd been sent to ask and then get the fuck out of here. Funny how he could remember the questions, but not the kid's name. "How many guys are in the Bangers Club?"

Six plus nine. Sixty-nine. Six plus nine. Sixty-nine. The kid's thoughts were a perverted chant. "I don't know what you're talking about."

Xander picked up his notepad, tilted it so the kid couldn't see, and scribbled $6 + 9 = 15$ onto the paper. "I need the names of all fifteen members."

Fifteen? How'd he come up with that number? He's guessing. "I'll tell you the same thing I told Good Cop and Bad Cop. I don't know what you're talking about."

"The names of all fifteen members."

Michael Blevins. Blake Johnson...

Xander listed the names until he lost the frequency. Five to ten seconds of silence in the conversation, and the connection severed. He stared down at the paper and cherished the absence of pain, then sucked in a few deep breaths, pumping himself up to reestablish the connection and restore the basketball thumping inside his head. "I need the rest of the names."

Bang! He jerked from the force of the blow inside his brain. God, that first hit—

Aiden Stacey. Trey Mitchell...

Xander listed all the names.

"What are you writing?" The kid half stood, trying to see across the table to Xander's notes.

"Names." Xander angled the notepad so the kid couldn't see his writing.

"I didn't say anything."

"Yeah, you did. Just not out loud."

What is he talking about? They sent in some mind-game expert? This shit isn't going to work on me. Just keep quiet and don't react.

"You're already reacting. I can hear it. You're breathing faster, shallower. Your pulse has picked up. You're not quite panicking yet, but eventually you're going to."

What the hell? What the hell? What. The. Hell. The kid did a stellar job of retaining his outward expression of entitlement. No one would ever guess he was on the cusp of an implosion.

"Between the fifteen of you, how many girls have you *banged*?" The word—the Bangers Club's word—tasted insectile on Xander's tongue, like if he didn't spit it out, it would burrow a hole through the roof of his mouth and have babies in his brain.

Fifty-seven. Twelve away from our goal—sixty-nine.

Jesus. The kid needed to be neutered.

There was no reason to ask for the girls' names. From what he'd been told, the Bangers Club didn't bother learning the names of their victims. "You ever been diagnosed with obsessive-compulsive disorder?"

No. The kid's brows rose and his head swiveled on his neck in a good imitation of a white-trash ho about to show her sass.

"Just asking because you seem awfully obsessed with the number sixty-nine."

The kid's jaw unhinged and nearly clattered onto the table. *Not possible. He can't really read my mind. He's guessing somehow. Or...did someone talk? No one would dare—*

"You're right. I'm not reading your mind. I'm listening to the things you aren't saying." As if the kid would believe that. Only one more question and Xander could walk out of the room, out the building, and be alone.

The last question was the most critical. From the dumbed-down version Xander understood, the kid had created a nearly impenetrable computer system that streamed all the Bangers Club bangs—for a monthly fee. The only way to shut it down was to access the original computer and enter the password—no mistakes, no guessing—or the entire system would go viral and start broadcasting live on all the local channels, even the small-town church TV station. Kids today were dangerously clever. "What's the password?"

6*2H95—London Bridge is falling down...

Xander wrote the numbers and letters on his paper. The kid was starting to catch on. Not that it would matter.

"Stop writing shit down. You're making things up." The kid's voice rode the ridge of hysteria.

"6*2H95. I need the rest of the password." Xander loved the way other people's brains just couldn't resist thinking.

O#ZR591H. No. No. No. London Bridge is falling down, falling down, falling down—

"6*2H95O#ZR591H. Keep going."

It took three more tries before the kid eventually spit out the entire password.

"The tech department wasn't kidding. This password is a monster."

No. This isn't happening. "Who talked? Someone is setting me up."

"You talked."

"I didn't *say* anything!" the kid yelled.

Xander felt the smile split open his face, felt the skin on his right cheek stretch in a way that wasn't familiar. Life didn't hold much amusement for him, but he always savored the moment when some asshole finally realized he'd been bested and was going to be sent on an extended vacation to criminal central.

Pushing back from the table, Xander got up and headed for the door. He stopped, hand on the handle, and turned back to the kid. "You come up with a creative insult yet?"

The kid leaned forward and smacked his forehead against the table. *No. No. No.*

"Guess not."

As Xander opened the door, a million sounds rushed his ears at once. A toilet flushing, typing, the hum and bump of the air conditioner, conversations—too many conversations. Sensory overload was imminent. The only question was how long before his brain shorted out, unleashing the Bastard in His Brain—that thing he always felt lurking in the darkest depths of his mind. When the Bastard took the wheel, there was no such thing as a happy ending.

He needed to leave. Now.

But Kent and Thomas, who'd been watching the interview, waited in the hallway.

He passed the notepad to Thomas, who sprinted down the corridor to get the names and password to the cyber division.

"Why the fuck was there talking during my interrogation?"

Kent gave him the same disapproving, annoyed, disgusted look he'd been giving him since Xander bloodied the guy's nose in the first grade.

Bam. Pain bounced inside his skull. Xander flinched. Goddamned tuning-in. "Quit with the look." They'd never been friends. Still weren't.

You're such an asshole. Acting like you're the only one working here. "Do you always have to be such a dick about us? The superintendent was watching." Kent headed in the same direction as Xander—toward the exit. *You need to make a decision about Camille.*

"The superintendent was the one talking. You pushed me to work here. You pushed them to hire me. You got a fat-assed bonus out of it. So if you, or the superintendent, don't like what I do, stop calling me. And what I do with Camille is none of your business."

"Keep your freak self outta my head."

"Only way to make it stop is by not talking to me."

Outside of work, Xander mastered in social isolation and conversation avoidance.

"Come on, man. She's my sister. We may not be real close, but I care about her. I'm not letting this go." *You're using her.*

Xander's neck got hot. He didn't argue with Kent's thoughts. He couldn't. The man was right. Camille never rejected him, never made demands on him, but she wanted commitment. He got that from tuning in to her thoughts. All he wanted was acceptance and uncomplicated sex.

The conversation lagged, and the pain vanished.

Xander exited the building. Low on the horizon, all that remained of the day was a single tiger stripe of orange. Already the June night was in full chorus. The whistle screech of a bat using its sonar-like system, the flutter of its wings overhead. The buzz of a trillion mosquitoes. The bass of a bullfrog two blocks away at the Sundew Park pond. Life pulsed all around him.

When he couldn't sleep, he'd lie in bed with the window open—listening, just listening. Not letting himself think, just focusing on the rhythm of the world. The sounds of nature were the only form of music he could tolerate.

He fished his truck keys from his pocket and pressed the unlock button.

"The superintendent is probably going to need you again tomorrow," Kent called from the doorway.

"Tell him to call me." Xander tossed the words over his shoulder.

"You going to answer the phone?" *Bet you don't.*

"Bet you're right."

—◦◦◦—

Death twined around Isleen Walker's body, whispering over her naked flesh, coiling around her heart and lungs, hugging the last sparks of life from her. Twenty-five years of being alive distilled down to a wish. A wish that death would hurry up and grant her its promised relief.

"I'm dying." She tried to warn Gran, but the words came out quieter than a breath. Her gaze roamed the room—their prison for the past eight years. It was just big enough to contain her and Gran and an overflowing waste bucket, but now it felt too small, too fragile to contain Isleen. Soon she would transcend this space, and no matter what Queen did, she wouldn't be able to tether Isleen here.

Gran slept, face tucked into the corner. Safety was an illusion—beating after beating had proven that fact—but still, they always gravitated to the corners. Gran's once-supple flesh sagged from her bones. Her spine protruded sharply in a pathetic row of spikes.

"...tobesaved. Not die....protectordiedtoo?" Gran spoke in a smear of barely distinguishable words. She'd been a sleep-talker for as long as Isleen could remember—even before they'd been abducted.

She used to wake Gran from her dreams, but had long since decided it was a mercy to let her stay inside them for as long as they hosted her. Maybe in her dreams, Gran still possessed her wits and all her faculties, and lived somewhere beautiful where nothing bad ever happened.

Footsteps pounded down the hall and stopped outside the door. The sound of the key in the lock scraped across Isleen's heart. Was today going to be a feeding day, a beating day, or a bleeding day? It didn't really matter. It was too late for food; a beating would finish her off; and she had no more blood to give. But there was Gran—

The door rasped open. Queen. Always Queen and only Queen ever entered their prison. If ever a name didn't fit a person, it was hers. Nothing about her was royal or regal. She was no whimsical fairy-tale ruler; she was a twenty-first-century reality. A simple-minded, delusional woman who took pleasure in domination and torture. Under a different set of circumstances, Queen would have been passing her days in a psychiatric hospital, medicated to the point of drooling.

Isleen could smell Queen's stench. Cigarette smoke so stale and foul and thick that Isleen could taste the bite of it in her mouth, feel the burn of it in her eyes. The pungency of flesh that hadn't been washed in years snuffed out the oxygen in the air.

Queen kicked her in the thigh. "The Dragon has not yet died."

A small gasp, not of pain, but of being startled escaped Isleen's throat. For as long as they'd been held captive, Queen had referred to her as the Dragon.

Queen cleared her throat. Mucus snapped and rattled. She hawked up a wad of nasty and spit it on the floor. "King decreed that if the Dragon shall linger—"

"You will suffer for everything you've done." Gran crawled out of the corner on all fours. "Her protector is on his way."

Queen's hunched shoulders straightened. "I am your queen. Bow before me." It was all a part of Queen's delusional mind—she was a queen and they were her subjects and the objects of her torture. Especially Isleen.

Gran didn't bow, didn't move, didn't understand.

"You will be punished." Queen opened and closed a giant pair of scissors. *Shkk. Shkk. Shkk.*

Dread burned a hole through Isleen's shrunken stomach. "It's not her fault. She doesn't understand." She tried to move, but her body was too weak, her limbs too emaciated.

"Your Majesty, I am sorry. I have committed the gravest of errors." Gran executed a bow of supplication, arms spread out, forehead to the floor. "Please accept my humble apology and know that I will never again speak in such a manner to one as powerful as you." Before Gran had lost her mind, she'd been fluent in kiss-up-to-the-fake-queen language.

Gran must be having a rare moment of clarity.

"Very well. I grant you a pardon. Know this—though I am a merciful queen, I will not tolerate such treasonous behavior again." She pointed a fat, stubby finger at Gran. "You have been warned."

Gran kept her pose. Good decision.

Queen turned her grotesque gaze to Isleen. She went through the same disgusting process of clearing her throat and then spoke as if she were making a proclamation. "King has decreed that on the sixth day, if the Dragon shall linger, I am to thrust my sword into its side."

Thrust my sword into its side. Isleen understood Queen's words; she just didn't fear them. No matter what Queen did to her now, it would be nothing—*absolutely nothing*—compared to the agony of living. A calmness nestled into her bones, curled up in her guts.

Gran lifted her face from the floor and challenged

Queen's authority by looking directly at her. "You don't have the power to kill her." Insanity warped Gran's tone.

Queen's attention snapped to Gran. "You were warned. Now, you shall be executed."

Isleen thrust words from her heart, words she'd always wanted to speak but never dared until now, when she needed to divert Queen's attention away from Gran. "You're not a queen. You're psychotic. You're a bitch. You're evil and stupid and mean. And…and… you smell bad."

Queen's wide-spaced eyes nearly bulged out of her block-shaped head. Her fat lips snarled back, revealing teeth so neglected they were the same color and texture as Fritos. She switched her grip on the scissors, fisting the handle, and stabbed the blades at Isleen.

She watched the scissors descend, heard the whisper and swish of them piercing her flesh. Felt only a vague pressure and presence of something foreign inside her body. Smelled sweetness in the air and tasted salt on her tongue.

Queen yanked the scissors from Isleen's body and held them up. Blood dripped from the blades, sending red streamers down Queen's doughy arm.

Warmth oozed from Isleen's side, the heat comforting her cold skin.

"Tomorrow, if you are still alive—off with your head!"

Gran waited until Queen locked them back in the room, then scooted next to Isleen. There were no bandages, no cloths, no tissues. Nothing to stop the bleeding.

"Hold on, baby girl. Just hold on. He's coming. He's got to be coming. He will release you. Save you." The worst part of Gran's mental breakdown was the delusion that someone would find them. In Isleen's most desperate of moments, she had allowed herself to believe Gran. Not anymore.

"Your dreams will come true. All of them. Remember the dreams about him. How you loved him and he loved you. Remember the dreams of sunshine on your face and the cabin you shared. Remember…"

There was nothing to remember. They had just been dreams. Silly dreams. No more powerful than Gran's sleep-talking.

You're not coming. You're not going to save me. Because you don't exist. Never have. I believed in you. Thought you must be real—Gran swore you were. But you were nothing more than hope's fatal dream. We're going to die, and no one other than Queen will ever remember we existed.

A rainbow of colors swelled in front of her eyes. Colors she hadn't seen in years. Colors so brilliant and bright and beautiful that her eyes watered. Death was an alluring kaleidoscope.

Chapter 2

A BLOATED MOON DANGLED FROM THE SKY, TOSSING silver light across the barren hilltop where Xander's cabin stood. He sat on the front porch swing, listening to the symphony of sounds only night could produce. A breeze full of relief from the summer sun whispered over his skin. From the woods encircling the yard, leaves rustled and branches swayed and clapped as if applauding Mother Nature's concert.

Xander closed his eyes—as close to sleep as he was going to get. To other people it was late, the middle of the night, but to him, time didn't matter. That's what happened when he couldn't sleep. The days and nights blurred and blended together with no division between them other than the color of the sky. It was an exhausting, endless sort of existence.

Tonight was worse than ever. His foot jittered against the porch floor. His insides twitched and trembled as if they were about to erupt through his pores. His brain itched. Itched. Actually fucking itched. Short of eating a bullet, there was no way to alleviate that particular sensation.

He couldn't sit there a second longer. He needed to go somewhere. Do something. Only he didn't know where or what. He'd figure it out on the way.

In less than five seconds, he was in his truck, cranking the engine. The pick-up turned over with a throaty rumble he usually enjoyed, but not tonight. He jammed his foot down on the gas, gravel chucking across the yard until the wheels got their grip and then rocketed down the mile-long winding driveway.

I'm dying.

Tension grabbed hold of his spine. His heart stuttered, stopped, and started again.

Those two words, spoken in that *female* voice, were not a product of the Bastard in His Brain. Those words were an auditory hallucination—another enduring effect of the lightning strike.

It'd been a long time since that voice had spoken to him. But still, there was only one sane way to deal with it—booze. There was another way to get rid of the voice, but that involved psych meds and a trip to the nuthouse. And he had a severe nut allergy.

He was ten minutes from the twenty-four-hour gas station with its beer cooler stocked full of liquid oblivion, but only ten seconds from driving past the main house. He should've moved years ago, but he couldn't afford a seven-hundred-acre tract of land as beautiful and isolated as the one his father owned. The benefits of extreme solitude continued to win over the reminder of rejection every time he drove past his childhood home.

He rounded the first curve in the driveway; the truck's headlights danced across the house's many windows. No lights shined from inside; no exterior lights illuminated the grounds. The place was a giant beast slumbering on the side of the hill.

Anyone else looking at the structure would be awed by the many gables and porches and stunned to learn that an entire medical facility was housed in the expansive basement. But to him the place was a mausoleum of memories. A place where he'd once been part of a family with his dad, his stepmom, and his teenage stepsister who all loved the child version of him. Until Gale left his father, taking Shayla with her, and his dad forgot Xander existed. He'd been just seven years old when love left his life. Twenty-five years later, he could honestly say anger had been a better friend to him than love had ever been.

He eased off the gas and coasted past the house, not wanting to make too much noise. He didn't want to wake Uncle Matt, and he especially didn't want to wake Roweena, the Stone family housekeeper. She might be an employee, but she'd chew his ass for driving around in the middle of the night as if he were still a teenager. She worried about—

You're not coming. You're not going to save me. Because you don't exist. Never have. I believed in you. Thought you must be real—Gran swore you were. But you were nothing more than hope's fatal dream. We're going to die, and no one other than Queen will ever remember we existed.

"Get the fuck out of my head." He yelled the words, breaking his number one rule—never talk back to the voice. Talking back meant he'd descended to a whole new level of cuckoo in the cranium. He clenched his eyes closed for just a second, hoping for a reset when he opened them.

A figure stood in the middle of the driveway, facing away from the truck.

"Shit." Xander slammed on the brakes, the truck skidding in the gravel before stopping only a few feet

away from a vehicular manslaughter charge. The sound
of his heartbeat and ragged breaths were as loud as an
air horn to his ears.

Dad.

His father stood in the middle of the driveway,
dressed in a pair of plaid pajama pants and a T-shirt. His
thick, gray hair smashed and bent, forming an unattract-
ive case of bedhead. What the hell was the guy doing?

Xander sat back in his seat and crossed his arms. He
wasn't making the first move. To acknowledge Dad
would be a violation of their unwritten code of conduct.
Each pretended the other didn't exist. It'd been that way
since Gale left them, taking his father's heart with her.

But that voice. How long before it started talking
again? He needed to get half-pickled to get it good
and gone.

Fuck the rules. He honked one short burst.

Dad didn't flinch or acknowledge he was standing only
feet from Xander's bumper in the beam of his headlights.

Xander rolled down the window. "Move." His throat
tingled from the force of his shout.

Dad acted oblivious. As if he weren't standing in the
middle of the driveway, in the middle of the night, in the
middle of Xander trying to get booze.

Xander tore open the truck door. Decades of anger
rode between his shoulder blades. Hundreds of unuttered
words flooded his mouth. He stomped toward his dad.
"What is your problem? I'm just following your rules. I
got the message ten years ago when you didn't show up
at the hospital after I was struck by lightning. When you
never even asked Row or Matt whether I was alive or
dead. Now get out of my…"

His words faded when he saw his father's face. Fine wrinkles flared out from the corners of his eyes and deeper ones cut furrows across his forehead. His mouth was turned down in an endless frown. The last time Xander had been in the same room with his father, the guy was in his forties. The man before him was two decades older and looked like he'd suffered a tremendous loss.

Tears streamed down the older man's cheeks, splashing onto his T-shirt.

Pain slammed into Xander's temple. He jerked and pressed his palm to the side of his head. He could practically feel his brain pulsing inside his skull.

Dad's gaze cut to him. "She needs me. I can feel her desperation, but I can't find her anymore. It's been too long." *I love her. She's my soul. My everything. I need her as much as she needs me.*

For a moment, only a moment, compassion chiseled away Xander's hard edges. But then blades of bitterness and rejection and anger stabbed through the tenderness. "This is about Gale? It's always been about Gale. It's been over twenty-five years since she left. Get over it. And get out of my way."

She's my fearless. Dad cast his gaze down the driveway.

"Here we go again." When Gale and Shayla first left, Dad had raged for weeks about some local legend and the bear totem that resided on the hill nearby. But that's all anyone knew—the rantings and ravings of a man gone manic in his grief. "You're not making sense." Xander grabbed Dad's arm and hauled him to the edge of the driveway. "Stare at the night all you want. But do it after I drive past." He got back in the truck and drove on, refusing to look back, or think about Dad or the voice. He'd think about beer. A chilled beer. He could practically taste the tang of that first swig. His mouth watered.

At the end of the driveway, Xander barely braked, just cranked the wheel to the right and skidded out onto the road, laying a strip of rubber and squealing the tires in a way any high school boy would admire. He gunned the truck's engine to get to the top of the tallest hill in Sunny County.

Alcohol was less than six minutes away. God, how he needed a beer. Or five. Fuck that, he needed a case. Hell, he should go straight for the tequila. Anything to kill the voice.

As he neared the top of the hill, his headlights played over a motorcycle parked along the wide berm of road and then snagged on a man. A huge beast of a guy stood staring up at the centuries-old carved wooden bear like it was his own personal savior.

The animal posed on its hind legs, mouth open in a frozen snarl, looking real. Alive. Ready to attack. It wasn't the kind of thing to attract tourists. It was more likely to repel them.

What the fuck was up with the carving? His father obsessed over it. And now this freak?

The man turned his face toward the truck, blinking from the brightness of the headlights. A thick black mark—what the hell was it—slashed up his face from mouth to cheekbone, giving him a sinister, half-evil look. He glared into the lights until Xander drove past.

Xander glanced in the rearview mirror. The truck's taillights tossed a bloody glow over bear and man, highlighting the play of muscle and sinew hacked into the wood and making the black mark on the man's face appear to be a gaping hole.

Xander's breath locked inside his lungs. As crazy as it sounded, he half expected man and bear to move. To charge after him.

The truck raced down the hill, the man and the bear fading from sight. Xander's gaze snapped to the road in front of him. Yeah, obviously, he was on the verge of losing it. *It* being his sanity.

Booze. Booze always helped. He needed to get some. Now.

Five minutes later, in sight of the gas station with its flashing neon BEER sign, a rush of energy stung his face and then rolled down his body—the Bastard in His Brain. The sneaky ass was about to stage a coup. Damn. All Xander could do was watch as he inexplicably turned the vehicle onto the highway and headed west—away from liquid salvation, away from reason and rationality, away from sense and sanity.

—⁓—

Three hours later, Xander parked on a mud strip that he suspected might have once been a driveway. The Bastard in His Brain had decided to take him on a vacation to Crazyland, where the only way out was *through* the funhouse. How else could he explain passing up alcohol and driving halfway across Ohio for this—a strange trailer secreted away among hundreds of acres of cornfields?

Despite dawn tipping the horizon in cheerful color, an ominous void and a bleak desperation hung over the place that went deeper than the structure's disrepair. One side of the trailer sagged lower than the other, giving the impression of an enormous teeter-totter. Windows were missing, their gaping maws covered with boards or plywood or simple cardboard. The screen door dangled by its bottom hinge.

Xander wanted to reverse the truck and lay twin strips of *fuck you* on the asphalt on his way down the road. *Wanting* wasn't enough—not nearly enough—to overpower the Bastard. He got out of the vehicle, leaving the keys in the ignition. He would run up, scan the inside of the trailer, satisfy the Bastard, then sort out his shit on the drive back home.

A miraculous hush fell across the landscape. No birds chirped, no insects chattered. No corn leaves rustled. Pure, undiluted silence invaded his ears, and it was more stunning and fascinating than anything he'd ever heard. He stopped. Listened. Nothing. Not one sound. He couldn't even hear the rapid *duh-dum, duh-dum* of his heartbeat.

He closed his eyes, savoring the quiet. Was this why the Bastard had led him here? To find relief from the constant barrage of noise? Was there something significant about this location? Something significant about the trailer? He needed to find out. 'Cause if this spot was devoid of sound, he was going to be moving.

He walked up the crumbling cinder-block steps to the trailer, his boots crunching loud and startling against the decay. So much for the complete-void-of-sound theory. He reached through the skeleton of the screen and jiggled the knob. Locked.

From the other side of the door, the thud of heavy footsteps approached. Someone lived here? The place looked like it should be inhabited by rats and rodents, not humans.

"Open the door. Now. Or I'm bustin' it down." The urgency in his voice surprised him. What surprised him even more—he meant every word. He'd get in this trailer one way or another. Didn't matter that he was trespassing or about to break half a dozen other laws. He *needed* to get inside. Not guilty by reason of the Bastard in His Brain—a.k.a. insanity—would be his defense.

A fist slammed into his temple—or at least it felt like a fist. Xander winced at the tuning-in. Damn.

The door cracked open. All he could see was a too-large-to-be-normal jaundiced eyeball staring out at him, locking on Xander's scars.

He bears the mark of the Beast. King warned me about him. He is here for the Dragon, but it is too late.

The mark of the Beast. Well, that was a new one. Xander touched the puckered skin on his cheek. He almost admired the originality. Almost.

"Go away. You're trespassing." The female voice was deep and thick, mucus snapping around each word. *King must confirm the Dragon's death before the body can be burned and the evil ashes soaked in holy water.* "I'll call the police."

"You won't call the police, or you would've called them already. Let me in. I won't ask again."

"Go away." *King would not permit such a risk to anyone, even one marked by the Beast.* The door slammed. A lock snapped into place. A chain rattled.

Was she fearless or stupid or crazy? He leaned toward crazy, considering her thoughts of dragons and kings. He shouldn't judge. He was short on sanity too.

Abandoning all of his self-control and the last of his logic, he rammed into the door, snapping the lock, busting the chain, and impacting with the heft of her body on the other side. He leaped across the threshold. The stench slammed into him—a physical entity that pushed him back a step.

Cigarette smoke so thick it choked the oxygen and clouded the room. Unwashed flesh so pungent and sour it burned his throat. And infusing it all, the putridly sweet rot of death. His throat kicked open, and he half coughed, half gagged, and barely managed to keep himself from vomiting.

The terrible throbbing in his head stopped, but his eyeballs took up the beat.

The floor was covered in trash. Old milk jugs, wrappers, empty boxes of food, strips of white paper that looked suspiciously like toilet paper. She obviously didn't understand the function of a garbage can, and the concept of trash day had to be about fifty points above her IQ.

Roach-like, she scuttled to block a darkened hallway. Sweat plastered her few strands of hair to her skull like a greasy comb-over. Her bulbous nose and wide features verged on downright ugly. Stains of various colors and textures trailed down the front of her tank top, over the bulge of her protruding belly. Everything—every single thing—about her disgusted him. Repulsed him. He didn't want to be in the same trailer with her, and he sure as fuck didn't want to be in the same room with her.

So why was he here? Why couldn't he force himself to leave?

She brandished a large pair of scissors and jabbed them at him like a roly-poly ninja. Under a different set of circumstances, he might've laughed, but her insanity sucked the humor from the situation.

And there was blood on the blades.

Dread fisted his lungs. "What have you done?" He braced, waiting for the frequency to be reestablished. His head jerked.

On the sixth day, I stabbed my sword into the Dragon's flesh. "A peasant should not question his queen." Her tongue slithered from her mouth and stroked over her lips, leaving a slime trail, before slipping back inside.

"I'm not your peasant." He might be on a visit to Crazyland, but she had moved into town, taken up permanent residence, and joined the Church of Unsound Mind. When in Crazyland, do as the crazy do. He packed his tone with authority. "I am your king, and you will tell me what you've done."

She froze, almost as if Xander had hit the pause button. *You don't look like King.*

Shit. "I had plastic surgery. Changed my entire appearance. That's why you don't recognize me." With the scars on his face, she'd have to be more than crazy to buy that line of bovine excrement; she'd have to be downright dumb.

Her face relaxed into a look of senseless understanding.

"Sire." She crossed one tree trunk of a leg in front of the other and curtsied. Fucking curtsied like she was some fancy-ass princess.

King is so pretty now. Except for part of his face. "I didn't know your new face."

"Show me what you've done."

"I have followed your decree. On the sixth day, I thrust my sword into the Dragon."

His gut coiled tight. "Show me."

"It might not be safe for you. I'm not certain the Dragon is dead."

He used his best I-am-the-king tone. "Show me."

"But Sire, you cannot risk being in its presence if it still lives."

"All will be well." He forced himself not to gag on his next words. "My queen, please, show me."

She turned and waddled down the short hallway. He followed her to a heavy steel door. The kind of door that wouldn't be standard issue in a cheap trailer. The kind of door used to keep intruders out. Or to keep something locked inside, something that bled, from the looks of her scissors. An animal? He *wanted* it to be an animal, but—damn—he knew he was going to find a human on the other side of that steel.

She unlocked the door and stepped aside. "Be careful, Sire."

Dim silver light from the open doorway slashed across the dark room, illuminating a body in the middle of the floor. The naked female, so devoid of muscle she qualified as a skeleton, had a vile ring of blood surrounding her, seeping from a gash in her side.

His lungs contracted, expelling the air out of him. "What have you done?" he snapped at the Crazy One and realized two seconds too late he'd broken character.

You're not King. You tricked me.

The woman on the floor needed an ambulance and mostly likely an extended hospital stay—assuming she was even alive. But the Crazy One still had those scissors in her hand. He wouldn't be helping anyone if she buried them in his spine. He put himself between the woman on the floor and the Crazy One.

"I *told* you." A croaky voice came from the shadows and muted planes of space the light didn't reach. "I *told* you her protector would come." Another skeletal body crawled into the light, face ravaged by torment and time, its attention focused on the Crazy One's scissors.

Something familiar plucked at Xander's memory, just beyond the reach of consciousness. Damn.

The Crazy One dropped the scissors. She stood, mouth hanging open, her flat slug of a tongue resting on her bottom lip. She backed away, one step at a time. *I must finish. I must finish.* She turned and ran down the hallway, each footstep reverberating through the floor.

"Take her. Protect her. Heal her. Save her from Queen." The malnourished figure crawling on the floor spoke again, urgency riding each of her words.

Save her from Queen. Recognition slammed into him, knocking him to his knees.

…and no one other than Queen will ever remember we existed. Queen—not a typical name.

"Fuck me." A burr gouged into his heart. The woman lying on the floor was *the woman.* The one inside his head. She wasn't a figment of a fucked mind. She was naked and emaciated and—oh, Christ—looked like a corpse.

Guilt choked in his throat—a lump too big to swallow, too awful to taste. She'd tried to tell him she was suffering and needed help. What had he done? Buried her words under a gallon of liquor and a barrel of self-pity. All those nights when he'd felt so restless, if he'd just gotten in his truck, would he have driven here? Found her before it was too late?

The woman's cheekbones jutted so sharply they nearly cut through the skin. Tufts of blond hair grew in patches along her hairline. And yet, superimposed over what his eyes took in, his mind filled in the gaps, added flesh to her cheeks, fullness to her eyes, and pale-blond hair to her head. Somehow, he saw beyond what lay before him to what might have been. She would've been beautiful. Radiant in an angelic way words couldn't adequately describe.

"Oh, God." He was the worst sort of asshole. Had always been a selfish bastard, owned that about himself, but this—this was a low he'd never be able to crawl out of. He couldn't just rationalize away his lack of action all this time.

The spot where his heart should be throbbed. His hand shook like someone coming off the sauce as he reached for her, touching her neck, feeling for a pulse, though he knew there was no way she could be alive.

Her skin nearly froze his fingers. Death did that to a person, stole their warmth along with their life. Her eyelids fluttered, stuttered, and opened, locking directly on him, pinning him with her gaze.

Logical thought tumbled out of his head, splashing onto the floor. His body went into suspended animation mode.

She swallowed, wincing as if the action hurt. "Xander?"

Every word in his vocabulary vanished behind a nearly impenetrable wall of shock and disbelief.

"Is it really you?" Her words were barely a breath of sound. "Or am I dreaming?"

He understood what she was saying, he just couldn't pluck any response out of the emptiness in his mind.

Her face scrunched up, and a soft, dry sob hacked in her throat. "You're just a dream. Why can't I just die?"

Seeing her hurting, seeing her pain, finally dissolved

his mental paralysis. "Oh, God. I'm here." He gripped her face in one hand. Her expression relaxed as if his touch eased her. "I'm real. You're safe." He swiped his thumb over her chin, felt it tremble at his touch.

Sorrow faded from her eyes, but other emotions filled the void—more emotions than he knew what to do with. He didn't need to be Freud to see the adoration and the hero worship. "Don't look at me like that. I'm not the good guy here." His tone was overflowing with self-loathing and guilt for not finding her years ago. "You know my name, but I don't know yours."

"Isleen." One side of her mouth twitched like she was trying to smile. "You're real. You're really real." The smile faded. "Where's Gran? You have to save Gran too."

Her eyes closed, her chest popped up and down in exaggerated breaths too unnatural to be normal. He yanked his cell phone from his pocket.

"Isleen, you stay with me now. You hang on." He dialed 911, waited for the operator to pick up. *Ring-ring.* Pause. *Ring-ring.* Pause. *Ring-ring.* "Pick the fuck up." *Ring-ring.*

"911, what is your—"

"The last road I remember is County Road 95. A trailer in the middle of cornfields. I just found two women being held against their will. They both need an ambulance."

"Sir, can you tell me…"

The growl of his truck's engine grabbed Xander's attention. The Crazy One—he'd forgotten about her— had stolen his truck. This day was full of happy damned surprises. The sound of his truck faded and got further away, but then the direction changed and the roar of pedal-to-the-metal screamed at him. What was she doing? Even as the question flittered through his consciousness, the answer came to him. His truck was about to meet the trailer.

He dropped the phone and grabbed Isleen.

The room exploded.

Chapter 3

KING FOLLOWED THE FOUR NAKED MEN TO THE RIVER. Languid anticipation warmed in his guts. Predawn light tinted everything in shades of onyx and silver. The only sound was the whisper of water and the splash of it against his Brothers' bare bodies, then against his own. Each step was a step away from technology and man-made things, away from his job and ordinary life, and a step toward divinity and the Lord.

The current—surprisingly warm during all the seasons—sucked at his calves, at his thighs, and then at his penis and testicles, stroking his sex organs with a delicate caress. All his Brothers would be aroused by the sensation, it was a natural part of the Ritual of Resurrection. Chosen One had assured them it was simply a biological reaction to being in the presence of the Lord.

When they were all submerged chest-deep, Chosen One pointed to each of the Brothers and directed them into position, their bodies forming the four points of a cross, with Chosen One in the convergence.

Their leader raised his arms parallel to the water and tilted his head back. The Brothers and King did likewise. He stared up through the thick tree branches reaching out over the river and watched as the world changed from muted tones to shimmery gold and orange. And all the while, they remained supplicant to the Lord.

King's sense of time and place morphed, and the memory of their ritual—performed four times a year on this spot for centuries—coursed through him. A breeze sparked against his skin. The Lord was in the air he took inside his body, in the water licking over his skin.

Chosen One spoke. "Lord, we offer our thanks and praise for your many sacrifices for us. On this day, we acknowledge the death of spring for the resurrection of summer."

King imagined what it would be like to be on the bank and a witness to the Ritual of Resurrection. To see all five men posed, filled with the spirit. The picture they must present as dawn illuminated the day. He couldn't breathe from the wonder of it.

"And now…" Chosen One's words were a cue for the Brothers to lower their arms. "We will all wash away our sins, cast them off into the current, and be reborn to serve you."

Chosen One gestured for King to move forward. Blood swelled in King's groin. Moving through the water with such an erection both pained and pleasured him.

His leader's face no longer reflected that of a kindly grandfather. His features had sharpened and hardened in an almost imperceptible way that portrayed power and knowledge and holiness. Chosen One stepped to the side and placed one palm on King's forehead, the other in the small of his back, his grip on the two points a reassurance.

"Brother King, do you seek purgation of your sins?" Chosen One's voice resonated across the river.

King could hardly breathe. "I do." A wonderful, warm tension pulsed through his organs.

"Brother King, do you seek to be reborn in the Lord's image with all the powers inherent?"

"I do." The tension transformed into an expectancy, a yearning—an urge so intense his knees quavered and he fought the desire the pump his hips.

"Brother King, do you seek to fulfill your destiny as the Lord has ordained it?"

"I do." He groaned the words, nearly lost to the sensations.

"Brother King, do you seek to die so that you may live?"

King nodded, unable to find his tongue or vocal cords amid the myriad of swelling passion, but he needed to speak the words, for saying them aloud made them a prayer. He tried twice before he actually uttered the sound. "I do."

Chosen One pushed against King's forehead, tilting his body backward until his neck, then his head met the water. His feet, no longer able to sustain the extreme angle, left the muddy river bottom. Chosen One supported King's weight with a hand underneath his back, and then he gently submerged King's face underneath the water. That's where King remained.

In the beginning, when he'd been a fearful boy of five, King had panicked and fought the sense of not being in control. Four decades later, he'd learned to anticipate the sensations. All of them.

Unable to draw air, his chest began to burn, but he forced himself to stillness. He wanted to draw out the experience, savor it like a sunrise. His lungs throbbed, his heart crashed, and the pain became unbearable. Just when he thought he couldn't tolerate half a second more, it happened—an endless moment where he felt heaven.

Only it wasn't a place; it was more like a sensation. The closest description he could come up with was that it felt like flying—not in a plane, but as if his body had released his soul and it soared. Oh, how it soared. The experience changed him, made him into a man blessed by the Lord.

His body bucked against the oxygen deprivation, and he slammed back to reality. He thrashed against the hands holding him under, and his penis released a stream of semen. The scorching liquid floated over his testicles in an elusive cloud of grace.

Only then did Chosen One lift him from the water.

King gulped in giant lungfuls of air, sucking river water into his mouth and up his nose, tasting and smelling the mud and algae searing his sinuses. In the river, bathed in dawn's divine light, the only sound was of his body snorting and snarling to find a new equilibrium after his return from death. It was a beautiful resurrection.

Chosen One's strong hands stayed on King's body, holding him up until his legs were strong enough to support his weight. Finally, when King calmed, Chosen One stepped away. With one finger, King pressed a nostril closed and blew out the waste in the other one, then repeated the gesture with the other nostril to complete his cleansing and resurrection.

"Thy will be done," King said, his voice thick, his body weak and shaky. He returned to his position to watch each of his Brothers go through the ritual.

By the time they were finished, dawn was an hour old, and heat and humidity and mosquitoes were an irritant. They waded back to the shore in the same order they'd entered the water. In the silence that followed the profound, they dressed. One by one, each of his Brothers bowed their heads to Chosen One and then left to return to their regular, routine lives. One brother was a lawyer, another a professor, another a doctor, and King was the chaplain for the local hospital.

"Brother King, would you stay a moment more?" His leader's tone was mild, but King sensed the urgency underneath.

"Certainly." A small smile of triumph teased his tongue and twitched his lips.

"Brother King, I sense a change. Your resurrection was particularly powerful this morn."

"It was." He drew in a breath. "I ordered Queen to kill the Dragon last evening."

Chosen One's eyes widened. "Rex!" He lapsed into using King's birth name and grabbed King's arms with both of his hands. "You completed your task." He brought King in for a hug, and King let himself be held by the powerful man who was more than his Chosen One. He was also King's father.

"I knew your simple sister would be of assistance to you. Serving you in this task has always been part of her purpose." Chosen One released him. "I am proud of you. You have struggled with this burden for far too long. You *must know*—especially today—that the Lord only chooses those who are strong enough to carry the burden of his destiny."

"I am pleased it is over, but my weak mind still struggles against…struggles to understand…the Lord's will."

"It is much the same for all who've been asked to complete such a task. We are here but to serve the Lord, not to question. You must now carry out the last rites, or the Dragon will never truly be dead. You do understand the importance?"

"I do." King's guts shriveled. He still needed to chop off her head, burn her body, soak the ashes in holy water, and inter them in holy ground. A nice little list of horror. But he hadn't struggled this long to leave his duty to the Lord unfinished.

Chapter 4

Only sound existed for Xander.

Heartbeats.

Two of them.

His beating rapidly, Isleen's catching only every third beat.

The whisper of their mingled breaths made a song—a rhythm only Xander was able to hear. He couldn't feel or see anything, but he wasn't freaked. It felt like they were in an odd sort of suspension, where only peace and grass-smoking hippies could thrive. A thought floated across his mind.

We should be dead. But we aren't. Our hearts are beating. We're breathing.

The rest of Xander's senses came back online in a rush of color and texture and sensation. He lifted his head, realizing he had buried his face against the span of skin where Isleen's neck sloped into her shoulder—an oddly intimate place for his nose and mouth. He found himself kneeling, knees on the grass, with Isleen crushed to him, her chest mashed against his. The way he held her was no sweet romantic gesture; it was determination to keep her with him. Keep her safe.

Overgrown weeds grew unimpeded toward the sky, and giant dandelions pocked the yard with their pretty color. On three sides of him, all Xander could see were cornfields.

Waves of malicious intent lapped at his back. He didn't need to twist around to know the trailer and his truck were behind him.

How had they gotten here? His memory provided no answers. One moment the trailer had exploded around them, the next they had been suspended in the weird place where only sound existed, and somehow here they were.

Flawless, fresh sunshine warmed his skin. God, just to be out of the darkness and despair of the trailer was a miracle. But now the extent of Isleen's misery was spotlighted. Every bone protruded against her translucent skin. Her eyelids were lavender; her lips nearly the same color. Wounds covered her entire body—some almost healed, some beginning to heal, and some heartbreakingly fresh. A meager stream of blood oozed from the gash in her side.

Underneath all the suffering, Xander saw something he recognized, something familiar, something he couldn't place and would have to ponder in order to understand.

The truck's ignition wheezed, chugged, and then caught. The roar of it rammed tension up his spine. He turned in time to see the vehicle bounce and jolt, trying to break free from the room it had plowed into. A small pile of debris was the only thing standing between them and a head-on collision.

No way had the grandmother survived. His thoughts shifted into hyperdrive, searching for options to keep him and Isleen alive. He wasn't the type to turn pussy and run. He was the type who enjoyed a good ass stomping. Didn't matter if he was the victor or the loser—either way was more satisfying than walking away with a limp dick. His hope sputtered and stalled. There were no options. But there was nothing to do. No way to fight. Here, in this situation, when he had to think about more than himself, the only fucking choice was to run.

With Isleen still pinned to his chest, he sprinted toward the cover of the cornfield. Maybe he could lose the bitch in the hundreds of acres.

The stalks weren't even as tall as he was and yet they stood as a formidable guard, blocking his entry into the field. He fought through the first row of corn, through another, and another—bashing, smashing, using his body and Isleen's to penetrate the field. The coarse leaves sliced at his face, his neck, his arms, leaving stinging cuts in their wake. He couldn't tolerate the thought of what they must be doing to Isleen's naked skin.

He glanced through the leaves, back to the yard. The truck broke free from the trailer and shot directly for where they had entered the field. Of course, it came right for them; he'd carved a nice path to their location.

He hunched over and changed direction, turning left to follow the row instead of going against it. The space wasn't wide enough for him, and certainly not for both of them. He ran in an awkward sidestepping motion.

The truck hit the corn in the spot they'd vacated less than ten seconds ago. For one fist-pumping moment, it sounded like the bitch was going to drive around in the middle of the field searching for them, but then the banging of stalks against the truck grille turned in their direction and got closer and closer as if she knew exactly where they were.

Xander bashed back through the sentry rows into the

yard and sprinted toward the trailer. If he could just get to the structure and hide inside, maybe the bitch would think they were still in the field. The angry growl of the engine was suddenly, inexplicably, obscenely close. The truck jumped out of the field no more than fifty feet behind him.

They weren't going to make it.

Not unless he suddenly sprouted blue tights and a red cape. The hope of escape morphed into despair and resignation and finally reckless pissed-off-ness. No fucking way was he going to die running. He stopped, turned, and faced the truck barreling toward them. The tires ate up the ground at an indecent rate. He clutched Isleen tighter to his chest. For her sake, he wanted it to be a quick death. No more lingering. No more pain.

That thought infuriated him. None of this was right. They shouldn't be on the verge of death. Again.

The truck kept coming—now twenty-five feet away.

Everything slowed, happening as if through the quicksand of time. A white dandelion floaty meandered on the breeze directly between them and the truck. His heart no longer ran a staccato rhythm. *Duh...dum.* Pause. *Duh...dum.* Pause.

His life didn't flash before his eyes. The future did. Isleen's future. In an ethereal dream beyond time, her skin was gilded by firelight, her eyes devoid of sadness and fear, her body whole and healthy. She smiled, an expression so full of warmth and tenderness and undiluted joy that it plunked itself down inside his heart and wouldn't leave.

He ached to create that kind of smile on her face, but their lives were over. It all could've gone so differently if he'd only listened to her, believed in her, found her years before now.

The air changed, displaced by the truck only a few feet from them. Heat from the engine blasted his face, smelling of burning oil, gasoline, and a scent reminiscent of popped corn. He locked eyes with the bitch. Her pudgy lips ripped back over her teeth in a snarling scream.

Xander knew anger—his best friends were fury and rage—but the look on the bitch's face went beyond mere anger all the way to unholy.

The truck imploded.

The sound was supersonic, a resonation that rippled through his skin and muscle to rattle his bones and shake the earth underneath his feet. Metal and glass and fire shot outward, skyward, backward, in a near-perfect arc of destruction. Flaming debris rained around them.

He stood there holding Isleen, watching it happen, not believing the message his eyes sent to his brain.

"What the...?" The last of the truck parts hit the ground. The pieces burned. That's all that was left— pieces. Nothing touched *them*, like they resided under an invisible dome of protection.

He glanced down at Isleen for an answer, but she was unconscious, her head lolling so limply on her neck it looked as if he was carrying a corpse.

The buzzing and drilling of unrelenting noise— conversations, beeping machines, TV, the rumble of the overworked AC—all threatened to shatter Xander's two-fisted grip on sanity. He sat in the emergency room waiting area, elbows on knees, hands cupped over his ears to filter out some of the chaos. The only consolation was that no one spoke to him. Tuning in on top of everything else would be a formal invitation for the Bastard to make a guest appearance.

The day had already gone to shit, but Xander didn't need the lowlight to be the Bastard going on an angry rampage that ended with him either in jail or in a hospital room recovering from bashing his face through a concrete wall. Been there. Done that. Twice. He didn't want to see what kind of charm the third time would offer.

It'd been four hours since the officer who'd found them had rushed them to the emergency room. Xander had tried listening in only to the conversations about Isleen, but trying to filter out all the noise to follow one thread was exhausting and overwhelming. The only thing he knew for sure—she could just as easily live as die.

His heart twinged at the thought. Isleen and the word *die* shouldn't be in the same dictionary. She deserved to live. He *needed* her to live. To have a life. A good life. One that made up for everything she'd endured. One that made him feel less guilty about drowning her pleas for help with alcohol and denial.

Across from Xander, a haggard mother tried to keep a grip on her writhing, squirming toddler. Twin braids of snot drizzled from the kid's nose. He sucked in his top lip, slurping up the mucus. The kid looked right at Xander's scars, then opened his mouth and coughed a wet snapping sound so full of phlegm that Xander cringed. God, he could practically feel the brat's germs splatting on his skin.

He looked around for another place to sit. A lone man holding a pink plastic bucket sat in the other section of seats. Xander stood to move to that area, but the man burped and belched and then barfed in the bucket. He wasn't a quiet barfer, and if the stench was any indication, it was coming out of more than one orifice.

Fucking goddamned public places. The man continued to vomit. The toddler started screaming. Xander's grip on himself slipped. A buzz of electricity sparked underneath his skin. The edges of his vision went white. That shit about seeing red was just that—shit. He saw white. He needed to get out of here. Now. Right now. The Bastard was on the verge of ballistic.

Xander sprinted through the maze of seats for the outside doors.

"…taking you to a scene in rural Prospectus. We don't have all the information, but we do know that two women were being held captive inside this trailer."

Xander's attention snapped to the TV and the wide shot of the trailer with its demolished back end, the debris of what used to be his truck, and the destroyed cornfield. Local law enforcement officers and BCI guys roamed the property, some examining evidence, others taking photos. He stopped sharp as if he'd hit a pane of glass.

His heart shifted into a higher gear. How had they survived? No matter how many times he replayed it in his mind, he didn't have an answer.

"It appears the women had been held for quite some time. Police officials say they are still piecing together what happened."

Nothing fascinated the masses more than stories of cruelty and violence. A media frenzy was about to erupt, and Isleen was going to be in the middle of it.

"This is Dwight Swineforth, the farmer who owns the

fields around the trailer. Mr. Swineforth, did you see any thing that would indicate what was happening inside?"

The camera panned to a grizzled farmer dressed in cutoff coveralls, work boots, and a baseball hat. The guy had to be pushing eighty, yet looked like a nerdy kid whose mamma still dressed him. *"Nothing. I mean, I never saw no one. When I'd be plowin', harvestin', or drivin' by checkin' the crops, I never saw a thing. Only reason I know'd someone still lived there was because sometimes there'd be a car in the driveway."*

The white at the edges of Xander's vision spread, engulfing more of his sight. He jogged through the doors to the outside.

Even though it was only late morning, humidity soaked the air, instantly dampening his clothing and moistening his skin. It was a relief from the noise. Oh, he could still hear it all, but now he was a layer removed. His vision returned to normal.

What a goddamned mess. The deputy who'd brought them to the emergency room had questioned him, but not as thoroughly as a detective would, or as Kent would when he got here. Xander's story had been far-fetched but plausible. He'd been lost, stopped to get directions, saw something wasn't right, and found Isleen and her grandmother. Any pig with half a brain would see through that shit shine.

Speaking of pork, Kent's oh-no-I'm-not-compensating-for-anything huge truck pulled into the lot. Xander sat on a bench in the shade of the entrance area and waited for Kent to take his sweet-ass time to park and stroll over.

Xander sucked in a slow breath. Held it. Waited for the slam of pain.

"You ready to give the real story? I've been out there. And I don't buy what you're trying to sell."

Bam. Xander flinched and then clamped his eyes closed for a few seconds too long to be normal before popping them back open. "Not my problem." He stared straight ahead. The goddamned pounding in his head had decided to pair up with his heartbeat to make a rhythm and a counter rhythm. The cadence might've been catchy if it wasn't rocking out inside his body.

"Gonna be your problem if you get arrested for murder. Right now, all that's left of that woman are pieces. The largest one I saw was a nipple—nipple ring still attached."

"Fucking Christ, man. Keep that shit to yourself. You didn't see her. You don't know how that image just burned a hole through my frontal lobe." Xander rubbed his thumping temple. "Media's already gone live with the story. You'll need to get someone here to protect Isleen's privacy."

"And you're gonna need a lawyer if you don't talk to me. No truck randomly explodes like that. There's a crater four feet deep in the yard. Your little tale about being lost? Sell it to someone else. Your truck had a navigation system and so does your phone."

An ambulance, lights flashing, but no siren blaring drove past where they sat to the ER entrance.

Kent gestured toward it. "They're bringing in the old lady. She was still alive."

Xander's jaw slowly sank open, and he struggled to assimilate that little knowledge bomb. "Whoa… She was in that back room. It was obliterated. I didn't think

she'd survived, or I would've looked for her." He stood
and headed toward the ambulance, pulled by curiosity
and maybe a little guilt that he hadn't focused more on
finding Isleen's grandmother.

The EMT guy pulled the gurney from the back of
the truck. A woman just as skeletal as Isleen lay in an
awkward fetal position. Isleen's grandmother looked
familiar. More familiar than Isleen.

The tuning-in slammed into the side of Xander's head.

"You family?" The EMT glanced at him and did a
double take at the scars. *Whoa, buddy. What happened
to your face?*

"Struck by lightning. It's called a Lichtenberg
figure," Xander answered without thinking. And then it
was like someone had hit his rewind button and he was
a little boy again, looking up at the face of the woman
who'd raised him. Until she walked out on him. On his
father. "Son of a bitch. This is Gale."

"You know her?" The EMT and Kent spoke in stereo.

"She's my dad's wife. My fucking stepmom."
Disbelief permeated his words. Reality shifted underneath his feet, but he didn't move, only watched Gale
being wheeled into the ER. He now existed in a world
where Isleen had been inside his head and she was Gale's
granddaughter. Where was Shayla then, Isleen's mom?

An image of Shayla laughing while she babysat him
burst into his mind. She'd been just eighteen when she
and Gale left, not quite an adult. He tried to picture her
as she would be now, a woman in her forties. Who had
a daughter—Isleen. Total mind fuck.

"What is going on here?" No mistaking the anger in
Kent's tone.

"I need to make a call, then I'll explain everything." Xander held out his hand. "I need your phone."

Kent slapped the phone into Xander's palm with the force of a bitch slap to the face.

Xander hoped the number to the main house hadn't changed since he was a kid.

"Stone residence," Row answered on the first ring.

"Row, I need to talk to Dad. Now." Silence on the other end of the line. "Row?"

"Sorry. My God, I never thought this day would come." A hitched breath. She might be the housekeeper, but to the family and to him, she was a lot more.

He wasn't able to tune in over a phone line, but with Row, he didn't need to. "You're not standing there crying, are you? I need to talk to Dad. Now." Over the line, he heard the patter of her feet on the floor.

"No, no. I'm on the way down to the Institute right now. Just a second. Hold on. Don't hang up. I'm in the hallway. Almost there."

Jesus. She was running. Probably didn't want to blow the one time father and son were actually going to communicate.

"Alex. It's…a phone call for you. Important," Row said.

Xander heard the shuffle of the phone being passed. "This is Dr. Stone."

Decades of training in noncommunication captured Xander's tongue. And right now, he didn't have anger riding him as a motivator.

"Row, I don't think anyone is there." Dad's voice went distant as if he had started to move the phone away from his face.

"Gale's in the hospital." The words shot out of

Xander's mouth at a volume louder than they should have. On the other end of the line, everything went quiet, except for the sound of Dad breathing into the mouthpiece.

"Where?"

"Prospectus, Ohio. There's another woman with her. A young woman."

"Shayla?"

"No. Her name is Isleen. Gale's her grandmother. They're both in bad shape. Not sure either is going to make it. I don't know what happened, but they both appear to have been held hostage, beaten, tortured, and starved."

"Oh God, Gale." Anguish soaked each of his father's words. "I knew she was in danger. I could've kept her safe. Everything would've been fine if she'd just listened. Listened to the legend. Listened to me." Dad exhaled, blowing into the phone and Xander's ear. "Why didn't she listen?"

The sincerity in Dad's voice shot a spike of panic through Xander's sternum. Like Dad really expected Xander to have an answer. What the fuck was he supposed to say?

"I'm on my way. Leaving right now."

Dad hung up, but Xander stood with the phone pressed to his ear. Their twenty-five years of silence had just ended, and Dad hadn't even acknowledged it. Didn't surprise Xander, but there was no denying the sting of it. He handed the phone back to Kent and then clutched the side of his head—a preemptive gesture.

"Keep in mind I've got this bizarre hearing thing that shouldn't exist, and yet you know it's real." The pain bulldozed into his brain.

"Oookaaaay." Kent stretched the word out into one long syllable.

"Well, that's only the tip of the glacier." He told Kent everything. Everything. About the woman's voice inside his head since the lightning strike, about how he'd always drowned it with booze, about how last night the Bastard in His Brain made him drive to the trailer.

Kent crossed his arms and gave him *that* look. "If this is the story you're going to stick with, you're screwed."

Chapter 5

Four days later...

SHE WAS DEAD.

> *Deceased.*
>
> *Departed.*
>
> *That was the only explanation for her surroundings.*

Isleen stood in an intangible space of airy alabaster. Delicate fingers of fog swirled and swelled, coiling around her like a sweet caress. The air smelled of white lilacs, of carefree times. Here in this space, there were no walls to confine her, no doors to trap her, no one to hurt her—no pain, no hunger pangs, no muscle cramps, no soreness from the latest beating.

She had to be in heaven.

Her heart fluttered as delicate as a butterfly trapped in a mesh cage. Her breath glided in and out on wings of sound. She felt so gosh-darned small, but expansive at the same time. The strange sensation scared her until her brain produced a name for the feeling. Freedom.

Tears slicked her vision, then skimmed down her cheeks, riding the wave of her jawbone to slip and slide down her neck. Gran had told her about this. About happy tears. They had both cried rivers and lakes in that room, but Gran—until she lost her mind—always reminded Isleen that happy tears happened too. And that they were chemically different from sad tears.

Isleen could feel the difference. These tears were full of peace and grace. These tears cleansed the wounds Queen had made on her soul.

The air became a visible thing—wavering and morphing into color and texture, as if an artist was painting the environment one feature at a time. Splotches of white swelled into the palest of blues, then intensified, and suddenly the blue separated from the white into a pristine sky, perfectly spotted by cotton-ball clouds.

The atmosphere rippled and pulsed. Green smears speckled the ground, then sharpened and defined and became tall grass. White blossoms dotted the meadow, then some of them transformed into gold, some into vivid purple, and the grasses became fused with beautiful wildflowers. Small birds, some brown, some red, some strikingly yellow, flitted among the flowers. A winding path cut a swath through the meadow and made Isleen want to stroll along and just exist in perfect harmony with the beauty surrounding her. This place was her version of paradise, of heaven.

A cloud slid away from the sun, and the entire landscape went to hyper-vivid color.

Heat blasted the environment—startlingly unpleasant. Her pale skin burned underneath the glaring rays of the sun. For the first time, she noticed a carved wooden sign next to the meadow entrance.

Prospectus Prairie Park.

Something about that sign wasn't right. It was more than the way the wood had faded to an indistinguishable shade between brown and gray. If she were in heaven, why would the sign be in disrepair?

Expectation and anxiety staged an emotional upheaval. Gone were the feelings of bliss and rejuvenation. Her happy tears dried to salt crust. Malevolence crawled over her skin.

A woman jogged past Isleen, so close their arms brushed. Isleen flinched from the invasion of space. The woman appeared completely oblivious to having side-swiped another human being. She just kept jogging, her body slender of muscle and form. She carried herself in a graceful way that reminded Isleen of a ballet dancer. Her mahogany hair was tied up in a perky ponytail that swished over her shoulders like a pendulum. Like a countdown. Like a warning.

Inside Isleen's body, something shifted and changed, but she couldn't put an exact name on the sensation. Impending doom thundered through her blood vessels. She could taste menace in the air. She jogged after the woman. Only she didn't want to jog after the woman. She told her legs to stop moving, but they didn't listen.

An entity held dominance over her, trapping her inside the rind of her skin, forcing her to be a mere observer to what was happening to her body. She pushed against the prison of her own flesh with the only weapon she had—her mind. Nothing. Panic ticked down her spine one vertebra at a time and then knifed her in the guts.

Stop. Don't do this to me. Let me go. Let me out. *She screamed the words, but no sound came out and her body continued to run.*

Breath sliced into her lungs, shot out, in and out, but oxygen seemed to be in short supply because she couldn't get enough. Her heart was a time bomb, ready to explode out of her chest from overexertion. Her legs wobbled, and a profound weariness smothered her. Still the thing at her controls continued to drive her. Sweat *dripped into her eyes, stinging and making them water. But still her legs kept churning over the ground and the sun kept burning down.*

The woman jogged over a fat culvert that served as a bridge for a dry streambed. A troll-like figure emerged from inside the massive pipe. His face was thickly bearded, his hair dirty and disheveled, and despite the distance, Isleen smelled his sweat and bad intentions.

He scrambled up out of the streambed and sprinted after the woman.

Watch out. Behind you. *The muscles in her throat strained to make noise, to scream, to warn the woman, but a stronger counterforce wouldn't permit a peep.*

The man sprang at the woman, launching himself as if he were a jungle cat taking down prey. They fell. A short, sharp snap of pain and fear slipped from the woman, then ceased when her body hit the ground. He landed on top of her. Neither of them moved for a few ticks of the clock, then the man lifted himself and shifted until he sat on her back.

The woman yelled nonsensical sounds of anger and terror. Her arms beat at the ground; her hands rucked up handfuls of dead summer grass. Her feet kicked, but her toes only succeeded in slapping the ground. Her hips bucked up and thrashed, trying to fling the man off her back like an angry bull, but he was too heavy.

Isleen stopped next to them. Immobilized. Paralyzed. Helpless. Forced to watch the man withdraw a knife from a sheath on his waist. The blade was subtly curved, wickedly curved, and smeared with rust. Only it wasn't rust; it was dried blood. Dear God, who else had he killed?

She pushed against the confines of her body, strained, tensed, tried to react, tried to catch that hand holding the knife, but it was already too late. He punched the blade down into the woman's back. The unholy shriek of pain from the woman branded itself on Isleen's brain, burning deep into her memory where she'd never forget it.

He raised the knife, then punched it into the woman's back—again, again, again—in a series of thrusts so rapid Isleen couldn't count. The sound of steel to bone snapped loudly against the peaceful backdrop of birdsong. Slurping, wet sounds now accompanied each slam of blade to flesh.

The woman stopped screaming.

—◦◦◦—

Xander jerked awake with a full-body shudder. Damn. The incessant noise of the hospital flooded his ears. Beeping and buzzing machines. Hundreds of conversations. The rattle and hum of the air conditioner. Christ. It hadn't seemed this loud until now. The sounds had been there, but somehow he'd forced them into the background. Now they were in the foreground, demanding his attention, depleting his hold on sanity, driving him closer and closer to a visit from the Bastard.

A streak of light snuck around the edges of the closed blinds, slashing across Isleen's empty hospital bed.

Empty.

Xander's heart went bucking bronco inside his chest. Where was she? He kicked to his feet and ran from the room. The hallway was empty except for Isleen in her hospital smock flashing her too-bony spine and creamy white ass to the world.

He darted back in the room, grabbed the blanket off the bed, and then raced after her, his boots clomping as loud as a Clydesdale's hooves against the tiled floor.

He didn't mean for it to happen, but his vision locked on the pale mounds of her ass, on the demarcation of each rib, on the expanse of all that ivory skin. He shouldn't be staring; he shouldn't be getting a monster rocket in his pants; and he shouldn't be thinking thoughts of—

What. Was. Wrong. With. Him. Especially when he could see the pale-pink outlines of so many scars that it hurt just looking at them.

She was only four days out of that torture trailer, three days free from death's grasp, and two days off the IVs and liquid food, and here he was, thinking about the ways he'd like to prime her pump. When had he become a goddamned pervert?

He caught up with her. "You're probably cold." The words gushed out of his mouth, sounding as awkward as the front of his jeans felt. He draped the blanket over her shoulders, arranged and rearranged it until her backside was covered to her knees. The whole time, she never stopped moving, never acknowledged him, just kept heading down the hallway.

"Where are you going? I can have them bring up a meal. Or if you need the bathroom, it's back there."

She turned into the small waiting area with its vending machines full of fake food. Row had saved him by hauling in as much home cooking as she could carry for Dad and him. She'd even gotten him a replacement cell phone and brought him clean clothes.

Isleen moved across the room and sat in a chair

directly in front of a window, staring out at the main entrance three stories below them.

News vans from every channel in Ohio had staked out the parking lot. Reporters and cameramen milled around, waiting, always waiting for a hint, a glimpse, a morsel of information about the two women held hostage in that trailer. The media had gone manic over their story.

"Goddamned vultures. I'm going to close the blinds, don't want them to see you." He pulled the cord, and the vertical blinds folded shut. She stared at the closed blinds, her face a blank slate, devoid of emotion and animation.

Shit. She was in shock. Didn't she have a right to be after everything she'd been through?

Her body seemed to be healing nicely, but her mind had stagnated. She ate when food was placed in front of her. She let the doctor examine her. But she never communicated. When Xander touched her, he felt more than actually witnessed her attention shifting from deep inside herself to him. After what she'd endured, she deserved any comfort he had the strength to give her.

He sat next to her and took her delicate hand in both of his oversized man hands. Over the past few days, he hadn't been able to resist touching her. Didn't know what that was about, only that it felt right to him and seemed to comfort her. A secret, crazy part of him thought his touch was the reason her body had been recovering so fast. But that was a thought his sanity couldn't afford to think.

"You're safe now. You're in the hospital. You're doing well. A little shaky at first. Your organs were failing, but now everything is functioning normally. The doctors can't explain your rapid recovery, but they are thinking of releasing you later today or tomorrow. They just wanted to see you up and around first." He touched her chin lightly, guiding her face around so it was aimed at his. "I've been right here with you the entire time. And I'll be right here whenever you decide to talk to me."

Part of him couldn't believe the words coming out of his mouth. When it came to her, his gonads had turned into nomads and taken off without him. Somehow, he was okay with that. Deep in his marrow, he meant what he said. He'd wait for her to come around. No matter how long it took.

He might've only met her four days ago, but she'd been inside his head for years, and somehow that made her intimately familiar. Not to mention that she'd waited all that time for him to find her and save her. The least he could do was offer the rest of his life as penance. If she needed time, he would give every second to her.

Her grip on his hand tightened, like she understood his words, but if she had, then why wasn't he tuning in to her? He focused on her, waited for anything in her expression to change, an opening for him to squeeze his way inside and help her heal.

Her room had been kept mostly dark due to her sensitivity to sunlight—being locked in darkness for an extended time had that effect on a person's optics. Here in the too-cheerful brightness of the waiting room, Xander drank in her features and let them imprint in his mind.

Her face had started to fill out, no longer seeming as skeletal as before. Her skin was no longer a shade of death, but a pale porcelain. Her hair amazed him—and everyone else. It was a near-perfect shade of white and had grown two inches in the four days she'd been in the hospital. Two inches. The doctors had no explanation for her hair's rapid growth rate. Not to mention her body's rapid healing rate. All her blood work just kept coming back impossibly normal.

There were so many things about her that defied explanation. She'd known his name. How? She'd been talking inside his head. How? He'd found her. How? The Bastard wasn't talking.

She stood, then tugged him by the hand like he was a reluctant toddler. She walked to the corner of the room and stared at the ninety-degree angle the two walls created.

Fuck. Fuck. Fuck. That kind of behavior gave a person a special invitation to a padded cell. "Isleen. Look at me. Snap out of this." Authority dominated his tone. "You *will* look at me." His voice went deeper, more forceful than he intended, the sound of it resonating through the space.

"What the—" Kent rushed in the room with that look on his face, the look he always wore in Xander's presence. "Don't speak to her like that." Kent's tone didn't carry the weight Xander's had, but the guy's face had gone radiant red with anger. *You're such an asshole. Treating her like that when she can't defend herself. Someone needs to put you in your place. Me. It'd feel like winning a championship to reacquaint you with my fists.*

Where was the slam upside the head? Xander waited for the pain. Nothing. "Say something to me." He spoke the words to Kent, but didn't take his gaze from Isleen.

"You're an asshole." *A sludge-eating loser who thinks he's better than everyone else because his family has money and he has an ability the BCI needs. The way you treat Camille like she's your personal whore makes you the lowest...*

What was going on? He still tuned in; he just didn't get the pain. Not that he was complaining. And when he was with her, the noises that would normally overwhelm him seemed so insubstantial. *When he was with her.* What was it about being with her that affected his hearing?

Isleen swayed on her feet. He snagged her by the arms, and a cool zing of energy tingled through his hands. Suddenly, he couldn't tell where his grip ended and she began. It was as if they had melded together. An ugly urge came upon him. The urge to shake her. Hard. And he did. One quick jerk that had her head flopping around on her neck. "Isleen. Snap out of it. Look at me." That weird force sounded in his voice again.

"You're hurting her." Kent tried to pry one of Xander's hands from her arm, but nothing could separate them. Xander had become an extension of her and couldn't be torn away.

Her eyes transformed from unseeing and unaware to full frontal clarity, their color an expansive sea of clear aquamarine, but underneath the surface, shadows of dark and dangerous things swam. "Xander?"

His heart went hot-air ballooning inside his chest. "You remember me."

Only a foot of space separated them, but she threw herself against him so hard he rocked back half a step. Her arms cinched around him, holding him tighter than he'd ever been held. He returned the favor. Didn't he fucking enjoy that? She fit into his hard angles like the final piece of a puzzle.

Through the thin blanket, he felt the protrusion of her spine and the ripple of each rib. He was intensely aware of her breasts mashed against his chest and the sharp points of her hip bones framing his happy place. It was more than bad timing that his happy place decided to grow ecstatic. *Christ.*

"He wouldn't stop stabbing her." Her voice bore the sound of prolonged suffering. "Blood was everywhere. Everywhere. On me. And I couldn't move. I couldn't make him stop. I couldn't even scream." Her body pulsated with fear, and Mr. Happy finally wised up and let some blood flow back into his brain.

"The things you've been forced to see. The things you've been through. I can't imagine. But, baby, it's over now. No one will ever hurt you again. That woman is dead. The trailer is destroyed. You are here with me. Safe."

"How did I get here? I don't remember."

"You were barely alive when a deputy sheriff found us and drove us to the hospital. You've been here for four days."

"No, I mean how did I get here from the park?"

"Huh?" The word popped out, making him sound like an imbecile.

"Just now. How did I get here from the park?"

He searched her eyes, expecting to see a crazy gaze aimed back at him, but her aquamarine depths were clear and lucid. "You've been here in the hospital for the past four days. I've been with you the whole time."

"No. I was just at Prospectus Prairie Park."

He spared a glance at Kent. The guy's eyes narrowed on Isleen; then he yanked his buzzing phone off his belt and read a message on the screen. *Really? She wakes up for the first time, and this is Kent's reaction?*

"Baby, you've been here with me. You've been sleeping a lot over the past days, pretty out of it. Then ten minutes ago, you got out of bed and walked down the hallway to this waiting room. I followed you. Put this blanket over you." He tugged the ends tighter across her front. "You were… You were all lights-are-on-but-no-one-is-home. And then you just snapped out of it."

Isleen had started shaking her head halfway through his speech. "Just now, I was at Prospectus Prairie Park. A woman was jogging, and a man crawled out of a culvert and stabbed her over and over. He wouldn't stop. I couldn't move. I tried." Her chin trembled, and her face scrunched into a grimace. "My head…" She grabbed her forehead with both of her hands. Her face went from hale and hearty to gray. "I don't fee…" Her eyes rolled back, her legs folded, and she collapsed. Xander caught her before she met the floor and swung her way-too-bony body up into his arms.

Kent was beyond useless. He stared at his phone as if the next winning Powerball numbers were being revealed to him.

"Nurse! I need a nurse!" Xander yelled as he jogged back down the hallway to Isleen's room.

"What happened?" The nurse assigned to Isleen rushed after him, huffing and wheezing as if she were running a marathon.

"She was up, walking around. Talking. Said her head hurt and then passed out." Xander settled Isleen into her bed.

You're so sweet, the way you haven't left her all this

time. Wish my Kelly could find someone as devoted. I bet she'd even be able to overlook your face if you treated her half as good as you're treating this girl.

Xander held his breath while the nurse took Isleen's blood pressure, listened to her pulse, and checked her pupils. "Everything seems normal. If she doesn't wake up in a few minutes, let me know and I'll call the doctor."

As if waiting for the cue, Isleen's eyes fluttered open and locked on Xander again.

"Baby, you okay?" he asked.

"I'm so cold and…" Her teeth chattered and a rash of goose bumps sprang out across her flesh, reaching up her neck and around the edges of her face. Damn. He didn't know goose bumps could do that. "And tired. I'm so tired."

"Here. You'll warm up in a moment." The nurse placed another blanket over Isleen. "You need to take things a little slower. Now, if you need anything else, you let me know. It's nice seeing you talking." The nurse rubbed Isleen's leg and then left the room, brushing by Kent, who was leaning against the doorjamb.

"Dude. We need to talk. Now." Kent's tone grabbed Xander's attention. The guy pointed to his cell phone.

No way was Xander going to leave Isleen. He glanced down at her. She had already drifted off.

"This can't wait." Kent's tone crossed the border from demanding into confrontational territory.

Great. Isleen didn't need to witness him and Kent going at it—and that's what was about to happen. He gave Isleen a final glance, then walked out of her room, heading toward the waiting area they'd just left.

The pain slammed into his head so unexpectedly

that he gasped and grabbed his temple. All the noises he hadn't noticed only moments before traffic-jammed inside his ears. What was going on with his hearing? All this time, days sitting at Isleen's bedside, the sounds hadn't bugged him as much as they did right now. Isleen was the key to a door he hadn't known existed.

He's hiding something. Or protecting her. Something is going on.

Inside the still-empty waiting room, Xander pivoted to face Kent. "I don't know what's got your big boys in a twist, but—"

"This." Kent shoved his phone in front of Xander's face. "I *just* got this message from one of the local guys."

Officer Decker: Female vic. Mid-twenties. Stabbed to death. Prospectus Prairie Park. Since you're in the neighborhood, you boys want in on this?

Chapter 6

Sunshine peeked through the closed blinds of the Dragon's hospital room, casting a divine golden glow around the space—a sign of the Lord's approval. But still, dread weighed heavily on King's shoulders, making each footstep to the bed a burden. He fingered the gold cross in his pants pocket, rubbing his thumb over the warm metal.

Chosen One's words came to him: *It is much the same for all who've been asked to complete such a task. We are here but to serve the Lord, not to question.*

"Lord, wrap me in your grace, protect me with your virtue, grant me your strength." King spoke the words at near-normal volume. Verbalizations carried more power than silent prayer. Though he'd dictated every moment of the Dragon's captivity, he hadn't actually *seen* her since he'd taken her—couldn't risk falling victim to her devilry. Only Queen—may his sister's soul be resting with the Lord—had been immune.

King remembered how the Dragon had looked back then, all platinum hair and big, baby-doll eyes too beautiful to be normal.

He stared down at the frail figure in the bed. Even now, her features carried a beguiling innocence. He could never allow himself to forget what he'd been taught: True evil never came with a warning; it masqueraded as beauty and grace.

"Why didn't you just die?" It had been his responsibility to eliminate the Dragon, but he'd been weak in his faith. So weak. He hadn't been able to bear the idea of murder. And if the Lord commanded thou shalt not kill, how was King to reconcile that with the Lord ordering him to kill? That paradox had been an infinite source of anguish. He'd spent days on his knees, praying—begging—for an answer, but the Lord had always remained silent, further testing King's faith.

So King had just contained the Dragon, temporarily keeping the world safe from her influence.

He spoke around the sob wanting to escape the confines of his throat. He needed to make a final confession before he fulfilled his duty. "I prayed—oh, I prayed—that the wrongness inside you was separate from your soul. I prayed it would vanish under the weight of your suffering body. I had you starved to deprive the evil. I had you beaten to make your body a hostile environment. I had you drained of blood to weaken evil's power. Nothing worked."

He licked his thumb and pressed it to the center of her forehead. Her skin was hellfire, burning through his flesh. He hissed a breath but forced himself to trace a cross.

She didn't move, didn't awaken, but her power blazed underneath his finger.

Sweat burst from his pores. "If only you hadn't left your prison…"

He slipped one hand underneath her head—and red-hot agony nearly buckled his knees. His palm smoked, and the scent of his burning flesh singed his nose. He didn't let her go. He pulled out the pillow and, with excruciating tenderness, settled her head back against the mattress. Tears watered his vision and then spilled down his cheeks. Guilt clogged in his throat, making it difficult to speak. "I never wanted you to end this way."

Sweat dripped from his temples and down his forehead, and mingled with his tears in a baptism of salt. He tightened his grip on the pillow, arranged it over her face. A moan slipped from his lips as he pressed the material down. "Forgive me. Forgive me. Forgive me." He sobbed the words, not knowing if they were for her or the Lord.

Her body gave a jolt and her arms raised, batting at him. He lay across the pillow, using his weight to suffocate the Dragon. She kicked and banged against the mattress. Muffled grunts of distress and panic filtered from underneath the pillow to mingle with the sounds of his own grief and guilt.

King had stood vigil at many a deathbed. It was part of his job as the hospital's chaplain. Over time, he'd learned that humans exited the world in different ways. Some screamed, some cried, some begged for life, some begged for death, some slipped away silently. No matter how a person died, they all shared one miraculous moment. At the moment when the body transitioned, the atmosphere—the veil separating humanity from the divine—parted and the Lord stepped in to escort his celestial creation to heaven.

Finally, her limbs went limp. King's body warmed, and he became aroused as he waited for the Lord to appear. A mini-eternity passed. Why was it taking so long? He lifted himself from her. The pillow still covered her face, her shoulders.

"Lord, please, please, please." His rib cage clamped tight, suffocating his breathing and squeezing his heart. "Lord, I have followed your will. Why are you forsaking me?"

An answer floated into his mind. The Dragon didn't deserve the Lord's grace. Relief washed away the fear in his heart. The Lord wasn't mad at him. The Lord was punishing the Dragon.

King lifted the pillow from her face. Even in death, she sustained an unnatural allure. As he rearranged her head on the pillow, touching her no longer burned. He retrieved the small golden cross from his pocket and placed it in the center of her forehead.

Later, much later, he'd find her body in the morgue and finish the last rites.

Chapter 7

THE CONFUSION OF HOSPITAL NOISES CLOGGED Xander's ears, and the relentless thumping inside his head distracted him from the thread of thought he should be following. He pressed his palms against his ears to muffle the turbulence and focused his eyes on the words displayed on the phone screen Kent still held in front of his face.

Officer Decker: Female vic. Mid-twenties. Stabbed to death. Prospectus Prairie Park.

Kent yanked the phone out of Xander's range of vision, but the words still blazed in bold type on his retinas, pulsing like flashing neon lights with each beat inside his head.

Add what Isleen had said earlier to this message, and it was clear. During her captivity, she had been forced to witness a murder. How had she survived, not only physically, but mentally? The things she'd endured were enough to snap a spine made of steel vertebrae.

Kent shoved the phone back into Xander's face.

Kent: Estimated TOD?

Officer Decker: Late morning

Xander read the lines. Twice. A question formed, one he didn't want to ask, but couldn't not ask. "When did you get these texts?"

"Five. Minutes. Ago."

Good, old-fashioned, concrete logic rebelled against

Kent's words. "Dude, I think your Officer Decker is funnin' with the big, bad BCI guy."

Kent's expression was as serious as grave gravel. No joke. No laugh. No humor. "He's legit. More legit than you'll ever be." *He's gone through the academy, knows protocol, respects the job and his fellow officers.*

"Ssshhiitt…" Xander couldn't find another word to sum up the situation.

"Yeah. Now tell me the goddamned truth. Who visited her? Did she leave the hospital?" *No way she could've known about this otherwise.*

"No one visited her. Does she look like she's been out visiting the local flora and fauna? Dressed in a hospital smock? With all the reporters out there? Use your oh-so-superior smarts."

"Then you"—Kent jammed a finger at Xander— "toss me an explanation that fits." *You're wanting me to buy shit that stinks.*

"Truth is fucking truth. She hasn't talked to anyone. She hasn't left the hospital. Maybe Queen told her that the murder was *going* to happen. You're the fancy BCI guy. You figure it—" Xander's brain went squirmy inside the cap of his skull, the brain itch. It felt like someone had opened his skull, taken out his thinking tool, rolled it around in a patch of poison ivy, then reinstalled it in his head.

He shook his head hard enough, violent enough, long enough to give himself the adult version of shaken baby syndrome. After his head stilled on his shoulders, his eyes hadn't gotten the memo because they continued to ping-pong around their sockets.

Kent was still talking. Xander's head was still

pounding. And still, the itch devoured everything with its unrelenting, unnerving, insatiable sensation. Xander's center of gravity warped the waiting room, transforming it into a fun house of distorted, disorienting images rushing at him from the walls and floor.

Against the imminent sensory overload, one thought dominated his mind—*get to Isleen*. He went with it, lurching away from his conversation with Kent without a good-bye, a kiss-my-ass, or a fuck-you.

In the hallway, his vision narrowed to a laser beam of focus on Isleen's door. Each step toward her room systematically eased the itch in his brain and faded the pain of the frequency connection until he stood outside her room—no brain itch, no pain. He had returned to a level of functioning that was better than his baseline. It had to do with her. Something about her affected the frequency connection and did something to him. But how? Why?

He pushed through the doorway—and froze solid as a glacier. Went as cold as one too.

Her mussed covers dangled off the bed, pooling on the floor. Her smock was tangled up on her bare thighs, her legs sprawled akimbo. Not even that image horrified him as much as what lay on her forehead. A cross, only it wasn't shaped the same as a Christian cross. It was squared off and sitting at an angle like a golden X-marks-the-spot. There was something wrathful and wrong about that piece of metal touching her. He ran for her and flung the offensive cross off her, sending it hurling across the room to bang into the wall and clatter to the floor. The silence that followed was deadly. His mind whirled through too many thoughts.

Someone had been in her room.

Someone was sending a message—but Xander wasn't fluent in the language of wonky crosses.

Someone had hurt her, and now she sounded dead. There was no thumping of heart pumping, no soft rasping of breath being inhaled and exhaled, no whooshing of lungs expanding and contracting. He couldn't trust his ears. They'd been fucking up from the moment he parked outside the torture trailer and heard nothing. But his eyes didn't lie. Her normally pale complexion had turned cadaverous, like she'd sidled up to death and was making cozy.

"No." Denial's favorite word flowed out of his mouth. "No. No. No." A scalding hot knife sliced open his heart—at least that's what it felt like—and cold fingers of dread reached in and squeezed the organ. "No, no, no, no, no, no." She couldn't be… No, he couldn't even think the word. Not after everything she'd been through. Not when her health had bounced back. Not when she had a chance at a new life. Not when he'd been just down the hallway, dealing with that fucktard instead of protecting her.

"Isleen, wake up. Right now." He shook her shoulder. Nothing. Shook her harder. The fist around his heart tightened, but he didn't care. Nothing mattered except her. He pressed his fingers against her neck, closed his eyes, and concentrated on finding the pitter-patter of her pulse, but…he wasn't in the right spot. He repositioned his hand. Waited. Nothing. He grabbed her cold face in his hand and yelled, "You have to open your eyes for me."

As if his words were a Simon-says of magical proportion, her eyes popped open. The cold grip on his heart vanished, and relief warmed him from the top of his head to the tips of his big toes. She was alive. As long as she was living and breathing, everything else was whipped cream and cherries.

She gasped and sucked in a breath so violent her torso thrust off the mattress. "Don't. No. Stop." Her arms and legs went wild, flailing in all directions. Her hand caught him alongside his scarred cheek. A sensuous zing raced throughout the network of his scars and down his neck, his shoulder, his torso, passing only inches from his happy place, before finally ending where the line of scars ended—on his calf. *Damn.* The sensation was a combination between a jolt of electricity and an orgasm. Never felt something like that before. Wanted to feel it again. And again. That response was the definition of bad timing.

"Isleen. It's me." He grabbed her arms and pushed her back against the bed, pinning her upper body, but her legs still kicked. He pushed his face in close and touched her nose with his. "Baby. It's me. Xander. Look at *me*."

Nightmare shadows swam in her eyes, then submerged, and she came back to him, her gaze lucid but tainted with terror. Her chin trembled. "Queen? I think she tried to hurt me again. I couldn't breathe."

He didn't move, just stared straight at her and hoped his message hit a bull's-eye through the heart of her fear. "That bitch is dead." Just speaking about Queen forced his facial muscles into a near-animalistic snarl that peeled his lips back over his teeth like a rabid raccoon. "Has been from the day I found you."

She assessed him, her gaze roaming between his eyes and his mouth and back again. "You're sure?" Doubt quivered her chin.

"I saw it happen. She was in my truck when it

exploded. Kent said the largest piece they found of her was—" Not telling her about the nipple with ring still attached. That was an image no one should have to endure. "—only a few inches in size." He eased the pressure on her arms. "I think you had a nightmare." The lie tasted pungent in his mouth and his scars burned, but it was the only explanation he was going to give her. No way would he scare her with speculation and suspicion that someone had tried to harm her. She had lived through enough terror in that trailer, and he was going to make damned certain nothing hurt her ever again, and that her life from here on out was a fear-free zone.

He released her arms and sat next her. She scooted into him, burrowing so close she was practically in his lap. *Oh, hell, why not?* He pulled her fully in to him and closed his arms around her. She was so damned tiny and fragile it was like hugging spun glass.

"I feel like I'm going from nightmare to nightmare and don't know what's real anymore." She spoke against his chest. "What's wrong with me?"

He leaned his cheek against the top of her head. "Nothing, baby. Nothing that time won't heal." For the first time since he woke up with supercharged hearing, he actually wished he could connect with her frequency and hear her thoughts. Not for himself, but for her. The urge, the desire to be inside her head to slay her fears, was a visceral need vibrating through his heart.

"Gran used to say that when we got out of there, we'd need time to heal from everything we'd been through. She said the world had kept going without us, and we'd be behind and have to work extra hard to catch up and be normal again."

"Your gran sounds like a smart lady." Xander owed himself a high five for that one.

Isleen's body went still as porcelain, but her heart overcompensated—*duh-dum, duh-dum*. The cadence was fast, the kind of fast that strolled along with fear. He flashed through their conversation, but couldn't fathom the reason.

"What's wrong?" he asked, tightening his hold on her. Whatever it was, he was gonna make it go away.

She swallowed, the sound verging on humorously loud, but nothing about this situation was funny. "I'm scared to ask. Afraid of the answer. Xander—"

God. The way his name rolled off her tongue captured him. Utterly and completely. If he was being honest, she'd owned him from the moment he had found her. The pisser was he didn't mind. Hadn't minded one moment of sitting next to her hospital bed, hadn't minded watching over her while she slept.

"—I'm so tired of being afraid."

Reality check. All his pink-pansy thoughts needed to be filed in the not-now-and-maybe-not-ever bin. More than just her body needed to heal. Her mind needed to mend. Part of that process was going to be adjusting and assimilating to her new reality. The hardest part was going to be packing up the past and placing it on a shelf in the back of her mind.

"Whatever it is, just ask. No matter the answer, I'll be right here with you."

Isleen wrapped both her arms around his waist, gripping him like she was either bracing for a blow or worried about being pulled away. "Gran?" Her voice was a whisper of sound that no one except him would've been able to hear. "Is she… Is she…"

"She's alive." Goddamn it. He should've thought to tell her first thing. Showed how much he knew about dealing with people—zero, zip, and zilch.

She ripped out of his embrace and aimed her gaze at him. "Really?" Hope charged through her—a visible entity squaring her shoulders and making her sit up straighter, bolder. Her features transformed from soft and scared to triumphant survivor. She was stunning. Radiant. Magnificent. All the words of beauty he could possibly think up. He'd do anything and everything to keep her looking this way.

"Really. Gale is stable. She's got some serious cuts and bruises, but nothing is broken. The major concern seems to be her cognitive deterioration. She's not talking. But then you haven't talked until today. So maybe…" He owed a two-ton-sized thank-you to Row for not being able to mind her own business or keep her mouth shut. Otherwise, Xander wouldn't have known anything about Gale's progress.

Sadness washed away some of Isleen's brilliance as she spoke. "She hasn't been right for a long time. At first, she couldn't remember the names of basic things like food, or colors, or my name. Then she couldn't remember things that had just happened. Then she couldn't remember me, or where we were. Those times were a blessing, an escape from our reality. The most horrible thing, the thing that hurt beyond everything else, was when she'd suddenly remember everything. Every—" Her voice choked off, her eyes clenched shut as if trying to not see the horrors replaying in her mind.

Words of comfort seemed shallow and hollow compared to the magnitude of what she'd survived. He said the one word, the only word that seemed to make sense to him and packed it full of compassion and support and caring. "Isleen. Oh, Isleen."

She snuggled against his chest, and he concentrated on the sensation of simply holding her. Of how her fragility made him feel strong, how her smallness made him feel large, how her touching him made him feel alive.

He'd never held a woman just to hold her. With Camille, it was about fucking—getting her off, getting himself off, and getting the hell out of there.

Bile frothed inside his stomach, threatening to roil up his esophagus. It was perverse to touch Isleen with thoughts of Camille in his head.

He forced his thoughts in a safer direction. There were so many sounds in a place like this, but just as it had been over the past days, they were in background, not all cramming into his ears and demanding his attention at the same time. Here with Isleen, he had control of what he heard, of whether to attend to it or not. And fuck—he didn't tune in with her. Not at all. What the hell did that mean? Was she some sort of antidote to his hyper-hearing? Were they making a weird trade-off— his protection for control over supercharged hearing? As long as she was happy with the trade, he was ecstatic.

From the moment he'd found her, their futures had woven together, then tied themselves in a double knot. The only question: What kind of future was it? The fluffy friendship kind or the I-want-your-sex kind? His dick went all rah-rah, sis-boom-bah for the sex kind. He rearranged his hold on her so she wouldn't feel his pecker poking her in the ass cheek—no telling how she'd react. No telling if she'd been sexually abused on top of the obvious mental and physical damage. A single beat of his heart pumped the urge to kill Queen— again—through his system. The Bastard in His Brain fell in love with the idea, sending a shock of electrical energy pulsing through him as if Xander had just jammed his finger in a light socket.

A powerful need to murder the already dead nearly overwhelmed him. Queen's quick, easy death carried no justice. She deserved to suffer. She deserved to be stripped of her flesh inch by inch, deserved to have each muscle ripped from its tendon, each bone broken. The torture he wanted to put her through was boundless. Nothing could ever make up for what she'd done to Isleen.

Isleen tightened her grip on him, the action dissolving his anger.

A mere shuffling of fabric from the doorway caught Xander's attention. His innards twitched in surprise. It had been a long time since someone had been able to sneak up on him without his ears alerting him. *Damn.*

Uncle Matt stood just inside the room, arms crossed spoiled-kid style, lips pinched into a belligerent grin. Matt's plastic-surgery-made-perfect nose wrinkled as if Xander and Isleen smelled worse than a roadkill skunk on a foggy morning. It amazed Xander that Matt and Kent weren't besties—their level of continuous contempt for Xander could've been the foundation for a great friendship.

"You fucking kidding me?" Anger and asshole dominated Matt's tone. "What is it with you and your dad? A genetic anomaly that turns you both into pussies around these women?"

Inside the circle of his arms, Isleen tensed and then withdrew from him. That his uncle's words had pulled her away from him hit the ignition switch on Xander's anger—after he'd just gotten it under control. "It's been a long time. Too long, probably. But you keep talking like that, and we'll be finishing this conversation with our fists."

"I assume you mean Gran and me, but I don't know you." Isleen's voice was surprisingly strong. "Explain why you hate us."

Isleen's words hit the brakes on Xander's anger. *Damn.* She was holding her own against Uncle Matt. It was a lovely thing.

"You're right. *We've* never met, but I know Gale. I've seen the heartlessness at her core. I've dealt with the devastation she leaves in her wake. And you are"— his gaze traveled from her to Xander and back again— "her granddaughter. That's enough for me."

"I don't know what you're talking about. How do you know Gran?"

The way Matt's mouth fell open might've made Xander laugh, if he hadn't felt his own mouth do the same. She must not have made the family connection quite yet.

"This is Matt. Alex's brother," Xander said.

She shifted further away from him, but continued to aim her gaze at him. "Okay, but who is Alex?" Her face was washed in total ignorance.

"You've got to be goddamned kidding me!" The words exploded from Matt's mouth, too loud to be socially acceptable in a hospital. "Gale never fucking mentioned Alex. Not once?" He didn't wait for Isleen's reply. "Xan, if you don't see this as the warning sign it is, you deserve the same fate as your father."

"Who's Alex? And what happened to him?" Isleen's voice carried obvious concern.

Matt snapped his lips closed, Xander's cue to explain. "Alex is your grandmother's husband." This time Isleen's lips parted and an airy whisper of sound escaped. "He's Matt's brother. And my father."

Her head jerked as if she'd been delivered an invisible slap. "Are you sure?"

What was going on that Gale hadn't told her anything? "Yeah, I'm sure."

She started shaking her head and looked down at the bedding. "I can't believe we're *family*." She spoke the last word as if she'd just uttered the world's worse curse.

"Yeah. I guess that's one way of putting it." Okay, that wasn't the kind of response he would've expected from her finding out her grandmother had been married. Though he couldn't quite say what a normal response would've been. He just suspected this wasn't it.

Matt started speaking, despite her continued head shaking. "The doctor is comfortable releasing her— especially with the facility being right there. We're leaving as soon as you sign the payment arrangement papers at the nurse's station. Alex is already on the way home with Gale—they're traveling via medical van."

"Home?" Isleen's attention snapped to Matt. "After all this time, I don't think we have a home anymore."

"Baby, he means our home." Technically, not his home, but he didn't feel like complicating an already crazy situation. "Gale and Alex's home. The Institute. Gale must've mentioned the Institute. She's still part-owner."

Isleen's gaze met his. There was something in her eyes, something he couldn't name that seemed to be pleading for—for what? He was lost, didn't understand what was happening.

Her chin began to quiver and her eyes went wet, but she blinked rapidly, fanning away the tears. She shifted away from him on the bed, out of touching range, and stared down at the mass of sheets and covers. "When do we leave?" Her voice was steadier than her chin.

"Ten minutes." Matt turned and headed for the door, then stopped. "Reporters are stationed at the lobby entrance and employee entrance, so you'll meet me at the ambulance entrance."

"Okay," she said. The word itself wasn't bad, the tone of her voice wasn't bad, so why did Xander feel bad like they were taking her back to the torture trailer or some equally terrible fate?

Isleen lifted her chin and aimed her words at Matt. "I need some clothes."

What was going on? Why was she talking to the family asshole when the guy who'd found her, the guy who hadn't left her side—except for a moment—was sitting a foot away?

One side of Matt's top lip curled up in an Elvis-worthy sneer. "Xander's in charge of that shit." He tossed Xander a WTF look and left the room.

Neither of them moved.

"Baby, what's wrong?" He scooted closer, but Isleen raised her hand in the universal sign for *stop*.

"I need clothes." She looked everywhere except at him.

He reached over, opened the drawer beside the bed, and took out a set of clothes Row had brought for her. He held out the bundle. "Tell me what's wrong." No, that was not the sound of pleading in his voice. He didn't plead. He didn't beg—at least not since he was child and his dad stopped speaking to him. Since then, Xander hadn't let himself care about anyone because this was exactly what happened whenever he cared.

Chapter 8

"ISLEEN. WAKE UP."

The richness of Xander's voice poured into her sluggish, sleepy mind like hot fudge. She basked in the warm sweetness of that special moment between sleep and waking, the muted crunching of gravel under the car tires a surprising lullaby.

"We're almost home." Xander shook her leg, his touch firm and full of reassurance. Every one of Isleen's nerve endings electrified and stood at attention, wanting and waiting for more of him. She could feel the energy of his body colliding with hers, pulling her toward him. Only there was something wrong with that, wasn't there? She searched her memory for why Xander's touch would be wrong, when all her dreams of him had been so—

Alex is your grandmother's husband...my father. Xander's father. Which meant Xander was her grandmother's son. Which meant he was Isleen's uncle. That made every dream she had of him—every feeling—sick, twisted, and wrong.

Her eyes popped open so fast she nearly lost her lids inside her brainpan.

She yanked her leg from his grasp and threw her body as far from him as the car door would allow. "Don't touch me. I just can't...can't..." Her mind searched for a socially acceptable explanation for her words, but no thoughts floated out of the abyss other than the scream echoing inside her head: *You're my uncle. You're my uncle.*

She shouldn't be surprised Gran had left out that humongous detail—that she'd had a son. Gran never spoke about her daughter, Isleen's mom, either. Or the past. Never. Not ever. Gran's motto—her rule—had always been "Focus forward."

"Understood." Fully aimed at her, his face was all hard lines and sharp angles. He probably intimidated most people, but to her, his face—seen so often in her dreams—had always been a salvation. Even his scars. They weren't angry or ugly; they were beautiful with their intricate, fernlike pattern spreading up his neck to decorate half his face.

He shifted his attention from her and aimed it out the windshield. She wanted to do something, say something, so he'd turn those gorgeous tawny eyes on her again, but that was stupid and risky. It wouldn't take a Mensa member to see she was love-starved and Xander was her favorite food. With effort, she forced herself to look forward at the driveway leading to her new life.

Xander drove them through an emerald forest toward a rainbow of color. The woods surrounding the car were a painter's palette of greens, from chartreuse to deepest sage. Dusk hugged the edges of the landscape, and ahead of them at a large opening in the trees, violent hues of scarlet tipped bruised clouds. A breathy gasp escaped her lips. She didn't want to look away. Monochromatic color had dominated her existence for so long that she had to blink back tears at the overstimulation.

Emotion burned the back of her throat and watered

her eyes. She swiped away the wetness before it could streak down her cheeks. "It's stunning."

"Wait until you actually see the house," Matt said from the backseat, his tone slightly sarcastic and laced with a dash of admiration. At least he wasn't being nasty.

They rounded a sharp curve, leaving the forest canopy behind to make room for the behemoth-sized house perched on the side of the hill. But the word *house* was too miniscule to contain the structure. The word *mansion* only fit because of the size. The word *castle* was close, but too harsh and cold to convey the whimsy of all the windows and wood.

Gables overshot the expansive second story, and a wide porch wrapped itself around the place like a hug. Plush wicker chairs and a porch swing invited her to sit and watch the sunset to completion.

"Wow," Isleen whispered. "This is where I'm going to live?" She stared out the window, straining her neck to take in the entire structure. Everything here seemed so large, so great, so unreal.

Xander parked in front of the massive arched entryway.

"Yep. This is your stop." Matt's tone carried a false lightness. "Unless you want to go home with Xander."

"She's staying here." Without a word to her or a glance in her direction, Xander got out of the car, slamming the door so hard it rocked the vehicle. He walked to the drive that went on past the house and farther up the hill. His shoulders strained the fabric of his T-shirt, and his legs consumed the ground in paces so large she would have to run to keep up. That's exactly what she wanted to do. Run after him.

All her muscles and tendons were poised, ready to

chase him down and set a world record in the hundred-yard dash. She grabbed for the door handle, the explanations flooding her mouth: *Your touch means everything to me, makes me feel whole and healthy and wanting so much more. You're my uncle and it's wrong to feel this way and I don't know how else to not want you.*

No. If she said that, she'd come off sounding like the love child of the demented and the perverted. She wouldn't go after him. She forced herself to let go of the door.

Restrained, unused energy vibrated through her, triggering a thousand memories. Memories of feeling that exact way inside their prison and the only relief, the only escape, was when Queen had beaten the feeling out of her. Physical pain was a distraction from the mental anguish and so much easier to handle.

Isleen clenched her fists tight, so tight they shook, so tight the slender, barely there muscles in her arms strained. Before her mind could decipher her body's intent, she punched down onto the fleshy part of her legs. Pain bloomed, a blessed distraction. She hit herself again. The desperate energy, the horrible urge to chase after him, eased. She beat her legs over and over—

Matt captured her wrists, locking them in his grip. "Stop it."

His voice punched her out of the trance she'd been in. She shrank back from him, but he didn't let go and didn't look away from her, refusing her the dignity of denial.

Shame blistered her face with its warmth, and the tip of her nose tingled. How had she not thought about Matt in the backseat? She'd been so absorbed in herself that she'd clean forgotten him. She yanked on her wrists imprisoned by his hands, but it was like fighting a pair of handcuffs.

"You done hurting yourself?" Matt's words themselves weren't kind, but the way they were spoken, slowly and deliberately, contained latent compassion.

She bobbed her head up and down, uncertain her voice was functional.

"I'm going to let you go, and if you hit yourself again, I'm taking you back to the hospital for an evaluation and immediate admission to the psych unit. Got it?"

He eased his grip on her wrists little by little, as if hypervigilant about waiting for her to start thumping on herself again. When she remained mostly paralyzed by humiliation, he released her from his hold, but not from his penetrating gaze.

His eyes were the color of a clear summer sky, but they contained none of the carefree happiness of a June day. He assessed her, judged her, challenged her. This she could handle. She'd known hate and intimidation at Queen's hand, and Matt's efforts were majorly lacking. She met him glare for glare, locked in a strange staring contest that she wouldn't lose.

Without warning, he stepped back out of the open car door and whispered, "Pull your shit together and pretend to be normal. Someone wants to meet you."

She barely had time to digest his words.

A woman stepped up beside Matt, and everything that had just happened vanished out of existence. The woman's hair was a captivating shade of lavender—the kind of color that could be both happy and sad at the same time. She wore a completely normal pair of shorts and a tank top, but what wasn't normal was her body covered from the collar down with brilliant, flowing tattoos. And with her face full of crumpled construction-paper wrinkles, the woman had to be pushing mid-seventies, maybe early eighties.

Isleen mouthed the only word that came to mind. "Wow." It was impolite to stare, but she couldn't stop looking. This old lady wasn't a sweet, kindly looking grandma. She was insanely spectacular.

"Isleen! Holy hell balls, girl! You're looking so much better." The woman's tone was that of a long-lost friend, as if they'd already met and known each other for years. "I sneaked some peeks at you while you were in the hospital, but you were always asleep. Christ on the crapper, look at your hair! It's grown at least three inches. How is that even possible?"

The woman paused to take in some oxygen.

"I need to get caught up on all the Institute work that's been back burnered since—" Matt moved away from them.

"Go. Shoo. Move. Get the fuck outta here." The woman flicked her hands in his direction but spoke to Isleen. "Sorry, sorry, sorry—you're probably wondering who the hell I am. I'm Roweena, but everyone calls me Row. I'm the maid, the cook, the laundress, and god-damned keeper of order around here."

Isleen sat stunned. She'd never in her life heard a woman cuss so much—and do it so good-naturedly. Row bent into the car, pulling Isleen out and into a warm hug filled with genuine affection. For some reason, tears burned in Isleen's sinuses. No, she knew the reason for her emotion. Gran used to hug her like this, but once her mind was gone... Well, it'd been too long since Isleen had experienced motherly affection. Without thinking about Row being a stranger with lavender hair and covered in tattoos, Isleen hugged her back, earning an even tighter squeeze.

Row shifted away and Isleen didn't mean to stare, but her gaze roamed over the vivid colors inked onto Row's skin.

"This one—" Row pointed to the beautiful cameo-esque tattoo in the middle of her delicately wrinkled chest. Shades of gold, orange, and sepia colored the image. Isleen moved closer to take in the intricate details. "—is a portrait of my Granny Maude. She swore like a sailor, smoked like a chimney, drank like a fish, and was kind as a saint until she died in her sleep at ninety-eight years old."

Isleen straightened from her examination of Row's tattoo. "You've got the swear-like-a-sailor thing down."

A smile fired on Row's face, but it was no ordinary smile. It was the kind of smile that surpassed age and transformed her wrinkled visage into timeless beauty. "That's a great compliment. Granny Maude refused to grow old gracefully—said that was for the unimaginative. So like her, I'm growing old fabulously." She laughed and ran a gnarled hand through her lavender hair. "One of the gifts of age is not caring what anyone thinks."

This woman was exactly what Isleen needed. Someone to care for her. Someone to care about. Someone it was easy to be around. "Thank you, Row." Isleen's vision got a little watery. "For being so awesome, so nice."

"Aww…" Row snatched her up in another hug and Isleen clung to the older woman, soaking up the affection.

"I'm all right," Isleen finally said. "I think I'm a happy crier."

"Nothing wrong with that." Row pulled back and visually checked Isleen over like any good grandmother would, then nodded as if confirming Isleen's words. "You've got be just about peeing your pants to see Gale. Alex, he's such a dumbass sometimes, didn't think about how badly you might want to see Gale before they left the hospital." Row's tone wasn't harsh or angry, but filled with teasing affection that ticked the corners of Isleen's mouth up a notch. Her cheeks were stiff, and it felt weird and right to be smiling for the first time since… She couldn't even remember the last time.

Row linked her arm with Isleen's and they headed toward the magnificent house. "I've got Gale set up in the library. It's the only private room on the first floor. After we visit with her…"

Isleen lost Row's words as they moved closer to the house, toward her new beginning.

There was so much about her life she didn't want to remember. The bad stuff in her past was too immense and diverse and horrific for her to analyze. If she wanted to make this new life work, she needed an amputation of everything up to the moment she met Row. But an amputation meant not only losing the bad memories, but the good ones—the happy moments of the time before they had been captured. Was she willing to sacrifice the good just to forget the bad? Yes. It would be worth it to be rid of the past, the pain.

Start here. Start fresh. Start focusing forward, just like Gran always did. Gran never spoke about painful things in her past. Never. Isleen didn't know how Gran did it, but she was going to bury all the bad under the rich, dark earth of her mind, then place the grave in the center of an endless labyrinth. If the bad ever escaped, it would be lost in the twisting, turning boundlessness of the maze and never find its way to her.

"Focus forward" had always been Gran's life motto. Now, Isleen was going to adopt it, coddle it, and care for it too.

Row pushed open the massive front door and motioned for Isleen to enter first.

She sucked in a breath of focus-forward determination and entered her shiny new life. One step across the threshold, her feet refused to move. The expanse and extent of the house held her captive in its cathedral-like majesty. Overhead, the ceiling soared so high it seemed a part of the sky. She felt miniscule compared to the wide-open space.

"Wow. Oh wow. Wow." She was stuck on repeat, not able to find any other words. The giant room possessed a hominess she didn't expect in such a large place. A kitchen was to the left, with a huge island and an even larger table that looked like it belonged in a fancy castle. The rest of the open space was filled with clusters of seating areas, some in front of windows, some in front of the fireplace, and some in the middle. It was the oddest, neatest place she'd ever seen.

Across the vastness, a spiral staircase wound up, up, up to an open second-floor family room. Cozy couches and chairs were set in front of a TV the size of a small movie screen. Wow. On either side of the loft ran open hallways with three doors on each side. Bedrooms she supposed. One of those was probably hers. Her own private place. How long had it been since she'd had privacy?

"It's pretty damned incredible, isn't it? Alex designed the place himself. He always said he wanted Gale to have a home that reflected the enormity of his love." Row's words contained the wistfulness of the past and the ache of love long lost.

"He built this for Gran?"

Row's brows pinched together, carving a new network of wrinkles across her forehead. "Yes, he did. I'm surprised Gale never told you."

"Gran's rule has always been to focus forward. I learned never to ask about the past. I never knew any of this existed."

"Sweet baby Christ," Row gasped as if Isleen's words stung her. "I can't flippin' believe... Yes, I can. Knowing Gale, I can believe it." She started shaking her head in that disappointed way only a grandmother could pull off.

Sparklers of anger sizzled inside Isleen's stomach and rocketed out her mouth. "Why do you and Matt act like Gran's a bad person? If you all hate her so much, why did you bring us here?" The moment the words left her mouth, she wanted to suck them back in. She shouldn't be acting this way when Row had been nothing but kind and accepting of her.

The question snapped Row out of her head-shaking. "Sweetie, I don't hate her. There's just a lot of history here between all of us that you don't understand. I'll tell you everything—I don't believe in that focus-forward bullshit Gale always spouted—but let's get you settled in first. About Matt... I suspect he really does hate Gale.

He has his reasons. And honestly, he's probably not too fond of you either simply because you're related to her."

Row's blunt assessment hit her hard, but Isleen much preferred the pain of bitter honesty over the caress of sweet lies.

"Come on now." Row wrapped her arm around Isleen's shoulders and guided her through the house to a door underneath the loft. She stopped a few feet away. "I need to warn you about Alex before you go in."

"Warn me? Why?" Isleen managed to close her lips before asking if Alex was going to try to hurt her. In her mind, underneath the soil in the middle of the labyrinth, she felt something writhing and roiling—a memory that wanted out, whose entire purpose would be to make her afraid. Nope. Not going to happen. She'd been a victim long enough and refused to be one ever again. If Alex wanted to hurt her, intimidate her away from seeing Gran, what Isleen lacked in physical strength she'd make up for with attitude.

She sucked the inside of her cheek into her mouth and bit down on it, not hard enough to draw blood, just hard enough to razor her focus to the doorway in front of her.

"Alex is…" Row trailed off as if looking for the exact right thing to say. "Hell, he's checked out of life—doesn't bother with living. Only his work matters. He and Xander haven't spoken in over twenty-five years. At least not until four days ago, when Xan called his father to tell him that he found you and Gale.

"I just wanted to let you know that Alex doesn't speak to anyone about anything except the Institute. He's brilliant and social and energetic when it comes to the Institute and its associates. Probably because he and Gale founded the place together and it's the only way he knows how to feel close to her. But he probably will ignore you and won't speak to you at all."

"So you're telling me he won't talk to me. And it's not just me. He doesn't talk to anyone unless it's business related."

Row let out a huff of relieved breath. "Precisely."

"Why? Why doesn't he talk?"

"The short answer: He lost his heart along with his voice when Gale left him."

...when Gale left him. Why would Gran leave him? Row opened the door, and the question vanished out of existence.

A pink, frilly gown swallowed Gran's tiny, gnarled body. The dips and valleys of her skull were painfully apparent through the sparse white hair corkscrewing out of her skull. Her skin was gray-tinged and sagged from her face like the jowls of a mastiff. She lay in the hospital bed, a quaint quilt of pastel colors folded at her waist. Bags of various fluids hung from poles, their tubes tethered to Gran at locations along her arms and hands. She looked so much better. And yet, she still looked horrible.

Isleen's heart tightened like it was trying to shrink down a size.

She had wanted—oh, gosh, had she wanted—the old Gran back. The one she'd grown up with who was healthy in mind and body. The one who always seemed so wise and promised her better days. But this woman lying in the bed didn't look like she was in her early sixties; she looked as if she were a hundred and twenty.

Gran stared, completely transfixed by Alex, an aged

version of Xander. He sat next to the bed, cradling Gran's hand between both of his and looked upon her with such a look of naked devotion that Isleen's throat clogged and her nose burned. It didn't take a love doctor to see he adored Gran, and Gran adored him. Their love filled the room so completely Isleen wasn't certain she'd fit into the space.

She forced herself to walk to the bed. "Gran." She bent over the only person who'd ever loved her and gave her a gentle hug. Hugging Gran was like hugging a mannequin—no response. When she pulled back, Gran's attention remained locked on Alex. It was as if Isleen didn't matter to her anymore.

Row stepped up next to Isleen and whispered in her ear, "They've been like this since we got Gale set up. It's kinda sweet how devoted they are. Like you and Xander in the hospital."

Isleen was going to have to follow up on that one later, because she sure didn't have any memory of staring into Xander's eyes with that kind of bald affection.

"Gran? I'm here. It's me, Isleen." She carefully clasped Gran's free hand. It was like holding bones. She willed Gran to look at her, to acknowledge her in some way, but Gran didn't and neither did Alex. Minutes passed and all Isleen could do was hope that Gran would turn her head and *see* her, even if only for a second.

"Sweetie, let's leave them alone. It's been a long day for everyone. You're probably tired. Come on." Row's voice was soft, as if she were speaking to an injured child.

Isleen settled Gran's hand back on the mattress and trailed Row from the room.

"Let's get you settled upstairs. While you take a shower and get dressed in your night things, I'll make us a late supper. Tomorrow, I'll show you the Institute and..."

Row chattered away, but Isleen wasn't listening. Maybe she was being selfish, but she couldn't help yearning for Gran to at least acknowledge her. Her cheeks stung, and she knew the reason—disappointment and rejection.

～w～

The color of angels, of heaven, of eternity surrounded Isleen in its infinite embrace. But she could find no solace in the space. With hyper-vivid clarity, she remembered what had happened the last time she was here. Something had entered her body and forced her to watch a woman being murdered.

Bristles of fear pricked her skin. She spun around, expecting to see something or someone standing behind her, but there was nothing beyond the eternal whiteness. For some reason, that scared her worse than if a chainsaw-wielding madman had stood there. Adrenaline primed her muscles and she couldn't stay still, waiting for whatever horrible thing was about to happen. She ran. She charged through the white nothingness, trying to outrun a phantom.

The atmosphere shifted. A subtle change in energy and function. Color invaded and shimmered, abstract and borderless, but then morphed, solidifying into shapes and images. A landscape formed and focused. She stopped running, mesmerized by the transformation.

She stood in a... Gosh, it had to be a waiting room.

A waiting room? Even with its cheerful blue paint and overflowing bins of toys, the place felt devoid of goodness, on the cusp of evil. Which made no logical sense. But then the prairie had seemed beautiful at first too.

A lone man sat hunched over in the farthest corner of the room. His elbows rested on his knees, his close-shaved head hung as if it were too heavy a burden for him to carry. The man's shoulders shook, and for a brief moment Isleen thought he might be laughing, but it wasn't quiet laughter that reached her ears. It was hushed sobs. He swiped a hand over his eyes and sniffled in that way little boys do when they are trying to be brave.

The collective of her pain recognized his pain, and her heart dictated that she do something to soothe him. She understood how it felt to be alone with anguish. It wasn't a fate she'd wish on anyone.

She tried to go to him, told her legs to move, to walk, to go to the man and offer him whatever meager comfort she possessed. Not one muscle responded to the message her brain sent.

"Mr. Goodspeed?"

Inside her skin, Isleen jerked at the unexpected voice. Her head turned and her eyes drifted in their sockets—only she wasn't the one controlling her head, her eyes, or her body's movements.

A woman who looked barely out of her teen years and still possessed the crisp beauty of youth stood in the entry to the waiting room. She took in the man with his hunched posture and the quiet sobs, but her face remained devoid of expression. "Mr. Goodspeed." His name came out in the firm authority of someone who knew what they were doing.

Isleen's head moved back to see Mr. Goodspeed.

He shoved the heels of his hands against his eyes and ground the wetness away. He sucked in a shuddering breath. "Yes. I'm sorry. I just... I just... I can't believe..."

"I'm Marissa Main"—impatience permeated her tone—"lead investigator for Sunny County Children's Services. I'll be supervising your visit today."

"I'm being investigated?" Confusion dominated Mr. Goodspeed's tone.

"Allegations of abuse have been made. Right now, that's all we have—allegations. It is my job to investigate those claims. Today's supervised visit is one way of working toward that goal. By seeing how you interact with your son, by seeing how your son reacts to you—"

"My ex is stuffing his head full of shit." Mr. Goodspeed stood and moved toward Marissa with the loose-limbed walk of a farm boy used to strolling through his fields. He towered over the investigator, but the way his shoulders hunched forward and his head hung on his neck lent him the defeated, saddened look of someone used to being a victim.

No way. No way would Isleen ever let herself look like that. Pitiful.

"Ever since the divorce, my ex has made my life miserable. It's been one thing after another." The look he gave Marissa overflowed with intensity. "I bet she told you that I drugged her for sex. That I hit her. That I locked her and Rory out of the house during a snowstorm. That I punish Rory by busting his ass with a belt. Oh, and her favorite claim is that I get off on touching him."

Marissa nodded her head at each of the ugly

statements, but wore the best poker face. "Those are serious claims."

"Rory is four years old. He'll say whatever his mother tells him to say. This isn't the first time she's said I hurt Rory. Every few months she concocts a new story. Always right after I've had him for the weekend. I'm sure you have a record. If you look closely, none of this started until she left me. Doesn't that tell you something? She's trying to take him away from me. And why aren't you concerned with her filling his head with lies about me? I want you to open an investigation on her. Fathers have rights too."

Marissa quieted. Isleen could practically see the wheels in her mind turning, processing Mr. Goodspeed's words. Score one for him.

Finally, she spoke. "This isn't about anyone's rights other than Rory's. We will still need to investigate, but I assure you our policy is reunification. We want you to be with your child. We're not against you in any way. We just have to see that being with you is a safe environment for him. That's all."

Mr. Goodspeed nodded his head. "I get that. So when he gets here, I want a moment alone with him to explain everything that's happening. He's a kid. He's got to be confused. I can help him understand."

Marissa cocked her head slightly to the side, her eyes squinting. The look either conveyed confusion or suspicion. Maybe both. "No. You are not allowed to be alone with him or to speak with him alone."

"He's my son."

"You are not allowed to be alone with him or to speak to him alone."

Mr. Goodspeed straightened from his hunched, victim-like posture. His face changed from concerned, conciliatory father to hard-edged, barely restrained rage. This guy had the Jekyll and Hyde thing down.

"You will not *prevent me from being with* my *son." His voice, so mild mannered before, boomed in the enclosed space.*

Marissa's impassive expression faltered, and she stepped back from the palpable menace emanating from the man. "Mr. Goodspeed…" Her voice trailed off when the door opened.

Isleen's head turned again. A petite woman entered, carrying a small, carrot-haired boy. The boy clung to his mother's body, arms locked around her neck, legs pinioned around her waist. Something about how he held on was sweet and sad at the same time.

Isleen's head swung back to Mr. Goodspeed so fast her eyeballs almost couldn't keep up.

The expression on Mr. Goodspeed's face was purely human—no animal could ever show so much hate and anger. "I told you what would happen, Molly. I told you. So this…this is all your fault."

"William, you're scaring Rory." The woman tightened her arms around her child and began backing away.

Isleen's attention locked on Marissa. Her cool demeanor had slipped completely away, leaving wild fear rolling in her eyes. "Mr. Goodspeed, if you—"

Kkkrrr. A gunshot. The blast shot the rest of Marissa's words—and her jaw—off her face.

Right after the blast, when the sound of it was only a ringing in her head, Isleen knew she was about to watch Mr. Goodspeed murder them all.

"No!" Isleen screamed, the sound echoing around inside the rind of her body, never entering the world. She fought the prison of her flesh, clawed at the confines of her skin. Tried to break free, to stop what was about to happen. Mr. Goodspeed aimed the gun at his wife, at his precious child. The monster at her controls had a moment of mercy and allowed her to close her eyes. But Isleen heard everything; the frantic screams of mother and son, the two shots used to take down wife and child, the slap and splash of blood dripping on the floor—just before the final suicide shot.

Chapter 9

XANDER PACED THE LENGTH OF HIS PORCH, HIS BARE feet padding across the wood, the sound pleasantly mixing with the chorus of nighttime noises rocking out on the hillside. But still turmoil roiled inside him. As much as he hated to admit it to himself, he was worried about Isleen. Worried about her health, her sanity, and—after finding that cross on her forehead—her safety. The thing that worried him the most was the simple fact that he cared at all. She shouldn't dominate his mind. Was Matt right? Did the women in her family possess some strange power to enchant the men in his?

A rhythmic sound invaded. He paused in his pacing, trying to place the origin. It was the crunch of gravel under feet. Someone was jogging up the driveway toward his place. He leaped off the porch, oblivious to his bare feet, and raced toward the sound.

His eyes weren't as sharp as his ears, but he knew—fucking knew—the figure that emerged from the curve was Isleen. She sucked and wheezed rapid breaths. Her heart beat a frantic *duh-dum, duh-dum* tempo. Her gait was all wrong—sloppy and disjointed, arms flailing almost as if she were swimming instead of running. With the way she'd acted earlier toward him, something had to be terribly wrong for her to seek him out.

Adrenaline bucked through his system, charging his muscles, readying him for a fight. He scanned the lane behind her, expecting to see someone pursuing her. Nothing. He listened for the sounds of a chase. Nothing.

He sprinted toward her. "What's wrong? What's going on?"

She didn't answer, didn't look at him, just continued on, ignoring him as effectively as if he were invisible. For only a fraction of a second, pissed-off-ness nearly got the best of him. Then he realized she was all lights-on-but-nobody-home. Again. "Shit." He chased after her, nabbing her by the arm. Her body swung around to face him, her forehead thunking against his sternum. The sound—an unnatural *wonk* of bone hitting bone separated by thick skin—reverberated through his chest. His arms trapped her close to him. "Goddamn it." The last thing she needed was a head injury caused by him. "I didn't mean to…"

He lost what he was going to say in the sensation of holding her. She was so petite, barely tall enough to reach his pecs, and yet she fit every angle and curve of him as if they were two pieces finally fit back together to make one. He held her until her heart shifted out of warp drive, then stepped back from her.

Moonlight silvered her skin, giving her a luminescent glow, but her face was completely devoid of expression. Her gaze fixed forward, locked on an intangible spot in the air between them. He'd seen this look at the hospital right before she spouted off about a murder she could not have known about. And yet, *did* know all about.

"Isleen. Snap out of it." His voice went deeper, carrying a strength beyond what it normally possessed. He shook her hard, one rough jerk that slung her head around her shoulders. "Wake up. Now." Wake up?

Where'd that come from? Did he honestly think she was sleeping? One moment she was lost, and the next, clarity and lucidity slammed into her features.

"Xander," she cried and flung herself against him, clawing at the back of his shirt with her hands and pressing herself so tight against him that it felt like she was trying to hide inside his skin.

"It was horrible. He killed her. He killed them all, and there was nothing I could do." Her words were run-on sounds, coming out so fast he could barely understand them. "I tried and tried, and all I could do was stand there and listen. I felt their blood... I felt their blood on my face, and I—"

"Shhh—take a breath." He waited while she sucked in air, then let it go. "I've got you. You're safe with me." He kept talking, saying nonsensical soothing things to her, rubbing his hands up and down her back, feeling each ripple and ridge of her rib cage and spine. When she calmed, he tried to pull back from her, but she clung to him like burr.

"Don't let me go. I think I might shatter if you do."

A precursor to a smile twitched the corner of his mouth. "I won't let you go." He meant it.

"Xander?" When she spoke, he felt the heat of her breath against his chest.

"Yeah, baby?"

"How'd I get here?"

He wanted to be surprised by her question, but he wasn't. This was exactly like in the hospital. "You ran."

"I mean, just a minute ago it was daytime and I was at Sunny County Children's Services and—" Isleen kept talking, and Xander kept listening to the fucking horror she was spouting about Mr. Goodspeed and murder. She had to be talking about a nightmare.

"You weren't there. It wasn't real. You were at the main house where I left you. Only two hours have passed. Not a day. It was a bad dream, and I think you were sleepwalking. Dad will know for sure. That's his job. He researches that kind of shit."

The relaxed, intimate way she clung to him vanished. She threw herself out of his embrace. Instinct had him stepping toward her to put her where she belonged. With him. Every step he took forward was one she took backward. He forced his body to stillness and his hands to fall to his sides. The heat of rejection ignited in his gut.

"I forgot. I forgot. I'm sorry." Her voice was a complete apology.

"Forgot what? Sorry about what? What are you talking about?" He tucked his hands under his arms to keep the traitors from reaching for her. She didn't want him touching her, so he'd abide by her rules. After what she'd endured, he needed to give her control whether it made sense to him or not. The best he could do was try to understand her feelings.

A pressured grunt escaped her mouth, and she slapped her palms on either side of her head as if she were trying to keep her brain from bursting out her ears. He was in front of her, his hands over the top of hers, before he even told his body to react. Where their skin touched, he went cool and began to sting—only *sting* wasn't the right word. The sensation was a cross between a sting and an itch and something surprisingly pleasant, something similar to what he'd felt when she accidentally touched his scar in the hospital. He closed his eyes, feeling the sensation move up his arms, across his shoulders, and down his torso. A shiver rippled through him. What was going on? Whatever it was, he liked it and so did she.

She stilled, simply standing beneath his hands, and moaned a sound not of pain, but of pleasure. The type of sound he could imagine her making as he pushed himself into her—

Whoa. Where did that thought come from?

"Why are you so hard to resist?" She spoke in a sexy groan that went straight to his dick.

"Why resist?" What? Was he flirting now?

"You know why." Her voice went sleepy sensual, and she moved the few inches into his body, leaning against him and trusting him to support her. "I'm so tired all of a sudden."

"No, I don't know why." He held his breath and spoke through his clenched molars. "Is it the scars?" He'd never cared what anyone thought of his face until her.

"Scars? No, silly. They are beautiful. I've loved them since my first dream of them." She yawned, and he felt more of her body weight leaning against his. He removed one hand from her head and wrapped it around her waist to support her in case she full-on zonked out. "I just wish… Oh, Xander, I wish you weren't…"

An asshole. Your father's son. Ugly. A piece of shit.

"…my uncle."

"What?" The word exploded out of his mouth, loud as a cherry bomb in the dead of night. He ripped his other hand from her head, severing the sensation that felt so wondrous.

She nodded against his chest and wrapped both

her arms around his waist. "I'm so tired. I could fall
asleep…just…like…this."

He pried her off his chest to look her in the eyes. Her
lids were at half-mast, her eyeballs floating upward,
not quite focused. "Wait, wait, wait. You think I'm
your uncle?"

"We're *family*. Gran and your dad are married."

The simplicity—the stupidity—of her assumption
shocked him. His mind rewound to their conversation
in the hospital. *Fucking damn.* It was right after she
found out about Gale and his dad that she pulled away
from him and started acting weird. No wonder. She'd
thought he was her uncle. Thank Christ that could be
straightened out. He'd been on the verge of going into
full-on creepy-stalker mode, sneaking around just to
check on her.

"I'm not Gale's son. My mom died after I was born.
Dad and Gale got together sometime before I turned a
year old. I think your mom was eleven or twelve when
they got together. That was why all of a sudden you
didn't want to have anything to do with me?"

She yawned. "I think I need to lie down." Her lids
fell, and she melted against him.

"Why are you so sleepy?" Even as he asked, he
understood. It was the same as in the hospital. There
was a pattern to this. A pattern only his father—the
world's most renowned dream researcher—would be
able to explain.

～～～

Isleen floated in that sweet spot between reality and
waking. The only thing penetrating her sleepy haze was

the scent of warm graham crackers and autumn leaves. It was a scent she was familiar with, one she loved. It was the scent of all her favorite memories. It was the scent of Xander.

A predawn haze of gray lit the room, touching everything with its soft color. Her head was pillowed on his shoulder, her face pressed against his neck, her body encased in the security of his arms, and he had one of his legs tossed over her thighs. Not since she was a little girl—too naive to know pain existed in the world—had she felt this absolutely safe.

Something strange seemed to happen whenever she was near him. The sheer power of his presence salved the wounds of her past and shaped her into the strong and capable woman she was meant to be. The real her. The person she would've been if she hadn't endured so much horror. The person she'd only had a chance to be in her nightly dreams of Xander. And weren't those dreams doozies?

Memories of him from her dreams flooded her mind, heating her body. Their nightly escapades had always been vivid and oh, so intimate. Her female parts wanted to nestle and squirm in closer to him, to satisfy the longing building from the mere memories of dreams, but she was already as close as she could get with her clothes on. Just what would happen if her clothes were off? Didn't that bring to mind explicit, triple-X-rated thoughts?

From her dreams, she knew what lay underneath his clothes, knew he was spectacular. Everywhere. And the hard length of him moving inside her, filling her so deliciously… It was a miracle that a body could feel so wanting and wonderful at the same time.

Her awareness of just how they were lying in the bed—groin to groin—gave her another flash of heat. Or was that longing? She could feel him through his pants, resting against her needy bundle of nerves. Her attention narrowed more and more until the only thing she could think about, the only thing she could feel was him right there, right where she wanted him.

She tried to hold still, not to move, not to disturb what was already the best moment of her *waking* life, but her body had other intentions. Excruciatingly slow, so she didn't wake him, she rocked her hips forward and back, rubbing against him. Instead of offering any satisfaction, need blazed brighter. If she didn't stop, she'd end up dry humping him in his sleep.

But then he pressed his hips forward, grinding into her. She gasped, nearly choking on air. What she'd thought had been pleasure went into pure bliss. Her dreams had always seemed so real, but they were old-timey black-and-white while this was vivid Technicolor, 3-D, HD, and surround sound all in one. His hand found its way underneath the back of her shirt, traveling up her side until it was just a whisper away from her breast. Breathing was too much of a distraction, so she didn't do it, all her attention focused on him and his hand.

He stopped.

"Don't. Don't stop. Please, don't stop." She wasn't ashamed to be begging. Not for this. Being with Xander was compensation—no it was a reward—for everything she'd endured. He was her rainbow after the destructive tornado that had been her life. Being with him would be a weapon against her past. It would be something *she* chose. Something *she* wanted.

"Isleen…" Her name was a languid caress of vowels and consonants, but underneath the sound there was something… Hesitation? Reluctance?

"Why did you stop?" Part of her wanted to pull away from him, to see the look on his face as he answered her question, but she was too much of a coward. If this was all she'd ever have of him, she was going to soak it up and store it in her mind.

"Baby, we just met."

"I've known you for years." As crazy as it made her sound, she couldn't not say the thoughts in her mind. "I dreamed about you." She whispered the words against his neck, still not moving away from him.

"Is that how you knew my name?"

"Yes."

"Were they good dreams?"

Oooohhhh, yyeeeaaahhh. They'd always had a happy ending, courtesy of his skill as a lover. Not that she was ever going to tell him about all her sex dreams of them together. Naked. Hot. Sweaty. And sweet. So achingly sweet she'd fallen a little deeper for him after each dream.

"Tell me"—Xander pulled back from her, dipping his head down to look into her eyes—"fucking tell me they were good dreams."

His eyes were an autumnal set of colors—brown near the pupil, fading to gold, surrounded by deep green. Fall was her favorite season.

"Fucking Christ, tell me." The words sounded angry, but his tone overflowed with regret and apology. "Were they good dreams?"

When he used that tone, she had to answer him. "The

best dreams of my life." Hunger and thirst for him was so prominent in her voice he'd have to be deaf to not know what she meant.

He relaxed against the pillow, facing her. "Thank God."

"You don't think that's weird? That I sound crazy?"

"Weird is relative. I…"—he winced and closed his eyes—"I've heard you inside my head for years." He opened his eyes and she saw something deep inside them, something she didn't have a name for, something that looked painful.

"It's okay if you had the dreams too. I'm glad." From the moment she'd opened her eyes in that room and realized Xander was really there to take her away from all the suffering, she'd known they were connected in a way that defied normalcy.

"No, it wasn't dreams." His hand, still on her ribs, squeezed, holding her tight as if she might try to move away from him and he didn't want that. Apology shone in his eyes. "I heard you… Holy Christ, I heard you inside my head begging for help. Begging me to find you. Only I thought—fuck—I thought you were a hallucination. I didn't know you were real. I thought I was insane."

Her heart halted its beats and hung limp inside her chest like a discarded plastic bag snagged on a tree limb. How many times had she cried for his help? Pleaded for him save her? To end her suffering? More than she could count.

He watched her, his gaze doing more than just taking in her response to his words. He was sorry and trying to understand everything she'd been through. There was no understanding, no rationalizing. Nothing was going to make what happened to her and Gran all right. The buried memories, all the things she never wanted to remember, threatened to stage a resurrection. *No.* She wasn't going to let the past steal her sanity and revoke her new reality.

Not now.

Not ever.

She took every word, every syllable he'd just uttered and planted them directly in the grave of memories.

Instead of moving away from him, like he seemed to expect, she scooted in closer until no space separated them. He hugged her tight and thankfully didn't say anything else. They remained that way for long, lazy minutes, until she found the exact right words she wanted to say.

"The past is the past. Right now is all that matters." She gyrated her hips against him. "And right now I want you."

He held perfectly still. "You're only five days out of that torture trailer. Your body is still healing. Everything is happening so quickly for you. I don't want—"

"I feel good. I feel healthy." She kissed his throat. "I want you like I had you in my dreams." Talking about her dreams was nothing compared to talking about her past. It just might get her what she wanted—him. And a distraction.

"I don't want you to go down a road you might regret later."

"I know what I want. I want you. How many more times do I have to say it?" Impatience crept into her tone.

He flipped her over onto her back and was on top of her, the steel strength of him covering her like a safety blanket of Kevlar. His beautiful, changeable eyes locked on her lips. "If I do more than hold you, if I kiss you, I'll want more than your mouth. I'll want to fuck you."

Chapter 10

"…I'LL WANT MORE THAN YOUR MOUTH. I'LL WANT TO fuck you." Did he just say that out loud? Yes, he had. He could tell by the way her lips parted in an enticingly stunned manner. He opened his mouth to…to what? Apologize? Nope. He meant every word; he just hadn't meant to be so damned blunt.

"Xander, I want you to"—cotton-candy pink splotches of color tinged her cheeks—"fuck me."

Her words went straight to his dick. She'd never uttered a word that could obliquely be called a curse word, and now she was dropping the f-bomb? Sexy as hell.

"Baby." It was the only word in existence.

She reached up, weaving her fingers into his hair, and tugged him to her mouth. He could've resisted. Yeah, he could've. Until he got his first taste. Her mouth tasted of sweetness and promise, of the past and future, of now and forever. Logic no longer existed. In its place resided a profound certainty that this was his destiny.

His heart banged inside his chest. Her heart—he could hear it—beat a counter rhythm. Her breathing, his breathing, only added to the melody. "I wish you could hear. Our heartbeats, our breathing." He whispered against her mouth, pressing his forehead to hers. "Together we sound beautiful." Maybe he shouldn't have said anything about his hearing issues. Not yet.

She put one hand over his heart, the other over hers and closed her eyes. "I can't hear it, but I feel it."

Fuck. This woman was something special. Rather than the thought scaring the shit out of him, he recognized the deep possibilities between them. She wrapped her arms around his waist, hugging him and holding him like he mattered more to her than anything on the earth. He soaked up her affection, letting it fill in all the dry cracks in his soul. Her cool hands slipped underneath his shirt, touching the skin of his back, running up to his shoulders and down in long, slow agonizing strokes that had his dick wishing those hands were lower. A lot lower.

She lifted his shirt and pushed it higher and higher on his back until it bunched underneath his shoulders. He sat back on his knees, straddling her hips, and tore the material over his head.

What was he doing? He shouldn't be doing this with her right now. Not after everything she'd been through. As if she sensed his hesitation, she sat up, never even glancing at his scars, and pressed her bare cheek over his heart, then kissed him there. His heart sucked against his rib cage, straining toward her touch.

"Baby, I want this." He grabbed her hand and settled it over his crotch. His dick—already hard—went to steel. He sucked in a breath and willed himself to not move or he might go off, just from her hand. On the outside of his jeans. What was up with that?

She squeezed him, the pressure a painful pleasure. He fought to keep himself from coming in his tighty-whities. "Christ, woman. I can't stand much more." He closed his eyes and balled his hands into fists to keep from ripping her clothes off. "Tell me how far you want to take this. I want to make it right for you."

As her hand moved away from him, regret flayed him open, and the loss nearly broke him. His closed eyes burned, and he almost wanted to cry like a goddamned baby. He wanted her that fucking bad. But he'd honor her wishes. He would.

"Xander, I want it all. I've wanted you for so long. Longer than you could possibly imagine." Then he felt her hands on the button of his jeans, tugging and struggling. His eyes snapped open. She worked the button through the hole and wrangled with his zipper.

He stilled her movements, then waited until her gaze flicked up to him. "Promise me something." There was only one thing he was afraid of when it came to Isleen and sex. Her past. She didn't want to talk about it, and he wasn't going to press her. He couldn't handle it. Thinking that Queen might've hurt her—in that way—was enough to shoot his anger to the spontaneous combustion level.

"Anything." The word came out breathy and full of yearning.

"If something doesn't feel right to you, if you don't like something, you tell me. Deal?"

"Deal."

He nipped the end of her nose, then got out of bed and began wrestling his jeans off.

"Can I see all your scars?" She spoke the words to his back.

He froze, pants halfway down his legs.

Right after the lightning strike, he'd been shocked by his own appearance. The thing that helped him most was hearing everyone's thoughts about the scars. The things he conjured in his own mind were always worse than what people actually thought. With her, he didn't have that advantage. He had no idea how repulsed she'd be when she saw the whole damned thing.

He heard her moving on the bed, shifting closer to him, then standing up behind him. Hell, he couldn't see her, but he could feel her at his back. Her hands lightly touched his hips, and he jerked as if she'd slapped him.

"I told you before… Your scars are beautiful." Her words were a cool caress across his spine.

She dipped her hands into his underwear, sliding them down until they met his pants and he lifted his feet out of them. It felt so weird—and oddly wonderful—to have her undress him.

He forced himself to face her. He stood bare-ass naked in front of her, his Mr. Happy waving at her. "Yeah, I know." He heard the resignation in his voice. "It's one big scar." He expected her to be staring at the deformity marring half his body, but her gaze was locked on his dick. The little fucker liked her looking and somehow got even harder.

She lifted her eyes to him and then reached for his face. It was crazy, but he almost flinched away from her. She touched the tippy-top edge of deformed skin on his forehead. A punch of energy surged through the network of scars, both painful and pleasurable. Shivers rolled over his shoulders.

"Is it sensitive? Hurt when I touch it?" Her eyes met his.

"No. It feels…odd and good. Way good."

"I'm glad. I've wanted to do this since the very first dream of you." With the tip of her finger, she traced the irregular flesh down his face and neck.

At his chest, she replaced her finger with her mouth. Each collision of lips to flesh was a percussion of feeling reverberating through him. Her touch was heaven and hellfire. Cooling and burning. Agony and ecstasy. He'd never felt anything like it. He wanted to feel it forever. He shook, his entire body trembling. He was acting like a damned virgin at his first prom.

She followed the pattern of scarring down, oh sweet Jesus, down to his hip, to the tangled branch of puckered skin that disappeared only when it reached his dick. Her beautiful thick hair whispered over him, and it was too much. A bead of pre-come oozed out, sliding down his shaft, and Christ, even that was an exotic pleasure. A tortured groan slipped up from deep in his throat. Her gaze flicked up to him, and it was all he could do to not grab her head and shove his dick in her mouth. He wouldn't do that to her. Not now. Not yet. Not until he knew that's what she wanted.

"Gotta stop right there." He spoke through clenched teeth and forced himself to take a step back from her. At this rate, he wasn't going to make it to the finale. He sucked in a breath, trying to calm his body.

"I want to be naked too."

All he could do was watch and make sure his tongue wasn't hanging out the side of his mouth. Her shorts and panties came off as one. There was no hesitation or shyness to her movements when she pulled the braless tank top over her head. She stretched her arms up, arching her spine and thrusting out her small, but perfect breasts. Her nipples were the exact shade of pink as the blush of her cheeks. Maybe it made him a pussy, but pink was his new favorite color.

Over the past few days, not only had her hair grown at an exceedingly fast rate, but her body had filled out. She was still too thin, but she no longer looked skeletal. Scars marred her skin, some pale with age, some red and fresh. God. After everything she'd been through, for her to be standing here in front of him wearing only a smile, was a miracle. She was a miracle.

"You have so many scars." Okay, not the most romantic words. He settled his hand over the healed wound on her side, the one that had oozed blood when he'd found her. Now only days later, it was completely healed. Somewhere deep inside, in a place of intuition and instinct, he knew he'd played a part in her recovery.

She smiled, but the smile was a sad one, the kind you expected to see on someone who'd suffered a great loss and was trying to hide it. Her shoulders slumped and her arms moved a bit in front of her body as if she were trying to hide her nakedness from him. Leave it to him to say the asshole thing, even when he wasn't trying to be an ass.

"Don't do that. Don't hide from me. You have scars. So do I. Do you think mine are hideous and deforming?"

Her head snapped up. "No, not at all. They're beautiful. So beautiful."

"All those scars on your skin are beautiful to me too. You know why?"

She shook her head, her gaze locked with his like what he was about to say meant more to her than anything in the entire world. Without even trying, she made him feel so damned… Fuck, he didn't even have a word for it. The best he could come up with was some hybrid of *special* and *important* and *adored*.

"Because they're evidence of your strength, of your

ability to survive. They are badges of courage. And you know—" He placed her hand on his shoulder where the lightning had entered him and the damage was the deepest. Again he felt that rush of electricity through the network of his scars. "—we match. Life has marked us both."

She rose on her tiptoes and kissed the spot on his shoulder before she hugged him. He didn't need to hear her thoughts to know he'd said exactly what she'd needed to hear. Instead of hugging her, he swept her up in his arms and laid her on the bed.

He scooted in next to her and leaned down, keeping eye contact as he neared her breast for a taste. No fear in her eyes, only wanting, and then her hand on the back of his head encouraging him. She tasted sweet and warm and of something that had no name but was purely her.

She moaned and arched up, and he caressed her other breast, rolling the nipple between his fingers. She started moving, gyrating her hips, pumping and thrusting—her actions showing him what she really wanted. Which was exactly what he really needed. He slid his hand down the jut of each rib, then lower, feeling the springy softness of her hair.

Her movements became frantic.

He smiled around her nipple. "Easy, I'll take care of you." His hand traveled lower and lower until he found the heat of her. "Open your legs for me."

No hesitation, she did as he asked. He slipped a finger inside. She was wet and slick and so fucking tight. He knew his dick didn't have a brain, but he swore the thing was imagining what it would feel like when it pushed into her—or maybe that was just him doing the daydreaming. She grabbed on to his hair and yanked him to her mouth.

He swallowed her moaning, taking her voice into him, letting the sound meld into his bones. Their tongues thrust in a cadence that matched the movements of his finger.

He couldn't wait any longer. He slid his finger from her. He shifted over her, bracing his forearms on either side of her face, needing to see for himself that she wanted this, wanted him. What he saw was himself reflected in her eyes. Saw how she trusted him, respected him, and felt complete with him.

He was there—right there—poised at her entrance. Ready. He tangled the tips of his fingers in her hair. Her hands were on his sides, sliding around to his back, her touch light, almost ticklish.

"Please." She arched under him, pushing up closer. That was all the encouragement he needed. Slowly, he pushed into her. Jesusfuckingchrist. Every nerve ending went on the alert, then exploded with sensations. He was lost in a wild combination of tranquility, euphoria, and awakening. He felt invincible, like nothing could ever hurt him, and he'd never let anything hurt her.

He felt her stiffen, heard the hitch in her breathing and how her heart's rhythm shifted—not in a good way.

He stilled.

"Xander?" Her voice was small, and fuck if he didn't hear a bit of fear in there.

Underneath him, her face scrunched up with no resemblance to flushed and relaxed.

"What's wrong?" Was that his voice? He sounded like a wounded animal.

"It hurts a little."

A thought air-dropped into his mind. She wasn't a

virgin, was she? "Um… We probably should've had this conversation before we went this far"—and son of a bitch, he should be using a condom—"but you've done this before, right?"

A hesitant little smile hitched up the side of her mouth. "Not in real life."

His brain must've been set on slow-mo—her words and their meaning took longer than they should have to register.

She was a virgin. Holy fucking Christ, she was a virgin. She was his. Completely his.

His heart went skippity-do-dah throughout his chest cavity. It was one of those things he hadn't known he wanted until he'd been freely given the gift. "I don't like that you are hurting, but you have no idea how happy it makes me that I am your only one."

"You will always be my only one." Her words were an arrow straight through all of life's bullshit, hitting the center of her target—his heart. He wanted to say something more, to let her know that he felt the same, but couldn't figure out how to say it right.

"We're just going to stay like this a moment, okay? Until you feel better."

"It already feels better." She reached up to his face, settling her palm over his scars. "I dreamed of this. Of being with you." The sweetest smile of promise teased the corners of her mouth. "We did this a lot in my dreams."

He chuckled, the action causing him to move a bit inside her. She closed her eyes and tilted her head back against the pillow. Shit, shit, shit. He didn't want to cause her pain. And then, she moved, pushing against him, releasing, pushing. He held still, letting her move, letting her guide this according to what her body needed. "Xander. Please...I'm good now."

Gently, slowly, carefully, he pulled himself through her slickness. The friction of her wrapped so tightly around him was a beautiful mercy. He paused, just the tip of him still inside her, then just as easy slid back into her heat.

"Damn," she said, her body matching his movements.

He settled more solidly over her, their bodies touching everywhere. He buried his face in her hair and continued the steady pace. Forced himself to go slow, when what he really wanted was to go at her with everything, all of him. Every little piece. He wanted all of her. He wanted her heart and mind and body and—fuck—her soul. He wanted to brand her, mark her, own her, make it known to everyone that she was his by burying himself so deep inside her that when he came, a piece of him would live inside her forever.

But this time—her first time—wasn't the time for wild, deep, and dirty pumping.

She shifted her hips and he slid impossibly deeper. "Xander. I need more. Harder. Faster."

His restraint shattered. His body exploded against hers. Pumping and thrusting, giving her what she wanted, what he needed. Faster and harder and deeper.

"Xander. Xander. Xander." She chanted his name as if it were magic. Her body clenched around him.

His orgasm gathered, pulling energy from his extremities, the power of it converging on his dick. Control vanished. He rammed into her. Her legs wrapped around his waist, and he couldn't tell who was saying what—hell, it probably wasn't even words—but they were fucking loud. And it was the most beautiful sound he'd ever heard.

———

Wow. Holy wow. Isleen giggled. She couldn't help it. The sound effervesced out of her on a wave of genuine joy. Never in her life had she ever felt what she'd just felt with Xander. He chuckled, his breath teasing her hair.

"Damn. That was ama—" His voice sliced off. He lifted his head and cocked it to the side, listening to something. Carefully he withdrew from her body, the friction of that small movement sending a spark of desire up her spine.

He tore out of her grasp so unexpectedly that her arms stayed around the airspace his body had inhabited as if she were holding on to a ghost.

"Shit. Fuck. Goddamn. Stay here." His tone wasn't friendly or even mildly cordial. He leaped off the bed, snagged his jeans, and rammed his legs into them, then ran across the bedroom and disappeared down the stairs.

What. Just. Happened? Isleen sat up in bed. For the first time, she noticed her surroundings. The bedroom overflowed with cheerful morning sunshine bouncing off the fat, blond logs of the cabin's walls. A railing overlooked the downstairs, but from where she sat, she couldn't see beyond the ceiling, walls, and windows. She scooted to the edge of the bed. "Xander?"

Somewhere downstairs a door opened.

"She's gone." Row's voice quivered with each word, making her sound her age. "I've looked everywhere."

"Row—" Xander tried to cut in.

"When she didn't come down for supper, I checked on her. Poor thing looked like she'd fallen asleep the moment she got out the shower. I didn't wake her up. But this morning when the front door was open—open, Xander—I knew. I just knew something had happened to her."

"Row—" Xander tried again, his voice louder this time.

"Your father is useless. Matt's already left for his run. I don't know what else to do. Should we call the police?"

Isleen snagged the sheet off the bed, wrapped it around herself, and headed to the stairs.

"Row—" This time both she and Xander said it at the same time.

Xander and Row turned toward her.

"Well, shit." Row clasped her hand over her granny Maude's portrait. "I just interrupted… I knew there was something special between the two of you." Row's wrinkled face took on a wise-ole-owl expression as she looked back and forth between them and chuckled to herself.

"It's not like that," Xander said.

Isleen's attention zeroed in on him, and she felt a wrinkle of confusion furrow into her forehead. It *was* like that. They'd just made love.

"No, no, no. No explanation needed. You're both adults. Consenting adults. What you do is none of my beeswax." Row jumped up and down and clapped her hands like an excited little girl. "But I am so happy for you both." She grabbed Xander, who stood at least a foot and a half taller than her, and gave him a squealing, happy hug.

Xander was tall and broad and made of muscle and male strength, but he melted into a little boy version of himself while Row hugged him. It was so sweet and tender that water came to Isleen's eyes. This happy crying was getting to be a bit much. But there was so much to be happy about, wasn't there?

She ducked back into the loft and dressed, then headed down the stairs to join them. Row latched on to Isleen the moment she was within arm's reach and gave her the same treatment as Xander. Isleen soaked it up like a flower in need of rain. "I'm sorry I scared you. I didn't mean to."

Row pulled back and clasped Isleen's face in both her hands. "Don't you ever apologize for being…" She trailed off, not finishing.

In love. Isleen's mind filled in the blank. She *was* in love with Xander. Had been since her first dream of him.

"Now you grab your honey and come on down to the main house." Row released her and moved out the still-open doorway. "I've whipped up a batch of my famous butterscotch pecan pancakes. They're Xander's favorite."

Isleen felt the smile in every muscle on her face, felt joy swelling inside her. This life here with Row and Xander and Gran was gonna be better than any dream she'd ever dared to imagine. She turned to Xander.

His scars were blood colored. "Go." His lips pulled back over his teeth in a sneer of disgust. The only thing missing was him spitting out the bad taste. "Go without me."

The fragile bubble of her happiness popped. "What's wrong?"

"Damn it, Row, that was pretty underhanded. Not gonna work."

Isleen heard his every word; she just didn't understand any of them.

Xander turned his attention to her. "Go with Row.
You shouldn't miss her pancakes."

None of this situation was what she'd expected to
happen after they made love. She'd expected to spend
the whole day lounging together, exploring each
other—body and mind. She hadn't expected this. Him
telling her to leave. Maybe what they'd just done meant
more to her than to him. Her stomach sank so low it hit
the ground.

"Don't order me around." She packed her tone with
irritation to mask the hurt. She turned her attention to
Row. "I can't wait to try your butterscotch pecan pancakes." She linked arms with the lavender-haired lady,
and they sashayed across the porch and down the steps.

Focus forward. Forward.

The grass was cool and damp underneath Isleen's
feet. A slight breeze ruffled her hair and was filled with
the scent of clean air and green growing things. A crown
of trees ringed the yard, and a strip of gravel came out
of the forest to stop at Xander's front door. They passed
from the open lawn to a whimsical trail carved through
the woods. It was the kind of path she'd expect to read
about in a book. Only it was real.

Sunshine filtered between the leaves and branches,
lasering cheerful yellow rays throughout the landscape.
Birds whistled back and forth, and a woodpecker hammered a hollow tree. The ground was mossy and soft
and the most brilliant shade of green she'd ever seen.
This place was the most beautiful place on earth.

"He's not mad at you," Row whispered. "He's mad

at me. Remember how I said he and his father haven't spoken in over twenty-five years? Well, Xan hasn't stepped foot in the main house since the day he became a legal adult. I think there are just too many painful memories there. And I—damn—shouldn't have used you to press him. I'm sorry. I'll talk to him after breakfast."

Her heart latched on to Row's explanation. Could it really be that simple? "Xander should've explained that to me. Not acted all… *Go. Go with Row*." She deepened her voice in an imitation of him.

Row chuckled. "Sweetie, he doesn't have a lot of experience when it comes to *relationships*. He's going to fuck it up a few times before he figures it out. And let's be honest—he was an asshole. All the Stone men are. It's genetic."

Chapter 11

Isleen's first shower post-torture-trailer had been last night. It'd been an efficient scrubbing-away-the-past kind of shower. Afterward, she had been so exhausted that she'd crawled in the giant bed, sunk down in the mound of pillows, and zonked out. Until she found herself outside with Xander.

But this shower, this one was pure pleasure. The shower nozzle rained warm water over her, sluicing and sliding down her body in the most soothing of caresses. Energy and excitement and gratitude coursed through her. Gran was alive. And Row was wonderful. And Xander... Being with him went beyond the physical into the mythical. They shared a connection that seemed only possible in fairy tales, but was somehow real. She could feel it in the way he looked at her, almost like he absorbed her, instead of seeing her.

Her new life was extraordinary. It really was. Happy tears swelled and spilled and mingled with the water as she washed her hair and body with beautifully scented soaps. The smells were a miracle to her nose so long deprived of appealing aromas. She rinsed the last of the suds from her body and then gave full freedom to the happy tears.

But her stomach tightened in on itself, tighter and tighter, until it felt like a heavy stone in her gut. Was she that hungry? Row's butterscotch pecan pancakes were waiting for her when she got out of the shower, but this didn't feel like hunger.

The stone in her stomach moved, traveled up her throat, and gagged her. She coughed, but the sound was no ordinary clearing of the throat. She recognized it for what it was—a sob. Before her brain could rein in the madness, another sob caught her, bending her double under its dark wave.

No. Life is good now. I'm happy now. I'm safe now. Her pep talk had no effect.

The past—all the things she'd shoved down into that grave in her mind—was about to rise from the dead. The eruption of horror and terror and ugliness was about to bury *her.*

Too weak to fight, she sank to her knees, crying for the happiness she'd only touched with the tips of her fingers. She could've had a wonderful life. A life where horror didn't exist. She wanted that life. She deserved that life. Not this fear. Not this pain.

She slammed her forehead into the tile floor. Lights glittered in her vision, and a starburst of agony burned in the middle of her forehead. An odd thing happened: some of the past sank back into its hole. She whacked her head against the floor—harder this time. Then again. And again. Until she'd reburied all those memories so deeply she'd need a deep-sea drilling rig to find them.

A hot poker of pain thudded in the center of her forehead, and it felt wonderful. Physical pain was easy. Cuts and bruises healed on their own with no effort on her part. She stretched out underneath the spray, her cheek resting against the tile wall, and closed her eyes. On

the back of her eyelids, red and orange strobes of color
pulsed and faded in perfect time with her heartbeat.

A knock on the bathroom door startled her upright.
Dizziness swayed her body, and her vision throbbed in
time with the thumping of her forehead.

"Isleen?" Roweena's tone carried the same frantic
edge it had when she'd thought Isleen was missing.

"Yes?" Isleen tried to pack as much normalness in
her voice as possible.

"No hurry or anything. I just wanted to let you know
that breakfast is ready."

"Um, go ahead and start without me. I'll be a few
more minutes." Isleen pulled herself to her feet, leaned
against the tiled wall until the world stopped rocking,
and then turned off the taps. Other than the pounding
in her head, she felt surprisingly all right. Almost as if
nothing had happened, when what had *almost* happened
was a mental eruption of volcanic proportions.

"Sweetie, is everything all right?" Row's voice,
speaking without the noise of shower, was laced with
compassion and concern.

"Yeah." The lie slipped out smoother than it should
have. "Just lost track of time."

"Well, I'll see you in a few minutes then."

"Yep. Just a few minutes." Isleen waited, breath
caged in her lungs, for Row to say something further,
but only silence stood on the other side of the doorway.

She rocketed out of the shower like a sprinter at the
sound of the gun. She dried and dressed and brushed her
hair and teeth and refused to think about what had just
happened beyond the evidence staring her in the mirror.
The center of her forehead was just a little red. No big

deal. She jogged from her room and didn't stop until she reached the staircase. Calmly, slowly, deliberately, she walked down the steps toward the clatter and clink of silverware on plates and the smell of breakfast.

The table was loaded with pancakes, syrup, eggs, bacon, and fruit—a glorious bowl of strawberries and blueberries. Her stomach roared at the sight. She barely stopped a dribble of drool leaking from her mouth.

"There you are." Row's lavender hair glowed from the sunshine streaming through the kitchen windows. Her tattoos somehow seemed more vibrant and shocking in the morning light. "Holy hell. What happened?"

Isleen stopped mid-stride, her mind whirling and searching for what Row could be talking about, but she kept coming up with nothing and more nothing.

"Your head." Row motioned to her own forehead.

"Oh…" She touched her forehead. The swollen hill of flesh, puffy and sore, hadn't seemed that bad only thirty seconds ago. "I bent down to get my towel off the floor and cracked my head on the sink." The lie flowed out so glossy and sleek she almost believed it. She didn't even blush or get flushed from the untruth. In all her years, through *everything*, she'd never been a liar until now.

"That's going to bruise. Let me get you some ice." Row scooted out of her chair and headed toward the fridge. "Sit wherever you'd like. And dig in."

Isleen turned her attention back to the table. Row's seat was at the head of the table—the power position. On her left sat Matt. He glared at her with a look that said I-know-you-did-that-to-yourself. But how could he know? He couldn't. It was in her mind. He was just looking at her like he always did   as if she were his enemy.

Alex sat on Row's right, silently eating. Isleen got to choose—sit next to Alex or Matt. Since Matt openly disliked her, that left Alex. She moved in next to him, but caught the smirking tilt of Matt's lips as if he knew exactly why she chose Alex. She bypassed Alex, walked around the table, and sat next to Matt.

The guy thought he could intimidate her? Yeah, she'd show him.

She reached for the empty plate and the silverware rolled in a napkin. Real cloth napkins. The kind fancy restaurants had. "Can you pass the pecan butterscotch pancakes? Please." She made sure—just for Matt—her voice was all sweet syrup.

Matt stared at her, the unyielding, half-angry expression pinching his lips, a futile attempt to be intimidating. She smiled at him, trying for one that looked genuine, but knew it came off as a bit forced.

Without looking away from her, Matt handed her the pancakes. The power of their heavenly smell drew her vision to them. Candied pecans were sprinkled over the platter, and the smell wafted into her nose. She closed her eyes and just breathed it in. God. Heaven on a plate. She forked one pancake on her plate, her hand shaking with excitement and the expectation of that first bite.

"Eat only a few bites. Small frequent meals until your body adjusts." Matt's tone was friendlier than his face.

"I know," she said and reached for the syrup. And then the eggs and bacon and fruit. She mounded her plate ridiculously full—knew she looked like a food hoarder, but couldn't resist the delicious look of everything. She sliced off a neat triangle of pancake and brought it to her lips. Flavor—butterscotch and butter and syrup—exploded inside her mouth. She closed her eyes and leaned back in her chair, savoring. She'd missed good food. She swallowed and finally opened her eyes.

"How'd you like it?" Row asked, handing her a fancy padded ice pack.

"Wow, Row. Best thing I've ever eaten."

A delighted smile lit Row's wrinkled face. "I'm glad you like them. I made some extras for you to take up to Xander's after breakfast."

Isleen nodded her head enthusiastically and shoved another bite of pancake in her mouth and then held the icepack to her forehead while she chewed. She wanted to bury her face in her plate and go at the food rabid-dog style, but the doctor had told her to eat slow, small meals. After she swallowed, she sat back, determined to wait a few minutes before her next bite.

Alex focused on his meal.

"Alex?" She used her best soothing-the-scared-child voice. Surprisingly, his head rose and he met her gaze. Triumph pumped through her. Maybe he wasn't as bad as Row made him seem. "How's Gran this morning?"

He looked at her as if he hadn't seen her before. With how devoted he'd been to Gran yesterday, maybe he hadn't.

"I see Shayla in you." His voice was a more gravelly version of Xander's.

"It's in the shape of her face, isn't it?" Row bounced in her chair like a happy ADHD kid, obviously unable to contain her excitement that Alex had spoken.

Alex set down his fork, folded his napkin, and settled

it neatly across his plate. "Where is Shayla?" His eyes were like twin icicles that pinned Isleen to her seat in a way Matt's attempts at intimidation never could.

"I-I don't know. Gran never spoke about her or the past or any of this."

Alex flinched as if her words had whipped him across his heart. "What happened to Gale? Why is she in the condition she is in? Don't you know how fragile she's always been? You should've protected her."

The pancake turned into a leaden lump in Isleen's stomach.

"Alex!" Roweena's tone was filled with shock and anger. "Don't you blame her. She barely made it out of there alive. Blame the person who held them captive."

"Gale's not the same. She should be getting better by being near me and she's not. I want you to tell me what happened to her." The ice in his gaze pierced Isleen's grave of memories.

"Alex. Leave." Row's voice was all angry mother. The tone could shrink an adult man to little-boy size. "Leave this table. Right now." She stood from her seat and pointed out into the house. He didn't leave; he just stared at Isleen, accusation chilling his expression.

"I didn't hurt her. I'd never hurt her. I tried to protect her." Images of torment and torture flashed into Isleen's mind—escapees from the memory grave. Things she never ever wanted to remember, things she didn't want to speak of, things she had to keep buried. "I'm not going to talk about it." She heard herself yelling and couldn't lasso her volume back down. "None of it matters now. It's done. It's over. And I'm done being hurt by it."

Xander shivered beneath the cold spray of water. Goose bumps prickled his skin, and chills racked his body, but he wasn't getting out until the goddamned urge to chase after Isleen passed. He wasn't going to set foot in that house, but goddamn, he was worried about her. Even under the frigid spray, his face fired with embarrassment that he'd had to call Row and ask her to check on Isleen. Row telling him that Isleen was okay, that she was just getting out of the shower, did nothing to calm him. It was like his body was primed in her direction, vigilant for a threat, ready to sprint to her rescue.

His phone on the sink vibrated loudly against the porcelain. It could be about Isleen. Naked and splashing water everywhere, he jumped out of the shower.

Kent calling lit up the display.

Fuck. He'd forgotten Kent intended to conduct his initial interview with Isleen today.

"Yeah," he answered, reaching for a towel.

"You going to be around after I interview Isleen? We need to talk."

"So talk."

"Face-to-face. Asshole." Anger sharpened Kent's tone, but Xander didn't care. Maybe talking on the phone was the way to handle the guy. No hearing his thoughts. No urge to go rage monkey.

"I'm busy." He wasn't intentionally antagonizing the guy. Okay, maybe just a little.

"Make time. I need some answers."

"Here's some answers for you. No. No. And, guess what? No."

"I don't have time for your shit. We're pulling up to the house right now. Camille wants to see you. Be ready to talk when I'm done with Isleen." Kent disconnected the call.

We're pulling up to the house right now? Camille wants to see you? Xander did *not* just hear those words. Kent was *not* saying that Camille was with him. No. It was a joke. Yeah, because they always enjoyed a good laugh together.

"Shit!" he yelled. Camille was here. He'd never invited her to his place. Hell, she thought he lived at the main house. She had made the assumption that was why he never invited her here—didn't want to welcome her into the family home for a fuck. She didn't know he had his own cabin on the top of the hill.

He hadn't expected Isleen and Camille's worlds to collide—at least not this early. Xander knew exactly what Kent was doing. The guy wanted Camille to stake her claim in front of Isleen and force Xander to *make a decision*. The guy was an asshole for doing that to Isleen. A whole new level of low in Kent and Xander's relationship was about to occur.

Xander yanked on a pair of jeans, the material scraping skin and hair off his damp legs. He jammed his feet into a pair of boots and sprinted for the main house.

She had yelled at Alex. Her words and tone hung in the air the way a piano chord still hums long after it has been struck.

A knock on the front door snapped all of their eyes and attention away from Isleen. Row headed across the house to answer the knock, while Matt and Alex left the table at the same time, both of them exiting the main house via a door underneath the balcony. Isleen stared down at her piled-mile-high plate that she'd only eaten two bites from, her appetite having disappeared.

"Isleen, you've got company," Roweena said and moved in next to Isleen's seat almost as if she were protecting her.

Isleen raised her eyes from the plate. The man from the hospital yesterday—she'd only seen him briefly—and a woman. They were a beautiful pair. Both had golden hair and stunning moss-colored eyes. He was classically handsome with sharp male features and carried a square-shaped duffel bag slung over one shoulder. She was the femininely beautiful version of him. Had to be brother and sister. She wore a dress the color of her eyes and a pair of heels that made her as tall as her sibling. She was stunning enough to be a model.

"You're looking good." The man's gaze roamed over Isleen's face, snagging just a moment on her forehead, then moving on to her hair. "You've made a miraculous recovery."

"I do feel better." She smiled at the pair. "I saw you yesterday, but I don't remember your name."

"Oh jeesh. Sorry. I'm Kent Knight. I work with Xander at the BCI—Bureau of Criminal Investigation. We're handling your case."

"My case? What case?"

"The investigation." He paused. "Into your abduction—"

Isleen flinched at the word *abduction*, and Kent stopped speaking. Uncomfortable silence filled the space until the woman stepped forward.

"I'm Camille, this guy's sister. I'm not with the Bureau. I'm just here to visit my *boyfriend*." She smiled, showing off a mouthful of white teeth that gleamed so brightly they almost glowed blue. "Xander."

Isleen's heart went cold, pumping frigid blood through her body. Goose bumps erupted over her skin. She shivered. No, it wasn't a shiver. She was trembling. She felt as if some prankster had just pulled the chair out from beneath her and she was falling, flailing, trying to catch herself before she splattered onto the ground. *Xander has a girlfriend. A girlfriend. A gorgeous girlfriend.*

Roweena put her hand on Isleen's shoulder.

She looked down at her flowing, pale-blue sundress. Row had stocked Isleen's closet with all kinds of clothes. Isleen had picked out the dress before she got in the shower because she wanted Xander to think she was pretty. But next to this woman, Isleen looked like a child. Camille had a sophistication that Isleen would never possess. How could Xander ever be attracted to her when he had Camille? Was that the real reason for his initial hesitation? He didn't want to cheat on his girlfriend, but didn't want to come right out and say it? Or maybe he wanted just to fuck her—his words—and then go back to his girlfriend.

Stupid. She'd been so stupid to think a fairy-tale happily ever after was going to happen to her. Gran had always said, "Loving men makes women messy." Now Isleen knew what Gran meant.

"Camille. It's so nice to meet you." Her lips seemed numb when she spoke, but at least her voice was audible.

"It's nice meeting you too. I've wondered about the woman monopolizing all Xander's attention." Her words were spoken in a kind voice, but the woman was looking Isleen up and down as if she were something harmful to be categorized as merely approach-with-caution or skull-and-crossbones deadly.

"He's all yours now." Isleen packed her tone with sincerity. Row squeezed her shoulder, and Isleen knew that the old woman wasn't happy with her words.

The kitchen door flew open, banging into the wall. Xander entered the house, his gaze finding her the moment he crossed the threshold, but she looked away. The sight of him was a pummeling her heart couldn't withstand.

"Camille, what are you doing here?" Shock sharpened Xander's voice.

"Busted," Isleen whispered, finally looking back at Xander. Row tapped her lightly on the shoulder. Xander thought he could get away with playing around with her, while he had a girlfriend on the side? Not going to happen.

"Hey, man," Kent answered, his voice and demeanor too light, not acknowledging Xander's obvious anger. "I'm going to talk to Isleen while you hang with *your girlfriend*. And then we need to go over some official business." Kent turned to Roweena, completely ignoring the way the scars on Xander's face flamed with rage. "Is there someplace private Isleen and I can talk?"

"How about out on the back porch?" Row pointed to the kitchen door still open. "Only the birds and leaves to hear you out there."

"Sounds perfect." Kent shifted the strange bag off his shoulder, carrying it in his hands, and headed in that direction.

Row bent down and whispered in her ear. "Don't be so mad at Xander. None of this is exactly how it looks."

Xander's attention snapped to Row whispering in her ear, then his eyes met hers. Isleen searched his gaze, hoping to see an apology, an explanation, something that would justify this situation, but all she saw was guilt.

Camille sidled up to Xander, pressing herself fully against his body as if she were going to hug him, but Isleen watched the woman's hand disappear into the space between their hips. Isleen's eyes jumped back to Xander who still looked at her, not his girlfriend rubbing his crotch. A muscle in his cheek ticked. His eyes went cold.

Isleen strained to pull in enough oxygen to keep herself breathing. Seeing Xander—*her* savior, *her* rescuer, *her* dream man—with another woman hurt more than a fist crushing her heart to pulp.

She tore her gaze away from Xander and Camille's PDA. On unsteady legs, she stood and moved to follow Kent outside.

"If you need me, I'll be right here in the kitchen," Row said. Isleen gave her a grateful smile. At least she had one friend in this house.

She closed the door behind her, closed Xander and Camille inside, and wrote "The End" to her and Xander's short story. Her body felt like crying, but her eyes remained dry. The future that looked so good only an hour ago was now a putrid mess. It was up to her to figure out how to be happy—without Xander, without Alex or Matt or Gran. Her happiness was her responsibility. She was strong. She'd survived *everything*. She'd figure out a way to thrive.

She sucked in a breath and sat on the swing facing out over a deep tree-filled ravine. No breeze moved the leaves, but the morning birds still sang.

Kent, who'd been staring out over the railing, took a seat in one of the wicker chairs opposite her.

"You don't have a very good view," she said. "You can sit here if you want." She patted the seat next to her.

"Actually, I think I have the best view."

Was he joking?

His square-cut features looked serious. "I saw you right after Xander brought you in. You were mostly dead, looked it too, and today—only five days later—you are a vibrant woman. It's like everything about you is a miracle. From how Xander found you, to you being Gale's granddaughter, to your hair growing impossibly fast."

She tucked a strand of hair behind her ears. "Today, life doesn't feel very miraculous."

"Hard seeing Xander with another woman?"

"Yeah." Confessing her feelings to a total stranger was only further evidence of how starved she was for attention and affection.

"I'm an asshole for bringing her here, but I knew Xander wouldn't tell you about Camille. He's been with her about ten years. Treats her like shit and she eats it up. I don't want that to happen to you."

"I guess he's not the person I thought he was." *Not the person I dreamed about.*

"I've got something that might lift your spirits." He reached into the strange-shaped duffel bag. Up close she could see the material was mostly made of mesh. He rummaged for a moment, then pulled out a little dog that was all skeletal legs, brindled fur, and ears three times larger than its head. It was the funniest looking canine she'd ever seen.

"Oh my gosh. He's so sweet. What's his name? Can I hold him?"

Kent's face went serious. "His name is Killer. And before you hold him, I need to warn you. He lives up to his name—Killer."

"He's mean?" Disappointment raised the pitch of her voice.

Kent lowered his voice to sound like a corny radio announcer. "He's a *lady*-killer. He doesn't look like it, but he loves the ladies. Hell, he loves anyone who loves him." Kent handed him over to her.

Killer's fur wasn't exactly soft; it was more bristly than anything. She settled him on her lap, but he twisted, stood on his back legs, his front paws on her chest, and licked her chin. His tongue was warm and... "Oh, his breath—"

Kent laughed, his features softening. "That's his Achilles' heel. I've done everything I can to get that stink under control. Mint charcoal doggy mouthwash in his water. No go. Doggy breath mints. No go. Brushing his teeth—that traumatized us both and still didn't work."

Killer settled back in her lap, his dark-chocolate eyes staring up at her. She didn't need to be the dog whisperer to know he wanted her to pet him. She scratched his ears, and he let out a doggy sigh of total contentment.

"I picked him up at the Humane Society about a year ago. I went in there looking for a dude's dog—you know, a Lab or German shepherd. I ended up with Killer. Just couldn't walk away from that face with those ears. It's taken him a while to adjust. At first, if I raised my voice—you know when you watch a game on TV or something—he'd start shaking, slink off, and hide like he thought I was going to beat him. He used to hoard his food too. He'd go to his food bowl, get a mouthful, then go spit it out in the corner of his bed, stockpiling it like one day I might stop feeding him or something. That's gone now."

"I can't believe someone could be cruel to him. He's the sweetest thing." Killer stood, turned two circles on her lap, then lay down, curling up in a tight ball. His eyes fell shut and he was out. "I'm in love with him."

"Told you. He's a lady-killer."

They sat quietly for a while, both watching Killer sleep.

"Isleen, I know it isn't going to be easy, but I have to ask you a few questions. Is that okay?" He removed a small recorder from his pocket and placed it on the seat next to her.

"No, it's not okay." Her voice came out soft and weak. She hated that. "I appreciate visiting with Killer, and I would like us to be friends." She harrumphed a feeling-sorry-for-herself sound. "I don't have any, other than Row. But I can't, Kent. I can't talk about—"

Kent scooted his chair closer, until only a few inches separated their knees. He reached out to her, covering both her hands with his. His grip was warm and dry and pleasant, but not the same as when Xander touched her. There was no electricity. No zing or zip. Only the comfort of human contact.

"Let's just start out with basic information. Like your full name, date of birth. You can stop this at any time. You're in control."

What did it hurt to give him her name? "Isleen Gale Walker. July Fourth—"

"You have a birthday in a few weeks. Let me be the first to tell you happy birthday. What kind of cake do you want?"

"Cake? It's been so long since I thought about cake." She paused, thinking back to the time before *everything*. "Gran used to make a chocolate cherry cake with chocolate frosting. Oh my gosh. It was incredible."

"Sounds amazing. All I ever got growing up was store-bought clearance cake. The crazy flavor of the week that no one wanted to buy. One year it was prune spice cake. *Prune cake* shouldn't be in the same sentence as *birthday*."

Isleen giggled.

"You laughing at my childhood trauma?" Kent asked in mock hurt. His eyes met hers and she saw something. It was more than the way the edges of his eyes tilted downward, lending his features a sadness; it had to do with the truth behind his joke. The light mood disappeared. "You still don't want to answer any of my questions?"

She shook her head.

"Okay, I won't ask you anything then." His hands covering hers tightened, his fingers stretched out to cover the insides of her wrists. "Here's what I know. I know that sometime between your junior and senior year at Prospectus High School, you vanished. When the truant officer finally got around to checking on your lack of attendance, he assumed you'd moved because the home you shared with your grandmother was empty."

Isleen's heart beat as swiftly as sparrow's wings.

"I know that you were starved, beaten, and drained of blood. I know that you've been enduring that for the past eight years."

Her insides shook, the sensation traveling outward on waves of fear until her entire body trembled. Deep in the grave of memories, Isleen felt the soil shift, felt for the second time today the memories trying to rise up. No. She was stronger than them. She would not let them take her over.

"Is…is Queen dead?" Isleen's voice shook when she said the name.

"Yes."

"Then none of it matters. It's over. It's done with. She can't hurt me or Gran anymore." The grave dirt stilled.

"Hey." Kent's tone was soft. The kind of tone a person used on a wounded animal. "I have to follow every lead. I have to make certain that you really are safe. That everything you've been through really is over. But, if you're not ready to talk about it today, we don't have to talk about it."

"I intend never to talk about it." She held his gaze, hoping he could see the promise in her eyes.

"Isleen, I've been doing this job for a while now. I have experience dealing with people like you. People who've experienced the worst life has to offer and survived. So I can tell you, holding it all inside is dangerous. It's a wound, and when you don't talk about it, it becomes infected. If not treated, the infection takes over and the nice life you want to build gets poisoned."

She pulled her hands out from underneath his and picked up the sleeping Killer, handing him back to Kent. She stood and headed toward the kitchen door.

Xander stood there. The memory of Camille pressing herself against him, her hand disappearing between their bodies, stabbed into Isleen's brain.

She turned back to Kent. "You're wrong. It's not a wound. It's an abyss."

Chapter 12

Fifteen minutes ago...

THE SWOLLEN PINK MOUND OF SKIN IN THE CENTER OF Isleen's forehead grabbed Xander's attention the second he walked in the door. What happened? He'd *known* something wasn't right. That's why he'd called Row to check on her.

Hurt and betrayal etched themselves on Isleen's face. Xander tried to go to her, to explain, but Camille—still pressed against his front—squeezed his dick dangerously hard, yanking his focus back to her.

You're mine. Not hers. Xander heard Camille's thoughts but experienced no pain from them. Just as he hadn't felt any pain when he burst through the kitchen door and the frequency connection opened with all of them—except Isleen. Usually, conversation with more than one person was a formal invitation for the Bastard in His Brain to make a guest appearance. Not today. All because of Isleen. Something about being near her helped him have control over his hearing. It was as though she healed the damage done by the lightning and made him almost normal.

Row's thoughts reached his ears. *I think she's going to blow him. Right here. In front of me.*

Jesus fucking Christ. It was bad enough having to deal with Camille, but Row's commentary—even if she wasn't saying it aloud—brought the situation to a whole new level of awkward.

"I haven't seen you in days, and you haven't been returning my calls," Camille said. *Kent told me you haven't left her side. You're spending too much time with her. Maybe I need to remind you why you're mine.*

Xander's gaze cut to Isleen following Kent out the kitchen door. God. Damn.

"Find us a private place," Camille whispered. "I know what you need. You need my mouth. You need me swallowing everything you've got." *You'll forget about her once I take care of you.*

The mental picture her words created in his mind wasn't erotic. It made him feel on the verge of a virile case of stomach flu. Being with Camille was wrong. Had been wrong for years, and yet he'd allowed things to continue because he was a selfish asshole who'd found someone willing to fuck him and not make demands.

Meeting Isleen had changed him into a different kind of person. One who no longer wanted a meaningless fuck. One who wanted more. He didn't know exactly what *more* meant, he just wanted it from Isleen, not Camille.

Does she not know I'm standing right here, listening to every word she's saying? Row's thoughts were an invasion into an already convoluted situation. *I thought her parents raised her better than this. And that my boy would involve himself with such a harlot—where did I go wrong raising him?*

He met Row's eyes. "This is on me, not you." Then he turned his attention back to Camille. Part of him felt horrible over what he was about to do to her—he'd been a pussy for not doing it sooner. The other part was still pissed at her possessive sexual display in front of Isleen. "Listen, I'm an asshole. You know that. Everyone knows that." He gripped her shoulders and physically forced her off his body. "But, there have never been any rules between us. There has never been a relationship between us. The only thing we shared is fucking. That's it."

"You don't mean that. You're just tired. You've been too busy playing nursemaid to *her*, but she's fine now. And I've missed you. I know you're not taking care of yourself." *Not the way I take care of you.*

He grabbed her by the arm and hauled her toward the front door and away from Row who wasn't shy about being nosey.

One day you're going to realize that you love me. And you're going to marry me. And we'll live here and be happy and—

"Marriage and happiness are two things we will never share."

She flinched at his words, taken from her thoughts. Her mouth opened to say something, but he sliced off her response with his own cruel words. "When have we ever gone on a date, Camille? Have I *ever* picked you up and taken you to the movies? Or out to eat? Or anywhere?"

"Well, no, but—" *That doesn't mean anything. It just means you don't like to be social.*

"Have I ever just called you, just to hear your voice? Or do I call with the sole purpose of schedule coordina-tion so we can fuck." He let go of her long enough to haul open the massive front door.

"But you're not dating anyone else. You've never dated anyone. We've been together for so long."

"Wake up. This"—he motioned back and forth

between them—"has only ever been about sex. And
now, I'm done. Done with this. Done with you." With
his hand on the small of her back, he guided her toward
the open door.

No... Oh my God. No. I can't be that stupid. Camille
stopped on the threshold. Her too-perfect mouth slack
with the realization. *He can't mean what he's saying.
He's confused.* "It's her. She's playing you, making you
feel like the hero to her damsel in distress. Wake up and
see what's happening. Are you willing to throw away
our years together over some girl who's not even pretty?
And her hair—it looks like she hacked at it with a pair of
pruning sheers. In the dark. Without a mirror."

Leave it to Camille, who managed a salon, to com-
ment on Isleen's hair. Anger curled his hands into fists.
He leaned in close to her face. "Don't. You. Ever. Talk
about Isleen that way."

Camille crossed her arms, not intimidated by him or
his anger. "There you go, playing her hero again." *You'll
see her for who she really is once she drops the victim act.*

"Don't call me. And don't ever come here again. I'll
tell Kent you're ready to leave."

*No. He can't mean that. Can't mean that we're really
over. He just needs to see that girl for who she really is.
A manipulative bitch who's moving in on my—*

He slammed the heavy door, the sound so loud to his
ears that it drowned out the rest of what Camille said.
Now to fix the damage done with Isleen. He turned to
see Row leaning against the kitchen island giving him
her most disapproving, disappointed look. The look that
made him feel like he was five years old and had gotten
caught stealing a candy bar from RaeBeck's Grocery.

"What?"

You know what. Row's expression didn't change. She was one of the few people who knew he heard on the frequency of thought. She knew how much it hurt him, too. So for her to be actually communicating with him like that, even she could see the changes Isleen brought into his life.

"I wasn't serious with her."

Row's right eyebrow rose just slightly.

"I wasn't."

You were fornicating with her.

"Jesus. When you put it that way, it sounds so dirty. I knew she wanted more from me, but I never delivered. Never gave her false promises. Never—" He stopped talking. Row's silence, both internal and external, didn't bode well for him. The one bright spot was that at least he was too big for a spanking. And he could outrun her if she tried to take a switch to him. Though if he was being truthful with himself, Row's disappointment in him stung worse than any switchin' he'd ever gotten.

"Okay, I made some bad decisions regarding Camille. But I'm trying to fix that now. And it looks like she's going to be"—he searched for the right word—"persistent."

Row rolled her eyes. "I want to know what you're going to do about Isleen. You hurt her by not informing her you had a girlfriend and by the display you two made." Xander opened his mouth to say it wasn't his fault, but Row shot him with the shut-up-and-listen look. "And Isleen's already had a rough morning."

"What happened to her forehead?"

"I'm not talking about that—though she *says* she

bent down to pick up her towel and thunked her head against the bathroom sink. What I'm talking about is your father. He verbally attacked her. Blamed Isleen for Gale's physical and mental state. Demanded answers. He really upset Isleen. And then, all this shit with Camille happened."

"Shit."

"Yeah. Now, go and fix this." Row flicked her thumb in the direction Kent and Isleen had left the house.

Xander was at the kitchen door before he'd even told himself to move. Hand on the door handle, he paused.

Isleen sat on the porch swing overlooking the ravine. Kent's mini-mutt was curled up sleeping peacefully on her lap, while Kent held both her hands in his—a comforting gesture that no one should be offering Isleen except for Xander.

He eavesdropped through the finale of their conversation—just another reason he was an asshole—then held the door open for her when she approached.

"Are you all right?" he asked as she walked into the house. He heard her heart thudding, her breath rushing in and out of her lungs. He settled his hand on her shoulder. "What's wrong?" It was a stupid question, but the only one that his vocals produced.

She whirled on him, shrugging his hand off. "You're asking me what's wrong?" Her chin trembled and so did his heart. "The easier question is, what's right? Nothing. Right now, nothing. And don't touch me. You want to touch someone? Go touch your girlfriend." She walked away from him.

He watched her until he realized she was heading toward the front door. Toward Camille. "Isleen, wait."

"I don't want you near me, so just stay away."

He didn't move toward her, wouldn't force her to be around him—not after everything she'd been through. "Camille's out there," he warned her.

"Good. We need to talk." She dragged open the heavy door and left him standing there with his regret and self-loathing.

"She's not happy with you." Kent said from behind him, not even bothering to conceal his amusement. *I'm glad she sees you for who you really are, even if my sister can't.*

It would be so satisfying to serve the guy a fist of five, but priorities were priorities. "Check out a guy named William Goodspeed. He should be arriving at Sunny County Children's Services today for a supervised visit with his son. He'll have a gun with him. And if someone doesn't stop him, he'll kill his caseworker, his wife, and his son."

———

Isleen shut the front door behind her. Before she could even take a breath, let alone a step, Camille invaded the bubble of her space, staring down at her with red-rimmed eyes.

Isleen understood pain and didn't want to hurt this woman anymore. "Are you okay?"

"Have you slept with him?" Hatred sharpened the woman's words.

"Yes." It didn't occur to Isleen to lie, when maybe she should have. Where was her self-preservation?

Camille glared at her, her eyes assessing Isleen's truthfulness. "I don't believe you. If you'd been with him, you wouldn't be calmly talking to me. You'd be just as angry as I am."

"Oh, I'm angry. Just not at you."

Camille smiled a downright cruel smile. "He's a machine, you know. Can fuck all night and still want more."

Not from her experience. And not in Isleen's dreams. In her dreams, he'd been tender and caring and passionate, but never mechanical. Never a machine. But then, her dreams weren't real. And what she had thought was real turned out to be smoke. The sooner she got that fact imprinted into her mind, the sooner she could begin to move on from him. Again. How many times was she going to let herself get hurt by him when they'd never even had a real relationship?

Camille stepped back out of Isleen's space. "You know he's only being nice to you because he feels sorry for you." Camille's gaze landed squarely on Isleen's hair, traveled to the swollen mound on her forehead, then moved down to take in the pale-blue sundress that Isleen had thought of as feminine and pretty when she picked it out.

The door behind her opened. *Please, don't let it be Xander.* She didn't have it in her to see him and Camille together again so soon.

"There you are," Kent said. "I was hoping to have a chance to talk to you before we left."

Relief unclenched muscles she hadn't realized were tense. Isleen stepped to the side to face him.

"Roweena was just telling me about all the trails. Maybe, if you are feeling up to it, we can take Killer on a walk tomorrow morning."

"I'm not going to talk about…" Her tone was filled with warning.

"You don't have to. Tomorrow will be a social call, just Killer visiting his lady friend. And since I'm his chauffeur, you get me too." Kent's features were so much softer and friendlier than his sister's.

Killer whined and pawed at the mesh dog carrier.

"How can I say no to that?" What else did she have to do between now and Kent's next visit? Nothing.

"I'll be by in the morning." Kent headed down the steps toward his truck, and Camille trailed silently behind him. If he'd been alone, Isleen might've asked him to take her with him. She didn't want to go back into the house and face Xander or Alex or Matt. The list of favorable people had dwindled to Row and Gran.

She could either stand out here all day feeling sorry for herself, not appreciating the awesome new life she had, or she could go in there and make the best of everything. Gran was alive. That was huge. More than she had ever dared to hope for.

Without giving herself another moment of pity-party time, Isleen walked back into the house. The massive space was wonderfully empty. She stopped outside Gran's room and peeked inside. If Alex was in there, she'd come back later. Gran lay in her hospital bed, her face turned to the window. The nurse sat in the chair Alex had used yesterday, reading aloud. Her finger moving across the line of text with each word spoken.

Isleen knocked lightly on the door. The nurse stopped reading and looked up. The woman appeared nearly as old as Gran, but she had color and vitality that Gran lacked.

"How's she doing today?" Isleen asked.

The nurse closed her book and moved out of the chair. "She's more spunky today. Aren't you, Mrs. Stone?"

At the name *Mrs. Stone*, Gran's gaze shifted from the window to the nurse, then back to the window. Gran had always been Mrs. Walker to Isleen. Hearing her called Mrs. Stone was foreign but elicited a response, and that was an improvement.

"She's asked for Alex a number of times. He had to take an important phone call and then said he would work from here." She gestured toward the laptop sitting on the dresser.

"Would you mind if I sat with her for a while?" Isleen asked.

"Go ahead. I'll take a quick bathroom break, then be just outside the door. You call if you need me."

Isleen waited until the nurse left the room, then scooted the chair over—blocking Gran's line of sight to the outside with her own body—and sat down. "Gran?" She smoothed a stray strand of hair off Gran's forehead. "It's me. Isleen. I'm here. I'm here with you." Isleen watched the miracle of recognition light Gran's eyes. Elation took wing inside Isleen's chest. She clasped Gran's hand between both of hers in a gesture that reminded her of how Kent had held on to her—an offer of sanctuary from the storm.

"Isleen." Gran started to smile, but it faltered and fell off her lips before it could even be fully born.

"Yes, Gran. I'm here. You're here." Her voice hid behind emotions she wouldn't let herself feel, so she whispered the words, "We survived."

Gran shook her head back and forth, over and over, her nearly bare scalp rustling against the pillowcase in a way that scratched the insides of Isleen's ears.

"I remember." Gran's eyes locked with Isleen's and

held on and on and on for an immeasurable moment as if she were trying to convey a message so powerful words wouldn't suffice. Gran broke their eye contact and turned her face away. "I remember, and I can't live with it."

"Oh, Gran…" These were the worst times. When Gran remembered every bad, awful, and terrifying thing they'd been through. "We're safe—"

"I can't live with what I've done." Gran's voice lowered to a rasp of sand over gravel, and she stared off into negative space.

"You're safe now. We're staying with Alex…your husband." Saying *your husband* felt weird on her tongue. "He's been taking such good care of you."

"I hurt him." Gran's chapped lips quivered. "I destroyed us by trying to save us. And I did this to you." The word *I* came out on an airy sob. A tear slipped down Gran's crepe-paper cheek. "It's all my fault. I'd take it all back. But, there's no take-backs in life."

"'Focus forward.' Your motto. Everything will be all right as long as we both focus forward." Isleen shifted her chair so Gran could see outside again. "Look out the window." She waited for Gran's head to turn. "See all the trees. Do you remember our little house? Remember how we used to walk down our lonely road to the woods and follow that old lane through the trees? You always used to say it reminded you of your favorite place." Gran's attention was back on the scenery outside the window. "I know what it reminded you of. It reminded you of here. And now you're here again. This will be your future again."

Tears rained down Gran's cheeks, but her gaze never

left the window. Isleen stayed with Gran until the old woman's breathing eased and her eyes drifted shut. Isleen kissed her on the cheek, then left the room.

Gran had the right idea. Isleen climbed the stairs to her room, then buried herself under a mound of blankets and a heap of denial.

Chapter 13

Xander parked his new truck on the same mud-crusted hunk of earth where he had a few days earlier. Police tape ringed the torture trailer like a too-tight belt. More of it crisscrossed in an awkward X-marks-the-spot over the sagging front door. The back end—the room where Isleen and her grandmother had spent years being tormented—was obliterated. Gone. The only indication it had been there was the debris strewn around the overgrown yard. The horrors that had occurred in that small space were beyond imagination.

His stomach squeezed with guilt for not listening to Isleen sooner. He'd carry that shame for the rest of his life.

He turned off the truck's ignition, got out—and made damned sure to put his keys in his pocket. Even though the crazy bitch was dead, no one could claim he didn't learn from his mistakes.

The corn leaves whispered among themselves, the abrasion of them rubbing against each other a low hum. Far off in the distance a hawk cried out, but Xander didn't see it in the sky. Summer sun beat down on his head. Hot and purifying. He hoped its rays had burned off the pain that once lived here.

He wasn't certain why he'd stopped here on his way to interrogate the Prairie Murderer. The superintendent had nearly laid a load in his shorts when Xander *called* him and volunteered to interview the killer and William Goodspeed. Xander had a motive the superintendent didn't know about—figuring out how Isleen was connected to these two men. And if she wasn't... Well, that meant he was about to go down a road with his father that he'd never intended to travel.

Maybe he was here to make sure things had happened the way he remembered—since what he remembered seemed as impossible as Isleen surviving. Or maybe to see if this place held any answers.

Wooden stakes protruded from the ground with police tape strung between them to mark off the hole where his truck exploded. He went up to the roped-off edge. No fucking kidding—it really was a crater. Looked nearly four feet deep and almost as long as his truck had been.

Memories flooded his mind, so visceral, so real, he could smell burned corn and feel the heat of the engine on his face. Feel the resignation that death was about to grab him and Isleen.

And then his truck and the crazy bitch driving it had blown up.

The BCI could find no reason for the vehicle to explode. It wasn't like he'd been hauling around a load of C-4. And there sure as shit wasn't any explanation for how he'd stood this close to the blast and neither he nor Isleen had been touched.

Beyond the yard, the cornfield was a mangled mess with wide swatches of flattened corn from his truck chasing him and Isleen through the field. The weeds and tall grass of the yard had been flattened and smashed in places from all the crime techs and officers searching for the smallest bit of evidence.

An odd furrow through the grass snagged his attention. It looked like someone had ridden a motorcycle through the yard and around to the back of the trailer. He was pretty damned positive the investigators drove cars. He listened. The noise from all the corn leaves rustling made it hard to pick up the sound, but he heard it none the less. A heartbeat. Breathing. Someone was behind the trailer. A sightseer or someone connected to the crazy bitch?

He followed the path, stopped at the corner of the trailer, and peered around it.

There was the motorcycle. A damned fine-looking piece of machinery. Flat black paint, skull on the tank. The kind of bike he'd love to spend some time admiring, then give it a test drive.

Beyond the bike was a giant of a man. He looked like he had a couple of inches and a dozen pounds on Xander. He wore jeans, a gray T-shirt, and boots. Same thing every other guy wore, but this guy's hair—whoa. That stuff on the top of his head flamed in the sun. It was the darkest shade of red hair Xander had ever seen. Wasn't there some fancy girly name for hair that color?

The guy faced out toward the field. Eyes closed, sucking in great breaths of air, holding them almost like he savored the flavor of oxygen before he exhaled slowly out his mouth.

Who the hell? And why the fuck did the guy act like he'd found a prime meditation spot—unless torture and pain were triggers for relaxation? Only a sadist would get off on the bad vibes this place emitted.

Xander moved around the trailer so the man could see him. "What are you doing?" His booming demand carried the weight of his attitude.

The guy didn't flinch, didn't startle, didn't react at all to Xander's voice breaking the silence among the fields. *He must be in one hell of a Zen state.*

"What are you doing here?" Xander headed toward the guy. A breeze blew from behind him, ruffling his hair.

The guy's eyes popped open, and he lurched around, fists clenched in a ready-for-anything stance. And Xander saw the other side of his face. A tattoo—a glossy, black feather spanning from the corner of his mouth up and over the apple of his cheek. As if that wasn't bad enough the feather had been broken and wept fat drops of red down the man's cheek and neck.

A tattoo like that made a statement.

Recognition hit Xander. This was the guy who'd been looking at the bear totem the night he drove to this decrepit patch of earth and found Isleen. With the bear carving so close to Xander's home and three hours from where they currently stood, no way was this encounter a big, happy coincidence.

"Who the fuck are you?" Pain slammed into the side of Xander's head. Goddamn. He blinked with every pounding pulse and pressed his palm to his temple until his body calibrated to the thudding.

Silence sliced the air for a few moments too long before Xander heard the guy's thoughts.

No one was supposed to be here. I was guaranteed privacy. "You need to leave. This is a crime scene, an ongoing investigation."

There was something odd about the way the guy spoke. It wasn't his words or his volume or anything Xander could easily label. It was almost as if he had a slight accent, but even that wasn't quite right.

"Yeah, I know. I'm a consultant with the Bureau of Criminal Investigation." Not an out-and-out lie. "You're trespassing."

The guy stared at him. Like take-a-picture-it-will-last-longer stared. Must be the scars. Though with that big-ass tattoo on his face, the guy shouldn't judge.

It was almost like there was a time delay on the guy's thoughts. Xander finally heard them.

He's not lying. This guy is a consultant. Then why the fuck did they call me in? Overkill. I could be home weeding instead of dealing with this shit. The guy nodded once. "I'm a consultant with the FBI."

Xander listened. Listened for the little hitch that would happen if the guy lied. Listened for his heart rate to increase. Listened for thoughts that varied from the words. Nothing. He was telling the truth. And seemed uber-serious about his weeding. "You're the big guns they called in?"

The guy shrugged. *Yeah. I don't look it. But neither do you.* "You're not what I had in mind for a consultant."

"Neither are you. I guess they like to hire the ugly ones."

Truth. Gospel fucking truth. A smile almost tipped the man's lips, but he didn't say anything.

"I'm Xander Stone, by the way." He held out his hand to shake.

The guy held up a gloved hand in a warding-off gesture. *Don't fucking touch me.*

It wasn't like Xander planned to molest the dude. "You got a name?"

The guy did that weird staring thing again, but didn't think the answer to Xander's question. A question like that and the brain couldn't help answering, and yet this guy—

Lathaniel Montgomery.

Guess this guy was just on a delayed reaction. Maybe Lathaniel here was a bit slow in the brain game.

"Lathan," the guy finally said. Omitting his last name.

Xander nodded and looked around the overgrown yard, then back to Lathan. "This one's personal."

Lathan watched him like every word coming out of his mouth was gold-plated and diamond studded. *Did he say it was personal? Was that what he said?*

"I'm the one who found the women." Even as he said the words, Xander pictured the moment he'd opened the door to that room and discovered Isleen lying there. A nightmare he'd probably have for the rest of his life.

More staring, then Lathan said, "No shit."

"No shit. You think the outside looks bad. Try going inside."

"Hell no. The stench is about gagging me out here. No way can I set foot inside." *There are limits to what I can do, and that's a hard fucking limit.*

Xander sniffed the air. Didn't smell a thing. "You find anything?"

"Not a damned thing everyone doesn't already know. There's a reason I don't work current cases or make house calls. But this one was so close to home the powers-that-fucking-be suggested I try it. I tried it. Sucked at it. Fuck the powers-that-be." He gave a middle-finger salute.

Xander couldn't help it. He kinda liked the guy. "Right on, brother." Xander imitated the salute. Since they were buds now, it was time to bring up what he *really* wanted to know. "I live near the bear totem. Drove by the other night and saw you there. What were you doing?"

Isn't that the fucking question I keep asking myself?
"You own it?"

Xander was half tempted to say yes, just to see Lathan's reaction. "No."

"Then I expect it's none of your business." Lathan's tone wasn't unfriendly; it just lacked the camaraderie they'd shared a moment ago.

Xander's phone vibrated. He yanked it out and glanced at the screen.

Kent: Where the fuck are you? Everyone is waiting.
Shit.

He shoved his phone back in his pocket. All the guy's attention was on him, wariness on his face, like he half expected Xander to attack.

"I'm late for an interrogation. You find anything, keep me in the loop. Contact Kent Knight at the BCI field office. Like I said, this one is personal."

The guy dipped his head in agreement, but didn't say—or think—anything as Xander turned and headed away.

Note to self: Ask Kent just exactly what kind of consulting Lathan does.

—∿∿—

The fluorescent light over Xander's head winked dim and then bright, the buzz of the dying bulb as annoying as a mosquito let loose inside his brain. Elbows on the table, he fisted his hands over his ears to drown the noise. Screw trying to look all invincible to the Prospectus County coppers observing on the other side of the interrogation room's two-way mirror. Remaining sane and not letting the Bastard in His

Brain make a guest appearance took top billing over
looking mucho macho.

A splashing dark stain on the ceiling tiles indicated
a leaky roof, and the gunk caked in the floor corners
proved the janitor—if there was one—wasn't being
paid to care. The sheriff's office seemed to be a victim
of underfunding and understaffing. With Isleen and
Gale's case and the murder in Prospectus Prairie Park,
you'd think the place would be overflowing with officers, but all staff on deck meant only a half dozen officers, making the place blissfully quiet. Except for that
goddamned light droning on and on and on.

The moment he'd seen Kent pacing in the corridor,
waiting for him outside this room, Xander had blasted
off with questions about Lathan Montgomery. Kent
knew less than he did, only that the FBI had called in a
local consultant. That was it. Nothing else. And wasn't
that weird? That there was a local FBI consultant that
no one knew anything about.

Xander waited three full revolutions of the minute
hand on the clock across from him, then spoke without
even facing the two-way mirror. "You want me to get
answers? Get him in here. Now. I don't have all day
to sit on my fucking thumb." He still needed to drive
back across the state to interview William Goodspeed.

The scraping squeal of the door being opened
practically lacerated his eardrums. He clamped his
hands tighter over his ears. The frequency connection
opened, the pain of it a fist to the temple. Without
meaning to, Xander flinched and held his breath until
the thudding in his head became a part of his body's
rhythm. He removed his hands from his ears and sat

up straighter while the officer cuffed the suspect to the metal table.

Asshole acts like a spoiled brat just 'cause he's a special consultant to the BCI. With a face like that, he probably hasn't been laid in a decade. The officer's thoughts were in line with how every other officer looked at him.

"Try six hours ago," Xander said to the officer, then locked his attention on the Prairie Murderer.

How'd he—

"There's a reason I'm the special skills consultant. Lock him down and leave." Xander examined the blond beast dressed in jailhouse tangerine. Yep. *Blond beast* was the best description. A thick scruff of matted beard shadowed the guy's face, and his hair fell in thick wheat-colored hanks over his forehead and into his eyes, obscuring the details of his features. But there was no hiding the indifference to sin shining bright in the guy's eyes. Simon Smith, a.k.a. the Prairie Murderer, looked more rabid animal than *Homo sapiens*.

After the officer left the room, Xander inhaled a lungful of pungent air tainted with body odor and the moist, greasy scent of unwashed hair. This was going to be one of those breathe-through-the-mouth situations.

Simon Smith's apathetic gaze roamed over Xander's scars. *He got what he deserved. Marked for life. Punished for life. Everyone will know about him. He's no threat.* His body betrayed nothing of his thoughts. He didn't move a muscle, didn't even blink.

"Who you talking about?" Xander asked.

You've been marked. You are no threat.

Xander's heart jackknifed inside his chest. Queen's words echoed through his brain—*Mark of the Beast.*

The wording seemed too close to be random. But coincidences did occasionally happen.

"You think I'm no threat? Because of my scars? My scars are what make me a threat." Actually, the lightning strike had caused his supercharged hearing. The scars were just the lightning's version of saying, "I was here."

Your scars are your punishment.

O-k-ay. They were having a one-sided conversation—Xander's side—and this guy acted as if that were completely normal. Someone had stepped over the loony line. The guy had to be off his psych meds. Xander would bet if they searched, they'd find a history of Simon Smith being in and out of the nuthouse. Better alert Crazyland—one of their residents had escaped.

Another coincidence: Queen was just as fruitcake nutty.

Xander picked up his pen lying across the legal pad and wrote in big, bold letters: YOU'RE MENTAL. When he looked up, Simon's gaze was still fixated on Xander's face. He held the paper up covering his scars, forcing Simon Smith to see his words.

I'm not crazy. I'm the only one who knows what's really going on.

"Yeah? I don't think you do know what's going on."

"Is this a joke?" The words came from the other side of the two-way mirror. "Your guy is talking to his damned self."

Should have known there'd be an interruption. Xander turned in his seat to face the mirror. "No talking, or I'm walking. And you can waste hundreds of man-hours trying to get the answers I can provide in five minutes. Choice is yours."

"How can he hear—" A scuffling sound on the other

side of the mirror, then the sound of something that sounded suspiciously like a body thudding into the wall. "I was just asking—" A door in the observation room opened and then closed, and Xander heard the guy panting in the hallway like a greyhound after a race.

"All clear. No more interruptions," Kent said from the other side of the mirror.

"Thanks, man." As soon as the words left Xander's mouth, he realized they'd probably just had the friendliest exchange of their lives. He turned back to Simon Smith. "How do you know Queen?"

"She the one I took down?" Simon's voice sounded as rough as his appearance. His beard was such a thick mat that Xander couldn't see the guy's lips moving. It was like conversing with a mangy mannequin. *She was a brunette. Wasn't such a pretty doe when I got done with her.*

"You *took down*"—the guy spoke as if the woman he killed was a game animal to be shot and field dressed and hung on the wall—"Courtney Miller. I'm not asking about her. I'm asking about Queen. How do you know her?"

"She a brunette?" *All the brunettes act like they're queens. They're all bad. I can't tolerate their sound.*

It was off the Queen topic, but Xander couldn't stop the question from popping out of his mouth. "What do you mean 'their sound'?"

The guy remained life-sized-dummy still, but Xander heard his heart rate speed up and the intake of his breathing go quick and shallow. So Simon Smith didn't worry about being caught or accused; he worried about the way a brunette *sounded*?

Their high-pitch sound makes me hard. They do it to torture me. But I'm not letting them get away with it anymore. I'm going to take them all down.

Xander scribbled on his notepad the essence of what the guy just thought, then sat back in his seat. When he had said Queen's name, the guy's mind would've automatically locked on to something concerning her if he'd actually known the woman.

There was one more route to explore.

"You know anything about two women being held hostage in a trailer?"

"They brunettes?" *I hope they—*

"You know anyone named Isleen Walker?" At least Isleen wasn't a brunette.

She a brunette?

"This is getting old. You ever been out on County Road 103?"

Where's that?

The guy knew nothing about Isleen, Queen, or even the road the trailer was on. Xander shoved back from the table and headed for the door. "Good luck in prison. The brunettes are going to love you."

—∿∿—

The awful whiteness surrounded Isleen—oppressive and claustrophobic. She turned in a circle looking for an escape. Nothing but infinite white. Panic frosted the edges of her mind, but she wasn't going to let it take hold. This time she was going to be logical instead of scared out of her wits.

White like this wasn't a place. No, the world and everything in it didn't just turn white. Something else was going on. A thought flared across her brain. Dissociation. The white and those moments where she was stuck inside her body—maybe she was dissociating. Could she be severing the connection between her mind and her body? It was possible. Gran had tried to teach her how to do that, how to find a safe place inside her head while Queen did terrible things to Isleen's body. But Isleen had never found such a place. Until now, it seemed.

The brightness shimmered, dappled, turned muddy and then dark and darker, until the environment was completely colored in shades of pewter and onyx. Her eyes adjusted slowly, the images in front of them gaining distinction by degree.

It was nighttime and she stood at Gran's bedside. Gran's gaze was fixed out the window on the lawn and shadowy woods beyond. Where was Alex? Where was the nurse? Someone should be with her. Gran looked so alone, so absolutely alone, that Isleen's heart cracked.

"Gran, I'm here." Only the words didn't come out— just bounced around inside her head. "Gran." She tried again. No sound.

Doom crawled over her skin like the hairy feet of a thousand roaches. She'd lost control of her body and was stuck inside her mind, looking out the window of her eyes, helpless to speak, to blink, to move.

She heard the quiet tread of footsteps on the wooden floor, but couldn't turn her head to see their source.

Sinister energy wavered in the air; she could practically taste evil on her tongue. Something terrible was about to happen. To Gran.

Isleen's heart tightened into a hard lump, bracing for

a blow, then banged around her chest, beating, pounding, searching for escape—a way to save Gran.

No, no, no. The words pounded through her blood. She wanted to fight, tried to fight, but couldn't move. Her body was no longer under her command, and all her words and thoughts and feelings were less than useless.

A man moved to stand on the opposite side of the bed and completely ignored Isleen. He moved with the assuredness of someone on a mission, his steps never faltering, never cautious. His hair shined bright—almost the color of pearl. His features were oddly pleasant and almost familiar. He didn't possess the look of a villain. He looked like someone's mild-mannered father. And then she noticed the chunky gold cross hanging askew around his neck and the square of white in his collar. A church collar—a priest's collar. Relief released her from fear's grasp.

If she'd been in control of her body, she would've sagged to the floor in a wet puddle of relief.

With complete affection and tenderness, the priest clasped Gran's hand in both of his. He flinched and tensed as if touching her hurt him in some way, but he didn't let go of Gran. "I have faith the Lord will be merciful." His voice was a breath, barely even a sound. "I have hope the Lord will forgive." His eyes shimmered, and tears slipped down his cheeks.

Gran's face transformed with recognition. "Rex." Excitement lit her voice on the first letter of his name, then dimmed by the last letter.

Gran knew him? Isleen shouldn't be surprised. Gran had an entire life here that Isleen had known nothing about until yesterday.

"Your trials didn't work. The evil never left us, no

matter how much we endured." Gran's words were a horror to Isleen's ears and brought memories of her conversation with Gran to mind. I destroyed us by trying to save us. And I did this to you. It's all my fault. I'd take it all back.

No-no-no-no-no-no…Gran had to be confused again. She couldn't know what she was saying.

The priest swallowed. "I prayed for release for both of you. But it never happened."

So the priest was going along with Gran's nonsensical thoughts?

Gran's gaze clung to him. "It's my turn to die, isn't it?"

An icy knife slipped down Isleen's spine, then into her guts, and twisted.

The priest nodded, his face so horribly full of compassion that none of this made sense. Was Isleen hearing things wrong, not understanding?

"It won't hurt. You'll simply go to sleep." The priest reached into his pants pocket and removed a vial. He lifted the stopper and then reached for Gran's head, propping her up enough to receive his poison. "Open your mouth for me, and it will all be over."

Move. Move. Move. Stop him. Isleen willed her body to lunge, to grab the poison away before one drop could hit Gran's tongue. She strained, tried run to him, to hit him, tackle him, jump on him. Something—anything—to keep him from killing Gran. Sweat dripped into her eyes, burning and blurring her vision.

But she didn't move.

She just stood there without making a sound and watched. Her vision went watery, her tears warm on her cheeks. She'd never forgive herself for letting this happen.

Gran winced as the clear liquid from the vial spilled into her mouth.

"I'm sorry." The priest's words were muffled with his own bizarre sorrow. "So sorry." He reached out and tenderly caressed Gran's wrinkled cheek. "For all of it. But it had to be done. Just as this has to be done."

"Thank you." Gran's eyes drifted up inside her head. Her lids slid shut, but stalled halfway. As if the scene were playing out like a bizarre slow-motion movie, Isleen watched Gran's jaw slowly, so slowly, fall open in death.

The truck's headlights blazed across the road, the parallel yellow lines a hypnotic path leading Xander home. About time. The day had gone in the shitter the moment Kent showed up with Camille way back in the morning. After that, there was the hour to get all the paperwork for his new truck completed, then a three-hour drive across the state to visit the trailer and question Simon Smith, then three hours back to question William Goodspeed.

And the only thing he learned was that Isleen had no connection to Simon Smith or William Goodspeed. Which meant she was likely dreaming about the crimes. And researching that kind of shit—dream phenomenon—was the reason Gale and Dad had established the Ohio Institute of Oneirology in the first place.

The carved bear totem at the top of the hill came into view. The thing had stood there for centuries and yet always looked good as new, like someone had just applied fresh coat of lacquer. Xander had passed this carving his entire life and yet somehow had never really *seen* it until a few days ago when he'd been compelled to drive across Ohio to find Isleen. For the majority of his life, he'd consciously ignored the totem because of his father. The thing represented all that was wrong with his dad—that his father believed in some secret legend more than he loved his son.

He saw the bike—flat black paint, skull on the tank—before he saw Lathan. What was the dude's obsession with the totem?

Xander whipped the truck over to the shoulder to get some answers.

Lathan was a statue in the headlights, unmoving as the truck bore down on him, almost like he dared Xander to plow right through him. It reminded him of what he must've looked like standing in front of his truck, holding Isleen's body—primed and ready to confront death head-on—when the crazy bitch tried to mow them down.

The truck skid in the loose gravel before coming to a halt. Xander leaped out of the vehicle.

Lathan just stood there, looking at Xander with flat, expressionless eyes. Paired with the tattoo on his cheek, they made him look like an escapee from a maximum-security prison. Not someone you'd have a friendly chat with in the middle of the night in the middle of nowhere.

"Hey, man." Xander raised his hand in a half wave. "What's going on? Why do you keep stopping here?" His voice was loud compared to the murmurings of night sounds.

Lathan's heart rate tweaked a bit, then settled back to normal. He gave Xander a hard stare. Not an if-looks-could-kill stare, but more of an apologetic look.

He didn't say anything. And the frequency connection didn't open. Didn't fucking open.

One of the universal rules of Xander's ability was that when he asked a question, a person's brain couldn't help but answer. He waited. But Lathan gave a big, fat doughnut hole of nothing.

Okay. There was definitely a level of not-normal going on. Not that Xander was the poster boy for normal consultants. Maybe that was the reason he and Lathan were consultants—they *weren't* normal.

Without a word, a wave, or a one-finger salute, the guy turned and walked to his bike.

"What's with the silent treatment?" They weren't besties and about to paint each other's toenails, but Xander had thought they were at least at the level of civil communication.

No response.

"Do you know the story behind this carving?" Xander called. Shit. He half hated himself for being curious about it.

The bike roared to life with a growl of pipes that was both obscene and thrilling to any man with balls. Lathan didn't glance back as he pulled out onto the road and sped off down the hill.

What the fuck was that all about? The guy never said a word. The frequency connection never opened. And Xander was left with even more questions. He'd have to ask Kent to pry into the guy. If for no other reason than Xander wanted—no, needed—to find out why the guy kept visiting the totem.

He turned his attention to the carving.

As always, the animal stood on his hind legs, big

and lethal looking. Lips drawn back to display deadly teeth. Eyes blazing hollow blackness. If animals were capable of facial expressions, this one looked pissed off. Funny how he had never noticed that before. It was hard to miss.

Xander got back in his truck, pulled out onto the road, and began his descent toward the driveway at the bottom of the hill.

A black sedan was parked along the median across from the property. That a car would just be *randomly* sitting across from their driveway seemed odd. Xander pulled up next to the vehicle. From his perch inside the truck he could see it was empty. Maybe some asshole got tagged for drunk driving. Or maybe… His brain flashed to the hospital and that cross on Isleen's forehead and the way she said she hadn't been able to breathe and had thought Queen tried to hurt her.

Right there in the center of the road, Xander rolled down his window and shut off the engine. The night chorus flooded his ears, and hot, humid air instantly dampened his skin. He closed his eyes, listening for anything out of the ordinary, but all he heard was a small animal scrounging around in the ditch and something larger, probably a deer, up the hill picking its way down one of the ravines. Something about the abject normalcy didn't feel right to him.

He was being paranoid. His new truck started with more of purr than a growl—he'd fix that later—and he pulled away from the car and pedal-to-the-metaled up the driveway. All the while, he kept seeing Isleen lying in that hospital bed with that vile X on her forehead. Who would try to hurt Isleen? Queen was dead. And there was no link between her and Simon Smith or William Goodspeed.

He was probably just tired and not thinking clearly. Though last night while he'd held Isleen, he'd actually slept. And the night before in the hospital he'd slept. That had to be a personal best. Maybe guilt drove him—for all those years he heard her begging for help and didn't listen. Maybe this was his penance. Always feeling like he had to make certain she was safe.

At the main house, he jammed the brake a bit too hard, fishtailing and making fun furrows in the gravel. He'd just run in, check on her quick-like, then get the hell outta there. He'd already spent too much time in that house. He forced himself to walk at a normal pace up the porch steps to the front door. The knob turned too easily in his hand. Why wasn't the door locked? He walked in and felt like he'd been swallowed by a whale.

The ostentatious size of the house made him feel diminished, like the little boy he'd been when he lived here. The little boy whose father would never look at him or speak to him or acknowledge him in any way. Sweat slicked Xander's skin just thinking about it. But that was then, and right now he was here because of Isleen. After he checked on her, he wasn't setting foot in this place ever again.

He walked slowly so his boots wouldn't bang across the wood floor and alert the household that he was sneaking into Isleen's room. Up the stairs, down the hallway, past his old room to the room next to it, the room that used to belong to Shayla. How many nights had she let him crawl in bed with her when it was stormy, or he woke up scared, or just didn't want to be alone? Now that he thought about it from his adult perspective, she'd been the best big sister.

After Gale and Shayla left, he'd sometimes sneak into Shayla's room and climb in her bed, praying that they would come back and everything would go back to normal. There was a reason he no longer believed in God. If God wasn't there for brokenhearted little boys, he sure as hell wouldn't be there for grown-up assholes like himself.

He lifted his shoulder and wiped the sweat off his face. Fuck. Just remembering burned.

Her doorknob was cold against his fingers. One look and then he was gone. He poked his head in through the opening. The room was flooded in tarnished moonlight, the bed empty, covers tossed and tussled like she'd just been there. He swung the door wide. His heart galloped in his ears; his own breathing bellowed in and out of his lungs. The sound of his body was so alarmingly loud, he held his breath so his ears could find her.

And then he heard her. A soft sob and a sound of pain from the far side of the bed. No longer caring about the noise, he ran. He found her sitting slumped on the floor, the pretty, pale-blue sundress she'd worn that morning scrunched up around her thighs. Her eyes cut him to the core. They were wide open, staring down at a nothing space. Tears dripped in a steady flow, slicking her hands and splashing onto her dress.

She was having one of those dreams again. And this one looked like a real fucker. He crouched down to face her and then snagged her by the upper arms, yanking her up straight.

Her skin was arctic, while he felt volcanic. He could practically feel his own heat thawing her. "Isleen? Baby, wake up. You're dreaming." He hated to do it, but it always seemed to work so he shook her, rattling her head around on her slender neck.

The tension eased from her muscles, and her eyes blinked and moved instead of being fixed on nothingness.

"You back?"

Her gaze shifted upward, her eyes brimming and overflowing, the tears a river of sorrow on her face. "Gran." Her voice quavered. Her chin quivered. "Oh my God. Gran." Her tone was filled with fear and horror. She wrenched out of his grip, turned, and scrambled on hands and knees until she got her feet beneath her, then sprinted out of the room.

What now? He'd thought she was awake. "Wait." He chased after her, out the door and down the hallway. For such a tiny thing, she was damned fast. "Isleen. Stop." His voice echoed through the cavernous house, and his boots slapping on the hardwood floor were mini-earthquakes of noise. What was going on?

"Xander? What the—" Matt's voice reached him, but he didn't have time or energy for a response. All his attention was focused on getting to Isleen before she hurt herself. He gained on her going down the stairs, the muscle memory of running down the stairs as a child taking over. At the bottom he reached out to her, but she darted behind the steps to Gale's room.

Isleen stopped in the middle of the room as quickly as if someone had hit her pause button. He crashed into her, sending her sprawling forward. Somehow he managed to grab on to her and haul her against his chest. He held her back against his front, her body limp and compliant, and he had a second—only a second—when he thought everything was going to be all right.

Then his gaze found the bed and the frail figure whose covers were pulled up over her head.

And then he noticed what he didn't hear: the rush and swoosh of Gale's heart pumping blood, or the suck and whine of air being processed through her lungs.

"No." Isleen's voice was a whisper and a world of pain. "No. No. *No.*" Each *no* got louder. "*No!*" She screamed the word one final time and then just screamed, bucking and fighting in his arms to go to her grandmother's corpse. He wouldn't let her. She didn't need to see whatever was under those covers.

"Jesus!" Uncle Matt rushed by them to the bed.

Xander whipped around and half carried, half dragged Isleen out of the room. Dad rushed by, not even glancing at them.

Isleen bit, she clawed, she tried to kick him, but nothing was gonna make him let go. She'd had enough trauma in her life without seeing her grandmother in death. The sounds coming out of her were pure undiluted pain and brought wetness to his eyes.

"Baby, I'm here." He didn't have any other words. Nothing to take away her grief. All he could give her was himself and the assurance that whatever she had to face, she wouldn't be doing it alone. "I'm here."

"Gale, wake up." Dad's voice carried out to them.

"I'm here," Xander said to Isleen.

"Wake up."

"I'm here."

"Gale. Wake up." Grief frayed the edges of

Dad's voice. "I'm touching you. Wake up. Wake up. Wakeupwakeupwakeup…"

Isleen's muscles and bones seemed to melt. Xander lost his grip on her for a moment, then locked on tighter and hauled her up in his arms.

"You killed her!" Dad stood in the doorway, pointing his finger at them, but the way his eyes shot hate beams at Isleen, it was clear just who he meant.

"Don't. You. Ever accuse her of harming her grandmother. She was already dead when we found her."

His father looked up at Xander, his face streaked with wetness. "I hate you for finding her. For bringing her back into my life. For making me go through this again."

"No sweat off my balls. But don't you dare hate Isleen. She's the granddaughter of this woman you loved. She's innocent. And she needs you to help her. She's been having dreams that come true. And this was one of them."

Chapter 14

Three days later...

"XAN, SHE'S HAD A BREAK FROM REALITY." UNCLE MATT spoke the words real slow, as if allowing each syllable time to be absorbed before moving on to the next one. The asshole didn't even bother hiding that he thought Xander was a weak-minded fool.

The muscles between Xander's shoulder blades went taut. He rolled his neck, both hearing and feeling the snap-crackle of restrained pissed-off-ness.

They sat at Xander's kitchen table, Matt enticingly close—so close it'd be no trouble for Xander to pop his fist into the guy's too-perfect schnoz.

For shit's sake, she's practically catatonic. Matt's thoughts were nothing Xander hadn't been hearing for a full three days. At least, when he chose to listen. He'd discovered that while within a certain proximity of Isleen, he could control what he heard and he never hurt. For the first time since the lightning strike, he could turn it off and on at will—the only silver lining in this funnel cloud of doom they were all swirling in. And he fucking hated storms.

"She isn't catatonic. She responds to me." That was a half-truth, and he damned well knew it. The only time she responded to him was when he got in bed with her. She snuggled up into his body, clinging to him as if she were about to be swept away by a rushing current of pain. He would whisper, "I'm sorry. I'm so sorry. I'm with you. I'm here with you." He didn't know what else to say. Eventually, her grip on him would relax—not let go. Just relax.

"Dad's the one who's gone crazier than a tin of mixed nuts." When Xander cared to listen to Matt and Row's thoughts, he heard all about Dad raving nonsense and trashing the house and the Institute. "There's a reason you're sitting here in my cabin, drinking my coffee. There's a reason Row is cooking in my kitchen, using my oven for her cinnamon rolls. Dad's lost his jacks, and neither of you want to be there. So don't tell me Isleen's the one with the problem."

"Hush now and eat." Row slid a plate in front of each of them. Her cinnamon rolls were a sweet nirvana and an effective diversion from the blowout he and Matt had been edging closer to for days. "I'll take one up to Isleen and see if I can get her to eat." *If she doesn't eat—*

Xander flipped the switch and turned off Row's thoughts. Control was a wonderful thing. He didn't need to hear any more about how worried Row was about Isleen. He had his own goddamned set of worries. There was no denying the situation was dire. She hadn't gotten out of bed in three days. Hadn't slept either. Not one wink. She just stared, but saying that wasn't accurate—to stare implied she was actually looking at something and she wasn't.

She'd barely eaten enough to keep a spring sparrow alive, and she wasn't talking. Not one word. But Xander clung like a burr to the fact that she sought comfort from him. She wasn't all gone. A piece of her remained.

They ate in the safety of silence, and Xander let his attention stray out the cabin's many windows. The sky was the color of sorrow. Birds didn't sing, branches didn't sway, leaves didn't rustle. It was kinda like the stillness of grief had pervaded the entire world.

Row came back downstairs and set the cinnamon roll on the counter. Only one bite was missing.

Matt's gaze landed on the uneaten roll, then bounced back and forth between their empty plates. "She needs to be evaluated by a psychiatrist."

Part of Xander recognized the truth in his uncle's words. The other part said she just needed time.

"I've contacted Dr. Hendrix. He's a trauma specialist," Matt said. "Once I explained Isleen was one of the women from the news, he agreed to make a house call this afternoon. After the funeral."

A cold jet of energy zipped along Xander's scars. He recognized the feeling. The Bastard in His Brain was preparing for a performance. "By some miracle, her name hasn't yet been leaked to the media, and you pull this? It'll only take hours before the news vans are lined up at the end of the driveway."

"He's a professional. A trauma specialist. He's dealt with this kind of thing before."

"I don't fucking care if he's Sigmund Freud. You are not making decisions about her, her mental state, or her future. If he shows up, he better be an MMA championship fighter wearing a bulletproof vest."

"You'd be content to allow her to continue this way? That"—Matt pointed over his head to Xander's loft bedroom—"isn't living."

"You didn't see the shithole she was imprisoned in.

You didn't see that bitch who held her captive. And you certainly will never see all the scars her body bears from what she's endured. She's been through the absolute worst life has had to offer, and she's going to come out the other side. She just needs time. And patience. Not you trying to force her into the nuthouse."

"She *needs* treatment. Medication. Counseling."

She needs me. I can heal her. The words floated around inside his mouth tasting sweet and true, but Xander clenched his teeth and didn't let them loose. They sounded insane and would only be lighter fluid on Matt's flickering flame.

"Xan, I agree with your uncle." Row had been strangely quiet for the past few days. She usually had too much to say on every topic and always sprinkled her language with expletives—unless she was upset. "You know I wouldn't say this if I didn't honestly believe it was the only way. You've given her time. She's not snapping out of this. How much longer are you going to let her deteriorate? You have to think about her physical health. She's already drastically underweight, and now she's barely eating."

"I won't have her trading one prison for another."

"The poor girl. What she went through… And Gale being…murdered… It's almost too much for me. I can't imagine what it's like for her."

Wasn't that the mind fuck they were all dealing with? Someone had snuck onto the property, into the house, and poisoned Gale. The only lead was the black sedan parked at the end of the driveway, and that had led nowhere. Xander even had Kent find out if the tattooed consultant guy had seen anything. Nothing.

The BCI was beyond puzzled. Why take out Gale?

She had dementia and memory problems. She was no threat. Isleen would've been the better target. Which scared the piss out of Xander—and he didn't do scared. The best the BCI could offer was an officer stationed at the end of the driveway, one outside the main house, and a guy outside Xander's cabin.

"I'll give her two more days. You refuse her treatment then, and I'll go through legal channels." Matt shoved back from his seat.

A cold electrical burn seeped from Xander's scars outward, infusing the rest of him with its anger. The Bastard in His Brain spread, taking over cell by cell. "You're asshole enough to do that, aren't you?"

"I'm the only one *thinking* about this. I'm not bewitched like your father was with Gale or you are with her."

Xander shoved back from his seat and stalked around the table to stand toe to toe, nose to nose with Matt. All he had to do was cock his arm back and let it fly. His hand curled into a fist. "You try to take her away from me, and I'll kill you." He was surprised by the vehemence of his words, but not their meaning. He would kill anyone that tried to come between them.

"You want to fistfight over her?"

"We've fought over less."

"Boys. Stop it. Right now." Roweena shoved her way between the two of them. "Matt, leave. Xan, calm down. Nobody is going to do anything today. Today we're supposed to be saying good-bye to Gale."

"We're not done." Matt backed off and pointed at Xander. "Little boy, you need to wake up to what's really happening here."

"You know what's really happening? I'll tell you, old man. You're jealous. Dad had Gale. Knew what it was like to be loved. Who have you ever had? Nobody you didn't *buy* and *pay* for. Not one person can tolerate you other than family. And we don't even like you very much."

"Xander." Row gasped his name as if he'd just shit on a holy relic. "That's low."

Something dark and dangerous contorted Matt's features. Something that promised payment for that truism at a future date. Without another word, he left, slamming the door so hard on his way out that the thing bounced back and forth, unable to latch.

"You two." Row sounded like an exasperated mother. "You're too much alike. That's why you've always locked horns."

"We've locked horns because he's an asshole."

"So are you," Row said and headed for the staircase. "I'll go help Isleen get a bath and dressed."

"Row?"

Row stopped at the bottom of the stairs, her face—the face of the only person who had ever loved him—turned to him, and he suddenly saw her age, every wrinkle cutting through her skin. The way her light-purple hair made her face sallow and almost sick looking. For the first time, her tattoos seemed garish and overdone. She was struggling as much as they all were. And he couldn't bear adding to her burden. "It's okay. I'll take care of her."

"Xan, that's not right. I think she'd be more comfortable—"

He went to her, needing to give her a hug, the same

way she used to always be able to sense when he needed one as a child. She squeezed him tight, and things seemed a bit better. Jeesh, maybe he was going pussy or something. But even that thought wasn't enough to make him pull away.

"Everything is just such a-a-a mess," she said. "There's just so much bad. Gale being murdered in our home. I don't feel safe now. Your father is a raving, destructive lunatic. What the BCI officers must think of us. You and Matt are fighting. And Isleen…" A breathy hitch in Row's voice almost melted Xander's heart into an ooey-gooey mess.

"It'll be all right. Things will work themselves out." The conviction in his tone surprised him. "We'll get a security system on the house. A gate at the end of the driveway. Dad will always be Dad. I'll try to not fight with Matt—as long as he doesn't…" He trailed off, not wanting to reignite his own anger. "Isleen's going to be all right. She just needs time. And to be with me. She feels safe with me. And that's something."

"I understand about her and you." She pulled out of his arms, then clasped his face between her hands, staring into his eyes. "I see so much of your father in you and so much of Gale in her."

He tried to shake his head in denial that she would compare him to his father, but she held his cheeks in a vise grip.

"The biggest mistake your father ever made was allowing Gale to leave. The second biggest was never going after her. Don't make those same mistakes. Promise me you won't."

The way she held his face mashed his lips together.

"I won't," he said knowing full well that he was making fishy lips. "Promise."

"Now say it again."

"I won't. Promise."

"Again."

"Okay. Now you're just enjoying this."

She laughed, patting him on the cheeks. "Wondered when you'd figure it out." She stepped back and gestured toward the loft bedroom. "Are you sure you want to care for her?"

"I need to, and I think it's what she'd want," he said softly, knowing Row would understand. "She's mine. My responsibility."

"Okay. I already set out her clothes, and there's a small bag of her toiletries. You want me to swing by after I change and help you get her to the cemetery?"

"I've got her. We'll meet you there." He walked Row out onto the porch. "Hopkins," he said to the BCI guy hanging out on his porch swing. "See that she gets home."

"Ms. McNeal, it would be my pleasure to be your escort this fine morning." Hopkins held his arm out to Row like she was a fancy lady, causing her to giggle like a girl. Xander was going to have to thank the dude later for being exactly what Row needed at that moment.

Back in the house, Xander went upstairs to the bathroom. He turned on the shower, adjusted to the temperature until it was perfect, then set out the clothes Row had brought for Isleen.

Something had to change with Isleen. Row was right. Isleen's body couldn't handle losing any more weight. He went into the bedroom and sat next to his girl.

"Baby." She didn't look at him. He threw back the

covers. She still wore the blue sundress she'd been wearing the day everything went to shit. He scooped her up in his arms and carried her to the bathroom. "You're going to take a shower. You're going to get dressed. And then I'm going to take you to your grandmother's funeral." His voice was firmer than he intended.

Gently, he settled her on her feet, keeping hold of her until he felt that she was steady and then stepped back. "Now, get in the shower, wash, and get dressed."

She didn't move or give any indication she understood his words. Maybe she just needed a little direction. By the hand, he guided her closer to the glass-enclosed shower. Without hesitation, she followed him, but that was it. She wasn't going to be able to do this on her own.

"Okay, we'll do this together." He shucked his boots and shirt, then opened the glass door and stepped inside. The water soaked his jeans, sucking them against his legs like sodden weights, but he'd deal. "Come on, baby." He held out his hand to her. All she had to do was reach out a few inches and… She stepped toward him. "Yes. Come on."

The first pellets of water splashed against the side of her face and arm. She flinched away from them, but he pulled her in tight, shielding her, protecting her from something as simple as water. "It's okay. It's just the shower."

She leaned into him, her arms sneaking around his waist. Everywhere their skin met was a miracle. Her touch perfectly comfortable in a way he'd never experienced. It soothed something inside him. Hopefully, something in her too.

While she clung to him, he reached for the shampoo

bottle. "Close your eyes. I'm going to wash your hair." He checked to make certain she was listening, then squirted the shampoo on the top of her head. It'd been only a week, and her hair was already past her shoulders. He massaged the suds into her scalp. "Row brought your shampoo, but I forgot to get it. I guess you're going to smell like me." Not that he minded.

He rinsed her hair, then just stood there under the spray with her. *Jesus. Just fucking do it.* It wasn't like he hadn't seen her naked before. "I'm going to take off your sundress now and get you cleaned up. You tell me if you've got any problems with this and I'll stop."

Slowly, he reached down behind her and gathered her dress up, then pulled it up over her waist to her arms. "Baby, raise your arms for me." She did, and he slipped the material over her head and tossed it in a soggy pile on the shower floor. With even more care, he slid her panties down her thighs until they fell and caught on her ankles. Throughout the entire process, she full-body leaned against him, shifting herself in response to his movements. At least she was aware of him, comfortable with him, and responsive to him—to a certain extent anyway.

He squirted his body wash on a rag and began at her shoulders, rubbing the cloth over her skin. Scars and cuts and still-fading yellow bruises marred her flesh. The sight of her skin reinforced his conviction never to allow anyone to control her life. Or hurt her ever again. If there was anything—anything at all—he could do to take away the pain of her grandmother's death, he'd do it. He'd happily carry the burden for her.

After the shower, he toweled her off, dressed her, and

helped her lie down on the bed so he could get his own shower and get dressed for what was to come.

Twenty minutes later, he led her down the stairs and out his front door. Her grip on his hand was firm, too firm to be normal, but it was something.

A bruised sky hung over them. A low rumble of thunder sounded from the west, threatening to rip open the clouds and pour grief over them. Xander's guts began trembling. He fucking hated storms. But for her, to give her the opportunity to be at Gale's funeral, he would suck it up.

He guided her across to the meadow of his yard to a path between two old trees. Green forest engulfed them the moment they entered. The sound of their feet treading on the moss-covered trail was the only noise. When had he ever heard things so quiet? He hadn't. Ever. Cemetery Hill rose before them. "It's only a bit farther, but it's all up hill. You tell me if you get tired. Okay?" He waited for her to answer, but she didn't, just kept walking beside him, her eyes straight forward.

Isleen's breath quickened from the exertion of walking uphill so he wrapped his arm around her waist, holding her tight next to his body, hoping to take some of the effort from her steps. Part of him was tempted to carry her, but maybe the exertion would be good for her and allow her to actually sleep tonight.

The path ended abruptly at the bald hilltop. White slabs of stone jutted out of the earth at crazy angles. The men, women, children, and babies buried underneath those markers were the first settlers of the area. Dad stood at the head of an open grave, staring down into the pit as if he himself were about to be buried alive. Roweena and Matt were together on one side of the grave.

It was no surprise Dad wanted Gale buried on the property. The guy was probably going to erect a tent and live on top of her grave. Even as the thought crossed Xander's mind, he realized he might do the same thing if the roles had been reversed and something had happened to Isleen.

He led Isleen to the open grave, stopping across from Row and Matt. If ever a coffin could be called beautiful, it was this one. The polished wood had been carved with flowing swirls of flowers and birds. It was ornate enough for royalty, but pretty enough for a princess.

Isleen's breath caught, and Xander heard her heart banging around inside her chest like it wanted to escape and jump in the grave with Gale. She was *seeing* this. No more zoned out. He wrapped both arms around her, holding her tight, wishing he had words to make this easier on her, but she had to feel the grief. Needed to feel it in order to heal. She clung to him, twisting his shirt in her grip.

"I'm here," he whispered against the top of her still-damp head. "I'm with you."

Dad looked up at them, his face haggard from the destructive power of grief. Only this time, he didn't look *through* Xander. For the first time in decades, his gaze remained. Flames of the old rejection and shame heated Xander's skin and dampened his pits. He slammed a lid on those emotions, shifted his attention from Dad to Isleen, and refused to look at his father. This was about Isleen's need for closure, not his dad randomly deciding Xander existed.

"I owe you an explanation." Dad's words were spoken more calmly than Xander had expected, but then silence followed. Only when it became as uncomfortable as a virulent case of jock itch did Xander finally look at Dad. His father's eyes softened, his face crumpled, and moisture slicked his cheeks. "I'm sorry. I'm so sorry. I thought—"

"Dude." No fucking way was he calling him *Dad* to his face. "This isn't about me. It's about saying good-bye to Gale. It's about Isleen getting the closure she needs to heal and move on."

His father's eyes shifted to Isleen. She still clung to Xander, but her face was aimed at the open grave. He sensed her—the *her* that had been missing for the past few days—close to the surface, ready to break out of the protective shell she'd formed around herself.

Dad pulled a small leather book from his pocket. The binding was frayed, the leather worn and smudged. "The Legend of Fearless and Bear began three centuries ago. Gale and I both thought their story was our story. We were wrong. Gale left. I let her. Our bond broke. Our story doesn't have a happy ending." He held the book to his face and began reading aloud.

A man, different than all others, used to roam this land. A man who was more than man. He carried a bit of spirit inside him. But even that bit of spirit was too great to contain within. Some of it showed on his skin.

The People, suspicious of all things unknown, believed a Bad Spirit had marked him—cursed him—for all to see. For all to avoid. For all to fear. The People believed the Bad Spirit wanted their souls.

So the man lived a solitary, nomadic life, nearly driven mad by isolation. One day a desperate loneliness overtook him. He tried to fight it, but was drawn to a field of women harvesting corn.

The women ran from him screaming.

A maiden stayed behind. Unlike the others, she did not fear him, but walked directly to him. Her face and arms bore the remains of a hundred healing wounds. He held out his hand to her.

She didn't hesitate, but settled her palm in his. A jolt of fire passed between them, but neither withdrew.

The maiden closed her eyes. "Take my life, and you may have my soul."

He stared at her, mesmerized by her fearlessness. Why would she want to die?

When death did not claim her, she opened her eyes and pulled her hand from his.

He saw a pain inside her greater than what her body had endured. "Why do you wish to die?" he asked her.

"I possess dream sight. I've seen my fate and would rather die than submit. Death would be freedom."

"Do you not fear me?"

"I fear this life more than you."

The sounds of many feet running through the forest came to man and maiden.

"Kill me now. I do not wish to survive another sunrise in the village."

"I do not take souls."

The maiden's face twisted as if in great pain.

"Come with me." The man held out his hand.

Men burst through the far side of the field.

The maiden hesitated only a moment before she

placed her hand in his. As one, they turned and ran—
together somehow swifter than the fastest of warriors.
They ran until the dark of night covered the earth and
the man no longer sensed anyone following them.

At a stream, they stopped. He lowered himself to
the ground and the maiden collapsed atop him, knocking him back against the earth. Fearing his curse had
claimed her, he grasped her shoulders and lifted her to
see her face.

Her eyes made great pools of water that rained down
her cheeks and fell upon his lips.

"Do not fear me." He tried to move away from her.
"I will not kill you. I will not take your soul."

She clung to him, pressing her wet face against his
neck. "I am not afraid. My eyes wash away the memories of the Bad Ones so I may live in peace."

Her lack of fear, her willing touch, astonished him.

He named her Fearless, and she called him Bear for
his great size and ferocity in protecting her. She soothed
his loneliness by her presence. And she found joy for the
first time. No longer under the control of the Bad Ones,
she smiled and laughed when she never had before.

Bear suspected the Bad Ones were trying to reclaim
Fearless and moved them constantly. Sometimes his senses
tingled, and in those moments, they would do as they had
done at the first. Run. Hand in hand through the forest.

Bear and Fearless grew closer and closer until Bear
began to worry over his feelings for her.

His fear came to life when Fearless was struck with
a deep affliction. She needed the medicine of a powerful
healer to save her. For weeks Bear traveled, carrying
her to the wisest medicine woman.

He was not permitted in villages or near dwellings. It was feared the Bad Spirit would claim a soul in each dwelling he passed, unless he himself offered his life. And he would, for he valued Fearless's life above his own.

He carried her to the village center, the location of the tribe's power. The tribe's men surrounded him, brandishing their knives and hatchets, waiting for the wise woman's command.

In the light of the fading sun, the wise woman cried a keening wail that hushed the people. She examined Fearless's wrist, spit on the star-shaped mark, and rubbed her tunic over the spot. Then she raised Fearless's wrist up for the tribe to witness. The people whooped and yelled, welcoming Fearless to the tribe.

The wise woman would care for her now. Bear laid Fearless down gently and tucked the heavy robes around her.

"You." The wise woman pointed her gnarled finger at him.

He stepped back from his only love, his head held high and waited for death.

"You are the answer to my prayers. My enemies had sought to destroy my power by stealing my babe. Every day I have chanted a spell of protection for her and prayed for her return. You are marked, yet nothing can destroy your bond. You are my prayers come to life. You are her protector."

"She is afflicted and needs strong medicine," Bear said.

"I do not have the power. She is with the ancestors."

Bear dropped to his knees beside Fearless. The light had faded from her, and he witnessed the truth of the woman's words. He lifted his head and howled.

The sound roared through the village, startling all who heard.

When he quieted, the medicine woman placed his hand over Fearless's forehead. "I do not possess the power to call her soul back, but you are her destined one. You alone have the power to heal her."

"I do not know the way."

"The Spirit inside will guide you."

Bear stilled, but the Spirit did not speak. The only thing in his mind was Fearless. He closed his eyes and chanted her name, remembered her laugh, her face, the soft sounds of her breathing as he lay with her.

Bear did not stop chanting until Fearless touched his hand. He opened his eyes. The light had returned to Fearless, the affliction gone.

The wise woman knelt next to them. "Daughter, you are returned to me a woman, but I love you as I loved the babe inside me." She grasped both their hands. "Together you create a shield stronger than the oak. No harm will come to either of you while touching the other. As long as light shines in one of you, the other will live."

At the wise woman's welcome, the tribe accepted Fearless and Bear. The wise woman taught Fearless her healing skills. Fearless's night sight—seeing in her dreams that which she couldn't see during the day— grew until she became the wisest woman of the region.

A time of great peace and prosperity settled over the land. From many moons away, people sought Fearless's healing and counsel.

The Bad Ones tried three times to kill Fearless, but they did not succeed. Nothing ever harmed Fearless and

Bear, for they remained always together. Their bond, stronger than the hills, kept them from harm.

As they approached the end of their earthly lives, Bear carved a totem on the crest of the highest hill to remind all in the region that good always triumphed over evil, for he would protect Fearless into eternity.

They went to the ancestors together. The tribe built a great funeral pyre in honor of them and anointed their bodies in bear grease before setting the blaze. Every village in the region witnessed the black smoke burning in the sky.

A week later, after the fire cooled, the tribe gathered the ash and rubbed it over Bear's totem to seal their power together inside the carving for eternity.

———~~~———

The world of Fearless and Bear was so real and alive that Isleen could smell the ash from their funeral pyre. Only it wasn't ash she smelled, it was the dark, earthy scent of fresh dirt. The kind of soil that could only be found when digging a deep hole. Like for a grave. An image of a beautifully carved coffin floated in front of her closed eyes. Gran's coffin. *Oh no.* She wasn't going to open her eyes. No way. It wasn't safe out there— outside the shell of herself. Her only chance of survival was to keep floating in the dreamy haze of another time and be held safe in Xander's arms. He wouldn't let anything out there hurt her.

A raindrop pattered against her arm, another one on the top of her head. All around, hundreds of drops splattered against the grass, the leaves, but one sound wasn't natural. The hollow thunking of rain against polished wood. *No, no, no.* She was not going to think about that.

A spike of thunder split the sky, the unexpectedness of it jolting her body. Xander tightened his grip on her, as if assuring her with his actions that he would protect her. But a fine, barely perceptible trembling traveled through his arms, up to his shoulders, and down his chest, until even the skin underneath her cheek twitched.

Something was wrong with Xander. She clenched her eyes shut, scrunched her face up, and held on tight to him. She couldn't, wouldn't, shouldn't open her eyes, or talk to him. It was dangerous out there. But what if the danger wasn't just to her? What if Xander was in danger? Because of her?

A low serrated growl rolled across the sky. Xander wheezed in a breath of air, his lungs expanding, then contracting so violently her body rocked against his. What had been a gentle trembling morphed into full-on violent quivering of muscle. The light of realization went on inside her brain.

They were in a storm. He had said he'd been struck by lightning.

"Xander?" Her voice was drowned out by another crack of thunder.

She tried to pull out of his hold to see him, but his grip was steel. "Xander. Let me go." Panic—not for herself, for him—edged into her tone. Her eyes shot open. "Xan—"

"Baby?" He didn't let go of her, just gave her room to pull back and see his face. His face was the color of milk, his scars the color of blood, and his eyes were an

unnameable color that could only be described as tortured. "You're back."

"Are you all right?" She raised her hand to his cheek,
needing to sooth the angry scars.

At her touch, he turned his face into her palm. "You're
asking if I'm all right?" His voice was thick, and he
seemed to struggle to speak at all. "Are *you* all right?"
Keeping one arm around her, he gestured to the side.

She didn't want to look, but her eyes moved before
she could stop them. What they saw, she could never
un-see. They stood next to the jaws of an open grave.
Gran's grave. Inside that exquisite box lay Gran's body.

Right after they'd been taken, she and Gran had
fought for each other, fought to keep one another safe
and sane, but when Gran's mind had started going,
Isleen had battled alone. Always struggling to protect
Gran, to keep her alive for when they were rescued. For
when they could start living again. But now, her fight
was over. She had failed. Gran was dead. And it was all
because of her.

*You are the Dragon, a vile beast set upon this earth
by the foulest of demons. Your evil will corrupt all. You
will slay everyone you love. It is your nature.* Queen's
words rose up out of the pit of buried memory and
echoed through Isleen's mind. She'd never believed
Queen until now. Until this moment of truth.

She'd watched the man pour that poison into Gran's
mouth. Had watched Gran die. And had done nothing.

Her throat opened, and a wild mix of anguish, grief,
and guilt spewed out of her in a sound so primal even
the storm around them seemed to diminish under the
immensity of her pain. A tornado of bad memories

swirled around her, only there wouldn't be a rainbow-colored Oz after this cyclone. There would be nothing left of her but the bad memories. She wouldn't survive if she had to remember *everything*. It was too much. Too much. Too much. She beat the sides of her head with her fists.

"Stop. Right now!" Xander's voice cut through the anguish at the same time his hands grabbed her wrists and forced them down to her sides. She tried to slam her head against his chest—physical pain being so much easier to deal with than the memories. He yanked her fully against him pinioning her arms at her sides and holding her tight. "I know what you're trying to do. You need to *feel* this."

"I can't. IcantIcantIcant…" Everything she never wanted to remember was right there in front of her mind's eye, and this time she couldn't escape. Grief stole her breath. Regret broke her heart. Guilt shattered her into a thousand tiny shards.

Chapter 15

REALITY AND ITS REPERCUSSIONS TORE ISLEEN AWAY from sleep's sacred oblivion. There was no moment of confusion between drowsing and waking. Nope. It was all right there with one horrifying memory ruling them all.

She lay on the couch where Xander had settled them after they'd gotten back from Gran's grave. Directly across from her, a wide window opened onto a swath of yard, sloping down into an enchanting thicket of trees where wood fairies and mythical creatures ought to live. Overhead, the sky was an elusive shade of blue more translucent and gossamer than any color created by man. This place was all so magical and majestic and, for her, temporary.

Because she remembered.

Everything.

She remembered every terrifying act done to Gran, done to her. Her body remembered the pain. And her soul echoed with the memory of Gran's death. The horrifying memory of watching the priest pour the poison into Gran's mouth and being forced to witness Gran's life and love and possibility die.

And Isleen had done nothing except watch. She should've done something. Should've forced her body to intervene. If only she'd tried harder.

When she had first remembered, the agony of her

lack of action had been unbearable, but she'd survived. Because of Xander. He hadn't let her go, and by the simple action of holding her tight, he'd glued all her shattered pieces together. So instead of being broken, she only felt fragile.

Salt crust from yesterday's torrent of tears gritted in her eyes. She didn't bother to rub away the grime. She'd cried herself to sleep in the safety of Xander's arms. He infused her with strength and injected her with courage. She inhaled a lungful of bravery, then held her breath. Nothing in the future could be as bad as what lived in her memory. Small consolation, but still a consolation. She exhaled all cowardice.

"Baby?" Xander's nickname for her warmed her in even the coldest places.

She turned away from the view outside to see him coming toward her, carrying a glass of water, and suddenly the comforting warmth turned into a bonfire of shame. When he found out she'd just watched Gran die… What if he already knew?

Her gaze locked on the clear liquid gently sloshing as he approached her. She pulled herself upright, continuing to stare at the glass. This was no time for denial and avoidance. It was time for honesty. Could she handle the look of condemnation on his face when he found out?

She'd just keep breathing, and that would keep her heart pumping. Basic system functioning would remain intact. Right? She forced herself to look him in the face.

"How'd you sleep?" Xander asked, holding the glass out to her. "No dreams? No nightmares?"

She heard him talking, but her brain wasn't linking meaning to his words. It was busy memorizing each detail of him for when she lost him. His scars wound up out of his shirt, over his neck, up his cheek then alongside his temple and flared out over half his forehead. They were stunning in a way that wasn't meant for words. She hoped Camille—his perfect, gorgeous girlfriend—loved his scars as much as she did.

Not knowing what to say, she nabbed the glass out of Xander's hand and began drinking. The water tasted sweet and refreshing, and she greedily slurped it down, not realizing how thirsty she was until the first satisfying swallow.

"Slow down. It's not a chugging contest. Don't want you getting sick."

She drained the last drop. "Wow. You have the best water." She gasped for air, having forgotten to breathe while drinking.

"There's plenty more where that came from. Come on, you need some food too."

He offered her a hand. No way was she going to resist an opportunity to touch him. His skin was warm and reassuring. More than anything, she wanted to step into him, have him wrap his arms around her and absorb into him, until she was hidden in the center of him where no one and nothing could find her or hurt her ever again.

He tugged her up to standing and guided her to his kitchen table, where he let go of her to pull out a chair. "How are you feeling?"

"Yesterday was a bad day. Today will be better."

"Every day will be better than yesterday. I promise you that. Now, eat." He set a giant cinnamon roll in front of her. "It's a day old, but still better than the best you can buy. Another of Row's specialties."

The roll smelled of cinnamon and sugar and cozy

memories from her childhood. Memories of her and Gran, and good and happy times before their world revolved around pain. "Looks delicious." She forked up a bite. Her taste buds had a mini party, but she couldn't enjoy it. She ate another bite and another.

Xander got a gallon of milk out of the fridge and poured her a glass. He was so thoughtful. So kind. Especially after everything he'd had to go through because of her. To him she had to be a pain in the backside.

But she wanted—oh, how she wanted—this to be her life. Something as simple as sitting across the table from him and eating cinnamon rolls together was all she'd ever need.

"You're looking at me funny." The sides of his mouth tilted up into a smile, and she almost stopped breathing. Normally, his face was all hard angles, accentuated by the scars, but his smile softened everything and made his eyes sparkle like gold. She resisted the urge to crawl over the table to him and press her lips to his.

"Thank you for…I guess everything. Saving us. Putting up with me. Being there for me yesterday." If these few moments with Xander were the only moments she'd have with him, she'd store them in a special place in her mind. For the rest of her life, she'd remember them as the times when she had felt the most alive.

"I was…" His voice trailed off, and he looked over her head a moment as if what he wanted to say was in a bubble cloud. "I guess the word would be *compelled*. I was compelled to find you. There's no need to thank me. I would never leave you when you needed me. I can tell you're better today."

"I am. I just feel a bit delicate and…"

When she didn't finish, he reached across the table and grasped her hand, lacing his fingers with hers. His touch was affectionate and full of reassurance, and just like yesterday, she could practically feel herself getting stronger.

"And what?" he asked softly.

Might as well be honest with him about what really happened. Her chin quivered so hard she wouldn't have been surprised if it fell off her face and flopped around on the table like a dead fish. Her throat constricted, imprisoning the words she needed to say. She forced herself to look at him while she spoke of her deepest shame. "Guilty. I'll never stop feeling guilty over Gran's death." Her vision went wet and watery. A tear from each eye raced each other down her cheeks. She had thought there were no more tears to cry, but obviously she'd been wrong.

The entire story overflowed the dam she'd built around it. Her words were fast and rushed as she told him what had happened—everything—and she didn't dare look at him until she'd said it all. "Xander, I-I watched her die and did nothing." The words jumbled out of her mouth, mixing with the sound of a sob.

"What?" The word exploded into the room. Her heart startled from the suddenness of it. His grip on her hand went almost painful. "Baby, it wasn't your fault. You couldn't help it."

Sincerity dominated his features. Which only made this all the harder.

"I watched him pour that poison in her mouth. And I didn't stop him." Saying it out loud, hearing her own words, hurt like a dull, serrated blade sawing and sawing until it finally tore deep enough to open a vein.

After a moment, the pain eased, then dulled, and she felt oddly lighter. Maybe that was because he hadn't let go of her hand. Maybe it was because his expression hadn't changed. She had expected revulsion. Disgust. Aversion. Not him gently squeezing her hand and his eyes softening with compassion. Compassion? Huh?

"That's not exactly what happened." He enunciated each word clearly as if her merely hearing him would change reality.

"Oh, Xander. I don't have the energy to argue with you over it. I *know* what happened."

He reached across the table with his free hand and brushed his fingers through the tear streaks on her cheek. His fingertips were rough against her skin, the friction so sweet and fierce her heart swelled with longing for more of him.

"You are wrong. I'll prove it to you." Without letting go of her hand, he pulled his phone from his jeans pocket, hit a button, and held it to his ear. "Yeah. I need a copy of my interrogations of Simon Smith and William Goodspeed."

"Goodspeed?" She blurted out the name. "You interrogated him?" Was it the same Mr. Goodspeed? Why had Xander interrogated him?

"Hold on." Xander spoke into the phone and then turned his full attention on her. "I'm an interrogation expert for the Ohio Bureau of Criminal Investigation."

"Oh…" How did she not know that? Another emotion joined her guilt—curiosity. Xander had interrogated Mr. Goodspeed? Before he killed everyone? The coincidence of it was a bit surprising, but what did that have to do with Gran?

"I'm back." He listened for a moment. "Of course I need them right now. As in right this goddamned second." Xander's tone was about two levels lower than mere nasty. "It's for Isleen. She needs to see them to understand what's going on." There was a slight pause while he listened. "Are you fucking kidding me? This isn't junior high. Jesus fucking Christ. Kent says to tell you hi, and that he and Killer will be stopping by tonight for a visit."

Despite her guilt and curiosity, despite the confession she needed to give to Kent, just thinking about Killer's sweet little doggy face lightened her mood and stretched her mouth into a smile. And here she had been thinking she'd never smile again.

"Tell him I said hi, and that I can't wait to see them both."

Xander rolled his eyes so far back in his head she thought they might get lost in his brain cavity. "You heard her, right? Yeah. She's better. A lot better. She's even smiling." His voice softened, and his gaze was warm when it landed on her. "Just send the files." He ended the call.

"Why are you so mean to him?"

"He's an asshole."

"So are you."

He chuckled. "Damn. I guess you really are feeling better."

"Kent tried to help me. Told me I needed to talk about things before I destroyed my future. He was right. If I had actually talked about what happened, maybe Gran would still be alive."

"I think you're confused about what's real. And I'm

about to prove it to you." He seemed so sincere that she wanted to believe him, but her memory wouldn't lie. Would it? "I need to explain what you're about to see." His hand around hers squeezed, then released— almost a quick imploring for her understanding. "Being struck by lightning did more than just scar me up. It supercharged my hearing, and now when I'm around people, my brain connects to their frequency and I can hear what they are thinking."

She stared at him, knowing her mouth was hanging open a bit, and yet not being able to close it as her own brain struggled to understand his words. What he was telling her seemed impossible, but that didn't matter. She believed him as truly as if it were her truth, not his. And that meant—oh gosh. Oh no. "So you've been hearing my thoughts from the moment we met?"

"Well…no. I don't know what makes you different. Sometimes when I'm not near you, I can hear you—like when you were in that trailer. But when I am near you like right now, I can't hear you at all."

"Thank God!" The words spilled from her lips before her brain could censor them. How mortifying would it have been if he knew exactly how she thought about him sometimes?

He chuckled. "That bad, huh?"

"No, not at all. Just the opposite."

"When I'm near you, I can still hear other people's thoughts, but it doesn't hurt like it normally does. For the first time, I can control it, censor it so it's not overwhelming. And I think I know why—" His phone buzzed and he looked at the screen. "Got it. Here. Watch this." He held the phone between them so they could both see the screen. "This is my interrogation of Simon Smith."

On the screen, the door to the interrogation room opened and the bushy-faced, scruffy-haired troll from under the culvert shuffled into the room. Fear froze her voice. She pointed at the screen with the hand Xander wasn't holding and finally found the ability to speak. "That's him. That's him. He stabbed the girl in the park. That's him."

"I know. His name is Simon Smith, and he really did kill Courtney Miller in the exact way you said it happened."

Isleen's attention fully locked on Xander having a one-way conversation with Simon Smith. Nothing about Xander's interview was normal. None of it made sense; none of it was logical. It mostly looked like he was having a chat with himself.

Xander didn't speak until the video clip ended. "He didn't know you. He didn't know Queen. He didn't know anything about the trailer you were held in. Didn't even recognize the road number. Courtney Miller's time of death was placed in the exact time frame while you were still in the hospital."

"But I was there. I saw it happen."

"You are right. And wrong."

He tapped the phone's screen and another video came on.

A man sat hunched over a table, his close-shaved head bowed so she couldn't see his face, but she instantly recognized him. "Mr. Goodspeed. He killed Marissa and his wife and son."

"No. He didn't."

"He did." Her words were firm. "I watched him do it."

"What you saw wasn't real."

"What do you mean, it wasn't real? I was right there."

"No, you weren't. You were here. What you saw was the future. What would have happened if your information hadn't stopped him."

He was speaking English. She understood what each individual word meant, but in that particular combination, it just wouldn't compute. "I have no idea what you are talking about."

"I told Kent everything you said about Mr. Goodspeed. He contacted Sunny County Children's Services and the local sheriff's office and had a plainclothes officer stop Mr. Goodspeed the moment he pulled into the parking lot. They found his gun tucked into the back of his trousers and a suicide note in his car. He had intended to kill them all and then himself. But the information from your dream stopped it before it occurred."

His eyes were the color of liquid gold and sincere, so gosh-darned sincere that she nearly believed him. Silence loitered between them while her mind rammed, bashed, and smashed into an impenetrable wall of disbelief. "My dream?"

Xander set his phone facedown on the table and grabbed her other hand in his. He looked into her eyes as if what he was about to say resided on the level of gospel. "Yes, dream. You are *dreaming* about these events."

The way he looked at her made her want to accept her own innocence. But the memory was so vivid, so intense, and full of horror—there was no way it hadn't been real. The strength of his personality swayed the logic in her mind. She let go of his hands, scooted back in her chair, stood, and walked across the cabin to stare out the window.

Outside, everything seemed so idyllic and calm. A lazy buzzard rode a current of air over the tops of the trees, then out over the yard. The sun shone through the bird's wings, backlighting them with an oddly angelic glow.

"It's real. Not a dream. I have felt the sun on my skin, the splatters of blood hitting my face. I see it. I hear it. I feel it. I can't move and I can't fight, but I'm right there…" Wait. Something had always been a bit off. She always got plunked down in a white nothingness that morphed into a picture, and then she couldn't control her own body. Could the explanation be as simple—and complicated—as a dream?

"You were with me when you had the first dream, the one about Simon Smith killing Courtney Miller. You got up out of your hospital bed and walked down the hallway and stared out a window. The second dream, I found you running up the driveway in the middle of the night. The last dream, I found you slumped on your bedroom floor, staring at nothing."

He was throwing her a lifeline, but she could only grab on with one shaky hand. Part of what he said made sense. She had thought she'd been to Prospectus Prairie Park. She had thought she'd been to Sunny County Children's Services. But she hadn't. Not really. But Gran… Those terrible memories had teeth that bit her to the bone.

"You weren't physically there when your grand-mother died. There was a suspicious vehicle parked at the end of the driveway that night. The BCI lifted prints off the front door that don't belong to any of us. They are analyzing the bedding for DNA. I know it's hard to wrap your brain around, took me interrogating those two yahoos before I'd believe it. There's no other logical explanation." He spoke from right behind her.

"You call that logical?" There might've been a hint of sarcasm in her voice.

"I threw out logical the moment I found you in that trailer. I'm operating on the what-feels-right theory. I know you loved your grandmother. I know you would never let her get hurt. I know that, and deep down you do too."

Her vision went sloshy. "Then *why*"—she said that word with cynicism—"why did William Goodspeed and everyone else in that dream live but Gran had to die?"

"Baby, I don't know. I don't have all the answers. I'm muddling through this too."

That bit of honesty tipped the scales in her mind and she believed him. He stepped up behind her, wrapping his arms around her. She leaned against him, hugging those arms that held her safe and secure.

And finally, she completely, wholeheartedly believed him. "But why would a priest kill Gran?"

A soft, faltering knock on the door stole Xander's response. He let go of her and walked across the room to answer the door. Void of his touch, she felt as if she'd gone from being warmed by the sun to freezing on the dark side of the moon. She wrapped her arms around her waist, a poor imitation of how Xander held her.

She watched him open the door. Watched shock knock him back half a step before he caught himself, visibly braced, then said, "What the fuck are you doing here?"

Chapter 16

"I'd tell you to get off my property, but it's technically fucking yours." The venom in Xander's voice was potent enough to take down a bull elephant.

With those words, she knew who must be standing there.

Alex.

One moment Isleen was clear across the room; the next, she pushed in next to Xander, primed and ready to provide support, backup, and a united front against the man who had never been a dad to Xander and who had verbally attacked her.

But the man standing on the porch didn't look like the Alex she'd met. The one she'd met had eyes that didn't see and showed no emotion—beyond anger at her and affection for Gran. This guy's face was pure expression. This guy looked like he'd endured multiple lifetimes of torment, and the memories were too morbidly obese for one man to keep hauling around. His eyes were a luminous light blue that seemed backlit from the bloodshot shine of unexpressed tears. Deep worry furrows lined his forehead and slashed down either side of his mouth. His thick gray hair was slicked back straight and severe, like a punishment.

Xander put his arm around her, drawing her to him as if ready to shield her from his own father. It made her look weak, but she didn't care. She leaned in to him, enjoying how utterly safe and protected she felt.

Alex wasn't going to be able to hurt her because in this moment she felt absolutely invincible.

"Xan—" Alex's timid tone overflowed with remorse and repentance.

Xander's arm cinched her tighter against his body, almost as if he were seeking comfort from holding on to her.

"Oh no. Don't you even. Don't you even go there in your damned head. I don't want to hear it." Xander's voice was a blade, stabbing each word toward his father. "No apology, no amount of sorry-my-bad is going to fucking fix what you broke over twenty-five years ago. No fucking way."

"Xan—" Alex held his hands up in a cops-and-robbers way of surrendering.

"You want to make me happy? Go back to pretending I don't exist." Xander stepped forward, neatly ushered her in behind him, and looked out on the porch. "Hopkins, escort him off my porch and don't let him come knocking again."

There was someone out there? She peeked around Xander to see a middle-aged man in oddly oversized pants and a baggy dress shirt step up to Alex. "Mr. Stone, you need to leave. Now." Hopkins' voice wasn't intimidating, but the bulky gun strapped on his belt was a clear warning not to mess with him.

Alex ignored the guy and scrubbed his hand over his mouth. She couldn't tell if the gesture was one of guilt or contemplation, or a stall tactic. Xander stepped back from the open doorway, reaching for her, pressing her into his side while closing the door.

"Did you really dream about what happened to Gale?"

Alex's words rushed out, powerful enough to stop the door Xander had been about to shut in his face. Isleen met the man's gaze. His eyes begged for another chance with her, with Xander. Maybe Xander would never see a way to forgive his dad, and maybe there wasn't one, but she wouldn't deny him the future possibility of having a loving father in his life.

A father. Something she'd never had.

"Don't you talk to her. She doesn't need your—"

"It was the worst dream of my life."

Alex's brows bounced halfway up his forehead, as if startled that Isleen had answered him. But then he picked up the opportunity she'd just tossed him. "A precognitive dream. Science has never been able to confirm their existence. Most claims are hoaxes."

"Jesus fucking Christ. Get in here. This isn't something we want to advertise." Xander stepped back from the door, and she moved fluidly with his body like they were one person, not two. Xander motioned toward the chair across from the couch. "You can come in, but this doesn't mean we're square. It means Isleen needs information about what's happening to her."

"I'll help any way I can." Alex stepped inside Xander's cabin, his gaze taking in all the surroundings while he moved to the chair Xander still pointed at. "You've really fixed this place up. Never thought it could look so quaint and cozy." Alex was worming his way in via her. And she was going to let him as long he didn't hurt Xander or her ever again.

"One topic only. The dreams." Xander's voice held no room for argument.

She and Xander moved toward the couch. They walked

as if they were a long-married couple engrained in each other's manners and ways. It felt so real and right to be close to him like this. "And there is no question about her dreams."

They settled on the couch, and she told his father about her dreams of Simon Smith and William Goodspeed. And Xander explained his interviews with the two men. His father asked a few clarifying questions, but never once indicated any disbelief.

The thing no one mentioned was her dream of Gran. Just as well. She wasn't certain she could speak about it anyway.

"If this is a recurrent pattern, do you realize the implications?" Alex aimed his question at her. Her mind conjured no implications beyond the horror of it all. "Lives that could be saved. Simply from a dream. Do you know how revolutionary that would be? And if I can document—"

"She's not your guinea pig or your favorite new toy."

"That's not my intention." Alex spoke directly to her. "Gale and I founded the Ohio Institute of Oneirology."

"Oh—what?" Isleen asked.

"Oneirology. We were pioneers in the field of dream research. We were the first to theorize that dreams were more than just a waste product of the brain. That they could be essential to cognitive functioning, creativity, mental health, and even psychic phenomenon. Did you know Gale was a sleep-talker?"

"Yeah." Her voice brightened, thinking about Gran. "She was always that way."

"She was also skilled at mutual dreaming. She could enter another person's dream—without them even knowing—and observe."

Isleen felt her eyes grow weirdly wide. "That's a real thing? Are you serious?" If Gran could enter another person's dreams… The things she dreamed about with Xander were not things she wanted her grandmother to see.

"Very. Her ability was incredibly fascinating. We were able to document her experience in the dream and compare it with the person who had the dream. It blew people's minds. Either that or they cried hoax and claimed we weren't conducting proper scientific studies. The one downfall to Gale's mutual dreaming was that after every dream, she had a seizure. Have you had a seizure after one of these dreams?"

Alex was asking her, but Xander answered. "She's never had what I'd call a seizure. When it happened in the hospital, she passed out for a few minutes, then came to and was cold and sleepy. When it happened here, she got the headache, but then it went away, then she got sleepy and cold again. The night Gale…" Xander didn't need to say it. "She passed out that night."

Fuzzy, fringe-of-her-mind memories matched up to Xander's words.

"Seizures come in varying forms. During a precognitive dream, your brain is doing double duty. It's guiding you through the cycles of sleep and operating as normal, but on a different plane of reality."

"Different plane of reality? What does that mean?" Isleen asked.

"The reason precognitive dreams are so hard to prove is because that different plane of reality only exists inside you. It's not something any test can measure or any scientist can observe. Only you can access it and learn from it. Your physical body remains here, but your mind is operating in two places at the same time. When you wake up, the brain can't handle the overload and shorts out—a seizure."

She stared into Alex's eyes, looking for even the slightest hint of humor, the joke, the punch line. Because if this wasn't a joke, then he was serious and she was going to have to decide if he was crazy smart or just plain crazy.

"The seizure is the price for being psychic."

Now she was leaning toward just plain crazy. "I'm not psychic."

"During your waking hours, you are correct. But in the midst of a precognitive dream, you are being given access to insider information about another reality—which makes you psychic."

Xander nodded his head as if he were receiving great understanding. "You've seen the interrogations. This is real."

"You'll need to spend a few nights at the Institute so we can measure and record your brain activity during the dream cycles. It would be groundbreaking to record a precog dream."

"Is there a way to cure it?" she asked, her voice soft and steady.

"Cure it? Why would you want to make it go away? You have a powerful gift."

"It doesn't feel like a gift. The things I've seen…" She trailed off, not wanting to access those particular memories.

"An innocent little boy, his mother, and a woman just doing her job are alive today because of that dream you had. Would you trade their lives just so you didn't have to experience that bad dream? How many other lives could your dreams save?"

That was a direct hit on her morality center. There was another way to look at her dreams. They weren't just horrible things she had to witness. They were important—a means to save people. No way would she trade lives for the ability to not dream. She could never be so selfish.

"Do you remember the story of Fearless and Bear?" Alex asked.

Their story was the only part of yesterday that didn't ache when she thought about it. "I remember."

"I suspect you and Xander are a modern version of them." He tossed that little bomb out there. Its detonation was quiet, but she felt the shock wave of it rock both her and Xander.

"You said it was your story." Xander's words were evenly spaced and perfectly clipped.

"It should have been. But now it's yours to finish." Alex's face was all sober expression, and the way he sat in the chair leaning forward conveyed his earnestness. Isleen glanced at Xander, who bobbed his head as if Alex's words struck a deep truth.

"You believe this?" Incredulity pushed her tone into the squeak range.

Xander turned his gaze to her, grim honesty shining in his eyes. "It makes sense. You see the similarities, right?"

The parallels between her and Fearless lined up nearly perfectly. Fearless had been kidnapped by the Bad Ones. Isleen had Queen. Bear had found and saved Fearless. Isleen had Xander. Fearless discovered she was gifted with dream sight. Isleen had precognitive dreams.

What about hard facts and truth? They had proof her

dreams could save lives—okay, she could buy in to that. But the story of Fearless and Bear was fiction. Oh, she *wanted* to believe it, only because she *wanted* Xander to be her destiny. But wanting a thing didn't make it happen.

"You wanna know the real kick in the ass?" Xander nabbed her hand. "The totem Bear carving sits on top of the next hill over. That fucking close this entire time, and I never really knew what it was until yesterday."

"I want to go see it sometime."

"I know. Me too. Kinda takes on a whole new meaning now." His words were filled with unquestioning belief in this.

Alex cleared his throat. "When Gale left—"

"Jesus fucking Christ. Time to leave. I don't want to hear—"

"Alexander. Patrick. Stone." Alex's tone was loud, sharp, and overflowing with angry father. "You will let me say this. And then I'll leave and you can go back to hating me." He didn't wait for Xander's agreement, just kept talking, although lowering his volume. "Gale left because she didn't believe. She swore something bad would happen to me if she stayed. When she left… I almost don't have words to describe what happened to me. I left too. I was gone. But not gone. I couldn't think clearly or see clearly or feel anything. Nothing made sense or computed right, except for work. The only clarity I could find was in my research. Maybe because it was the only link I had to Gale.

"It wasn't until…" His voice warbled, high and low. "Until…she…died that I finally broke free from the prison I'd been locked inside all that time. Free to feel all the guilt, anger, and, my God, the regret." He aimed tortured eyes at Xander. "I know everything I missed. I know I wasn't there as a father, a mentor. I wasn't there for all the small wonderful moments of your childhood, and I especially wasn't there when you almost"—his voice faltered—"died. I will carry that responsibility and remorse for the rest of my life."

In the silence following Alex's speech, no one moved. Her heart turned puffy soft with compassion toward both of these men who needed each other so badly, but the distance of time and pain separated them.

Alex nodded his head once, stood, and waited as if he expected Xander to say something, but when the quiet continued, he headed toward the door. He paused, hand on the door handle. "It would've been more merciful if someone had just shot me in the head and put me out of my misery." He opened the door and looked back at Isleen, pinning her immobile with the intense sadness of his gaze. "Don't you ever do to him what Gale did to me."

—◦◦◦—

If Isleen responded to Dad's parting words, Xander couldn't hear it. He was lost inside his own thoughts. If this thing between him and Isleen was similar to what Dad claimed to have had with Gale, that granted Isleen the ability to annihilate him. To turn him into the same person as his father. That Xander had let himself go down this road—refusing to listen to Matt's warnings—made him fifty kinds of stupid.

Shit fucking goddamn. Matt had been right all along. Wouldn't the guy just about get wood from being able to say *told you so*?

Xander forced himself to his feet, fighting the physical urge to be close to her. He refused to look at her and fall under her alluring spell. Oh, but his body wanted her, and yet his mind knew the consequences. He needed time to think, time to figure things out, time alone.

"I got some work to do." *Liar, liar, tighty-whities on fire.* He walked to the front door. "I'll have Hopkins walk you back to the main house." He opened the door and peered out at the BCI guy stationed on his porch. "Hopkins, see that she gets back to the main house."

"Will do." The guy nodded one of those professionally curt nods, then looked beyond Xander to the interior of the cabin. Hopkins' eyes softened, his facial features melting into a soft, slightly girlish look of pure compassion and sympathy. He glanced at Xander and his expression went terminal, as if Xander were a hot, steaming pile of fresh dog shit mashed into the grooves of his brand-new tennis shoes. What the fuck was that about?

Xander flipped on the listening switch. From habit, he tensed, waiting for the first thump from the frequency connection opening, but Hopkins thoughts glided into his ears on a wave of no-pain.

After everything she's been through, you do this. Dick.

"Do what?" Xander asked, more than a little attitude in his tone. What was it with every guy—except his father and Matt—always acting like he wasn't treating Isleen right? He'd never hurt her.

Hopkins ignored him and held out his hand. "Miss Isleen, don't worry. I'll see that you get there safe. No one will hurt you. I promise. There's no need to cry."

She was crying? Xander whipped around so fast he nearly ass-planted on the floor. She stood in front of the

couch, chin quivering, tears slicking her cheeks. "I can't
go there, yet. Gran… It was the last place… I don't think
I can face it. Is there someplace else I can go? Someplace
that's not here or there." She might be crying, but her
words were strong, spoken in a quiet voice that carried
latent power and neatly sliced through his bullshit. Jesus
fucking Christ.

Hopkins was right. After everything she'd been
through, Xander had been about to abandon her on
Dad's doorstep. Total dick move.

He slammed the door without even looking at
Hopkins and started across the room, but she held up
her hand in the universal sign for stop. He obeyed.

She stood up straighter, lifted her chin, and looked
him square in the eye. "I am tired of being the victim. I'm
tired of feeling like everything happens to me and I don't
have control over any of it. I can take care of myself. You
don't have to feel obligated to take care of me." She used
the palms of her hands to wipe the residual wetness off
her cheeks. "I *am* going to cry. I can't seem to help it. But
that doesn't mean I can't handle things or that I'm weak.
It just means I need to feel things."

"I know you're not weak. A weak person wouldn't
have survived what you did. A weak person wouldn't be
telling me to step off for wanting to baby her too much."

"I'm not telling you to step off. I enjoy—" She
looked straight ahead at where his heart resided in his
chest. The organ seemed to sense her gaze and pumped
a little harder as if flexing and showing off its muscular-
ity. "It's just that I don't want you to feel forced to take
care of poor wittle Isween." She spoke her last words in
a pouty-child tone.

"Baby, I don't look at you like poor wittle Isleen." He mimicked her tone. Her lips twitched and ticked up by degrees until a full-on smile blazed out at him. "I look at you like a woman who's been through shit and then got shit on again, and has just walked out of the shit pile, but some of the stink is lingering."

She giggled, the sound a symphony to his ears. "Are you saying I stink?"

"I'm saying it might be awhile until you find your new normal. I know what it's like to have normal destroyed. After the lightning strike, I was lost and adrift and desperate to adapt."

She came to him, wrapping her arms around his waist and hugging him tight. Holy fuck, she felt so perfect, so destined, so inevitable. There was no resisting her. That's what scared the shit out of him.

"Why did you really want me to leave?" She spoke against the fabric of his shirt, the heat of her breath a caress. "What do you feel about the Fearless and Bear thing? About us? And what about Camille?"

And damn. She'd just shoved the elephant in the room into his arms. His choices were to keep quiet and lug the bastard around or answer her questions and set it down. He stepped back from her, needing the distance to formulate coherent thought. He ran a hand through his hair, then scratched the top of his head—pure delay tactic. Jesus. Was he really this much of a coward? Not normally.

The temperature seemed to be ratcheting higher and higher until it felt like he stood on the outer ring of hell—only it wasn't his AC suddenly taking a dump, it was his own damned wimpiness at having to talk about his feelings.

Might as well answer the easiest question first. "Camille is a non-issue. We fucked. That's it. There was never a relationship. No matter what she or her fucktard of a brother say."

Isleen narrowed her eyes at him, like he might not be telling her the truth. "Kent said you've been with her a decade."

"We've fucked for a decade. She never made any relationship demands. On the surface, she seemed fine with our arrangement, but I heard her thoughts—knew she wanted more, and I knew I'd never give it to her. It makes me an asshole for not stopping it when she wanted more. I own that."

"Is that what you're doing with me? Just wanting a fuck? How do I know you're not going to get tired of me at some point, dump me like a dirty diaper, and move on to someone else?"

The wrongness of her words knocked him back a step. "I would never do that to you."

"Did you say the same thing to Camille? That you'd never do that to her?" Her face wore an odd expression of both suspicion and longing to trust him.

"With my history, you've got no reason to believe me, but I would never do that to you. With you, everything is different. I'm different." And here his feelings were, lining up and getting ready to shoot out of his mouth. "The Fearless and Bear thing feels right in a way that isn't based on logic but resides somewhere on the level of gut feeling and instinct. I don't know how I feel about that. I enjoy touching you. I want to be close to you. I feel something for you that I've never felt for another woman. I want more of you. I want all of you."

He hoped she got what he meant. "But if it means, in the end, that I'll turn out like Dad? No way. I'd rather walk away right now while I am still me."

She listened to every word he said, never blinking, never looking away, just focusing all her attention on him. Wasn't being the object of her focus sexy as hell? She made him feel seen and heard in a way he'd never experienced.

"So you'd rather hurt me than be hurt." Her voice carried a concrete certainty.

"No." Her very words were abhorrent to his ears. "God, no. I'd never hurt you."

"What do you think is going to happen to me if you walk away and leave me like Gran left your Dad?"

"Hadn't thought about it like that." The idea of her being like his dad had been—and it being his fault—made his heart almost rupture.

"Maybe we need to think about it like that. If we both have the power to kill each other's souls, then we need to figure out how to trust each other."

Trust. When had he ever trusted anyone besides Roweena? She'd been the only person in his life who'd never let him down or cast him off like yesterday's dirty underwear.

"Xander, I already trust you. I know that you'd never intentionally hurt me. I know who you are. I know because I've spent time with you. I have history with you from my dreams."

His heart went all warm and fuzzy, but his mind doubted and questioned. "Trust doesn't just *poof* magically appear."

She reached for his hand and placed it over her

heart. Under his palm, the swell of her breast had his dick doing some swelling of its own. She settled her other palm against his scarred cheek. Energy surged through him.

Her gaze locked with his—locked so hard the entire world vanished and all that existed were her and him and his hand feeling the steady beat of her heart. Whatever the fuck she was about to say, he was gonna believe her. She could tell him he was a two-headed, purple squirrel, and he'd go out, find a nut, and climb a tree.

"Xander. I vow to protect you from pain. I vow never to leave you unless you want me to leave. I vow never to hurt you the way Gran hurt your father. Because hurting you would be hurting myself. Your pain is my pain. And my pain is yours. But together we are strong and invincible. Don't you feel it when we touch? It's all I can feel. All I want to feel. You and me. Us. Together."

Her words did more than enter his ears; they melded into him as bone-deep truth. He'd never do anything to hurt her and—damn—he trusted that she wouldn't hurt him. As sick as it sounded, maybe his faith in her was born from the suffering she'd endured. She *understood* pain. Understood the depth and damage pain caused in a way few others ever would. That kind of knowledge made her incapable of wounding anyone else.

"Say something. You're looking at me funny." Her voice trembled just a bit. He could practically hear her doubting whether she should've spoken the words of her heart.

"What you said… Those words…" Christ. He didn't have experience talking about his feelings. "Everything."

She cocked her head to the side, questions wrinkling her forehead.

He was screwing this up. "Your words mean everything to me." He could show her easier than he could tell her. He slid his hands up her neck, framing her face, staring at her, absorbing every detail. "You're my..." *Fearless*. He caught himself before he said the word. To base how he felt on a story wasn't real. She was real. And the emotions warming him were real. "Everything."

He lowered his mouth to hers. She tasted sweet, of cinnamon and sugar, and for some reason, his heart ached with a fullness of feeling it had never experienced before.

He scooped her up in his arms, cradling her to his chest, his mind flashing back to the day he found her—and to holding her this same way. God, she had weighed so little, had seemed so fragile, but she was strong. Stronger than he'd ever be. Knowing what she'd gone through, what she'd survived—yeah. *Strong* was too weak a word to describe her.

He carried her up the stairs to his bedroom, his mouth never leaving hers. With a gentleness born of reverence, he settled her on the bed. He broke the kiss to stare at her once more. Her eyes were closed, her face relaxed, her lips deliciously puffy and pink from a good kissing. He fucking loved pink.

Slowly, her eyes fluttered open, finding him. A lazy smile stretched across her mouth, full of sweet, ornery secrets he longed to discover. He was gonna spend the rest of his life learning all those hidden thoughts tumbling around inside her head.

"You keep looking at me funny." She reached up and settled her palm against his scarred cheek. Something hot and primal zinged through his scars and then settled heavily in his groin. Jesus Christ.

"That's just my I'm-in-awe-of-you face."

"In awe of me?"

"Yeah, you." He nipped the end of her nose, pecked a kiss on her mouth, and then moved lower to her shoulder. Her skin was cool and soft against his lips and tasted of his favorite flavor. Her. "I want you bare," he whispered against the fabric covering her chest.

She sat up and lifted her arms over her head. He pulled the somber black dress over her head and let it drop on the floor. Later, he'd toss that wad of material in the trash. That was the last time she was ever going to wear the color of mourning. He'd make sure her wardrobe was full of sunshine, sky, and flower colors. Nothing but happy shades for her.

She leaned back against the pillow, her pert breasts snagging all his attention, and he changed his mind. She didn't need clothes. He preferred her like this. Naked, except for a delicate pair of lace panties. And those would be coming off in about thirty seconds. He shucked his clothes while she watched—her gaze hungry, devouring every inch he revealed. She licked her lips as if he were her favorite meal. She could eat him up whenever she wanted.

He crawled back onto the bed and skimmed his hands down her ribs. The ripples and ridges of bone were still too prominent against her skin, but time and Row's cooking would take care of that. He bent down, kissed her belly button, and tugged her panties down. She shifted her weight, allowing him to sweep them off and toss them over his shoulder.

Bare to him, the light blond curls between her thighs were caught by a ray of sunshine slanting across the bed, glinting shades of gold. She was perfect. Not in the way of supermodels or porn stars, but in a way that she was everything—that word again—he'd never known he needed. She filled in his hollow places, rounded his sharp edges, and made him feel something other than anger for the first time in twenty-five years. "Baby." He almost forgot how to speak beyond the endearment. "You're so lovely. Let me see all of you. Open for me."

Without hesitation, she spread her legs for him. She had no fear in bed. She'd said she'd dreamed of them together. Maybe that was why. The reason didn't matter. He loved her lack of inhibitions.

He moved between her legs, slid his hands underneath her ass, and lifted her to his face. She was pink and glistening with her desire for him. His already-hard dick went to steel, wanting her so badly he ached. But it was an agony he'd gratefully endure. He bent, inhaling the primitive scent of her desire just before he licked her. She tasted warm like sunshine on a salty sea. She tasted of promise. She tasted of good things to come. Together, they were going to make something spectacular.

"Xander…" She breathed his name, the sound as powerful as a physical caress to his dick. He moaned against her opening and then suckled her clit, laving the bud until she writhed against his face with uninhibited exuberance, wanting and needing what only he could give her. He couldn't wait a moment more.

In one fluid movement he rose over her, positioned himself at her core, and slid home. Home. She was his home. So hot. So tight. So…right. Being with her wasn't about fulfilling his body's craving for release. Being with her was about fulfilling himself, becoming the man he was meant to be. The man she made him.

"Xan—oh God."

Her orgasm pulsed against his dick, urging him to fuck her. Really fuck her. But this was sweet. Too sweet for hard fucking.

"Over. Roll over." She gasped the words, but he didn't understand language anymore. Only sensation existed. Her heat wrapped around him. Her body sliding against his.

Somehow his body submitted to her will and he found himself on his back, her riding his dick with gusto and strength.

She fucked him. Fucked him with her head flung back, body pumping against his, taking all of him—body, heart, and soul. It was a goddamn beautiful thing.

Tension built in his balls. He gritted his teeth, trying to contain the mounting explosion. He wanted to give her more. Give her everything. She slid herself down his shaft, and he touched heaven. All his fancy-assed ideas about control vanished. He grabbed her hips, thrusting up while she slammed down. Their rhythm messy and frantic and perfect.

"Xander. Xander. Xander."

His fucking name on her lips while she came triggered his own orgasm. Cum burst from his balls, and he ground against her while pleasure ripped through him.

He collapsed boneless, as the aftershocks of what they'd done gently hummed through him. She slumped forward on his chest with him still inside her. Not that he minded. He could live an entire lifetime right here and die a happy man.

A sweet giggle of dazed satisfaction came from her. He chuckled too. Being with her, he felt something he'd never had before.

Happiness.

Chapter 17

A THUMP.

A moan.

Xander bolted upright in bed, his hearing on hyper-alert for Isleen. Had he been sleeping? Must've been. He heard the rapid rhythm of her breathing coming from downstairs. That thump, that moan had come from her. He knew it.

"Isleen?" He called loud enough to be heard throughout the cabin and got out of bed.

Evening sunshine shimmered through the bedroom window, splashing russet rays around the room and giving the atmosphere a lazy, timeless quality.

Bzzz. His cell phone vibrated against the nightstand.

Kent calling lit up the display.

Fuck the phone.

From the top of the stairs, the entire living room was visible. Isleen huddled on the floor, clutching her head and rocking. Xander flew down the stairs, feet barely touching the steps. Another dream. Only this time he hadn't been there to wake her up.

"Baby, you'll feel better in a minute. Just hold on." He slid in next to her, laying his hands on top of hers.

A great sigh of relief slipped from her lips. Coolness swelled over him. A tingle and zing started in his palms and moved up his arms to his shoulders and then spread out from there. Holy wow. It felt so good and right and oddly satisfying to do this for her, like it was his soul's destiny to ease her suffering. To heal her.

His phone, still upstairs, started vibrating again. The guy was going to have to wait.

Isleen slipped her hands out from beneath his, but he continued to hold her head, weaving his fingers into her hair. She scooted in closer and closer until she crawled up on his lap, straddling his hips and latching on to him like a baby monkey. And still he didn't let go of her.

"What's it feel like to take my pain away?" Her voice sounded wobbly, and he felt dampness on his bare chest. She was crying, and it cut a chunk out of his heart that she had to endure any pain. If he could, he'd take all the hurt away from her, gladly shoulder her burden, and make it his to bear.

"It's cool and feels good in a way. Almost the same way it feels good to scratch an itch."

She lapsed into quiet, more of her tears wetting his skin. More of his heart wept for her having to go through this.

"How's your head now? Are you feeling tired, dizzy, disoriented?"

"My head is good. I think I'm all right." She spoke as if a sob clogged her throat.

He let go of her head and wrapped his arms around her, pressing her so hard against him that air whooshed out of her. "Tell me about the dream. You'll feel better." He nuzzled his cheek against her hair.

She pulled back from him. Her eyelashes were spiky from wetness, her eyes bloodshot and glistening. And yet courage and determination sharpened her beauty. "It was the worst one."

Nnkk. Nnkk. A knock sounded at front door.

"Fucking goddamn it." Probably Kent at the door. The guy had said he'd stop by this evening with his cream-puff canine. Xander stood, still holding her body to his. He ought to walk to the door and open it just like they were—to show the asshole on the other side that he'd been interrupting—but that might embarrass Isleen. He settled her on her feet and held on to her for a few extra seconds to make certain she was steady.

Nnkk. Nnkk. Nnkk. Nnkk. The asshole on the other side of the door started knocking again.

She clung to him like she was afraid of letting go.

"Xander?" She'd only spoken his name, but he heard so much more. He heard her fear, her hesitation, and her caring. Such a strange combination.

"Baby, what?" He rubbed his hands up and down her back, wishing his touch could infuse her with everything she needed to feel good.

Nnkk. Nnkk. Nnkk. Nnkk. Nnkk. Nnkk. Nnkk. Nnkk. More pounding on the door.

She released him, stepping away from him and smiling, but it wasn't a real smile. It was one of those fake ones that only touched her mouth, not her eyes or her soul. The smile looked sad and scared and stubborn all at the same time.

Something was wrong. Only he didn't understand. Was it the dream?

Nnkk. Nnkk. Nn—"I'll be there in a second," he bellowed loud enough that Isleen flinched and Row probably heard him down at the main house. That persistent fucker on the other side of the door was about to meet Xander's fist.

"Let me get rid of this asshole." He stalked to the door, nearly ripping it off the hinges.

Kent held his mini-mutt, and—of fucking course—Camille stood right next to him. Kent just couldn't leave the Camille issue alone.

Hopkins stood behind them, looking on the verge of pissin' in his pants. The guy was a BCI agent, for shit's sake, and petrified of a little interpersonal conflict? Where did they find these assholes? Probably the same place they'd found Xander. Rejects-R-Us.

"Seriously? You're pulling this again?" His volume wasn't quite in the shout range, but close.

"What?" Kent's voice carried false innocence, his expression phony concern.

Xander wasn't going to flip the switch and listen to Kent's thoughts. No way. Not today. He didn't need the aggravation on top of everything else.

Isleen moved in next to Xander, wrapping her arm around his waist and leaning in to his bare chest. Her actions were a clear sign of ownership. He was hers. And he didn't mind at all. A smile spread across his lips, stretching the skin of his scarred cheek.

"You fucked him?" Camille's face morphed into a mask of ugly jealousy.

"I told you that the last time we talked." Isleen wasn't intimidated by Camille. Not even a little bit. "You chose to not believe me."

Kent's mouth fell open, and damn if Xander didn't feel his own jaw hanging slack. Isleen had told Camille they'd been together? Whoa. Isleen had a giant pair of girlnads.

"You know"—Camille's tone was abnormally calm—"he's only with you because he feels sorry for you."

"Cam—" Kent's voice was full of rebuke.

Xander slid his arm around Isleen, telling her with his actions that Camille was wrong. "Don't talk to Isleen like that." He spoke slowly to give the words time to penetrate Camille's concrete skull.

"Camille, I can see that you are having trouble adjusting to this situation." Isleen's tone carried no anger, no malice. "I understand. I know the kind of man Xander is, so I know what you're losing. I feel bad that you are hurting."

"You feel bad that I'm hurting?" Camille's voice rose to a she-demon screech. She lunged for Isleen. Xander stepped between them, blocking her path.

"Cam. What the hell?" Kent shoved the dog at Hopkins, then grabbed his sister from behind, hauling her down the porch steps. She struggled and screamed terrible things at Isleen. "Stop it. Right now. If you don't get yourself under control you're going to get arrested."

Those seemed to be Camille's magic words. She went limp, all anger and hostility gone.

"Take her home." Xander pointed to Kent's truck. "And don't bring her back."

Isleen moved in next to him again. "Xander, I need to talk to Kent about my case. He needs to know about the priest. Maybe you should take Camille home. She shouldn't be here right now. It's not good for anyone."

"You need to talk to Kent?" He parroted her, couldn't think of anything else to say.

"Just about my case." Isleen seemed sincere, so why did he have a suspicion in his heart that everything good in his life was about to get flushed down the shitter? She reached up to his neck and tugged his face down to hers.

She kissed him, her lips sweet and cool, and if emotion could pass through the barrier of skin, he swore he felt her complete devotion. But still something didn't jive.

Or was that all in his head? He had zero relationship experience. All he knew was what little he'd had with Isleen. Was he smothering her? Was this her way of getting a bit of space? There shouldn't be anything wrong with leaving her to drive Camille home. Not that he wanted to leave Isleen, but it would give him a chance to apologize to Camille. And nothing bad could happen while he was gone. Kent and Hopkins would see to that.

He shrugged into a shirt and nabbed his keys from the dish by the door.

"Don't you let her out of your sight," he said to Kent. The guy nodded, and for all the shit between them, Xander trusted him with this. "I'll be gone thirty minutes. Not one second longer."

"I'll be here," Isleen said.

So why did he feel like he was about to lose her?

———

Camille's perfectly composed face slipped and fell. She didn't cry, bawl, or scream, but pain sank into her features. It hurt to watch. Xander didn't say anything, just opened his truck's door, waited while she climbed in, and then jogged to the driver's side.

Isleen stood in the yard, cradling Kent's mini-mutt to her chest and smiling so sweetly that Xander stopped and couldn't move. Behind her, the sun had already slipped into the horizon, shooting shades of molten fire across the sky. The image of Isleen and the sky together was epic, the kind of vision that inspired people to write songs of love and beauty and the fear of loss.

He wished he had a camera to capture the grace of the moment. He settled for staring at her while she scratched the dog's ears, memorizing the way the light made her hair glow golden, her skin luminescent, and her lips deeply rose, begging to be kissed. She looked up, catching him watching her. The smile she gave him carried enough wattage to keep his happy sensors running on full power for the rest of his life. Damn.

She lifted her hand and waved a carefree gesture, then used the dog's paw to wave at him too. He waved back, but deep in his gut, a worm of warning latched on and began feeding on his happiness, reminding him that good things never happened to him. She could be in danger.

Someone had been in her hospital room and left that cross on her head. A priest had killed Gale. That same someone might be after Isleen. She should be safe here with Kent and Hopkins. Two guards on her. Another guard at the main house and one at the end of the driveway. That was four trained agents watching out for her. But there were no guarantees in life.

Okay, maybe he was being a bit paranoid, not to mention jealous of anyone besides him spending time with her.

She had wanted to talk to Kent. She had wanted Xander to take Camille home. And he wanted to make her happy. He would deny her nothing.

The solution: Be fucking quick about it.

He got in the truck.

"Why did you fuck her? What can she give you that I

can't? Why didn't you tell me you lived here? I thought
you lived at the other house with your family and that
was why you never invited me over." Her quiet questions rushed him like a linebacker. At least she wasn't
trying to rip his face off. "Why? I don't understand any
of this."

He started the truck, tore a swath through the gravel,
and sped down the driveway. Pain slammed into his
head. A breathy grunt escaped his lips. The frequency
connection opening. Fucking damn. It'd been a while
since he'd actually felt that pain. Then again, it'd been
awhile since he wasn't either with Isleen or near her.
Another reason that being away from her made no sense.
She took away his pain and gave him control over his
hyper-hearing.

*I feel so stupid. But how could you be with me all
that time, and it was only ever about sex? Ten years.
Ten years of my life. How could that just be about sex?*

"I could ask you the same question." She jerked from
him answering her thoughts. It was too fucking difficult to respond to only the oral shit. "You never made
demands, and I never gave explanations." He worked on
keeping his tone soft, because his words were harsh and
his head pounded.

He whipped the truck out onto the highway and sped
toward town. Headlights from an oncoming vehicle pulsed
with the throbbing in his head. He rubbed his temple.
Three minutes away from Isleen felt like three years in a
torture chamber.

"It was about more than sex to me." *It was an investment.*

"But it wasn't about love. You don't love me. We
were two lonely people craving human contact to ease

our isolation. I needed someone who didn't judge me and accepted me without strings. You gave that freely to me. I appreciate you for that." He glanced at her. He'd never seen her look so forlorn and lost. "I am sorry your feelings are hurt. I wish I would've done things differently so we could've avoided this."

Love? I don't need love. I can picture us in that house living together.

"You deserve to be happy, to be loved. To be some-one's everything." And, wow, did he understand that now. "You are a beautiful, passionate woman. There is someone out there for you." He almost couldn't believe the words coming out his mouth. When did he turn into a relationship expert?

She stared out the windshield. "Do you love her?"

Love. That was a word that hadn't existed in his vocabulary until recently, and yet something about it and Isleen being paired in the same sentence felt honest and true. Maybe he was a pussy, but the first thing he was going to do when he got home was tell Isleen he loved her. He'd never said those words to another person in all his life, and now he was as excited as a kid with a secret to share. "I do love her." And fucking damn, he was half tempted to turn the truck around and race back to her. He needed to be near her. Life felt wrong without her.

Camille gasped and flinched as if his words had bitch-slapped her. "You just met her. You can't love her. You don't even know her. You have to be confused." *What's wrong with you?*

"You don't need me. You don't need any man. You're a strong, powerful woman."

He sped into town, not caring about speed laws, only

caring about getting her out of his truck and getting back to Isleen.

What does she have that I don't? Just tell me and I'll change. I'll be what you want me to be.

Holy Christ. Her level of desperate-to-not-be-alone surprised him. It wasn't like he saw her every day or even every week.

"She's wrong for you. She's all simpering and fake nice. You'll get bored with her."

He turned into her trendy apartment complex and parked outside her door.

"I bet she can't give you what I can." She put her hand on his crotch and squeezed his dick, and damn if his balls didn't shrivel away from her, hiding themselves somewhere behind his liver.

He grabbed her wrist, tore her grip from him, and shoved her away. "Don't."

The silence growing inside the truck and in Camille's mind seemed lethal.

He'd said what needed to be said, and now he needed to get back to Isleen. Camille didn't look back at him, just opened her door, and stepped out of his truck. He reversed out of the space and sped for home, his mind locked on Isleen. Always Isleen. She was his guiding star, his reason for living.

Chapter 18

He'd lived his entire life on the same property, been up and down the steep, curving driveway so many times he could probably navigate it with his eyes closed. But tonight everything seemed off in some indiscernible way.

In the periphery of his truck's headlights, the trees speared the sides of the lane, their sharp vertical trunks like raised pikes supporting the shrouded sky. Branches arched over the drive, hulking monsters ready to crush and smash. He heard his own damned heart pick up a faster pace. Tonight, nature felt oppressive and unfriendly.

He jammed his foot on the gas, going faster than what was safe on the gravel.

The worm of warning in his gut grew to the size of an anaconda. He shouldn't have left Isleen. Call him possessive, controlling, jealous—whatever—he'd own it. But that didn't change the bone-deep certainty that he wasn't going to feel normal until he was with her again.

His vehicle tore out of the woods, revealing the clearing the main house resided in. Kent's oh-no-I'm-not-compensating-for-anything huge truck was parked in front of the arched entryway. Inside the house, lights were on, but the outside remained dark. Exterior lighting in summer attracted every insect in a ten-mile radius.

Why wasn't Kent waiting at Xander's cabin? The asshole was supposed to be guarding Isleen, and she hadn't wanted to come to the main house. Had something happened?

He stomped on the brakes, and the ABS stuttered and jerked. The tires lost traction on the gravel and went into a long skid. He rammed the truck into park and was out the door before the vehicle stopped moving. Fuck his transmission. The only thing that mattered was Isleen.

He full-on sprinted for the house, his boots crunching through the crushed rocks, overwhelming all other sounds. He rounded Kent's truck and saw her.

She stood on the top porch step, Hopkins right beside her, his hand resting on his service weapon as if Xander were a potential threat. Another BCI guy stepped out of the shadows. At least they took their job of protecting her seriously.

"Why aren't you at home? What's wrong?"

She came down the porch steps, heading for him, and he met her halfway, wrapping her in his arms. All the pressure, all the worry evaporated. He held her against him. Yeah, he might be a foot taller, twice as broad, and have close to hundred pounds on her, but when she put those arms of hers around his waist, he fucking felt safe and a little bit invincible.

She hadn't answered his questions.

He pulled back to see her face. "Did something happen?" Starlight colored her features in shades of slate and silver. Her eyes were wide, unblinking—she looked worried—and he'd do anything to get that emotion off her face.

"Nothing happened."

He heard the quivering undertone. He heard the change in her heart rate, and the way she stopped breathing, holding her breath to see if he bought the lie she was trying to sell.

Tension fisted between his shoulder blades. "I can hear the lie in your voice. Now I want to hear the truth. What happened?"

Her gaze darted between his forehead and his mouth, never meeting his eyes, but she didn't step away from him. She kept her hands on his sides, her fingers twisting in his shirt.

He glanced up at Hopkins. The guy practically sprinted to the far end of the porch. Either he didn't want to get involved or Xander's Frankenstein face scared him.

Kent walked out of the house carrying a feminine tote bag. The same style of bag as the one Row had brought to Xander's cabin with some of Isleen's clothes. He wanted to chalk it up to Kent getting in touch with his girly side, but Xander wasn't stupid. He knew how to add.

Kent + Isleen's tote bag = Isleen was leaving with Kent.

Every muscle went taut, bracing for the final blow to his heart. Xander forced his arms away from her, forced them to hang at his sides.

Roweena followed Kent, her jaw thrust out, her arms crossed over her chest. Xander knew that look. He'd been the recipient of it daily during his teen years. Row was pissed and aiming her anger at someone other than Xander.

"Row, what's going on?" He flipped on the switch to hear Row's thoughts. Out of habit he flinched waiting for the pain, but it never came. And neither did Row's thoughts. She said what she was thinking.

"I don't care what excuse she gives, she shouldn't leave you. It's not right."

He aimed his next words at Isleen. "Tell me what she's talking about." He spoke deliberately, making sure his tone was even. She still wouldn't look him in the eye, but she still held on to him. If she was leaving, why wasn't she letting go?

If you let her go, it'll be the biggest mistake of your life. Row directed her thoughts to him, knowing he'd hear her.

Kent's thoughts overlapped the end of Row's. *Yeah, asshole. She's leaving you. Wants to spend the night with me. Not you.*

The air punched out of Xander's lungs.

Row's and Kent's terrible thoughts bombarded him, echoing over and over inside the cavern of his skull.

If you let her go...

Wants to spend the night with me.

If you let her go...

Wants to spend the night with me.

"Xander?" Isleen stood directly in front of him, no more than a foot away, but her voice seemed faint as if it had traveled a great distance.

"You want to leave me for him? I'm not going to beg you to stay." His voice came out rough-hewn and primitive, and anyone really listening would hear his own lie. It made him a motherfucking pussy, but he would beg her to stay. Anything to keep her with him. "And in case you were wondering—I don't share." That at least was the truth.

Isleen grabbed his waist tighter. "Xander, stop it. It's nothing like that." Her mouth puckered up like she'd eaten something sour. "I just need to go with him for the interview. There are so many questions I need to answer—about what happened at the trailer. About my dream of Gran…"

"I don't believe you." Oh, he wanted to, but he could still hear that little shiver, smaller now, but still there.

"I can't wait. I want to get it done. Now. Get it all out. I want to find the person responsible for Gran's death. I won't relax until he's caught."

Keep pressing it, asshole. You'll see she doesn't want you around. Kent's thoughts were begging to meet Xander's fist.

"What's really going on?" He looked back and forth between her and Kent, who still held that girlie tote in his hand. "And why do you need an overnight bag if you're just being interviewed?"

She seemed to try for a reassuring smile, but missed the mark. "I thought if I got tired, I could lie down for a bit."

"There's some truth there, but you're still lying about something."

No one said a word. Nature sounds filled the void, and for a moment Xander wished he could go back to that night on his porch when he got that brain itch—and fucking ignore it. Save himself the pain and suffering Isleen was about to cause him when she ripped open his chest, cut out his heart, and stomped on it.

"You want truth? Here's some truth. I'll be back in the morning. I promise. Nothing is going to happen between me and Kent. We are just friends. He is going to interview me. I have a pair of pants and a sweater in the bag in case I get cold. If I get tired, I might take a nap. But I want to do this now. Right now. Not later. Not tomorrow morning. Now."

She was telling the truth, but something wasn't right.

Ask to come along. Ask to wait on her during the interviews. Ask her.

Xander recognized Kent's thoughts for what they were. A trap. Designed to maim Xander in the deepest way, but it was a snare he couldn't resist. "Okay. I'll drive you. I'll wait for you until you're done." A fist of dread closed around his windpipe.

"It could be all night. You stay here. I'll call you when I'm done."

Fucking goddamn. She was lying again. He had to be sure. "I don't mind waiting."

"You should stay here. It'll just be boring, and they probably won't let you…"

See, asshole? She doesn't want you around. She wants to be with me tonight. Not you.

"You don't want me around." The words came out in blocks of concrete certainty.

Through the entire conversation she still clung to his shirt. "I'll be back in the morning. After I've done the interviews and—"

After I've spent the night with her.

Kent's words hit Xander's anger ignition switch. "Dude, you better fucking walk away right now before my shit gets too hot."

"I have a right to be here. She asked for my *help*." The way the guy accented *help* made it sound like he was saving Isleen from Xander. "Asked me. Wants to get away from here. From you."

"Kent! That is not what I said. Or meant."

A jolt of energy Xander couldn't deny or control—and didn't want to—landed directly in his shoulder. He grabbed Isleen's wrists, pulled them off his shirt, then took two steps away from her—all the time he needed to funnel the anger into his fist. He swung at Kent.

Fights in real life weren't like in the movies where everything was perfectly choreographed. In real life, there were misses and failed maneuvers because fury, not intellect, drove the body.

Kent flinched at the last second. Xander's knuckles didn't connect with bone; they just scraped Kent's face hard enough to burn them both.

Before Kent could recover and react, Xander mashed his other fist into Kent's gut. Surprise was going to determine who won this battle, but Kent didn't go down from the gut punch. Must've been prepared for it. He and Kent were too similar. They'd grown up fighting. Taught each other how to brawl through the experience.

Kent launched himself at Xander, tackling him low in the waist and driving them both back. Xander's boots couldn't keep up with the momentum and went airborne. He landed ass first, spine, then shoulders on sharp shards of gravel. Might as well have been a bed of nails. Kent used Xander as a landing pad, driving each gravel spike a bit deeper into his flesh. He ground his teeth to keep from groaning.

Street Fighting Fact 1: Keep standing. Don't go down.

Street Fighting Fact 2: If you go down, be on top.

Street Fighting Fact 3: If you are on the bottom, you are fighting two people—gravity and the asshole on top of you. Yeah. And Xander was underneath two hundred pounds of Kent's temper.

Everyone started shouting. He could pick out each

of their voices—Isleen, Roweena, Hopkins, the other BCI guy—

Kent's fist caught him in the jaw. The sharp crack of flesh against flesh was something he heard both externally and internally. Acrid warmth filled his mouth. It was low—he knew it and didn't care—but he spit the blood and saliva in Kent's face. The guy startled, giving Xander an opening. He bucked, knocking Kent off balance, and then flipped the guy over, landing on top.

Kent knew the rules. He wrestled Xander for top. Top being more important than landing any blows. They went into an alligator roll. The world flipped over on itself again and again as they battled for primary position. Xander lost all sense of direction, of up and down, top and bottom.

The spinning stopped. Kent crushed Xander's skull between his hands and slammed his head back. Twinkling stars of pain burst in his vision. Guess he was on bottom. He punched the guy in the ribs. Heard a satisfying grunt.

Isleen shouted, but Xander's brain wasn't working fast enough to understand her words. His gaze found her. The BCI guy—the one Xander didn't know—held her from behind, arms around her, pinning her hands to her sides. She fought his grip, throwing her head back to butt him, but he was too tall and she hit his chest.

Part of Xander understood why the guy was holding her. He was trying to keep her away from the two grown-ass men going at it with their fists.

Pain exploded in his cheek. Spit and blood slung from his mouth. Kent had used Xander's distraction to get in another shot.

The other part of Xander—the Bastard in His Brain—didn't understand logic. All he saw was someone holding Isleen against her will. She'd been there, done that, and he'd be damned if he'd let anyone ever hurt her again.

Xander's world went white, Bastard in His Brain officially in control. The only color that existed was Isleen. Quick—one, two—he landed a double punch to Kent's ribs, then threw him off as if he weighed no more than a toddler. Xander was off the ground and in front of Isleen before any of them had a chance to react. He popped his fist into the BCI guy's nose and snatched Isleen to his chest, so the guy wouldn't take her down with him.

And he did go down. Fell straight back. Unconscious.

"Don't fucking touch her." He spat the words at the world, blood dripping from the side of his mouth and over his jaw, then sliding down his neck. Everything had gone still and silent.

"Xander..." Isleen reached up to him, sticking her hand in the mess on his face. He flinched away from her, but the moment she touched him, everything changed. The Bastard in His Brain receded, taking all Xander's tension and anger with him. The hundred points of pain in his body eased and vanished. A cooling tingle spread through him. Was this what she felt when he took her pain away? Was this her healing him?

"You feel this?" he whispered, his gaze locked on her. "This is why you can't leave. We are special together."

Her chin quivered, and water glistened in her eyes. "I had a nightmare. You died." She choked on the words. "I'm given these dreams in order to save lives. To stop these bad things from happening. It's my duty. So I *will* stop this dream from happening, but the only way is to find the guy who killed Gran. And use what I saw in the dream to stay away from any situation that may re-create what happened. So I can't be around you at night. I have to leave." Truth resonated in each of her words.

His naive heart buoyed inside his chest. She had been trying to protect him, not leave him.

"Baby, I'll be all right. We'll be all right. But I need you to trust me."

"I do trust you, but that's not what this is about. It's about my faith in a story. I want to believe the Fearless and Bear story. I want it all to be true. It feels like it should be true, but is it fact? No, I can't take a chance with your life. What I dreamed… You wouldn't be able to come back from it. You'd be dead. I couldn't live with myself if you died and I didn't prevent it."

He wanted to argue with her, deny her words, but he didn't have a logical comeback.

She gripped his face with both of her hands and stared him in the eyes. "I don't *want* to leave you. I *have* to leave you. Or else you could die."

Pain swam dark and deep inside her beautiful eyes, and he knew some of it—his refusal to let her go—was caused by him. That almost broke him. He had sworn never to hurt her. He fell to his knees, wrapped his arms around her waist, and pressed the side of his face to her abdomen. He opened his mouth to apologize, but that's not what came out. "I love you."

The night insects, all the people around them, even the stars in the sky seemed to stop and pay homage to the words torn out of his soul.

"Xander…" She started crying, quiet sounds so filled with anguish that they punctured his heart. "I love you too. I always have. From my first dream of you. That's why I have to go."

Chapter 19

"I was a shitbox. Shouldn't have acted that way. It just pissed me off that he scraped off Camille like she was a leech or something, and... I hope you know he doesn't deserve you." Kent started the truck. "Are you sure about this? Sure you want to leave." He eased off the brake and pulled away from the main house. Killer whined and pawed at his carrier on the floor between her feet.

Isleen nodded, unable to speak through the knot of tears in her throat. For Xander's sake—for his survival—she needed to be away from him. She twisted in her seat belt to see Xander out the truck's back window. He stood in the driveway, arms hanging limply at his sides, desolation and loneliness wafting off him like greasy smog.

It tore her chest open, seeing him that way and knowing it was her fault. But she had to leave him tonight. If she stayed... She couldn't take the chance. She lifted her hand to the glass, touching his image. Kent drove around the first curve in the driveway, and Xander disappeared from her sight. She stared out the back window for a few seconds, then faced forward again.

"You don't have to do this. We could put extra guys on you both. Figure out something." Kent glanced at her and then back to the driveway.

Her cheeks were wet. She palmed the wetness off

her face, but the tears wouldn't stop flowing. "No. The only way he'll be safe is if we catch the person who killed Gran."

"Jesus. You've got his blood on your hand and are smearing it all over your face."

She didn't mind. She'd wear Xander's blood like war paint—a way to protect herself, ward off enemies, and carry him with her.

Kent leaned over, hand outstretched to the glove box. "I've got some napkins—"

The air fractured into an explosion of sound. The wheel jumped out of Kent's hand. He slammed the brakes. Her head whipped forward, her torso slammed into the brace of the seat belt, stealing her ability to breathe. Tires locked, the truck skidded through the gravel. And then she watched as they headed straight for the tree-lined ravine on the edge of the driveway.

She screamed. Kent yelled something, but his words were muffled and muted under the weight of what was before them. The headlights illuminated their horrifying path straight down.

Xander. She shouted his name in her mind. Willed his image in front of her eyes and clung to it.

The truck crashed front end first into the ground with a cacophony of sounds. Weight smashing against solid earth. Metal crunching metal. The shrieking of bending steel. Her body's forward momentum abruptly, painfully stopped by the seat belt securing her torso and hips. Breath expelled out of her as if she'd been gut punched. Her arms and legs flopped around completely at the mercy of inertia.

And then, sweet silence.

Something in the engine pinged and popped, and she realized her eyes were clenched shut. Had she blacked out for a moment?

The dashboard had been blown out by the air bags. The windshield dangled off the hood in a mass of crackled glass. Beyond the front window was grass.

"Kent?" Her voice came out quieter than she'd meant. She cleared her throat.

He hung in his seat belt, arms on either side of the wheel, chin touching his chest. Seeing him gave her brain a framework for how she was positioned in the truck. She was suspended over the dashboard, facing out the hole where the windshield should be.

"Kent!" She shouted his name this time. He didn't move. Adrenaline pumped through her. She had to get him out of the truck. He needed a doctor. She probably needed one too. A quick body scan revealed that—yep—everything hurt.

Her hands shook so violently they practically blurred the air. *Calm down. Caallmm doowwnn.* She sucked in a slow breath and reached for the seat belt release. Her fingers trembled, and she couldn't figure out where to press—

Her body went weightless, her head smacked on the roof, and she tumbled out of the truck and down the hood, landing in a messy jumble of arms and legs. She rolled onto her back. Overhead, the night sky was brilliant in its dark beauty. Starlight pierced the black velvet, winking and glittering like the facets of exotic jewels. If this had been another time, another set of circumstances, she would've enjoyed just lying there watching the show.

But her head throbbed, her body didn't feel right, and she needed to get Kent out of the truck. She inhaled a breath of pure determination and pushed herself upright to kneeling and then got to her feet. The world swayed, then evened out.

Kent. Have to get Kent. She stepped up to the hood of the truck, grabbed hold of the opening where the windshield should have been, and hoisted herself up next to him.

A shivery, whimpery whine snagged her attention. Killer. She reached down, grabbed the carrier, and then maneuvered it out of the truck, leaning out the windshield to set it on the ground. It was the best she could do for the little dog until she took care of Kent.

"Wake up." She knelt on the dashboard and shook his shoulder. Nothing. She reached out, grabbed his head in her hand, and tilted his face toward her. It was hard to see in the dark, but he seemed to have a bruise on his temple. He groaned.

"Wake up, wake up, wake up." She raced through the words, hearing the frantic tone swelling in each of them.

"Imwake." His voice slurred.

"What hurts?"

"Evrythn."

"I need to get you out of the truck. It's not good for you to be hanging like this. What if there's a gas leak or it explodes or…" Enough with the worst-case scenarios. "Can you move your arms?"

He flopped his hands through the air like they were rags instead of flesh and bone. She almost laughed. At least he was trying to cooperate.

"Now, find the steering wheel." She guided his right

hand to the wheel and waited until his left one found it. "Hold on tight. I'm going to release your seat belt, and I don't want you falling out of the truck and injuring yourself. Ready?"

"Mmm…"

She braced her arm across his chest to help hold him. "Hold tight. I'm releasing it now." She jammed her finger into the seat belt release. His body, with her arm underneath, slammed into the steering wheel. Pain burst through her arm and shoulder. She cried out. Bad decision—thinking she could help brace over two hundred pounds of male with only her arm.

"Srrree."

He pulled back enough for her to slide her arm out from underneath him. It flopped down at her side, useless. She tried to raise it, but it refused to move. Was it broken? Odd that it didn't hurt. "Kent, look at me."

His body was draped over the steering wheel, head half hanging out the front window. He didn't look at her so much as turn his head in her direction.

"I need you to slide your legs toward me, get them up and over the dashboard, and then we can get you out of here." With her only useable hand, she reached down to his leg and guided it in the right direction. He followed her instruction, twisting and turning his torso and hips until his legs hung out the windshield.

"Okay. Hold on. I'll get out and help you down. Just stay here."

She positioned herself next to him in the same manner and slid down the hood, landing on her feet, then falling back on her ass. "Oomph." The landing jarred her arm, sending stabbing pain racing up and down the limb. Numbness had definitely been favorable to the throbbing ache.

She got to her feet. Fell. Didn't even know why she fell. She just blinked and was back on the ground. Slower this time, she stood and walked to Kent's bottom half dangling from the front window. "Okay, now slide down slowly. You only have a few feet and you'll hit the ground."

No movement.

"Kent?" She reached out to shake him, but his entire backside was right there. What did it matter? She smacked him on the butt. "Kent. Wake up."

Nothing. She tugged at his belt, tugged harder. His body began to slide. Yes. And then it was sliding too fast, and she had two options. Let him fall on the ground and possibly injure himself worse, or try to catch him, a.k.a., be his cushion. Her hesitancy made the decision for her. He fell back into her, and she fell back—into arms.

Strong, sure arms caught her from behind before she landed on the ground. Kent slid harmlessly off her. Not a graceful fall, but not one that would injure him.

"He's hurt. He needs a doctor."

The grip on her tightened. The pain in her arm ignited again. "Ouch. My arm." The way Xander held her didn't feel right—too firm, almost painful. "I think it's broken. But Kent needs…" Xander's touch had always brought her comfort, but now she felt the opposite of comfort.

A terrible truth pressed into her mind. It wasn't Xander behind her, holding her.

"The Dragon would put another's needs before its own?"

Her blood froze into a thick sludge. Her heart rammed against her chest, trying to force the congealed liquid through her body. That voice belonged to the man who killed Gran. To the man who killed Xander in her dream. To a man connected to her and Gran's torture inside that trailer. No one had ever called her the Dragon, except for Queen.

She thought about struggling out of his grip. She thought about running. But she wouldn't leave Kent defenseless against a murderer. "Who are you?" The question popped out before she had a chance to censor it.

"I am but a sorry soul sent to fulfill my duty to the Lord." He spoke slowly, resignation and sorrow giving his tone a drowning sort of weight.

Resignation and sorrow? As if *he* needed sympathy. Anger flicked into flame inside her, but she smothered the blaze before it consumed her. She needed her sanity, sense, and shrewdness to deal with this man. She needed to find a way to keep Kent safe and keep this man from hurting Xander. She needed to figure out how to capture him. "Kent needs medical attention."

"I carry a gun in my pocket. If you run when I release you, I will be forced to use it on the young man."

"I won't run. I just want to make sure he's okay." She didn't need to try to sound cooperative. She was cooperating. For Kent.

He released her and moved to Kent without looking back. She stared after him for a moment, then followed, kneeling on the opposite side of Kent while the man checked Kent's vitals. She watched, ready to attack with her good arm if he tried to hurt her friend, but the man seemed sincere in his ministrations.

For a murderer, he looked surprisingly friendly. His face was square and pleasant, and his eyes crinkled slightly in the corners, giving him a harmless appeal. His hair was thick and almost white in the starlight—the kind of hair a bald man would pay for. A large, squared-off gold cross hung from his neck.

And despite how he looked, she hated him. Her fingers and toes tingled with the force of her loathing.

"Was he wearing a seat belt?" The man's voice carried concern.

"We both were."

"Has he regained consciousness since the accident?" He patted his hands along Kent's body, feeling for any broken bones.

"Sort of. His words were slurred and sleepy sounding. He tried to cooperate with the plan to get him out of the truck, but I think he passed out at the end."

"I don't feel any broken bones. But I do suspect he has a concussion. Internal injury can't be ruled out yet, but the odds are in his favor since he was wearing a seat belt." He reached into his pants pocket and pulled out a small pendant the same shape as the one he wore around his neck. He placed it in the middle of Kent's forehead. "He will live."

"Who are you?" This time her voice carried a bit of bafflement. "You're treating Kent as if his life matters, and I'm glad for that." Her tone filled with hatred, contempt, and loathing. "But what makes his life more important to you than my grandmother's?"

"You've had a vision."

His words startled the anger out of her. How did he know about the dreams?

He sat back on his haunches and stared at her. "All life is important to me. *Especially* yours and your grandmother's."

"Huh?" Did she hear that correctly? She replayed what he said, searching for a hidden meaning to his words. But there was no other message. She felt her face twist in disgust. "How can you say that? You know that Queen called me the Dragon. That means you were involved with what happened to Gran and me in the trailer. You know what she did to us. You killed Gran. And you expect me to believe that Gran's life mattered to you? That my life matters to you?" If her tongue hadn't turned to sandpaper, she would've spit at him. So much for keeping the anger under control. "You. Are. A. Liar."

He sighed, his shoulders slumping as if she'd just defeated him in some battle of wits that she hadn't known they were playing. "From the moment I took you, I have been trying to save your life."

She reared back, his words slapping her. Neither Gran nor she remembered anything about being taken. They'd both gone to bed in their little house in the country and then woken up in their prison. "You? You took us? Gave us to Queen to torment and torture at her pleasure? That wasn't *saving* us." He had to be crazy. Her voice rose and fury flowed out. "How could you think being locked in that room for years, being beaten, starved, and drained of blood was saving either of us?"

"I was trying to save your souls." His voice hitched as if he were trying not to cry.

"By killing us?" She screeched the words at him.

"By killing the demon inside each of you." He clutched the squared-off cross hanging from his neck.

His words hung in the air between them.

What? Ookkaayy...

What should she say to that? Should she ride along with him on the crazy train, waiting for an opportunity to save Kent and herself? Or should she try to convince him of his insanity?

He raised his gaze to the sky. "There shall be none among you who practice occultism, no seers or spell casters, nor any who use prediction, prognostication, or prophecy. Whoever commits these acts is an abomination to the Lord. And the Faithful shall drive out the demons to become righteous in the eyes of the Lord."

He *was* talking about her dreams. About Gran's ability to enter another person's dreams. But how could he know those things? She hadn't known about her own dreams until recently.

"I am a faithful man, but this task tested me. I tried to save you by making your body a hostile environment for the evil. I was ever hopeful it would leave you, but its roots had grown into your heart and twined themselves around your soul. And now your evil has grown powerful—"

"Isleen!" Xander shouted her name.

She whipped around. He stood next to a stream she hadn't noticed before. Starlight glinted off the water, and the picturesque bank called to mind another image—one of death. Xander's death in her dream. No. This couldn't be happening.

"You've hurt her enough, asshole. I won't give you the chance to hurt her again." Xander walked steadily forward.

"No." She finally forced the word from her dry mouth.

Xander's full attention was aimed at the man. "You just keep praying to your Lord, keep asking for his protection. You're going to need it. I intend to kill you with my bare fucking hands." His tone was a feral growl.

"Xander. No. Go back. This is my dream." The words sped from her lips.

His concentration on the man wavered and slid to her. Confusion, surprise, and rabid determination flashed in his eyes.

Kkkrrr. A gunshot.

She startled. So did Xander. Only he didn't really startle; it was the impact of the bullet slamming into his head. His face went slack, his legs crumpled, and she saw the neat hole in his forehead. He fell facedown with a solid *thunk* that jarred the ground underneath her.

She squeezed her eyes shut. This was a dream—a bad, terrible, horrifying dream—and she was going to wake up. She had to wake up. Pain would wake her up. She balled her hand into a fist and punched her broken arm. White-hot agony rolled through her. She almost vomited. She cried out and opened her eyes.

Xander lay where he had fallen. She punched her arm again. Pain blinded her for a blessed moment, then ebbed, and reality swallowed her.

"Nonononono…" It was the only word that existed. Somehow she ended up next to him. He lay facedown. She didn't want to turn him over, didn't want to see confirmation of what she already knew, but something stronger than herself reached out to him, tugging his shoulder with her good hand until she finally flipped him over.

The neat, round hole on the side of his forehead was an abomination on her soul. Death stared out from his unseeing eyes. Her insides felt like they were being ripped from her body. Her mind tore from its skull. She heard herself crying and screaming and bawling, even as she laid her hand over his wound, willing herself to heal him, heal him, heal him.

He'd told her that taking away her pain felt cool and satisfying. But all she felt was the scalding heat of his blood trickling from the wound and, underneath her palm, a shard of skull poking her. "You can't be dead. You can't be. You have to live. You have to. I can't do this without you. I need you." Her voice vibrated with grief and terror.

"He heard me. Heard my thoughts. He was possessed of evil too. I had to... I had no choice. Forgive me. Oh Lord, forgive me."

Isleen heard the man talking, but didn't pay attention to his words. The only thing that mattered was... "Xander. Xander. Xander." She chanted his name over and over.

Sirens sounded in the distance, ringing out over the low hills and through the shallow ravines.

"You must come with me now. We need to leave this place." The man grabbed her arm.

"No!" She turned on him, baring her teeth at him like a cornered raccoon. Her reaction startled him back a step. She wasn't leaving Xander. She was going to heal him.

Chapter 20

EMERGENCY SIRENS SCREAMED THROUGH THE DARK, mixing and blending with the Dragon's anguish until King slapped his hands over his ears just to be able to think beyond the grief and guilt.

He'd been watching and waiting for an opportunity to steal her away. He'd spread the road spikes when it appeared she was finally leaving. Of course, he hadn't anticipated that the truck would end up in the ravine. Number one priority: Get her away from here so the proper ritual could be performed.

When he pulled his hands from his ears, they were damp, the gun slick and slippery in his grip. He tightened his hold on it. Weapon shaking, he aimed it at the man who'd been in the truck with her. The last thing he wanted was to kill an innocent, but she didn't know that.

The Dragon wailed and howled her grief, the sound a vise of guilt tightening down on King's chest. He'd killed. Again. It was the decades of indoctrination that had raised his hand and squeezed the trigger. It was fear. And it was his *duty*. As one of the Faithful, it was his responsibility to eradicate evil from the world. The man had been inside King's head listening to his thoughts.

Logic dictated that King end the man. But murder… Eliminating a corrupt soul was supposed to be right, so why did it constantly *feel* so wrong? In his mind, King could hear Chosen One saying, "*It is not for you to question the laws of the Lord. It is for you to prove your faith in the Lord.*"

But still, the Dragon's sorrow paralleled the horror in King's heart.

"Leave with me now, and he won't be harmed." His voice cracked.

The Dragon's hand covered the wound in her man's head. The desperate and determined way she pushed palm into flesh made it seem as if plugging the hole in his head would guarantee his survival. Pure denial.

He witnessed it every day on the faces of people whose loved one had died. Denial always made a short show before fizzling out. Years of training and experience had taught him how to handle the emotion. Speak the truth with compassion. "Your man… He has passed on to…" King usually followed it up with a reference to heaven, but this time he couldn't. He didn't know what the Lord intended to do with her man's soul. Or hers, for that matter.

The sirens were closer. So many of them. Probably every squad car in the county. "It's time to come with me, or I hurt the one still living."

Slowly, she lifted her hand off the wound, then examined the hole in her man's head, fingers dancing around the rim of the damage as if she didn't trust her vision. Denial again.

Her bitter gaze landed on King. She raised her hand to her face and slathered blood over her forehead, cheeks, nose, and chin. The result: A warped, morbid mask of death and despair. She looked every bit as evil as the demon inside her.

Revulsion squirmed underneath King's skin like freshly hatched maggots.

Slowly, laboriously, she stood, cradling her broken arm close to her body. She swayed on her feet. Good thing he hadn't planned on her walking the two miles to his car. She wouldn't have made it.

He motioned with the gun, and she walked past him in the direction he indicated. He followed, holstering his weapon and unclipping the stun gun from his waist. He flipped the switch and pressed it into her shoulder. A squeak of pain and surprise slipped from her. She melted to the ground, sprawling on her broken arm. He couldn't help it; he grimaced, knowing how badly that had to have to hurt.

"The pain will all be gone in a moment." He knelt next to her and pulled the syringe from his pocket, pushed the needle into her neck, and depressed the plunger. The drug should take effect before she recovered from the electrical charge.

Quiet tears slid down her cheeks. Her eyes were the only part of her face not covered in blood. They were big and luminous, like one of those cartoon princesses, but unlike make-believe, they reflected sorrow and suffering and a soul ravaged by real evil. So much pain carried by one small woman. It wasn't natural. Or right.

He couldn't help it. Compassion ached in his throat. He wanted to say something to make things better. It had always been his job to offer comfort and solace to those who were hurting. Now was no different. Despite the blood, despite the evil, he wiped her tears with his fingers.

The moment his skin touched hers, he remembered she would burn him. Only this time she didn't. And wait.

He had grabbed her bare arms when she was helping the
man out of the truck. He hadn't even thought about it.
She hadn't burned him then either.

Evil had departed from her soul, leaving her…just her.

Optimism, delicate as dragonfly wings, fluttered in
his heart. This changed everything. *Everything.* Every
moment he'd spent on his knees in prayer had led to this.
A miracle. She was free. And he owed it all to Chosen
One and the Lord. Chosen One had been the one to sug-
gest that the ancestor and the Dragon's evil might be
linked. Killing the ancestor had saved the girl.

He reached out and settled his hand on her head—just
like his father used to do to soothe his upset. "Go to
sleep. Everything will be better when you wake."

In a soft, low lullaby voice he began singing his
favorite hymn.

> *Devout is my soul,*
> *When all the world looks on.*
> *Pure is my will,*
> *When sinners cry my wrongs.*
> *Calling me to the Lord's Brigade.*
> *Calling me to the Lord's Brigade.*
> *Lord, will you take me,*
> *A soldier in the midst*
> *Of earthly evils,*
> *When devils whisper to me?*
> *Calling me to the Lord's Brigade.*
> *Calling me to the Lord's Brigade.*
> *Cleanse my heart, oh mighty One.*
> *I'll fight for you, oh mighty One.*
> *Blood in your name, oh mighty One,*

When I must stay strong.
Calling me to the Lord's Brigade.
Calling me to the Lord's Brigade.

Her eyes slipped shut. Her body relaxed into the drug.

The sirens were all around them. Under the shrieking noise, he heard the rumble of gravel under tires. They were coming up the driveway. Would they see where the truck went over the side?

He wanted to pray over her, but now was not the time for prayer. It was the time for action. Using her good arm, he hauled her up and over his shoulder and then began a slow jog through the dark forest. Any sound he made was hidden by the sirens still blaring on and on.

Her body jostled against his, her head and arms slapping and smacking his back. He didn't want to think about how holding her in this position was further damaging her broken arm. Couldn't be helped. He followed a barely discernible animal trail, brambles and bushes grabbing at them both.

He'd spent many a night out in nature. Had found that communing with God's creation comforted him. But tonight the forest seemed dead. Dead quiet. Where were the peepers and crickets? The only sounds were of his footfalls and the fading emergency sirens. To be so surrounded by the natural world and hear only man-made noises was odd.

It felt like forever and no time had passed when he finally emerged next to his car. He'd hidden the vehicle two miles from the property on an isolated dirt road. He'd learned from his mistake of parking too close.

That had nearly gotten him caught the night he killed the ancestor.

A dog howled in the distance. A pet? Or a scent dog? Didn't really matter now.

Oh, so gently, he settled the Dragon in the passenger seat, draping her broken arm across her body, but it kept sliding. He shouldn't take the time for this, but he couldn't leave her injured. He stripped off his outer shirt and tied it around her neck in a makeshift sling. By the dome light, he saw the area just above her elbow swelling. He threaded her hand into the sling, adjusting the fit until her joint was stabilized. The best he could do for the moment.

He got behind the wheel and drove. The car's headlights illuminated an unfamiliar world of winding, hilly, remote back roads. Where he lived, the land was absolutely flat. The night scenery here was eerie and beautiful at the same time. So much like the Dragon had been.

They passed no other vehicles. If it weren't for the occasional solitary house with its lights on, King would've sworn they were the only two people on earth. He reached over and pressed his fingers into her neck, searching for a pulse, wanting to make certain she didn't have an adverse reaction to the drug.

After driving an hour—surely a safe distance away—he pulled over alongside an abandoned road and flipped on the interior lights. She sat exactly as she had the entire drive. Her body leaned against the passenger door, still asleep from the effects of the drug. Tenderly, aware of her broken right arm, he adjusted her position in the seat and turned her head to face him.

He wanted to see her. Really look at her. Take her in.

Even when he'd captured her, he hadn't been allowed the time to drink his fill of her appearance. It had been feared that any contact with her could corrupt him.

He grabbed a handful of tissues from the travel-sized box he kept in the console, wet them with the half-empty bottle of water, and began wiping the blood from her face. The tang of tarnished pennies choked out the oxygen. The air was so thick with the scent he could practically taste it on his tongue. His stomach soured, the contents curdling and threatening to erupt, but he pushed on, cleaning her skin until she was fresh-faced and lovely.

He tossed the wad of soiled tissues out the window, then let himself absorb her appearance.

Her face was…his face. He saw himself in the shape of her brows and eyes, in the curve of her lips and the color of her hair. It was as if Shayla contributed nothing to the makeup of their daughter. She would've been so pleased. She had always said she wanted their child to look like him.

Shayla… No. It had been decades and still he couldn't think of her.

He refocused on the young woman in front of him. "Isslleenn." Her name—the name Shayla had picked for her—felt awkward in his mouth. He'd never spoke her name aloud, had never allowed himself to think of her as *his daughter*. Calling her by Queen's name for her—the Dragon—had always been safer.

But now, things were different. They could have a future. He'd teach her everything he knew about the Lord. He'd make certain the evil never again took root in her. He'd protect her and keep her from harm. Forever and ever. Amen.

—⁓—

The road ran parallel with the water, winding and curving with the river. Sunshine peeked from the horizon, slanting brilliant rays of gold over the landscape. No matter how many sunrises King experienced, on the river they were a pure, majestic thing to behold, a time when nature and spirit combined to make a godly moment.

He slowed and pulled in next to Chosen One's car. Chosen One leaned against the hood of his expensive sedan, staring out at their sacred place upon the water. He was dressed for work—fine tailored suit and expensive tie, the exact attire one expected from the mayor.

King cut the engine, checked her pulse once more, waited for the thump of it against his fingers, then adjusted the sling on her broken arm. He looked up from his ministrations. Chosen One stood at the hood of the car, glaring in the window. King understood how it looked, and he'd best explain quick before Chosen One—

"You've been corrupted." Chosen One's voice hit every note of disgust on the scale. His lips peeled back over wide, square teeth in a sneer that made King feel like the bad little boy he'd once been. The vein in the center of Chosen One's forehead—the one that swelled and turned blue when he got angry—bypassed blue and went to apocalyptic.

Oh no.

King grabbed the door handle and yanked it. Locked. He hit the unlock button. The window slid down. He jabbed another switch. The side mirror moved. Why couldn't he find the right button? He punched another knob. *Trnk*. The locks disengaged, and he shot out of the vehicle and fell to his knees in front of Chosen One. His father.

Father raised his hand—a hand slightly gnarled with age—and swung.

It had been decades since Father had last punished him, but King felt as if it were only yesterday that they were here upon the river, going through the same motions about the same things. Only before it had been about Shayla.

King tensed, braced for the blow. His head jolted back, his cheek burned. Father packed enough force to ring a church bell, and the crack of palm to cheek seemed as loud. King wanted to press his hand over the heat on his face, but he didn't move. Wasn't allowed to move.

"You have shamed me, shamed your brothers, and shamed the Lord." Condemnation was a poison dripping from each of Father's words.

"No. No, Father, it's not like that." King grabbed the cross dangling from his neck, kissing the warm gold. "See? I'm not corrupted. I'm not. I've done nothing wrong."

"Silence." Father's voice boomed, quieting even the river. "You deny you were *touching* her?"

"I do not deny I was touching her. She no longer burns me. You were right. Her power was linked to the ancestor. She has changed. I can no longer feel her evil."

Father listened, then looked beyond him into the car. "Stay here."

King didn't move. He kept to his knees and didn't dare look anywhere except forward. He heard the passenger-side door open, then heard nothing else.

Dear Lord, please please please let him see that she is saved. Please please please... He chanted this over and over until Father returned to his line of sight, carrying Isleen in his arms. He walked past King to the demon box on the bank.

Nooooo. The primal scream echoed inside King's head but never made it out into the world. His chin trembled, his body shuddered, and he couldn't remember how to breathe. This was *exactly* the same as with Shayla.

Father meant to lock her inside the iron box for six days and six nights. If she survived, it would be proof of her evil. If she died, she would prove her innocence. Either way resulted in death. King wanted to chase after Father, wanted to steal her away from him, drive off with her and never look back, but he couldn't move. An entire lifetime of obedience kept his knees on the ground and his protests in his mouth. He couldn't defy his father, his leader—the one man who communed directly with the Lord.

Father dropped her in the box like an armful of dirty laundry.

Her arm. Her broken arm. The pain was going to be excruciating when she woke.

Father slammed the iron lid. The clang of it reverberating over the river. He locked each side with a black key, then walked back to King, whose gaze never left the box containing his daughter.

"Rex, my eldest son"—Father stroked King's chin and then forced his face up—"evil's power is boundless." His voice was soft and kind. "You know it could be masquerading as dormant to fool us."

"Her touch no longer burns me. It no longer burns

you." He tried to keep the defiance from his tone, but he wasn't successful. He braced, waiting for another slap.

"We cannot take the chance that this is a ruse."

"That's what you said last time." King whispered the words, not daring to say them full volume. When Father didn't strike him, he continued. "Father..." Liquid sorrow flowed into King's eyes. "She's my daughter. Your granddaughter. Our blood flows in her veins. She could learn to be strong in our faith. Can we give her a chance?"

"No." The word was flat and full, offering no room for argument. "I cannot allow this. I have been lenient with you regarding her because I understood your struggles, but we will not squander this Lord-given opportunity."

King could no longer bear the sight of his father, his leader, this man who was respected and revered in their community. He clamped his eyes shut.

"Have faith. Let the Lord in. He will ease this burden just as he has eased the burden of what went before."

The Lord had never eased that burden. The only way King could live with what had happened to Shayla was to not think about it. To carve that memory out of his brain and bury it so deep inside himself that he couldn't find it.

"If it eases you, stay with her. Offer her counsel, educate her in the ways of our Lord so that her death will be a release instead of a condemnation." Father sighed. "That is the most mercy I can offer either of you."

King nodded, but he didn't open his eyes.

Father let go of him and settled his hand upon King's head. "Find peace, my son."

Chapter 21

"I'M SORRY. I'M SO SORRY."

The words penetrated Isleen's sleep, acting as a tether pulling her into awful awareness. It was dark, so dark. Where was she? She didn't know. With her good hand, she searched for the source of the voice in the dark. Her fingers trailed over the smooth floor, then up the wall next to her, then over the ceiling above her. Her mind mapped the dimensions of the space.

She was in a box. No, it wasn't a mere box.

It was a coffin.

She should be freaking out. She should be pounding on the sides, trying to find a way out. She wasn't doing any of that. All the fight had left her.

Memories and pain hit—searing, burning, throbbing. The ferocity sucking the air out of her. She remembered this kind of pain. Only this time it was worse, so much worse. This time she didn't have her dreams of Xander to sustain her.

He was dead. And if by some vicious fate he wasn't, he would be a vegetable. No one survived that kind of bullet wound to the head without the severest of consequences.

In those woods, she had tried, had poured every ounce of will into healing him, had waited to feel something, but nothing happened. Fearless and Bear—she and Xander—had been nothing more than an alluring story.

"Xander…" Her voice snapped and broke over his name. A beautiful name, a strong name, the only name that ever mattered to her.

Heavy, ugly sounds of sorrow spewed out of her.

Everything hurt.

Breathing hurt.

Living hurt.

She'd thought she'd known pain in the trailer. She'd thought she'd known pain when Gran died. She hadn't known pain at all. Hadn't known that pain was a dull ax blade hacking, cleaving, severing heart from soul. Her heart from Xander's soul.

"I'm sorry." The voice—the voice of Xander's killer—penetrated her grief, but her mind had no room to question him, no room for anger. Every thought, every feeling boiled down to one terrible truth. Xander was probably dead. She cried until her throat was scraped raw, her face hurt, and her stomach muscles ached from the force of her sobs. And then her soul cried until exhaustion settled its blanket of oblivion over her.

Consciousness slammed into her, jerking her out of sleep's numbing embrace and thrusting her back into reality. Pain hammered at her arm and a dull, diffuse headache saturated her brain, but something was different with her. She didn't hurt. Oh, her body still ached, but her heart no longer wept and her soul no longer bled. Everything that mattered—feelings, hopes, dreams, Gran, and Xander—had separated from her.

She had fractured. She'd broken like a wishbone

snapped in two, and all that remained of her was a body that hadn't died yet and a mind incapable of emotion. Or could this lack of feeling be an indicator that she had died?

Darkness surrounded her, blinded her. The exact opposite of that endless white from her dreams. She blinked hard to clear her eyes. Nothing. No shapes. No shadows. No shades of color. Maybe this black void really was death.

"And the Lord commanded"—the words sounded odd and diluted—"all his Faithful to rid the land of demons and devils. And the kingdom of…"

Nope. Not dead.

She recognized the voice. The man who killed Gran and Xander. Just thinking about Xander should be devastating, but her emotions were blessedly anesthetized.

The man continued to spout Godly phrases and holier-than-thou platitudes, but she wasn't listening.

"Where are you?" she asked more out of curiosity than any real caring, cutting him off in the middle of some prayer.

"You're awake. Bless the Lord. I'm here. Outside. There's so much I need to tell you before the end."

She supposed he meant to kill her, and yet she didn't feel any horror at the thought of dying. Honestly, she couldn't wait. She'd simply reached her limit. She had no more tolerance for this life that had given her nothing but terror, pain, and heartache, with only the briefest glimmers of happiness.

"Mister, why don't you just kill me and get it over with?" Her tone was all attitudinal teenager trying to get her way.

"I do not like you referring to me as *mister*. I'd prefer you to call me Father."

"Oh yeah. I forgot. You're a priest." Psychotic laughter bubbled up from somewhere inside her. "What are you preaching to people? Thou *shalt* kill?"

"I am an ordained man of God, but wish for you to refer to me as Father because Shayla was my wife and I am your father." He spoke with the same authoritative tone Alex had used on Xander.

White sparklers of color exploded in her head. She had to have heard him wrong. But her ears still rang with those words. *Shayla was my wife and I am your father.*

Chuffing, sniffling noises came from outside. "Shayla… She… She…" He hiccuped a sob. "She died. The same way you're going to."

"You killed her? I'm not surprised." The person speaking these words, using the bored tone of voice, wasn't her. It was her broken self.

More evidence of the fracture her psyche had suffered: The old her would've been clamoring for more information about her mother. Any detail. Anything about the woman Isleen had never met and knew nothing about. But this version of her had moved beyond pain to a state of apathy. Her mother was just another loss on the necklace of bones hanging from her neck. And this man claiming to be her father…well, she didn't need to know anything about him other than he'd killed Gran and Xander and her mother.

"Your mother was vivacious and alluring. The type of woman every man noticed and few had the courage to approach. I was so brave back then." He was having a moment. She heard it in the nostalgic way he spoke, as if he were in another decade, inhabiting another space. "As simple as it sounds, it really was love at first sight for both of us."

She didn't care—didn't want to care—about anything he said. "Well, Daddy-o, let's get this funeral started. I'm going to die like my mom. Let's go."

"I loved everything about her, and she loved me. She was the only person to ever love me unconditionally, at least until the end. Then she hated me. And I hated myself even more. I've never gotten over what happened to her. I try to not think about it, to pretend she never existed, but it's like lying to myself. I always know I'm lying."

"What did you do to her?" The question popped out before she could contain it.

"While she was pregnant with you, she began having these dreams. Odd dreams about benign things, like getting invited to dinner by my father or that the car wouldn't start one morning. And then those things would happen. I chalked it up to bizarre coincidence. But then her dreams turned dark. She kept dreaming this one dream over and over—my dad, my brothers, and me killing her. It tested her mind. She withdrew from my family, became paranoid they were going to hurt her. And then she withdrew from me. Not in any outward way, but it was like I was no longer with all of her. She was keeping part of herself secreted away. She swore it wasn't true, but I could feel it. I could feel the loss. Finally, I mentioned her dreams to my father. I figured he'd know what to do. I figured he'd offer me guidance on how to help her. I hadn't figured his answer would be to kill her."

Isleen didn't want to listen, but she heard every nuanced word. If she didn't know him to be a killer, she would've sworn he sounded contrite and heartbroken.

"My father—your grandfather—is a very special man. He's the Lord's Chosen One, and my brothers and I are the Faithful. We were raised on the verse: 'There shall be none among you who practice occultism, no seers or spell casters, nor any who use prediction, prognostication, or prophecy. Whoever commits these acts is an abomination to the Lord. And the Faithful shall drive out the demons to become righteous in the eyes of the Lord.'"

He had said that to her in the woods, just before Xander—

"Chosen One said Shayla, my wife, my life, my only love, would have to endure the demon box as soon as you were birthed. Six days, six nights in the box. No food. No water. No shelter from the heat. If she died before the lid was lifted on the seventh morning, she had been innocent. If she still lived, it would be proof of the demon inside her. And then she would be baptized in blood and holy water."

Isleen grabbed on to each of his words. When he didn't say anything more, she prompted, "What happened?" The silence seemed endless and empty. She strained to hear anything from outside her own demon box. "Are you still there?"

"On the seventh morning, the lid was removed and she was still alive. Her eyes found mine. They were filled with so much emotion—love and hate and longing for me to save her—but I couldn't. She had been spawned from the devil. I didn't think I'd be able to complete the ritual. I was completely wrecked, but she eased that burden for me. She died the moment we removed her from the box."

The words punched the breath she been holding out of her. What had she expected? "You just let her die? How could you ever say you loved her?"

"It was my duty as the Faithful… We are here but to serve the Lord, not to question." His voice changed like he was mimicking something he'd been told.

"Who told you that? Chosen One? Sounds like he doesn't want anyone questioning him."

"Do not speak ill of what you do not understand."

"I understand better than all of you. I understand that your Chosen One gets off on controlling you. I understand Queen got off—as in *got off*—on hurting Gran and me. And I understand that you are too weak or too brainwashed to see that you have been killing good people who only want to do good things in this world. And that's a sin that the *real* God will never forgive." She sucked in a breath.

"Your grandmother understood. She took you and raised you. Carried the burden of her own evil, realized no human—not even herself—should have the power to change the Lord's destiny. She was baptized in the ways of the Lord and agreed the stain of evil should be removed from you both."

The words entered Isleen's ears, then exploded in her mind. Doubt crept among all the things she thought were facts. She remembered what Gran said to him right before he killed her. *Your trials didn't work. The evil never left us, no matter how much we endured.* "Gran knew? She condoned you killing her daughter?

You taking us? Queen torturing us? Me? No, I don't believe you."

"She didn't want your fate to be the same as her daughter's. She wanted you saved. As did I."

"Saved? You call what we went through being saved?" Isleen's mind flashed through a thousand horrible memories and landed on the last words Gran spoke to her. *I can't live with what I've done. I hurt him. I destroyed us by trying to save us. And I did this to you. It's all my fault. I'd take it all back. But, there's no take-backs in life.*

Then she remembered their last day in the torture trailer. *Hold on, baby girl. Just hold on. He's coming. He's got to be coming. He will release you. Save you. Your dreams will come true. All of them. Remember the dreams about him. How you loved him and he loved you. Remember the dreams of sunshine on your face and the cabin you shared. Remember…*

Why would Gran encourage Isleen's dreams if the dreams were bad? Was that a product of her mind slipping? Or was this guy—her father—lying? So many questions lined up, but there would never be answers she could trust. Gran was dead. And Isleen was next in line, so there was no point in thinking about any of it.

"If I make it to the seventh day, will I die after I'm baptized?"

There was a long pause. When he spoke, his voice was quiet as a whisper. "Yes."

"Good." The word came out loud, firm, and clear.

"Don't say that." He spoke in the whiny tone of a miserable kid.

"Sounds to me like all roads lead to me dying. The

only question is if it's going to happen sooner or later."
She was just being practical.

"I don't want you to die. Sooner or later."

"And yet you won't do a thing to get me out of this
box, will you?"

"I can't. Chosen One… The Lord…"

"Guess we're in agreement on one thing. You won't
be saving me, and I don't want to be saved. I just want
it over." Even she was surprised at her flippant tone.
But not surprised by her words. She meant every one
of them.

———— ✺ ————

The heat woke her. She was hot. Too hot. In-an-oven
hot. Sweat ran from her pores and evaporated almost
instantaneously. The air was so thick with her body's
moisture she could practically taste herself every time
she breathed.

Outside her coffin, the man—her father—sang
some off-key hymn she didn't care to listen to. She had
stopped talking to him, but then he'd started talking
nonstop about his Lord, or he sang hymns or prayed or
quoted scripture. He obviously wasn't going to let her
die in peace.

Her stomach spasmed. She recognized the feeling.
Hunger. She wrapped her good arm around her middle
to ease the pangs a bit. All her muscles were cramped,
and her joints felt loose-hinged and hard to move. She
knew that feeling too. Dehydration.

She welcomed starvation and dehydration. That
dynamic duo were her new best friends. They were
going to be her salvation.

The line between consciousness and sleep blurred. Isleen lived in that indeterminable in-between space where time lost all meaning. Minutes became hours, hours became days, and days were an endless expanse of forever and always. She forgot a world existed beyond her coffin and the voice constantly talking outside it. She forgot about Gran and Xander. She forgot everything except for pain and suffering and the relentless wish for it to be over.

The overwhelming darkness that had been her constant companion relented, and shapes and shadows formed. Fresh, cool air swept across her skin. She inhaled deeply, taking in the wonderful aroma of growing things and the crisp scent of water. Her sluggish mind took longer than it should have to interpret the message her eyes sent to her brain. The lid of her coffin had been opened. The end—her end—was near.

Overhead, a dainty splinter of moon pierced the pre-dawn sky. A lone bird began to sing a morning song. A beautiful song. A funeral song. It was silly, but she wished she could thank that sweet little bird for its kindness at her last sunrise.

"Behold, the Dragon still lives." The voice boomed through the stillness.

Her heart gave a sad slap against her rib cage. Not because she feared the voice, but because the sudden glaring sound of it had startled her. She was used to her father's low praying and singing.

A murmur of male assent came from all sides of her box. Cloaked figures wearing monk-like hoods looked down on her. Each man wore a large, squared-off cross around his neck. One of them was her father. Dark circles ringed each of his eyes, and his skin sagged from his skull as if he wore a mask of devastation and destruction that was too large for his face.

She almost felt sorry for him. He *had* kept his word and stayed with her—at least every time she was conscious, she heard him outside her coffin. But it seemed traitorous to admit that she'd found comfort in his voice and constant presence.

"Witness the beguiling innocence of the Dragon's form. Do not be fooled by the outward appearance of virtue and purity and weakness. Evil lives in its heart and has devoured its soul. Six days have passed in the summer sun with no food or water and see how it survives? A mortal would've perished."

She stared at her father. His hair was the same color as hers. She recognized herself in his features. How had she not seen it in her dream of him killing Gran?

"No one man can kill it. Brother King has tried. He has since removed the ancestor, suspecting their power may have been linked. So today, together, it will be our sacred duty as the Faithful to end this evil."

"Sounds good to me." Her throat and mouth were gritty as desert sand and no sound came out.

"The first light of dawn is but thirty minutes away. Remove her from the demon box."

She possessed no fear. The only emotion that existed for her was longing for this life to be over. She'd suffered enough.

Her father reached into the coffin, sliding his hands beneath her body and lifting her out. His hold on her was gentle—he even tried to avoid jarring her broken arm—and he held her like a revered possession, cradled close to his chest. She was too weak to move, but if she could have, she just might've hugged him. Just once. Just briefly. And only because she wanted to feel what it would be like to pretend to have a loving father.

He laid her on the ground and smoothed her hair back from where it had caught on her cracked lips. His gaze upon her was tender and sad, and tears welled in his eyes. He arranged her left arm straight out to her side but didn't touch her broken arm. Then he arranged her legs—spreading them obscenely wide.

Were they going to rape her? She couldn't dredge up any horror at the thought. The worst had already happened. Nothing they could do to her would hurt as bad as Xander's death.

A man moved to stand at each of her limbs, and one stood at her head—the Chosen One. Her grandfather. She didn't look at him.

Her father was her right-hand man. Her lips twitched at the pun.

"Lord, we, your Faithful, pray for strength and courage to fulfill our scared duty." Chosen One's voice boomed with authority. "We ask that you bless us and our actions as we wash away this stain of evil with our blood."

The urge to fight and resist flickered inside her, but the flame was too weak to catch.

"Brother King—"

How fitting his name was—King. A perfect match to Queen. She should've seen that one coming.

"—are you faithful to the Lord?"

Morning birds began to sing—one and then another,

then five more—until it seemed hundreds of birds chirped, their choruses uncoordinated and yet soothing and majestic.

Her father swallowed, tears racing down his cheeks. He sniffled and wiped his eyes on the sleeve of his cloak.

It was strange… He was trying to kill her and yet he felt so sad about it. She swallowed, cleared her throat, dug deep to find the energy to speak. "It's okay."

His gaze snapped to hers, searching her face.

She didn't know what he was looking for, what answer he hoped to find. "I want to die."

He turned his attention to Chosen One. "I am faithful to the Lord," he whispered, the words sounding less than confident.

"Demonstrate your faith." Chosen One passed a knife to King. The hilt of it was in the shape of the cross each of them wore.

She watched King, expecting to feel the pressure of the blade against her flesh, but he didn't move toward her.

Instead he sliced a line across his palm, squeezed his hand into a shaking fist, and let his blood weep onto her chest. Each drop against her skin an inferno. Each drop a death knell.

"Thy will be done." King's voice was heavy.

He passed the knife back to Chosen One.

"Brother Bartholomew, are you faithful to the Lord?"

"I am."

Again the knife passed. This time the man sliced his palm without hesitation. She didn't want to watch. She closed her eyes and listened to the birds while blood dripped on her flesh and the knife was passed to the men at her feet.

Her body went cold. So cold. Colors swirled and danced behind her closed eyelids, then faded to dull gray.

"Brothers. Are you faithful enough to endure?"

"We are."

"Bare yourselves to the Lord."

She heard the rustle of fabric from the men around her. Felt the whisper of air as each man dropped his robe. Definitely not opening her eyes now.

"Wash away the stain."

They lifted her by her wrists and ankles, their grip on her slimy and slippery. Her broken arm popped. She heard it but didn't feel it. Her father gasped and dropped her. The other three dragged her. Her back scraped the earth and her head bounced on the ground until her father got hold of her again. This time he lifted her at her shoulder instead of at her wrist. At this point, what did that little kindness matter?

Cold water brushed her backside. The beautiful birds still sang, and water lapped a bank she couldn't see. The men carried her into the water. They adjusted their grip on her, each of them holding her underneath her body— shoulders and buttocks—keeping her afloat.

Her head bobbed on the surface, her ears under- water, taking away the lullaby of birdsong. She opened her eyes. Overhead, giant trees spread their branches out over them, and the sky had lightened to burnished gold.

Chosen One spoke more words, but she couldn't understand them. Water ringed her face. Her entire head was submerged except for her mouth, nose, and eyes. Her gaze found her father's once again. She should hate him for taking part in holding Gran and her captive. She should hate him for killing Xander and Gran. But she couldn't hate him.

It wasn't his fault. Not all of it. He had been brainwashed by Chosen One. And she really was the Dragon, destined to destroy everything she loved. Queen had been right about that. Isleen recognized the truth now.

Chosen One placed his palm across her forehead and pressed down. Water covered her face. She closed her eyes and waited for her body to need its next breath. Her lungs began to burn, and she began to thrash—her body fighting for a life she didn't want.

Chapter 22

THE FIRST THING XANDER NOTICED WAS THE BANGING inside his brain. His smarts center seemed to be bashing itself against his skull with all the vigor of a death-row inmate fighting for a stay of execution. Nausea undulated in his stomach, each slow roll getting closer and closer to coming up. Until it did. He gagged, the sound erupting out of him, part violent groan, part esophagus working backward.

Somebody rolled his body onto its side. Something cool touched the side of his mouth—a puke pan. His stomach made a valiant attempt at coming up his throat. Nothing came out. Not his stomach and not even a dry hint of anything else. Finally, the spasm ended and he rolled onto his back.

His head throbbed. He reached up and felt a thick mass of gauze over his forehead.

He's fucking waking up. Thank you, little baby Jesus. He's waking up. Now you just keep the miracles coming here. I don't want my boy being a stick of celery. I want him exactly the way he's always been. You got me, God? Exactly, like he's always been.

Hearing Row's thoughts didn't hurt, but then his head couldn't hurt any worse than it already did without blowing off his shoulders. The air conditioner hummed, an elevator dinged, and someone was having a conversation about Mr. Needlemeyer needing his catheter reinserted.

A hospital. He was in the hospital. Again. Had he been struck by lightning? No, this time there was no stench of burned, rotting flesh. But exactly like last time—no Dad. Only Row was here with him.

"Row?" His voice didn't sound like his own. It sounded like it belonged to someone weak and helpless. He cracked open an eye. Only one. Didn't want to overload his already angry brain.

Row stood over him, her deeply lined face split wide open with one of those genuine Row smiles that transformed her into an aged beauty. "I'm here. Holy hell balls, I can't believe you're awake. And you know my name."

"Why wouldn't I know your—"

"Do you know your name? Your birthday? Your dad's name?"

"Whoa… Slow up with the questions. My head is fucking killing me."

"Not surprising. Your noggin took a bullet."

Memories exploded in his brain. Vile memories of seeing Isleen with that man, of knowing that he intended to deal the same fate to her as he had to her grandmother. "Isleen!" He shot straight up in bed. An invisible fist punched him repeatedly in the temple, his vision pulsed, and yet he scanned the room for her. "Where is Isleen? Tell me!" He bellowed the words and saw white for a moment.

He heard footsteps—three people—running toward his room. Just let a nurse, a doctor, or a rent-a-cop try to calm him down.

"Don't you use that tone with me, boy." Row jammed a knobby finger at him, the expression on her face fierce enough to make him feel ten years old again.

His room door burst open. Dad, Matt, and Kent crammed into the opening like some bizarrely modern version of the Three Stooges until his dad broke free, unclogging the dam, and they all practically tumbled into the room.

Hooollly fuuuck. He's alive.

Holy shit.

I knew it. I knew they were connected.

Xander's ears jammed with the thoughts from all three men. His already maxed-out brain went into the red zone, threatening a nuclear meltdown. He pushed his fingers into his ears, though that wouldn't do much good. Another reason on the list of reasons to get her back: she made him normal.

Dad stepped up to him, bending down to peer into Xander's eyes. "What's my name? When's my birthday? Do you know—"

"Quit with the fifty questions. I'm not brain damaged." Though he wasn't so sure if that was accurate. He unplugged his ears and tried for a calmer tone, not because he felt calmer, but because his brain might blow to bits if he yelled again. "Where's Isleen?" He swung his legs over the side of the bed, the hospital smock riding high on his thighs. "Somebody better tell me where Isleen is, or somebody—probably all of you—is going to get hurt. And I need some goddamned clothes."

Row jumped to action, but the three guys just stood there.

He's going to go apeshit, batshit, and shit storm when he finds out. Matt's thoughts were loud inside Xander's head.

"When I find out what?"

Row handed him a pair of jeans and a T-shirt.

Kent cleared his throat. "She's gone. No trace. We brought in scent hounds. They led us a few miles away, but then the trail died. We brought in a chopper to get the eagle's-eye view, but nothing. Yesterday, we brought in Lathan, that local consultant the FBI keeps under wraps. Nothing. He said the trail was too old. She just vanished. No one saw anything—except you, and you weren't talking. The only thing we had was a weird gold cross found at the scene. Prints not in the system."

"She didn't vanish. He took her." Xander stuffed a leg into the jeans.

"Who?" Everyone asked the question at the same time.

"The man who killed Gale. He's some Jesus freak or something. I heard him reciting verses when I found them." He jammed his other leg in the pants and stood to pull them up. The world wavered and wobbled. Row—tiny Row—grabbed him by the waist to steady him and pushed him gently back to sit on the bed.

"I can have a sketch artist here in thirty minutes." Kent pulled his phone from his pocket.

"No time for that. I found her once. I'll be able to find her again." At least he hoped he would.

Oh shit. He doesn't know. Kent looked at Alex, then at Matt with a someone-help-me-here expression, but Xander's family was famous for not lending assistance. "I never should've taken her from the house. She was safe there. I should've just put more guards on her, instead of letting my hatred of your ass cloud my judgment." Kent's face went stop-sign red with anger, shame, and self-loathing. "Xander, it's been…too long."

"Too long?" He shoved his arms through the shirt-sleeves. His body was weak and his head felt atomic, but needing to find Isleen put things in perspective. He could deal with feeling weak and being in pain, but he couldn't live without her.

"It's been a week." Kent's tone was flat and full of regret.

Xander's stomach fell until it was lodged somewhere near his ankles. Icy hands of dread choked off his air supply. His arms, stuffed into the sleeves, dropped to his chest. His head fell forward, and he squeezed his eyes shut. "A week? Are you sure?"

"Xan—" His father moved up next to him. "You were shot in the head. In a coma. We thought you were gone." He swallowed, reached out, and touched the bandage on Xander's head. "We pulled the plug on you yesterday."

Xander's head shot up, his gaze locking with his father's.

"But you didn't die. You just kept on…" Dad's eyes went wet. "I'm so glad I get this second chance with you." Dad hugged him, a fierce man hug that nearly made Xander feel like a kid again. Row stepped up to them, and Xander wrapped an arm around her too. She reached out to Matt, dragging him into their hug fest. Matt grabbed Kent and shoved him into the mix, until they all surrounded Xander in one big, sissy ball of emotion that actually felt kinda damned nice. "Now finish getting dressed. If you're still alive, that means she's still alive, and we're all going to help you find her."

His estrogen level had to be weirdly high because tears burned in his eyes. He blinked them back, swallowed, and then still couldn't speak, so he nodded.

Their group hug broke apart.

"Tell me what you need. Law enforcement will

cooperate. We're searching for a murderer who's abducted Isleen."

What did he need? The answer came to him in the form of instinct rather than thought. "I need to go to Prospectus County. I need to go to the torture trailer."

—◦◦◦—

Red sky at morning, take warning. Xander didn't remember where he'd heard the phrase, but it felt appropriate.

The rising dawn hurled bloody smears of cloud across the sky, casting everything in an eerie crimson glow. Kent drove them through the endless fields of corn and beans that seemed to swallow the entire world. It all seemed so bizarre, but it was real.

Xander's brain thumped in percussive blasts that jerked his head and rattled his vision. He felt hot and cold at the same time—fucking miserable. The constant whir of the car's engine and the buzz of tires against asphalt—added to every man's heartbeat, every suck and whoosh of their breath—frayed Xander's already shredded nerves and combined to make it all sharply real.

He craved quietude the way an addict craved their next fix. Actually, he craved Isleen. She gave him silence and peace. At least Kent, Dad, and Matt had done very well at playing the silent game. Xander wouldn't have survived the three-hour drive if he'd had to listen to everyone talking and to their thoughts too.

The car bounced and rocked over the cheaply paved country road. In the distance a sign became visible— white with green letters that he couldn't read until they were right on top of it.

ENTERING PROSPECTUS COUNTY

Kent pointed at the post. "We'll be at the trailer in about ten minutes." *Why would Isleen's abductor take her back to the trailer? If he did, it'd be an episode for the World's Stupidest Criminals show.*

Xander's head pounded too hard to feel the pain of the frequency connection. "She's not going to be at the trailer, asshole." He spoke through clenched teeth, the anger in his tone sounding deadly. Only he wasn't angry at Kent. Yeah, the guy had driven her away from him, but Xander had let her go because that's what *she* wanted. Was he angry with Isleen? No. Yes. Maybe. He didn't have time or brain space to ponder it right now. He just needed to get her back. "Sorry. I'm the asshole. I just need to go there. It's somehow connected to the man who took her."

Kent glanced back and forth between Xander and the road, fucking pity in his eyes. "You okay? You're shivering and sweating." *Never seen him like this.*

"No, I'm not okay. I'm not going to be okay until Isleen is safe."

Kent nodded. "You should know this: The plot of land the trailer sits on doesn't exist. The county records show it as part of the farm, but the farmer said the land has been in his family for over a hundred years, and there's always been a dwelling of some sort—not owned by him—on it. Another dead end."

"You look into the farmer?" Xander remembered the picture of the guy from the news. He'd looked like an overgrown child.

"Yeah, we looked into him. Dug as deep as we could go. The guy's got farming smarts, but that's the beginning and end of his intellect. I can't imagine he'd have anything to do with this." *All you'd need is one conversation with the guy, and you'd understand.*

"How could a plot of land with a trailer on it—the electric, septic, gas—get past the township, the county, the government?" Matt asked from the backseat.

"There was no electric. We found a kerosene heater. No running water. The place was completely off grid. We suspect someone—possibly in the local government—has been falsifying and erasing records and greasing the right palms to keep the land and dwelling off the records. Our investigation turned up no one suspicious." *No leads. Not one. Nowhere to look. Not even a direction to go. We're not going to find her.*

"I don't need your negativity right now. I've got enough of my own. I already know this is fucking impossible. I already know…" His voice cracked, and he couldn't speak beyond the lump of dread in his throat. At minimum she'd spent the past week captive and scared. That thought was bad enough. He didn't dare let himself think of the millions of other things that could've been done to her when she'd already been through so much. And what if he couldn't find her?

The thought punched him in the throat, cutting off his oxygen and filling him with bone-deep fear.

He's going over the edge. This is gonna get ugly. Glad I'm in the backseat. Matt's thoughts weren't exactly helpful, but they provided enough motivation for Xander to drop-kick the worst of his fears out of his mind. If he was going to go all cracked nut, he'd do it later. After this was over.

"Listen. My head is throbbing. I feel like dog shit. I can't concentrate with everyone talking and having to listen to the thoughts. But I'm not going over the damned edge. Not yet anyway."

Dad scooted forward and placed his hand on Xander's shoulder. His grip was firm and fatherly, and goddamned if Xander didn't almost melt. He wanted his dad to solve it all. Wanted him to fix it and make it all better. But he wasn't a little boy anymore, and his father couldn't fix this one.

"Xan, you can find her…" *I wish I could tell you how. I wish I could offer you some guidance, but the link isn't something that can be found with words or directions. It's something inside you.* "…the same way you found her before."

The brain itch. The restlessness. Only his head hurt too bad to feel anything other than pain. And his body was too spent to feel restless.

He closed his eyes and thought back to the story of Fearless and Bear. Bear had called Fearless back from the ancestors by touching her and chanting her name. He couldn't touch Isleen, but he could call to her. Maybe she'd answer. Yes. Maybe like before, he'd hear her inside his head.

Isleen. Isleen. Isleen. Her name was an incantation, a spell, begging her to hear him, to respond, to help him find her. *Isleen. Isleen. Isleen.* He thought back to his best memories of her. Being inside her and knowing she was his. Watching her stand up to Camille. That ornery smile she so rarely showed. *Isleen. Isleen. Isleen.* He called to her, pleaded with her to answer…

Nothing happened. Not one goddamned thing. Tears burned in his sinuses and threatened to leak from his closed eyes. His breathing went shaky—hell, his whole body trembled. He wrapped his arms around himself to keep from rattling apart. He rocked in his seat like a nutjob. Okay, now he was going over the edge.

Everything went blessedly quiet.

No more engine humming, no more tires on the pavement. No more heartbeats from the men in the car. No more whoosh and suck of lungs working. His ears just stopped working. His muscles unclenched, and he melted against the seat. His mind went blessedly blank. He bobbed on a wave of nothingness. It fucking felt wonderful.

And then he remembered: The day he'd found Isleen, there'd been a blast of perfect silence too.

"Stop the car!" The absolute quiet vanished. In its place was control. Control of his hearing.

Kent slammed the brakes. Tires screeched against the pavement. Momentum pushed Xander against his seat belt. He braced his hand against the dashboard until the car stopped moving, then was out the door searching the landscape.

Cornfields on all sides except one. On his right was a bean field, and a mile beyond that, a snaking line of trees. A fencerow? A creek? Didn't matter what it was. His body hummed, pulled him in that direction like a magnet seeking its mate. "There." He pointed straight across the field at the trees. "She's there."

Only a minute ago, Xander's head had felt on the verge of exploding, his body spent, but all that had vanished. What remained was anticipation and worry and restrained rage that she'd been taken from him.

The guys all stood by their open car doors staring at him.

"That worked?" Kent didn't bother to hide his skepticism. "As in, really worked? Like she's really across the field? How could you know that?"

"It's their connection," Dad answered for him. "There is a bond between them that defies definition."

"Jesus." Matt's tone wasn't merely doubting; it was downright pissy sounding. "Here we go again—you and your mystical connection shit."

Kent ducked inside the car and got a pair of binoculars from the glove box. He looked down the road in front of them, then down the road behind them. "I don't see a way to get over to those trees. The closest road was a few miles back, meaning we'd end up backtracking, and even then I'm not sure we'd be able to get to that specific chunk of trees. I don't see any road turning off in front of us either."

"I saw a shortcut. Everyone get in." Xander rounded the hood of the car, heading for the driver's seat. Kent wasn't going to like his shortcut, but the guy could go fuck himself.

"You saw a road back there?" Kent got in the passenger seat. "I don't see anything, and I don't remember—"

Xander pedal-to-the-metaled it before they'd even closed their car doors. The engine roared and they shot forward. He cranked the wheel to the right. They slid, bounced, and plowed into the bean field.

"What are you doing?" Kent shouted.

"The shortest distance between two points is a straight line."

The car fishtailed in the soft dirt, and he wrangled with the wheel until the tires found traction. And then they were sailing through a field of beans.

Kent had more to say, but his voice was drowned underneath the leafy green stalks slapping the car, sounding like a hundred pairs of shoes tumbling around a dryer. The noise sent Xander back to the day he'd found Isleen and that bitch driving his truck through the field. Here he was, about to find Isleen again.

He'd learned a lesson. Isleen wasn't going any farther than arm's length away from him. If he had to cuff her to him, he fucking would.

Dead ahead, the line of trees meandered through the landscape, the trees' heights contrasting sharply with the fields surrounding them. A quaint gravel road ran alongside the wood line. He hadn't seen that little lane until just now.

"You see that road?" he asked Kent.

In dawn's bittersweet light, it all appeared to be a picturesque scene. Something he'd expect to see on a calendar or a postcard. But there was something intangible— maybe the way the trees clawed toward the sky, maybe simple bad juju—that made the place bizarrely unappealing. A shiver ripped through Xander's entire body.

"There are cars parked among the trees." Kent pointed. "I count…five. Shit. Best-case scenario, five men. Worst case, if every car was full, twenty-five." Kent pulled his cell off the clip on his pants and hit a button. "This is Kent Knight with the BCI, badge number 5487, requesting backup and a bus to my current location." He ended the call without giving them any more information. "This is one of those better-to-ask-forgiveness-than-permission situations."

"Yep. I know the feeling." Xander was actually starting to like the guy.

"We don't want to go in asses flapping in the wind, outnumbered and outgunned. So I need you all to listen to me. When I tell you to do something, do it. Don't fucking question me. We're going to pray like monks no one hears us coming. Pull out of the field over there." Kent pointed to an area just past the last parked car. "And then we're going to hang back, evaluate the situation, and proceed accordingly. Everyone down with the plan?"

Dad and Matt voiced agreement. Xander mumbled something that could pass for yea or nay. Fuck Kent's plan. Xander had a plan of his own. Get to Isleen. Period. The end.

Kent kept talking, kept giving orders, but Xander tuned him out. All his attention zeroed in on a point through the trees. Her location. What had she been through this past week? Beatings and starvation like before? Or this time had things been worse? Nightmarish images from every horror movie he'd ever watched flashed through his mind. He clutched the steering wheel so hard he wouldn't have been surprised if it snapped in half.

Stop it. Stop thinking that way. No matter what she'd been through, she was alive. She'd only been gone a week. Not the years she'd endured before. This couldn't be as bad. It couldn't. His heart didn't believe the lies his brain was trying to sell.

Even though they didn't have to travel more than a mile across the field, it felt like a small bit of forever until Xander let off the gas and pulled the car onto the gravel road next to the tree line. He rammed the car into park and then bolted from his seat, ignoring Kent's loud whispers for him to stop. What was the guy going to do? Shoot him? Not likely.

A pathway opened off the road, so he darted onto it and found himself sprinting through a serene copse of trees. The sun shot beams of light through the leaves, casting a warm golden glow over everything. Birds sang chipper songs. He heard the rush, gurgle, and slosh of water. He smelled moist earth, river water, and the terrible tang of blood.

Through the screen of trees, he saw everything. Its magnitude and severity so much worse than anything his imagination could have conjured up.

Chapter 23

TIME BROKE, GIVING XANDER'S MIND SPACE TO TAKE IT all in. Memorize it. Relive the horror of it in his nightmares for the rest of his life.

A coffin-shaped box of black metal on the shore, lid open. She had been kept inside that steel prison. Beyond the box, sunshine dappled the water, casting a pink gossamer shimmer over Isleen's drowning body.

Four naked men held her. A fifth man cruelly shoved her face under the water.

Xander's stomach collided with his heart. Something inside him popped, the feeling similar to a pressure release, like the cork on his sanity had just blown. He stumbled and nearly went down, but caught himself and kept running toward her.

"Iisslleen!" He howled her name, the sound somewhere between wounded animal and feral dog.

The man with his hand over Isleen's face lifted his gaze. His eyes were cold and lacking a conscience. He raised a large knife in the air and still held her under the water. A ray of sun glinted off the bloody blade. "I command you to stop, or I will slay the Dragon with my sacred sword."

Every cell inside him screamed to keep going. But he wouldn't make it to her in time to prevent that knife from piercing her flesh.

He stopped, his feet sliding in the soft mud at the

river's edge. "You touch her with that blade, and there will be blood. I'll make all of you bleed." He made eye contact with every goddamned one of them. Even the man who took her. Xander paused. In the morning light the man looked...fucking familiar.

The man nodded at him as if they'd just reached a private agreement. "Save her!" he yelled and then tackled the knife guy.

What the... He didn't have time to question. Needed to save Isleen, and he'd just been given the perfect opportunity.

Every ounce of worry, guilt, terror, and anger distilled into one primal emotion—rage. A white sheen slid over his vision. An electric zing slid from the top of his head down to the tips of his big toes. His skin prickled and twitched—the Bastard in His Brain. This time Xander didn't fight him. Instead, he unclipped the leash.

Go and destroy.

One moment Xander was on the bank, and the next he was in the river drawing back his arm. Fist connected with nose. Cartilage crunched. Blood gushed. The man screamed a sissy-girl sound and flew back into the water.

Xander felt a malicious smile twist his lips. That had felt fucking fine.

One down.

He turned on the next man. The pussy raised his hand to block his face.

"Lotta good that's going to do." Xander served a thumper into the man's stomach so hard his knuckles brushed spine. The man's mouth formed a wide-open *O*, but he didn't make a sound.

Two down.

The last man let go of Isleen. Xander grabbed her

limp body, pressing her against his side with one hand
and keeping his other hand free. A quick jolt of cool
healing passed from his body into hers.

The man clasped his hands in front of him as if in
prayer. "Lord protect me."

"The Lord ain't here, asshole." Xander lunged forward and kicked. His foot slammed into the man's
exposed testicles. The soft give of flesh and the soprano
scream satisfied something in Xander's soul. It was
gonna take a surgeon to remove the man's stones from
his ass cavity.

In the shallows, the two other men continued to fight
over the knife. *Let 'em fucking kill each other.*

Not ten seconds had passed from the moment he'd
hit the water to the moment he emerged with Isleen.
Pale blue tinged her skin and lips. She'd lost weight,
her bones protruding nearly as sharply as they had
when he'd found her at the torture trailer. "I've got you.
Everything's going to be all right."

He laid Isleen on the bank, just as Kent, Matt, and
Dad ran up. Xander didn't give two shits about anything
except her.

He bent close, placing his ear against her chest.
Nothing. No. Couldn't be nothing. She had to be alive.
He was alive. She *had* to be alive. That was the rule,
right? And then he heard her heart and lungs—so quiet
they were like the whisper of butterfly wings. "Come on,
baby. Wake up for me."

He placed one hand over her heart and cupped her
cheek with the other one. A soothing coolness began
where his palms touched her and spread up his hand,
arm, shoulder, and then throughout his body. The

sensation began to sting and itch—so weirdly satisfying and pleasant. He was healing her.

"Xan—" Dad crouched down next to him. "Will you let me check her over? Do what I can for her? It might help in some way."

"Okay." It was the only word he could manage. The sensations in his body overwhelmed his speech center.

Dad picked up her wrist to try for a pulse, but froze. "This arm is broken." His tone was graveyard somber. "I need to immobilize it."

Xander felt like he was falling, flopping, and flailing through an endless abyss. He couldn't get air into his lungs; he couldn't feel his heart beating. A part of himself was dying. Seeing her like this, knowing that those men had kept her locked in a box and broken her arm.

He ripped his shirt over his head, tossed it to Dad, then placed his hands back on her. "Do something about her arm."

Dad made a crude but stable splint using the material and a few sticks.

"Baby, come on. Wake up for me. You're safe now. I've got you." He kept talking, going over and over some version of the same words. She was breathing more normally, her color better, but she hadn't awakened. Yet.

"Xander." Matt laid a hand on Xander's back. "I think you need to let the experts take over."

"She needs *me*." He didn't have the energy to explain—again—the connection he and Isleen shared.

"It's been thirty minutes."

Matt's words were a stop sign smacked upside Xander's head. He froze. Lifted his gaze, looked around for the first time. "What?" It seemed only minutes had passed. Cops were everywhere. The naked men all lay on their stomachs, hands cuffed behind their backs. Two paramedics stood off to the side, a gurney next to them.

"Xan—let them have her." His uncle's voice was filled with compassion. "They'll take care of her. You can even ride with her to the hospital."

"You don't understand. Isleen needs me. She doesn't need doctors or the hospital. She needs me." He recognized how his words had to sound to everyone else. He just knew something they didn't know and wouldn't understand. "They're not taking her. You're not taking her. No one is taking her."

Everyone on the scene paused and looked at him. Pity, sympathy, and sorrow on all their faces.

"What are you all looking at? She's going to be all right. She just needs time!" He yelled the words like a deranged psycho.

Some of them looked away, and some shook their heads. Some of the cops put their hands on their service weapons as if Xander were on the verge of needing to be taken down. "Fuck you!" he shouted. "Fuck you all." He gathered Isleen into his arms and stood. "Dad—" He spoke soft so only his father could hear him. "You've been a shit father. Haven't done a goddamned thing for me since the moment Gale left. And hey, I get it. But I need something from you right now. You have to keep everyone away."

"I'll make sure you have all the time you need." Dad turned to the crowd of people who stared at them. "I'm a doctor. Her vitals are stable, and I've field-dressed her injury."

Xander walked away, headed toward the river, and

followed a short path to a colossal sycamore. The tree was something from an epic movie. Its trunk immense, branches fanning out in all directions—some toward the water, some toward the sky, some dipping down offering shelter. Its bark was mottled white and tan. Giant gnarled roots hunched out of the ground. He settled in between those roots, the tree cradling him in the same way he cradled Isleen.

He shifted her around in his arms so she sat between his legs, her back against his chest. He wrapped his arms around her, hugging her tightly to him. The tingle and itch of healing pulsed through him. She was getting better. He could feel it. It was only a matter of *when* she'd wake up.

He rested his head against the top of hers. Her hair had dried and smelled of river and algae.

In front of them, the water swirled and eddied, slapping and rippling against the shore. A blue heron descended from the sky like a miniature flying dinosaur and landed in the shallows. The bird stalked through the water, his head tilting side to side, looking for a meal. Water bugs darted and glided over the surface like skiers on a slope.

She would wake up soon. She had to.

Unless she didn't *want* to wake up. After everything she'd been through, why would she seek out this life with all its pain? She'd been offered nothing but shit. Imprisoned in that torture trailer for years. Locked in that box. Starved. There had been five naked men. Five. Had they taken turns? Passed her from one to the other?

His mind conjured up horrors his heart couldn't take. His throat kicked open and he leaned away from her to gag, but a sob came out instead. His eyes stung; his vision went watery. Warmth sprinted down his cheeks. Tears. Fucking damn. He didn't cry. Hadn't cried when Gale left, when Dad rejected him, when he'd been struck by lightning, when he'd nearly gone crazy from all the noise. But this—confronting what she'd been through—hurt like a heart amputation.

He held her tight, buried his face in her neck, and wept.

He cried for everything she'd endured. She was so petite, so fragile, and yet she'd been forced to grow a steel spine. The worst she had suffered had only temporarily bent her, never breaking her. But even the strongest metal fractured after too much pressure. Was this her breaking point?

"If I could, I'd endure all your pain. Take it on myself." He spoke between sobs, his words rushed and running together. "Willingly. Gladly. I never want you to be hurt, in pain, or suffering. I want to give you happiness and joy. I want to see you smile and hear you laugh."

He started rocking—forward and back—with her. He was goddamned losing his shit and couldn't help it. "There's so much you've missed out on. So much I want to give you, so much I want to show you." Everything in his mind gushed out of him in a torrent of longing. "There's a pond on the property where I used to swim as a kid. The fish would nibble my toes, and it felt so strange and funny at the same time. I know you'd love it.

"I want to show you Fearless and Bear's totem. I want to take you to see the fireworks on the Fourth of July. I want to spend Thanksgiving with you, eating and lounging on the couch watching football all day. I want to see you playing in the snow. I want to see you by the light of our Christmas tree. I just want you in my life. I want you happy."

He cried until he had nothing left inside, and then he clung to her until he felt strong enough to lift his head from her neck.

Across the river, on the opposite shore, stood a doe and her speckled fawn. They froze as if sensing Xander watching them. The doe's ears flicked, searching for a warning sound, while the fawn bent to the water and drank.

"I wish you could see this. They're so beautiful," he whispered, his voice hollow. Probably because he felt like his heart had been removed from his body.

"They are beautiful." Her words were a breath of sound.

His empty chest bloomed a wild bouquet of hope and joy. He couldn't speak, couldn't move, just joined her in watching the deer on the opposite shore.

When they disappeared into the brush, she shifted against him, turning to see his face. "Am I dreaming?" She reached up, winced from the movement, and put her hand over his mouth. "No, don't tell me. I don't want to know."

That was the first thing she'd said to him when he found her in the torture trailer. Did she believe good things could only happen in her dreams? The goddamned spigot behind his eyes opened, clouding his vision of her.

He gently tugged her hand from his mouth. "This is real. I'm real. You're real." He scrubbed a hand over his eyes, not wanting tears to obscure his vision of her.

She moved her hand to his forehead, her face

flickering in pain from the movement. She brushed his hair back to see the puckered scab. "I didn't think I'd ever see you again. I thought you were dead."

"I would've been if it hadn't been for you."

Emotions and memories blazed in her eyes, but they passed so quickly he couldn't grasp them.

"How bad do you hurt?"

"I feel like I've been hit by an ocean liner and have the flu." A barely perceptible smile tipped the edges of her lips. "I've been worse."

He wanted to ask her more, but couldn't find the words and wasn't certain he'd be able to handle what she had to say.

"Hey, I'm okay. Really." She must've seen the concern on his face. "Nothing some sleep, some food, and some time with you won't heal." She sounded sincere. She looked sincere. But something wasn't right.

He should be happy she'd survived relatively unscathed. But that itself was the problem. No one could go through what she'd been through and not be affected. He'd never been a poster boy for mental wellness, but he did know she should be reacting to what she'd been through. Hell, it hadn't even happened to him and he had reacted all over the place.

Was this what denial looked like? Could it masquerade as sanity?

"They need time alone." Dad's voice carried from the opening of the path that led to the sycamore.

"He can't deny her medical care." Kent was using his asshole voice. The guy might've toned down his asshole vibe for the ride here, but he was back to full power again.

Isleen could hear them arguing too. They weren't using their indoor voices.

"One of the nudes over there said they kept her in that box for six days. No food. No water. I'm not a fancy-ass doctor like you, but she needs medical care."

"She's going to be fine."

"Excuse me if I don't take your word for it."

Bring it on. Xander had reached full capacity on Kent questioning every goddamned thing he did. He stood, gently pulling Isleen up with him. She swayed on her feet and he wrapped an arm around her waist, tucking her in to him.

Kent rounded their tree—funny how Xander thought of it as *their* tree. The guy stopped, his gaze raking over Isleen. Taking in her splinted arm and the fact that she was actually on her feet.

"Kent, I'm okay." Her voice sounded light and airy. "I'm just tired and don't feel the greatest, but I'm good." She sounded too chipper, like she'd just gotten over a cold, not been kidnapped and tortured.

"Jesus Christ." Kent's head wobbled on his shoulders. "You should be..."

"It's their connection." Dad moved in front of Isleen to look into her eyes. He reached out, pressed up one of her eyelids, and looked close. "I don't get why you and Matt refuse to believe what's in front of you." He checked her other eye. "Well, young lady, unless you prefer to go to the hospital, we can take care of all your injuries back home. The Institute is a fully equipped medical facility."

"I want to go home. But I need to..." Her voice trailed off, the false brightness in her tone flickering and fading.

"Baby, what do you need?" Whatever it was, Xander would find a way to give it to her.

"Kent…" She aimed her attention at the guy but said nothing else.

"What is it?" Kent asked.

Xander could see the guy would do just about anything to make her happy. Same as him. That was part of their problem—Kent was pissed because Isleen kept him in the friend zone.

She pressed herself against Xander. He could hear her heart galloping, her breathing wild. Whatever the fuck she was about to say upset her. He tightened his arm around her, offering her his own solid strength.

"Well…my mom…" Isleen's voice dissolved.

"Shayla." Dad said the name, expectancy dominating his tone.

"Yeah." Isleen nodded. "She…died. They killed her. The same way they were trying to kill me. My father said he buried her nearby. Underneath the largest sycamore tree. He said Gran condoned him taking us and letting Queen torture us to get the evil out. That she was trying to save us—me—from the same fate as my mom."

Her words were a grenade. The explosion of them sending shards of thought through his mind. *Her mom. Her father. Her father killed her mom. Buried her. Largest sycamore tree.*

"Fffuuuucccckkk…" He looked up at the tree they all stood under. Glanced around. No mistaking they were standing near the grave.

"Not Shayla too." Dad began shaking his head as if the action could dodge the words, keep them from sinking home.

"Your father? What… Who…" Xander didn't even know what he was trying to ask. He knew less than zip about her father. It'd just never come up. A lot of things hadn't come up. But this—this was big shit.

"The man who took Gran and me. The man who ordered Queen to keep us captive. The man who killed Gran, who shot you…" The silence drew out, skating on the edge of a blade. "He's my father."

Her words were a shock wave of sound, nearly knocking him back a step.

And yet, Xander had known. Not in the conscious part of his mind, but somewhere underneath he'd known the moment he'd made eye contact with the guy. A piece of him wanted to deny that the truth—not for himself, but for what the truth meant to her. Her own father had killed her mother, killed her grandmother, forced a life of torture on his daughter, and then had tried to kill her too.

"Baby…" He didn't know what else to say. No words were going to make that okay. Dad's eyes were bloodshot and brimming. Kent stood there like a metal post in the middle of a storm. Both men had apparently gone mute.

"It's okay. I'm okay. Really." Her words came out too rushed. "I know I should hate him. But I don't."

Her eyes were wide and full of… Xander tried to name the emotion, but couldn't quite find it. Then it hit him. Her eyes were full of empathy. Empathy. For the man who'd tried to kill her. "What the hell?"

"He stayed with me. Never left the entire time I was in that box. He told me how sorry he was, how he didn't want me to die, but that Chosen One demanded it and he couldn't defy Chosen One because he's my grandfather. See? He's not all bad. Not all of him."

Xander had heard every word she spoke; his mind just wanted to reject them. How could those words pass her lips? Her father had stolen her life when he placed her in that trailer. Murdered her mother and grandmother. Attempted to murder Xander. Participated in trying to kill her today—would've succeeded if she and Xander didn't have a special connection. Yeah, her father had provided Xander the opportunity to save her, but only after she should've already been dead.

"Who you trying to convince? Me or yourself?" He hadn't meant to say it so harshly.

"You don't understand. He—"

"I do understand." He tightened his hold on her and stared into her eyes. "An evil man eased your torture, and you think that was kindness when it was still torture."

Isleen flinched as if he slapped her. Shit. What was going on with his mouth? He couldn't control what decided to shoot out of his lips.

"He's not like the others. He didn't *want* to do any of the things he did. Chosen One made him."

"Baby." Xander softened his tone. He didn't want to hurt her. Christ, she'd been hurt enough, but the way she was thinking about this was an infection— one he needed to scrape off of her. He wouldn't let her father infect her mind. The man had hurt her body, left her with wounds that would scar over and be constant reminders of what she endured. But Xander refused to let that man stay inside her head. "He *killed* your grandmother. He *shot* me—Chosen One didn't force him to pull that trigger. Your father held you, *let* Chosen One force your face under water. And they were all naked." His volume rose, couldn't help it.

"What did he let all those naked men do to you? What did he do to his daughter?"

"Xander." Kent said his name as if he were about to draw his gun on him. "That's enough."

But he wasn't done. He had to finish lancing her mental wounds. "We're standing on a grave. Your. Mother's. Grave." He pointed at the tree. "Where your father buried her. How can you possibly think he's got an ounce of goodness in him?"

Isleen shoved away from him. Her eyes were misty and murky, bad memories swimming in their depths. And if he cared to be completely honest, he saw a bit of betrayal in her gaze. She'd thought he'd be on her side. But he couldn't be. Not about this. He needed to rip every trace of that asshole out of her mind.

Her chin trembled, and the first of her tears cleansed a path down her cheeks. She stumbled. He reached out to her, but she held her hand up to ward him off. Didn't matter what she wanted. What mattered was what she needed. And she needed him. He grabbed her, pulled her to him. She beat her fist against his chest, two hard thumps of anger, of resistance, and then she sagged against him, sobbing against his heart. The sound cut him to the bone, but crying was good. It meant she was feeling this. Not hiding from it. And not trying to put a shine on the shit.

She was going to be all right.

Chapter 24

ISLEEN STOOD OUTSIDE THE CLOSED INTERROGATION room. Xander's arm was around her, pressing her to his side. She could feel the tension and anxiety in his muscles. He didn't agree with what she was about to do.

"We shouldn't be apart. Bad things happen when I'm not with you." Xander's grip on her tightened. She knew he was thinking about the night she drove away from him and everything that happened after. She was thinking about that too. But she needed to see her father. And she wanted to do it alone.

Kent walked out of the interrogation room, shutting the door firmly behind him. "He's ready. I've got him chained to the table and practically bolted to the floor."

"Thanks, Kent. I appreciate you making this happen." She tried for a reassuring smile to ease the frown he wore on his face. Xander wore an identical expression.

"You don't have to do this. Kent can handle it." Concern crinkled Xander's forehead.

"Yeah. No problem. Just let me take care of it." Kent jumped in, so quick to agree with Xander. "You don't need to deal with him, especially with what you've got going on later."

Later she had a funeral. Her mother's funeral. The coroner had finally released the body, and they were going to have a sunset service. Somehow the funeral tonight made her want to do this all the more. It sorta brought things full circle—if the circle was a misshapen blob. Doing this—meeting with her father one final time—was part of taking back her life and owning her fate. "I will do it."

She went up on tiptoe and kissed Xander's chin. "Don't worry. I'll be fine. He can't hurt me, and there's nothing he can say that he hasn't already said to me."

"I'll promise you one thing." Kent spoke to Xander. "He pulls any shit, and he's gonna have an accident." Kent's tone was dead serious.

"Baby, I'll be right here. One fucking step away, listening to everything. He hurts you—I'll fucking kill him." Fury dominated Xander's tone. She suspected if he got within arm's reach of her father, he'd try to kill the man. Xander bore his own set of wounds over what had happened.

"I'll just be a few minutes." She sucked in a giant breath, stepped away from Xander, and opened the door. Her legs were numb as she walked in the room and closed the door. The space smelled like a boys' locker room—dirty clothing, old sweat, and guilt. Her father sat, hands cuffed to the table, his head bowed as if in prayer. He didn't look up.

His hair was the same pale shade as hers. From his profile she could see the shape of her own nose and lips, see the similarities in the way their brows arched. After all these years, it was odd seeing her features on another human being.

She didn't mean for it to happen, but tears came to her eyes. One of the aftereffects of everything she'd been through was those dratted tears. They flowed when happy, when sad, when she saw something beautiful, when she felt safe. It was just one of those strange things about her. She decided to embrace it instead of fighting it.

Her father lifted his head. His eyes widened. He gasped and tried to stand, but the cuffs kept him locked to the table. "Isleen…" His gaze locked on her tears.

"Don't think these tears are for you. They're not." She moved further into the room and sat in the hard plastic chair across from him, meeting him stare for stare. "They're for what might've been. For all the ways our future could've played out but didn't. For all the possibilities that died when you killed my mom."

"I—"

"Don't." Her voice was a strong pop of sound. She held up her hand, halting whatever he'd been about to say, then wiped the wetness from her face. "I didn't come here to have a conversation with you. I came here to make you listen." Her tone was unyielding, the words themselves offering her power. "You've taken from me, but that stops right now. It doesn't matter if Gran condoned our treatment at Queen's hand. What matters is that I *know* Gran loved me. And I won't let you steal that from me.

"You will never be anything to me other than the man who kidnapped me and commanded Queen to torture me all those years. You are a coward for not saving your wife from that box, and something lower than a coward for not saving your daughter. Forever you will just be someone who hurt me. Never my father. After I walk out that door, don't ever try to contact me. I want you to forget that I exist because that's what I'm going to do. Forget you."

She stood up. Stared down at him. His chin trembled—Just like hers always did. Tears slicked his cheeks, but he didn't say anything. Silence was his only gift to her.

As satisfying as it had been to speak her words, there was one last thing she needed to say to him—the entire reason for her visit. "You decided to believe Gran and I were evil because of our abilities. You are wrong. Last night I had a dream. This afternoon, an inmate will be placed in the cell next to yours. He's going to have red hair and an eye tattooed on his cheek. He's going to ask you to come closer to the bars to pray with him, and then he's going to stab you in the neck with a sharpened plastic knife. You'll die. That was my dream. So you see, this thing you always thought was so evil about me… I use it to save lives. Even yours."

His face morphed through a menagerie of emotions, stopping finally when his features crumpled and he began sobbing. He looked directly at her while he cried, not even bothering with the dignity of trying to hide his emotions.

She turned and walked from the room.

Epilogue

IT PROBABLY MADE HER A BAD PERSON, BUT ISLEEN couldn't help it—she didn't want to go to her own mother's funeral. In so many ways it would be like attending the funeral of a stranger. The sun dipped behind the tree line, kissing the forest with a warm golden glow as she and Xander made their way up Cemetery Hill. Xander squeezed her hand, the simple gesture conveying so many emotions—strength and reassurance and concern. He worried too much about her. Not that she blamed him. After everything they'd been through, it was understandable. Only time would ease his mind.

The graveyard was old, the stones mere white slabs, names long ago worn off by wind and weather. The clearing where it rested was peaceful and quiet and filled with a serenity she hadn't noticed the last time she'd been here, but then she hadn't exactly been in a sane frame of mind.

Her gaze found Gran's grave. Isleen braced for an emotional blow at being in this place again, being reminded of everything that came before, but only soft sorrow caressed her.

A new mound of fresh dirt resided next to Gran's grave. Her mother's grave had already been filled in. No empty hole. No coffin. No glaring reminder of death.

Next to the two fresh graves, a large red-and-white-checked blanket was spread on the ground. Row, Alex, and Matt all casually sat there as if getting ready for a family picnic instead of a funeral.

"I don't understand what's going on." Isleen's legs stopped moving, her mind unable to assimilate the graveyard and the cheerful picnic blanket.

Xander put his arm around her and kissed the top of her head. "This isn't going to be like last time." His arm around her nudged her forward.

Row glanced up as they approached. In the late day's sun, her hair seemed darker—almost eggplant in color, while her tattoos seemed bolder. "They're here." She announced as if Isleen and Xander were special guests. "I'm in charge of this here party. And that's what it's going to be. A party." She threw her hands out theatrically as if introducing the stage production of *My Mother's Funeral*. "This is going to be a celebration of life—your mom's and yours—instead of a damned melancholy rehashing of all the fucking losses." She held out a fat square book to Isleen. On the cover in bold letters: Photos. "You sit down and look through these pictures before you lose too much of the light. And we'll tell you about your mother."

Isleen's body reacted before her mind fully plugged in to Row's words. She took the album and sat on the blanket like a kid waiting for story time. Finally, she was going to learn about her mother. She had so many questions—a lifetime of questions that she'd stored up—but in this moment, she couldn't remember any of them.

Xander sat behind her, spreading his legs out on either side of her. Even though she was among friends, she felt as if he was protecting her, blocking her from any potential threat and buffering her from pain. He looked over her shoulder at the album in her hands.

"Go ahead. Open it." His breath was warm and sweet against her temple.

Anticipation warmed her chest. She held a great gift in her hands. One she'd never expected. "Thank you." The words burst from her. "I never thought I'd get to see pictures or hear stories."

Her hand trembled as she opened the book. A beautiful, dark-haired girl—not quite a child, not quite a teenager—held a rainbow bouquet to her nose. Her face alight with pure joy. She looked like Gran. It was in the warm color of her eyes, in the tilt of her head, in the shape of her features. "This"—she pointed to the photo—"is my mom." It wasn't a question. It was a statement of awe.

"Yeah." Xander breathed the answer in her ear and reached down to run a finger over the picture. "She loved picking wildflowers. She put vases of them all over the house during the spring and summer. She even put them in my room, but I was too much of a boy to appreciate them."

"But she didn't always care if they were wildflowers." Row's eyes were misty with memories. "She once picked every bloom in Gale's zinnias patch and made bouquets with them before anyone could tell her not to."

"Don't forget about the roses." Alex leaned in to see the picture. "Gale couldn't keep a bloom on a rosebush. Shayla would wait until her mother wasn't looking and then snip them all off and put them in a pretty vase, or make a bouquet, or just float them in a bowl of water."

"No matter how many times we explained to leave

some flowers on the vine, she just couldn't do it. Said they should be enjoyed." Row turned around and began rummaging in the large picnic basket behind her.

"We all thought she was going to grow up to be a florist." Matt's voice was soft and full of genuine affection. Something Isleen hadn't witnessed before. He had cared for her mom. "She knew I wasn't into the whole flower thing, so she'd make me a bouquet of dried willow branches or pinecones. They were pretty clever." He leaned over to take in the photo. "It's a little worse for the wear, but I still have the pinecone bouquet in my room."

"I would love to see it."

He sat back and seemed to pull his mantle of surliness back around himself. "Sometime."

Isleen flipped the page, but the dusk had faded and it was more dark than light out. She held another picture up close to her face, willing herself to see the image.

An older version of her mom—maybe in her early teens. She lay on her stomach on the floor with a board game open, smiling at the cutest little boy—Xander.

His face hadn't been scarred yet, his gorgeous hazel eyes untouched by life's pain, and he wore a smile of pure angelic mischief.

"Aww… How old were you?" she asked, turning to hold the photo up for Xander to see.

"I don't even know."

"I got him that stupid game for his fifth birthday." Matt's tone was nostalgic. "Everyone hated that damned game and wouldn't play it with him, except Shayla."

"Five years old…" The light had dimmed so the image was no more than shadowy shapes, but Isleen couldn't take her eyes off the picture.

A bright golden glow lit their small circle. She looked away from the photo to birthday candles burning atop a cake. A chocolate cake with a sweet mound of cherries in the center.

Her breath caught in her lungs.

"Happy Birthday to you." Everyone sang together, their individual voices off-key and not quite in unison, but perfect. Beautifully perfect. Their smiling faces all lit with an orange glow. This—these people, her new family—was what her life was going to be about. "Happy birthday to you. Happy birthday, dear Isleen. Happy birthday to you."

"Christ, that sounded awful." Matt laughed.

Happy tears swelled and spilled. Isleen laughed and wiped them away.

"And many more," Xander sang softly in her ear.

"How did you know? I totally forgot. I wasn't even paying attention to the day."

"Kent told me. And told me about your favorite cake." Row held the cake in front of her. "I just happened to have Gale's recipe. You blow out the candles so we can dig in to this while we watch the show."

The show? She didn't have time to ask. Her candles were burning. She closed her eyes to search for her wish. And found it. She sucked in a breath, opened her eyes, and blew out twenty-six candles. *I wish happiness for all of us.*

A pop in the sky startled her.

"The fireworks are starting." Xander pointed overhead. "It's Sundew's celebration. We just happen to have the best view." A flash of white burst in a perfect circle above them, tendrils of color fading as they fell. Another flash. Pink and green exploded across the sky.

Isleen turned in his arms, needing to do more than just feel him around her, needing to see him. The hard angles of his face were lit blue from the rockets exploding. His gaze on her was full of… Words were too small to describe the look of love he bestowed on her.

Her heart practically leaped out of her chest to be with his.

She placed her hand on his scarred cheek. "I love you. I love your family. And I love the life we're going to have." She tugged him down to her mouth as a kaleidoscope of color and a future of happiness burst over them.

Keep reading for a sneak peek of the next book in the Fatal Dreams series

Hunt the Dawn

MINDS OF MADNESS AND MURDER. THE GLOSSY POSTER advertising today's seminar was taped to the closed auditorium door. Someone had drawn tears of blood dripping from each of the *m*'s.

Lathaniel Montgomery's gut gnawed at his backbone, but not because of the poster or the bloody tears.

Holy Jesus. How was he going to manage being in an audience surrounded by hundreds of people, with all their smells, all their memories?

Gill touched his arm like he always did to get Lathan's attention. "Going in?"

"Yeah." But Lathan's feet had grown roots into the floor. He hated how nothing in his life was normal. He hated the fucked-up sequence of genetic code that had enlarged the olfactory regions of his brain. He hated that he smelled everything. And he especially hated the ability to smell the energy imprints of people's memories. Scent memories. Memories that could overwhelm him and annihilate *his* reality.

Gill stepped up close and examined Lathan's left eye—the eye the SMs always invaded first, the eye that would roll around independently of the other one, making him appear in need of an exorcism.

"Quit with the eye exam. I'm all right." For now. Concentration kept the SMs out of his mind. Vigilance kept them under control.

"Your seat is directly in front of the podium. You won't have any trouble reading Dr. Jonah's lips. After the presentation, introduce yourself. He'll recognize your name." Gill gave him the don't-screw-this-up look. "Convince him about the Strategist."

The Strategist.

Lathan's freakish ability had generated leads for nearly every cold case he worked. Except for the Strategist's.

"Explain how each person has a scent signature. Explain that you smell the same signature on thirty-eight unsolved murders. Explain that the FBI won't do anything unless *he* confirms there is a connection among the kills."

"Save the lecture. This whole fucking thing was my dumbass idea." Could he maintain control of the SMs long enough to make it to the end of the presentation? "If I—"

"There is no if. You're not going to lose control." Gill had read his worries as easily as Lathan read his friend's lips. "Maybe I should go in with you."

"I don't need you holding my hand." Lathan showed him a raised middle finger—a salute they always used in jest, forced a smile of bravado across his lips, and then pushed through the doors before he made like a chick-enshit and bolted from the building. Barely inside, the SMs hit. Millions of memories warred for his attention, tugged at the vision in his left eye. He sucked air through his mouth to diminish the intensity, to maintain control.

Never in his life had he been around so many people at once and been coherent. Maybe he should leave.

No.

He clenched his fists. Knuckles popped, grounding him, giving him an edge over the SMs.

He strode down the steps toward the front of the room. Thank whoever-was-in-charge the presentation hadn't started yet.

An empty seat in the front row had a pink piece of paper taped to it: RESERVED. Lathan would've preferred the anonymity of the back row, but he couldn't see Dr. Jonah's face from that far away. He ripped off the sheet and sat in the cramped space.

His shoulders were wider than the damned chair. His arms overflowed the boundary of his seat. The woman on his left angled away from him, the cinnamon scent of her irritation infusing the air. Typical reaction to his size. And with the tattoo on his cheek, she probably assumed he'd served a sentence in the slammer.

The woman on his right reeked. But it wasn't her fault. The rot of her body dying was a stench he recognized, along with the sharp chemical tang of the drugs that were killing her so she could live. Cancer and chemo. Her emaciated features evidenced the battle she fought. And yet, she was here. At this presentation. She was a warrior. And he was a fucking pussy for bellyaching about the SMs.

His ears picked up a faint snapping noise. Clapping. Everyone applauded enthusiastically.

Dr. Jonah walked to the podium. His clothes were baggy and ill fitting, his face wrinkled, his head topped with a mass of fluttery gray hair. Even though he looked like he'd just awakened from sleeping under an overpass, he possessed the look of frazzled genius. The look of someone whose work mattered more than living life. The look of the nation's most respected profiler.

A door on Lathan's right opened. A young woman lugged a folding chair across the room. Toward him.

He held his breath.

No. She couldn't be there for him. No one here knew him. Knew about him. Except Gill. And Gill wouldn't—

She opened her chair and sat facing him. With an overly enthusiastic smile that showed the silver in her back molars, she started to sign.

He looked away. A long bitter whoosh of air escaped his lips.

He didn't need an interpreter.

The combination of what little hearing he still possessed, speech reading, and his nose worked just fucking fine. Most of the time.

Anger burned a gaping hole through his concentration. The interpreter's memories invaded the vision of his left eye.

She swiped a quick stroke of mascara across her lashes and examined the effect up close in the bathroom mirror. Good enough. Getting the day over with, getting back to Cara mattered more than her makeup.

"I should go." Her voice lacked as much conviction as her will.

"Baby, come on back to bed, just for a little while." Cara threw back the covers. She'd strapped Big Johnnie around her waist. He pointed proudly perpendicular.

She glanced at the bedside clock. She was going to be late. It'd be worth it.

The SM continued to play in front of his left eye. His

right eye focused on Dr. Jonah. Lathan pressed his left eye closed with his fingers to block out the images, but they projected on the back of his eyelid. Hard to focus on reality. Disorienting as hell. *Don't lose control.*

His right-eyed vision of reality wavered. Almost like a double exposure, he was able to see the stage, see Dr. Jonah, but superimposed over it was the interpreter and her sex bunny having a girls-only party.

Lathan's heart punched against his chest wall, pumping so hard he felt the echo of it in his damaged ears. Fuck. The SMs were about to stage a coup.

"I'm out of here." Did he shout the words, whisper them, or even speak them at all? Didn't know. Didn't care.

He sprinted out of his seat and up the auditorium stairs, feeling the weight of hundreds of eyes watching him.

Gulping giant fish-out-of-water breaths through his mouth, he slammed through the door, burst into the hallway, and then barreled out the exterior door.

Away from the people, away from the damned interpreter, the SMs vanished. His sight returned to normal. He'd figure out some other way to talk to Dr. Jonah. No way was he taking that kind of risk again.

The stark fall afternoon held a hint of winter chill, but he didn't mind. He was always hot, and the temperature suited his mood. He hurried across the lawn to his motorcycle.

A wisp of scent tickled his nostrils. The fleeting aroma possessed a sickening familiarity that felt out of place for his surroundings. He plugged his nose against the smell, refusing to allow one bit of air to enter his nose until he was on the road.

Someone grabbed his arm from behind.

His heart stopped. Adrenaline shot from his brain straight to his fist.

He swung at the same time he turned. Punch first, ask questions later—his body's default reaction ever since the attack that cost him his hearing.

He barely stopped himself from impacting with the guy's face. Lathan lunged forward a few steps, feigning aggression, expecting the guy to retreat, and he did, tripping over his own feet, almost falling on his ass. Good. That was one way to get someone to realize he took his personal space seriously.

"Don't fucking touch me." From the force of the vibrations in his throat, he had yelled the words. He didn't care. He forced himself to breathe from his mouth. Didn't want to look like more of freak than he already did by standing there plugging his nose.

The guy swallowed and nodded, then swallowed again. "I'm Dr. Jonah's partner." The guy's mouth formed the words in perfect precision. "Dr. Jonah wants…return…presentation."

The words *you, to, do, new* all looked identical when spoken. Conversation with a stranger was a recipe. Mix the bits of sound he heard with the speech he read. Sprinkle in the context of the sentence. And bake with the emotions he smelled.

Why would Dr. Jonah want him to return to the lecture? Why would Dr. Jonah stop the presentation to tell his partner to come after him? He wouldn't. Lathan must've read the guy's words wrong. He sure as hell wasn't going to ask the guy to repeat himself. Every time he did, people spoke in such an exaggerated manner even God wouldn't be able to divine the words leaving their mouths.

The guy opened his mouth to say more, but scratched at a spot on the side of his nostril, blocking every word from Lathan's view. His ears only picked up random sounds, nothing that added up to a word. The best way to handle not understanding speech: silence. Anything else ended with people looking at him like he was stupid.

He sat on his bike and flicked the ignition switch. Underneath him, the engine pulsed; the vibrations traveled through his body. His heart, his breath, the engine all moved in one synergistic rhythm. The closest he ever got to music.

The guy stood in front of the bike, waving his hands like an amateur cheerleader to get Lathan's attention.

He backed the motorcycle from the space.

The persistent little pecker jogged next to him.

Lathan kicked his Fat Bob into gear and shot out of the parking lot. He needed to be alone. Alone meant no SMs. He needed to be home. Home meant sanctuary. But every sanctuary was part prison.

"What time you off work, Evan?" Carnivorous anticipation spread across the trucker's face.

At some point during every shift at Sweet Buns and Eats truck stop, Evanee Brown was grateful the label maker had run out of ink halfway through her name. The patrons spoke the name on her tag with a familiarity that made her stifle her gag reflex. If they had used her complete name… Well, full-blown barfing would've been bad for business.

She pasted a super-huge smile across her mouth and lied, "Oh, I'm, uh, working a ten so, hmm, whatever time ten hours from now is." Hopefully, her voice carried the right amount of empty-headed dingbat. Acting stupid earned better tips than being smart.

"Evan, one of these times I'm passing through I'll have to show you the inside of my truck. It's real nice." He stretched the words *real nice* into one long taffy-like string.

She smothered an eye roll.

The trucker was old enough to have known the original Casanova, yet still made the same X-rated offer every time he came in. She glanced at the clock hanging above the door. Any minute, Shirl—her replacement—should be arriving. Couldn't happen quick enough.

"How about an Ernie Burger, rare, everything, side of onion rings?" She worked to maintain her light tone. She wanted the twenty-dollar bill he always left for her tip.

"You remembered my usual." He smiled, his teeth a post-apocalyptic city—abandoned, jagged, decayed. "You know I can't resist an Ernie Burger."

She scrawled his order on the slip and then left the table, feeling the slime of more than one man's gaze on her body. That was to be expected when the uniform requirements were four-inch heels, shorts that barely covered her ass, and cleavage. Lots of cleavage.

Ernie liked his girls barely decent, said it was the best business decision he'd ever made. He was right. Sweet Buns was packed twenty-four seven, three sixty-five. Most days, the tips were great. Hell, there wasn't anywhere within forty-five minutes where she could earn as much as she made at Sweet Buns.

Ernie met her at the kitchen window with a pair of tongs in his hand and anger on his face. His sharply slashed brows met over his eyes, a scowl constantly gripped his lips, and the strange vibe of restrained violence intimidated most everyone and kept the patrons from being too grabby-feely. He looked like a homicidal hashslinger, but didn't have any bodies stashed in the freezer. At least none she'd found.

Acknowledgments

A simple list of wonderful people—and animals—whom I owe a big, giant, huge THANK YOU.

Dan: None of my books would exist if it weren't for your unconditional love giving me the courage to write them. Thank you for being my best friend and my favorite human being. You've given me the world.

Margie Lawson: You showed me how to be the writer I wanted to be. It wasn't easy and I went through 863 highlighters along the way, but I got here! I owe you more than a THANK YOU. I owe being published to you!

Michelle Grajkowski: My super awesome agent lady. You were the first industry professional to have faith in me. You have no idea how many times when I felt like my writing sucked that I said to myself, "Michelle believes in you. She wouldn't be your agent if she didn't." Thanks for always being supportive of me and my dark writing. I'm glad you're in my corner.

Deb Werksman: My all-time favorite editor. I'm so glad you understood my dark and different books and never asked me to dumb them down. I enjoyed our phone conversations and that you get my need to ponder things before finding the solution. I'm so happy to be working with you.

Sourcebooks: You all have been fantastic to work with. I know there are many people behind the scenes working on my book—people I've never met and never heard of. I want to offer each of you a personal thank-you for all that you do. Also, I need to thank a few special people who've been wonderful to interact with and have answered even my dumbest questions without making me feel dumb: Rachel Gilmer, Laura Costello, Susie Benton, and Diane Dannenfeldt (copy editor extraordinaire). I need to offer a super special thank-you to Beth Sochacki for orchestrating an awesome cover reveal. And, and, and… My hat is off and I am bowing low to Dawn Adams and Kris Keller for creating the most AMAZING cover for *Race the Darkness*. It is gorgeous beyond my wildest imaginings! THANK YOU!

Brinda Berry: You. Are. The. Best. Thank you for always telling me the things you love about my writing and the things you hate. And then letting me pick apart every detail of why you hated it so I can figure out how to make you love it. You're so generous with your time—always answering my dumb questions, and I have a lot of them. You're always helping me out with something. What you give to me I can never repay. And I owe you a special thank-you for writing *The Lord's Brigade* for this book. You really are a talented song writer—even when you're writing an old-style hymn.

Dreamweavers: Being a Golden Heart Finalist was one of the best things that's ever happened to me. And being a finalist alongside all of you—was the icing! What a great group we have.

Readerlicious Wonder Women: Christina Delay, Jennifer Savalli, Jenn Windrow, Kathleen Groger, Brinda Berry, Kelly Crawley, N. K. Whitaker, S. B. McCauley, Sandy Wright, Carol Storey Costley. Thanks so much for inviting me to be a part of this awesome group. I'm truly honored to call you all friends.

Naomi: You are my cheerleader. My coworker. My partner in crime. You've always supported me. No matter what crazy new idea I had. Blue hair. Tattoos. Writing! Thanks for just being you. You're one of the best human beings I know.

NEORWA: You guys win the most supportive chapter award. I love you all so much for always stepping up and supporting me even though I live two hours away and never make it to meetings. You guys rock!

My Critique Peeps: Christina Delay, Brinda Berry, Jennifer Savalli, Jenn Windrow, Celeste Easton, Pamela Stewart. You guys critiqued this before I ever sent it to my agent. I had some real stinkers in here until you all read it. Thanks for saving me from looking bad. I'm so grateful for each of you!

Dobby and Brindle: You're the best fur babies. One of you always warms my lap while I'm writing. At this point I'm not sure I could write a book without one of you sleeping on my legs. And, Dobby, in case you didn't realize it—you were the inspiration for Killer.

Emmanuel: Dude… If I can write a whole novel and get it published—you can do anything! Don't ever forget to be awesome. Being your aunt has been one of the best things ever.

Mom, Dad, Laura: Thanks for encouraging me to read as a child. I know you must've spent a small fortune on books for me. I remember getting in trouble because I was always in my room reading, but you never made me stop reading—I just had to sit downstairs with the family to do it! Loving reading is what made me want to be a writer. Without each of you, I wouldn't be the person I am today.

My clients: Your tragedies and triumphs inspire me every day. I really do have the best job in the world.

You: My books are nothing without you. Thank you for investing your time and money in my novel. You have no idea how much it means to me. I salute you, dear reader, and hope you will return for my next novel, *Hunt the Dawn*.

About the Author

Abbie Roads is a mental health counselor known for her blunt, honest style of therapy. By night, she writes dark, emotional novels, always giving her characters the happy ending she wishes for all her clients. Her novels have been finalists in many Romance Writers of America contests including the Golden Heart. *Race the Darkness* is the first book in the Fatal Dreams series, which features dark, gritty romantic suspense with a psychological twist.

Be sure to visit her website at www.abbieroads.com and sign up for her newsletter to receive exclusive content and special giveaways.